The Magnificent Spinster

The Magnificent Spinster

A novel by
MAY SARTON

W · W · NORTON & COMPANY
New York   London

The text of this book is composed in Gael, with display type set in
Baskerville. Composition and manufacturing by The Haddon Craftsmen, Inc.

First published as a Norton paperback 1988; reissued 1995

Library of Congress Cataloging in Publication Data

Sarton, May, 1912–
The magnificent spinster.
I. Title
PS3537.A832M3   1985   813′.52   85-4893

ISBN 0-393-31249-6

W. W. Norton & Company, Inc., 500 Fifth Avenue, New York, N.Y. 10110
W. W. Norton & Company Ltd., 10 Coptic Street, London WC1A 1PU

1 2 3 4 5 6 7 8 9 0

In Memoriam
Anne Longfellow Thorp
1894–1977

Contents

The Magnificent Spinster

Prologue, Part I

For the second time in my life—and I am now seventy—I am embarking on an effort which may well come to nothing but which has possessed my mind, haunts, and will not let me sleep. The first time was long ago and it was the war in Spain, but whatever is relevant about that experience will find its place later on as this second act of commitment on my part proceeds. I mention it here only because in the forty years between these two adventures so little has happened and I have led such a sedate, quiet life in the groves of academe.

What then has driven me to attempt so late in my life to write a novel? Quite simply the unequivocal need to celebrate an extraordinary woman whom I had the good fortune to know for more than fifty years until her death a year ago. I am vague about dates these days, but it must have been a year ago because the Unitarian Church in Cambridge, that rather cold, white, pillared interior, had become a bower of spring flowers—iris, daffodils, narcissi, anemones, an unforgettable explosion of beauty in the midst of a February snowstorm. How appropriate the brilliance, the glow, and the innocence of all those flowers seemed! Jane Reid had died after a long, full life, so the funeral became a celebration rather than a time of mourning. One of my classmates gave the eulogy and it was just right, though I remember very little of what she actually said. I do remember she opened with a line of Stephen Spender's, "I think continually of those who were truly great."

It was very fine, but what moved me to tears was our each being given a sprig of spruce from the island as we left the church. For those of us who had been to the island (and I expect many of those at the funeral had) it was a gesture of such intimacy and remembrance that it brought tears. Jane Reid always slipped a sprig into a buttonhole as every guest embarked for the shore at the end of a visit, and now she herself, one felt, was saying a last "Godspeed." I expect that her friend Sarah, her companion all the last years, must have engineered this, and it was perfect.

Snow was falling fast as I walked home that day, thinking about Jane. Was she "truly great"? Yes, I decided, she was. I lit the wood fire in the library and sat for quite a while as elation turned to depression and I realized that in a few years everyone who knew Jane would be dead. Who would remember her? In fifty years who would know she had existed? She never married. There would be no children and grandchildren to keep her memory alive. She was already vanishing like sand in the ocean. ... Then, almost without thinking, I went into my study, forgetting all about lunch, and began to write. It was chiefly quick notes, whatever came with some urgency as I sat there. But in an hour that spurt of energy had gone, and by the time I heated up some soup I realized that I could not possibly sustain such an effort, and even if I could, self-doubt was eating into the impulse, for whatever tiny fame I have achieved has been in medieval history, and that, a matter of some papers on the trade routes, is of minor importance. I have no illusions. I shoved the notes into a drawer and that was that.

Months later, by a curious stroke of fate, I was brought face to face with the Jane Reid I had first known when I was a student at the Warren School and had had her as my teacher in the seventh grade. Over the years a few of us from that memorable time had kept in touch, and one day Anne Strange turned up in Cambridge—she lives in Oregon—and called me on the telephone to see if she could come and see me. So there she was, recently widowed. She knew my dear friend Ruth had died some years ago, so at first we talked mostly about how one handles these losses of a central person in life. But, as always when students of Warren get together, we ended by speaking of the school and of Jane Reid. And, rather shyly, Anne took a small black leather notebook out of her purse, and said, "I thought you might like to see this." It was an extraordinary moment, for what I saw written out in Anne's clear hand was a whole book of poems four of us had written after we left Warren and were in the public high school. I was bowled over by the intensity of these poems, so much so that I could not read them, and asked if I might keep the book for a week and send it back.

And when I read it alone in bed that night, the past came back like an explosion. Had I ever felt that intensely? Had I really written such impassioned poems for anyone, for Jane Reid? I had. The evidence was before me of a whole emotional landscape I had buried for almost sixty years! Of course a crush on a teacher is fairly common, I expect. But how often does it take the form of such disciplined and impassioned utterance? And what was it about Jane Reid that had elicited such feeling?

I knew I could not escape the effort now. I must try to celebrate her somehow, in some way. And I began to imagine how I might approach the task. I saw that what had stopped me in the beginning was not so much doing it as *how* to do it. And little by little I became certain that a novel and not a memoir

15

or biography had to be my way. At least a work of fiction would free me from the struggle with minute detail, with dates and facts. I had had enough of that in my professional life over the years. The essence was what mattered, after all.

Today it is snowing, as it did on the day of her funeral. My old cat, Snoozle, is asleep in a round black ball on the couch, and in the marvelous silence of the snow I dream of a summer morning almost seventy years ago on the island.

Jane Reid is a child.

Part I

"Children Dear, Was It Yesterday?"

Childhood is a place as well as a time. For James Reid's five daughters the place was "the island," as it was always called, although it has a name, Wilder. Their father bought the island off the Maine coast, and the old farmhouse on it, in the nineties, when he had already as a young man amassed a fortune from lumber in Minnesota, where he was born. At the wooded end Mr. Reid built one of those Henry Jamesian arks prevalent north of Boston, shingled, ample in porches, with a private bathroom for each bedroom, but then and up to the present no electricity—Aladdin lamps downstairs and candles to take up to bed. Cooking was done on a huge coal range. There were sailboats and rowboats to "mess about in," and a captain to ferry guests back and forth from the mainland in an elegant canopied motorboat, *West Wind,* that kept a tranquil pace and bore no resemblance to the motor launches that whizz around making an infernal noise these days.

Jane's summer world had nothing to do with luxuries. Hers was the world of secret hiding places in the "moss drawing room," a part of the forest floor covered in emerald and pale-green mosses like a sumptuous carpet. Her world had a great deal to do with escaping the grown-ups, and also escaping Snooker, who had been brought from England as a nanny for the two youngest, and would remain in the family, a cherished friend, until she died in her nineties. Jane's world was running off with her sister Alix to pick blueberries, lying for hours in the soft warm grass, filling their baskets, or simply sneaking off to explore, if possible get lost, and frighten themselves with imaginary dangers, and frighten Snooker by being late for lunch.

The narrator has said enough. Let me begin with a sample day on the island in 1910, when Jane was fourteen and Alix twelve.

"Can't we get up, Snooker? It's nearly seven," Jane whispered at Snooker's door.

"What's that?" a sleepy voice murmured.

"We want to go and see the fish hawk's nest—please let us!"

By then Snooker had dragged herself out of sleep and put on her dressing gown. "You'll be soaking wet; there is dew on the grass—"

"Please, Snooker. You forget that I'm fourteen, after all. I'm not a baby."

"We'll hold up our skirts, over our knees," Alix said and began to giggle at such a scandalous idea.

"Sh—sh—you'll wake your mother and father. Very well, be off with you. But don't be late for breakfast—blueberry pancakes, cook said last night."

"Darn it, I've got a hole in my stocking," Jane said, by mistake aloud.

This brought Snooker out of her room, a twinkle in her eye, "It might be better to darn it, than say 'darn it.'"

"It's in the toe, Snooker. It doesn't show."

"Be sure and give it to me when you come back. . . ."

But her whisper got lost in the departure, as sneakered feet sped down the stairs, creating an impression of a mild thunderstorm.

Outside the house, the two girls stood quite still for a moment, listening, and drinking in the piny scent, the cool of fresh morning air. Then they were off, walking fast, Jane's long pigtail bouncing a little, so she pulled it round her neck and let it hang down in front.

Usually they talked a blue streak but the stillness in the woods, the excitement of a wholly untouched morning world, made them silent, made them stop often to stand and drink it in. The white-throated sparrow repeated his three-note song and somewhere far off they heard a thrush. They were following the path along the shore that would bring them in a quarter of a mile or so to a tall pine that had been struck by lightning and topped. There, in the top of the broken trunk, fish hawks had built their raggedy nest.

"There—look! There he goes!"

The great wings had lifted off just before they could see the nest itself. They watched the huge bird fly away.

"It makes a lump in my throat," Jane said.

"You're not crying, are you?"

"No."

"You've got tears in your eyes."

"I don't know . . . the wildness."

"It's funny to cry at beautiful things."

"I guess so." Jane suddenly laughed, breaking through the moment's mood of awe, "I'll race you home . . . you take the moss path. I'll go by the lumber road."

There was something thrilling about running alone as fast as you could through the woods. Jane pretended she was a deer being chased by hunters (occasionally in winter deer swam over from the mainland but were rarely seen). She was running fast now, bound to win, when she fell headlong to the ground, her foot having caught on an exposed root. It was so sudden that she lay there for a moment, stunned, then slowly felt her ankle,

21

which hurt quite a lot. She found she could stand on it and even walk in a gingerly way, but it was humiliating to hobble home and find Alix, triumphant, waiting for her on the porch.

"Dearie, do you have to be so violent?" Snooker asked, not cross but concerned. "Why tear through the woods, why not walk?"

"I don't know. I'm just so full of everything, I have to let off steam."

"Anyway, I won!" Alix said. "And we have blueberry pancakes for breakfast!"

They were just finishing when Mamma and Pappa arrived for their breakfast before the older sisters and two young men, beaus of Viola's and Edith's, made their appearance. Breakfast was apt to be an extended feast on the island, where the Reids wanted life to be as flexible and free as possible for all concerned. Very occasionally, cook rebelled and announced that she would not serve breakfast after ten.

"Can we sit with you till they come?" Alix asked, standing behind her father's chair, her arms laced round his neck.

"Tell us about Vyvian," Jane begged, sitting down next to her mother. And then before a word could be said she added, "Is he going to propose?"

Pappa laughed. "He's only just arrived . . . you're in a great rush, aren't you?"

"Viola is dying to get married. She told me so the other day."

"I should think she'd enjoy having all those beaus and not making up her mind," Alix said. "I'd like that."

"I'd hate it," Jane said passionately. "They suffer."

"You make them sound like a school of porpoises," her father teased.

"Vyvian is handsome," Alix murmured.

"I'd call him pretty . . . he's not made anything of himself yet," Jane said.

"Well, in that case, why are you so eager for him to propose to your sister?" Allegra Reid turned to her daughter with an amused, tender look.

"Oh, well . . ." Jane looked embarrassed. "It's just that I'm dying to hear someone propose . . . how it's done . . . does he go down on his knees?"

"Fat chance he'd do that with a little sister hovering around," Alix giggled.

"I'm going to hide, that's my plan, in the cupboard where the newspapers are."

"Jane!" Her father was serious. "You can't do that. Eavesdropping! We can't have that."

"You'll have to wait till someone proposes to you, dearie," her mother said gently.

"I'll never get married," said Jane with complete conviction.

"Don't we set a good example, your mother and I?"

"That's it. That's the trouble," Jane answered. "You and Mamma are a little too good to be true. I never see anyone anything like you, Pappa. They're all so dim."

Fortunately perhaps, the conversation ended there as Martha came and sat down, and Jane went around the table to give her father a hug, and kissed him.

"What are the plans for today, Pappa?" Martha asked, pouring syrup on her pancakes.

"Well, I presume Vyvian and Lawrence will want to play tennis with the girls later on. And Mr. Perkins is coming at four. We might all be down at the dock to welcome him."

"Can we go over with Captain Philbrook and fetch him at the town dock?" Alix asked.

"What do you think, Allegra?"

"I think Mr. Perkins would be gratified, especially if Jane puts on a clean skirt and ties a ribbon round her hair."

"An excellent idea," Viola was standing in the door with Vyvian at her side. "You look as though you had been climbing a tree!"

Jane flashed her sister an angry glance, then melted as she took Viola in, impeccably dressed in a striped blouse with starched white collar and cuffs and dark blue skirt.

"I fell," Jane said. "We were racing, Alix and I!"

But, suddenly self-conscious, she then got up and went upstairs to Snooker, and lay down on the bed while Snooker rocked in her low rocking chair and mended the toe in Jane's stocking.

"I'll never never look like Viola," she said crossly. "It's hopeless."

"Well, she's an elegant young lady, there's no denying that, but you're yourself, Jane. And if you ask me, she'll never have your look."

"What's my look? Oh, I wish I knew what it was!" she said passionately.

Snooker lifted her head and smiled, "And if I told you it might go to your head!"

"Viola and Edith treat me like nothing, as though I were a little girl. I'm fourteen, after all, it's an awful age."

"It won't last long. Next year you'll be putting up your hair."

"The trouble is, I don't want to. I don't want to grow up, Snooker."

"Dearie, there's no way out of that."

"I suppose not." She got up then and took the mended stocking Snooker handed to her. "I don't know what I'd do without you, Snooker. Somehow you always make me feel better."

The cuckoo clock announced the hour, ten "cuckoos." Jane counted them and ran off down the stairs singing out "The Duchess! The Duchess! Oh, my ears and whiskers!"

Alix was dressing her large teddy bear down in Pappa's office. "Where is everybody?" Jane asked. "We'd better hurry."

It was always like this on the island. The day began at a slow, casual pace and gathered momentum, and for Jane and Alix time began to leap and carry them away long before noon.

"Come on, Alix. They'll be playing by now with no one to chase balls—you're too old to be dressing bears."

"Am I?" Alix looked startled. Then said firmly, "I intend to dress this bear until I die."

"All right, you loon, but *please* come now. I'm bursting."

Snooker went down to the kitchen for a cup of tea with Cook and Daisy, the waitress. They all three enjoyed a half-hour of peace and quiet with everyone launched on the day. The dishes were still piled up in the pantry, but they could wait, and soon someone must put more coal in the stove, but that could wait too.

"Mrs. Reid wants strawberry shortcake for dinner, but I'm not sure Captain Philbrook can find enough for eleven. Mr. Perkins will be here for tea, you know. And what will I do if there aren't strawberries? A lemon meringue pie . . . he's fond of that."

"Is his beer on the ice?" Snooker asked.

"Naturally," Cook answered as though she would forget!

"Does he have beer, now?" Daisy, new this summer, asked, astonished, for not a drop of wine or liquor had been served in the house so far.

"Mr. Perkins is privileged," Cook said, smoothing down her starched white apron with an air of complicity.

"I've always wondered how he managed it about the drinking," Snooker said, shaking her head.

"And who is Mr. Perkins?" Daisy asked. It seemed quite dramatic that he could come onto the island and expect such preferential treatment.

Cook glanced over at Snooker, who was the one who knew everything.

"He's an old bachelor, a cousin, I think, of some friends of Mr. Reid's in Minnesota. He's been coming for years. Always brings a huge box of Sherry's chocolates with little crystallized violets on the top. And that's all I can tell you about Mr. Perkins!"

"Oo, I've never tasted a violet!" Daisy said, her eyes sparkling.

And Snooker promised to steal one if she could.

"Time to get back to work," said Cook. "There are vegetables to peel and cut up, Daisy, after you've done the dishes."

Outdoors the tennis players were starting their second set. Viola and Vyvian had won the first one, six-four. Lawrence, a spectacled young man with a ruddy complexion and rather floppy chestnut hair, was an erratic player and kept the girls busy chasing his balls, and Edith, who hated losing to her older sister, couldn't help showing that she minded when his second serve was out again.

"I'm sorry, Edith," he said, taking a big white handkerchief out to wipe his face. "I'm out of practice."

"Practice will never make him perfect," Alix whispered to Jane.

"Sh—sh . . ." Jane said fiercely, trying to control a fit of uncontrollable giggles.

Edith gave them a cold look. But it was no use. Alix gave Jane one look and they were suffused with giggles.

"Come on, Lawrence, they're only silly girls—let's play," Viola commanded, and this time the nettled Lawrence's serve was hard and flat, and they ended by having quite a long rally.

"It's getting late," Jane, who was getting restless, said to the world at large, "and Alix and I have to help Martha pick lettuce for supper and beans for lunch!"

"Run along, for heaven's sake!" Edith called after them.

"Little sisters should keep their place," Jane said, winking at Alix. They walked along, then, at the bend in the road, turned to look back at the tennis court through the pine trees. "Poor Lawrence!"

They found Martha already picking in the vegetable garden, very glad to see them. "It's so hot," she said. "Let's hurry so we can go for a swim." In a short time they walked down together to the low, shingled bathhouse, a series of cubicles which opened into a roofless area so the temporary inhabitants could dress and undress in sunlight and open air. This summer there was a swallow's nest in Jane's and Alix's cubicle and they had sometimes been frightened by the mother swallow when the babies were small, as she dive-bombed the intruders. But it was worth it, Jane told her father, "because we have seen everything, Pappa."

The big salt pool, a long rectangle, with a shallow, enclosed place at one end for the little children, was quite close to the shore. On very hot days Jane and Alix sometimes went in to the icy ocean itself, screaming when they finally brought themselves to take the plunge.

On this day Allegra and James Reid were sitting in the big wooden armchairs in their bathing suits when the girls came sauntering down through the field. Allegra had on an old, rather faded suit with a sailor collar and wide dark-blue bloomers, and, of course, stockings and flat black sneakers. She was wearing a white hat. Jane had never understood why women had to be smothered in clothing when going for a swim while Pappa looked so comfortable in his long blue shorts and vest.

"Do I have to wear stockings, Mamma?"

"Dearie, the young men will be here shortly, and I think perhaps you do have to." Very occasionally when only the family was present this humiliation could be avoided.

"I'm only a child, after all," said Jane, lifting her chin as she did when she was feeling stubborn. Unfortunately, it gave her a rather grown-up air.

"You have such long legs, Jane," her mother said gently.

"What difference does that make?"

But then they heard voices and Jane knew there was no hope, as the four tennis players came round the bathhouse. Lawrence gave a whoop of delight at the sight of the pool and ran out on the diving board as though he was about to dive in fully clothed. Jane watched him and suspected that this enthusiasm had to do with getting away from tennis and into a sport where he could excel. He had been on the swimming team at Exeter.

When Jane and Alix came out from their cubicles ready to swim, their mother and father were already in, Allegra doing her breast stroke up and down for a daily stint and James floating on his back. The girls ran to the beach to watch a yawl go sailing past and wave to it.

"It's the Emersons, Mamma. They've got *Alice* out!" At this four heads appeared over the cubicle walls, as Vyvian, Lawrence, Edith, and Viola stood on the benches to see. In August the harbor was full of boats of all kinds and the island was an excellent observation post, set at the harbor's mouth a quarter-of-a-mile from the mainland. Every Saturday they had grandstand seats for the races on the big porch.

"I'm too hot," Alix announced. "I've got to swim."

And in an instant she and Jane had plunged in from the deep end. "Whew! It's freezing, Mamma!" Jane called out, but within a moment she felt a kind of ecstasy at being in the water, the delicious shock of cold and something she enjoyed without defining it, her arms and legs as free and fluid as the element they swam in, for once not constricted by bodices and petticoats and skirts. Oh, to be a seal!

They were joined by the two young men, who showed off

CHILDREN DEAR, WAS IT YESTERDAY?"

their dives, Lawrence managing a superb jackknife though the diving board was really not high enough. Vyvian threw the big red ball in, and by the time Edith and Viola emerged, Alix and Jane were screaming with joy as they threw the ball around. Allegra and James left them to it, after Allegra's head had been soaked with spray.

"Oh Mamma, I am sorry!" But Jane's eyes were sparkling with the joy of it all, and who cared about getting hair wet? Mamma certainly did not.

Nevertheless, when Edith and Vivyan joined in the game she and James went back to their chairs to watch and dry off in the hot sun.

Allegra drank the scene in, the activity in the pool, and then beyond it the long field, gold in August just before the haying, rippled in lovely waves by the breeze, and rolling right up to the farmhouse. Beyond it, sky, today a rather rare day, not a cloud in sight. She turned to her husband with one of those warm smiles that seemed to enfold him and the whole world around him in joyful appreciation and love. And he reached over and took her hand in his. They stayed on until Jane and Alix pulled themselves up the ladder and lay on the edge, panting.

"It's awful to feel so heavy again when you get back into the air," Jane said, lying on her back, looking up at the sky.

"You'd better get dressed, dears. You've been in a long time."

"Just one more swim, Mamma!"

"Very well, but someone might pick a bunch of flowers for Mr. Perkins' room . . . black-eyed Susans and Queen Anne's lace, on the way up to the house. I'll do a bunch for the table myself."

"We'd better get started . . ." Alix murmured. "The suits have to be rinsed, and everything."

Of course they were dressed and on their way up the winding

path that meandered around the emerald golf greens long before their parents followed. They picked assiduously, though the black-eyed Susans were tough and sometimes a whole plant got tugged out. But it was necessary to stop quite often and look out over the harbor to see what sail was gliding past, and to take a deep breath of the Mount Desert mountains, dark blue in the distance, ancient and round like sleeping elephants, Jane thought. Or to look the other way at the forest edge, spreading out from the tall trees to a tapestry of blueberry and wild cranberry bushes.

"I wish there didn't have to be a golf course," Jane said, "it spoils the wildness."

"Well, yes," Alix considered this. "But Pappa loves it."

"Croquet's a much fiercer, better game," Jane said. "And you don't need all those clubs and things."

"Anyway," said Alix, "it's just about a perfect place, you have to admit."

By the time the three-tiered Japanese gong had been rung with emphasis by Daisy, the whole clan quickly assembled. Allegra's bunch of delphinium, salpiglossis, and dahlias in a blue Chinese jar was glorious but hardly dominated the huge table on the porch, set for ten. Allegra and James sat opposite each other at either end, the older girls and their beaus facing the bay, Snooker between Jane and Alix, and on the other side Martha, on her father's right.

For a moment there was silence as Daisy laid a platter of swordfish before Mr. Reid and went back to fetch vegetable dishes. Allegra and James exchanged a glance and bowed their heads, and Allegra, unhurried, thought for a second or two before saying:

> "I will lift up mine eyes unto the hills
> from whence cometh my help.

My help cometh from the Lord, which made
heaven and earth."

"Why didn't you say it all, Mamma?" Jane asked.

"I have an idea everyone is rather hungry . . . and the swordfish is getting cold."

"It was just right, dear." James began to cut judiciously and gave Daisy the plates one by one to go down to Allegra for the beans and hashed brown potatoes.

"Martha picked the beans . . . and don't they look delicious?" Allegra noted, smiling down at her daughter at the other end of the table.

"Now you get your reward," James said as her plate was set down.

An atmosphere of tender regard was tangible in the way the family treated Martha, and it seemed sometimes as though she floated on the calm sea of family life, entirely happy, entirely accepting of the fact, which must have been hard to accept, that she lacked the beauty and magnetism of her two sisters . . . Viola so elegant and poised, and Edith so warm and open to life.

Once they were all served, conversation flowered as James turned to Lawrence with a teasing smile to ask him whether the Harvard football team had a chance of beating Yale this year, well aware that Vyvian at Yale might wish to argue the point.

"Ah!" Lawrence turned to Vyvian. "What do you think?"

"I don't think you have a chance!"

"We've got an Italian halfback, Rizzo, who will show Yale a thing or two—wait and see!"

Then Viola reminded her father of the awful thing he had done when she was about nine and they had walked through the Square on the day of the Yale game, she in a blue dress. "He told me everyone would think I was for Yale!" she said, smiling mischievously at Vyvian. "I've never been so humiliated."

"You burst into tears and your father felt like a criminal," Pappa chuckled.

"Do you play football, by the way?" Vyvian asked Lawrence.

"No, I'm on the freshman crew."

"That's something I really envy," said Vyvian.

"I'm a little better at it than at tennis, anyway."

Jane observed the two young men from across the table. They seemed so conscious of being in some way superior to any girl. They took it for granted that a stupid conversation like this must be interesting to everyone. Even Pappa went out of his way to make them shine and feel important. And there were Viola and Edith apparently entranced! It was a total mystery.

Luckily the conversation took a turn for the better as Vyvian noticed a purple finch at the feeder that swung from the porch beam, and this led to talk about the birds on the island and gave Jane a chance to describe the fish hawk's nest.

"Do the great horned owl," Alix begged.

"Oh yes," Lawrence said. "Please do that!"

"I don't know whether I can. . . ." Jane had actually seen a great horned owl the summer before apparently trying to get the attention of another great horned owl . . . an unforgettable sight which had immediately to be imitated for the family when she got home. "I have to get up to do it," she announced. "I need room."

So she stood behind her mother's chair and began hunching her shoulders, her arms turning visibly into wings that suddenly flapped while she called out from deep in her chest, a strange repeated hoot. It was a remarkable performance and was greeted with roars of laughter and applause.

"Why is it so funny, Snooker? It's exactly what it was like," said Jane, a little dismayed by the hilarious effect of her performance.

Snooker herself was laughing so hard it took her a moment

to calm down. "You're just so unlike a horned owl and so like one at the same time," she finally uttered.

"Where's the strawberry shortcake?" Alix asked, greatly disappointed to see a bowl of cut-up oranges being brought in by Daisy.

"We're saving that for Mr. Perkins, tonight," Mamma explained.

"There are brownies," Daisy whispered as she went past.

The best time, Jane always thought, was after luncheon, when they sat on, sipping demitasses, reluctant to leave the porch and separate. The best talks took place then. Sometimes they could persuade their mother to tell tales of her childhood in Cambridge, and especially of the autumn when her recently widowed father, the famous novelist, took her, his eldest child, to England and they were invited to several great houses for weekends, for Benjamin Trueblood was then at the height of his glory and received like a prince. How modest life in America had seemed by comparison! The carriages, the horses, the incredible numbers of servants. That is what Jane loved best; her eyes grew dreamy hearing about the wonderful gardens, the fountains, the artificial lakes, and everyone they met being a lord, or so she imagined.

But today Pappa was in a philosophical mood and the talk turned on what a hero is and whether Teddy Roosevelt could be called one. Lawrence felt he could most decidedly and defined a hero as brave and kind. But Vyvian disagreed, "Too full of himself and too brash for my taste." Viola felt strongly too, and suggested that there was something too undignified.

"Why does a hero have to be dignified?" Edith asked.

"Could a writer be a hero?" Jane broke in, thinking of her grandfather.

"Oh no." Lawrence was positive. "A hero must act! Must do something heroic, I mean, don't you agree, Mr. Reid?"

33

Pappa's eyes were twinkling. He enjoyed discussions like this and so did Jane, but Allegra was apt to feel that things might get a little too tense. Jane's passionate outbursts troubled her. And it was she who ended the discussion by rising from the table with one of her smiles, "It's time to think about a nap, James."

The mail pouch was lying on the dining room table inside and had to be rifled for possible letters. Viola, as usual, had one, and Martha. "I'm furious," said Edith. "David promised to write as soon as he got to France."

Snooker went up with Jane and Alix to tuck them in for the required hour's rest after luncheon, and begged them for once to close their eyes and try not to talk. They lay down and closed their eyes, but Jane recited the whole of Francis Thompson's "The Hound of Heaven," her favorite poem that summer, and Alix followed with a large chunk of "Hiawatha," after which there was silence for a half-hour. But who could rest with so much going on? And it was dismal to realize after a careful count that there were only thirty days before September tenth, when they would have to take the boat back to Massachusetts and school. "How can we bear it?" whispered Alix, informed of this fact.

"By then maybe Viola will be engaged."

At three Snooker came back with clean middy blouses and white, pleated skirts, and wide pale-blue ribbons to tie in a bow at the top of their pigtails. "You'd better hurry. Captain Philbrook wants to start at three."

"We're much too dressed up," Jane groaned. "It's not Sunday, after all."

It took Snooker years to get the bows right, but at last they were free and ran down to the dock, taking deep breaths of pine. . . . In midafternoon on a hot day there was a wonderful mixture of smells, the wild roses, seaweed, warm grasses, and pine needles, the island smell to be quaffed like an intoxicating drink.

"Right on time, Miss Jane." Captain Philbrook lifted his cap. It was low tide, the gangway to the float was steep, and Jane ran down so fast she bumped right into him.

"You could run right on into the water," he teased.

"Oh, I'm sorry. . . ."

"*West Wind* is all ready, so step right in, Miss Alix, Miss Jane."

He was at the wheel now and Alix and Jane stood on each side of him as he swung out and into the channel. "Very little wind today, hardly a breath. . . . I have an idea there'll be fog tonight. It's a weather breeder."

But the girls were not paying attention. They were in one of their trances of pure happiness sitting in the stern, not even talking.

Mr. Perkins was standing on the town dock and took off his Panama hat and waved as *West Wind* approached, and the girls waved back. It was always so exciting to meet someone, and especially someone familiar. There he stood in his white suit, with his stiff white collar and black tie, and his black boots. He was tall and thin, with a surprisingly round red face and bright brown eyes behind glasses, and he always seemed to be enjoying some private view of life that was entirely his own.

"He's just the same," Jane whispered to Alix, "that's what's so wonderful."

And perhaps he felt the same about them, for he said after the greetings, "You haven't changed, dear girls."

"I'm an inch taller," Jane said, teasing him. "I'm fourteen now and Alix is twelve. We're nearly grown-up."

While Captain Philbrook took charge of the suitcase and an elegant dispatch case, Jane had received the large package tied with a thin gold ribbon, her eyes shining in anticipation.

And Mr. Perkins observed her with evident pleasure. For

everything that was happening inside Jane was reflected in an extraordinary way in those blue eyes, so the anticipation of chocolates from Sherry gave her now a special radiance, and this elicited a wink from her observer, one of his rare winks that she recognized as a shy form of admiration.

For those taken into the world of the island, part of the charm was surely that nothing changed. Long before the dock came into sight, Mr. Perkins was standing ready to wave, but when they drew nearer and he could see six people he became a little nervous.

"I don't see very well, but who are all those people, Captain Philbrook?"

"Oh, you must mean the two young men . . . Vyvian and Lawrence, friends of Miss Viola and Miss Edith."

"Ah . . ." Mr. Perkins nodded, taking in the white flannels and blue and red sweaters, and lifted his hat and waved as Allegra and James, his old friends, stood apart smiling and waving their welcome, James so tall and loose-limbed and Allegra small, compact, round, looking especially charming today in a wide-skirted pink linen dress.

"Well, well," he said, shaking hands all round.

And then as the procession started up toward the house, Captain Philbrook bringing up its rear with the luggage in a wheelbarrow, Allegra took his arm and they talked, and laughed as she pointed out that Jane was carrying the big box of chocolates like a sacred object, leading them all. "You shouldn't have, Donald, but of course the children are crazy about chocolates!"

"Jane is becoming a beauty," he whispered.

"Oh such a gangling girl," Allegra said, shy of such praise, and unwilling to admit that Jane was almost a young woman. For the little ones, she felt, must stay children as long as possible. It would be too sad when no one was a child any longer.

"It's her eyes. I've never seen such eyes."

But sensing the slight withdrawal on Allegra's part he added, "In a way we are contemporaries. Jane is fourteen, she told me, and I have been thinking that it must be about fourteen years ago that we came up to look at the island. James wanted my advice, you remember."

"I do indeed . . . and that you were hesitant."

Mr. Perkins looked quite solemn, "It seemed a rather large undertaking at the time."

"It did, didn't it, Donald?" James, taking Allegra's free arm under his, joined them. "But I have to say now that I've never regretted it."

It would have been hard for any of them at this point to imagine life without the island.

Alix had left the group and was picking raspberries, wild ones that grew on either side of the path. Now she ran to Mr. Perkins to offer him a handful.

"Thank you," he said, smiling happily, and ate them in one mouthful. "The island has a taste too, doesn't it?"

Later, after Mr. Perkins had settled in to his room, the guest room with a balcony where he spent long hours reading and writing on the chaise longue and watching the sails float past, after he had hung up two suits and washed his hands, he joined Allegra, James, Snooker, and the girls for tea on the big porch. The girls sat in the swing, a couch suspended on chains, and swung back and forth, dangling their legs.

"It's just a long soak in happiness to be here," he said, "and yes, I'll have a second cup."

"I presume the two couples have gone for a sail?" James asked his wife.

"Yes, Captain Philbrook thinks we'll have fog tomorrow, so they took the chance. . . ."

"Not much wind."

"Come and play a game of croquet before supper," Alix begged.

"Mr. Perkins must be tired," Snooker said, shaking her head. "He's had a long journey, you know."

"I slept very well on the train, as a matter of fact. And why not a game of croquet?"

"Hurrah!" Jane was on her feet. "Mamma, Pappa, let's all play!"

Pappa had work to do in the office, but Allegra decided to come along and do some gardening while they played. But on the way she sat down on the cushioned bench in the office for a little talk with James. Vyvian had now been with them for nearly a week, and she was not entirely happy with the idea that this time Viola, surrounded by admiring young men as she had always been, might be serious. Vyvian certainly appeared to be. "Has he talked to you, James?"

"No, but I have, I think, seen that look of an impending talk in his eye."

"Oh dear."

"Why not, after all? He's handsome enough, and very rich, from what I have learned."

"That doesn't matter," Allegra said firmly.

"Viola is so sure of herself—I would prefer she married someone well enough off so she would not rule the roost in that area at least. Besides, Viola wants a life of fashion, you know. She has that air already of a woman of the world, as they say."

Allegra caught the twinkle in his eye. He knew very well that this family into which he had married prided themselves on not being worldly at all. It was one thing to give a million dollars to the Annex of Harvard, where women students were relegated; it was quite another to give balls and opera parties as Boston society did. The Truebloods were Cambridge and Cambridge was plain living and high thinking.

"We've produced a bird of paradise," she said. "It seems very unlike us, James."

Then they both laughed and Allegra got up and kissed the top of his head.

"If you think they'll be happy, dear . . ."

"That really cannot be foreseen, can it? One can hope, of course. . . . I like Vyvian. He has a sense of humor and seems a balanced young man. She could do worse, Allegra. Remember that Italian count?"

She remembered all too well. Luckily all that was left of him was a pale-blue officer's cape that Viola wore to dances.

And Allegra walked up to the garden, thoughtfully, comforted by the shouts of laughter that greeted her as Mr. Perkins and her little girls shared some secret joke. Nevertheless, she was frowning as she picked dead heads off the dahlias and salpiglossis, the velvety salpiglossis she loved. If only Viola could fall in love with an unworldly young man!

Though it was still light on the porch and the candles had not had to be lit for supper, when they all trooped into the big room, it was dark enough for the Aladdin lamps to be needed. The room was a little like a cave, shadowed on one whole side by the porch, and dominated by a great stone fireplace with a black bear rug before it, surrounded by deep sofas and velvet armchairs. This was the hour Jane loved almost best, the hour when they all gathered for an hour's reading aloud, the hour when she curled up on the bear rug, hugging its head, and listened dreamily to her mother's voice, sitting in the big chair under the lamp. Sometimes the logs crackled so loudly, and occasionally made a sound like a pistol shot, that it was quite an interruption, but tonight Daisy had lit the fire early and it had quieted to a lovely red glow. James sat opposite his wife, smoking a cigar. Mr. Perkins chose the corner behind the lamp, and the two couples were squeezed onto the big sofa. Alix had taken a cushion and was sitting with her head against Pappa's knee.

"We've just begun *Nicholas Nickleby,*" Mamma said, "but I'm sure you remember it, Mr. Perkins? So I'll go on to chapter two, if I may."

In Jane's view Mamma's reading was perfection. She had a gentle voice capable of every inflection and irony, and enjoyed herself so much that the pleasure was contagious. And soon the attention was absolute, punctuated by a ripple of laughter now and then. When Jane lifted her head to exchange a glance with Alix she noticed that Vyvian held Viola's hand firmly in his. Whatever Dickens had to say at that moment went unheard, as Jane suffered one of those explosions of feeling that brought tears to her eyes. She buried her face in the bear's comforting head so no one would notice, but she felt acute discomfort and didn't know why, except that Vyvian and Viola were drawing a magic circle around themselves that excluded everyone else, and that would, eventually, break into and even destroy the precious family circle. I don't want it to happen, Jane thought fiercely. I don't want Viola to go away. I don't want anything to change. In some terrible way it seemed the beginning of the end. Mamma and Papa hadn't changed yet, but Jane in her gloom saw them grow old and die. Did passionate love always bring the shadow of death with it?

It was a relief when Allegra reached the end of the chapter and Snooker suggested that it was time for bed.

"Jane was fast asleep already," said Alix, for once not in tune with her sister, and handed Jane her candle already lit. They said their good nights and, preceded by their long shadows, climbed the wide staircase, each holding her candle flickering in the air currents, so it must be shielded with one hand.

I have to admit that I am very disappointed with this first attempt at novelizing. There seem to be so many details, and it was so hard to get at the core of the matter. Maybe it will be easier when I myself appear as a character later on, and when memory rather than imagination can operate. But for now I feel I must cheat and tell the reader something of what had to be left out, or what I lacked the art to render effectively. What was most in my mind was to suggest that the island was both a real place, as it still is, but also a metaphor—the island and the life lived there in 1910 are a vanished world. Jane was a child at a time when there was strong belief in the perfectibility of man, when nothing immediately threatened peace, in the world before 1914.

Those who experienced that world could not be prepared for cataclysm, or even for the income tax, which would make great wealth a little harder to come by. James Reid was already a rich man at thirty, when he married Allegra Trueblood, who was, herself, the inheritor of a fortune at a time when inheritance taxes were minimal. In those days a man could not propose marriage in their circles unless he could support his wife. But added to all this, the Reids were an especially close-knit family and the island enhanced the privacy of family life. I have hardly begun to suggest how rich and various this was through the summers when five daughters were growing up.

James Reid had grown up in Minnesota and had with his three brothers become an experienced woodsman and camper long before he went East to Harvard College. At least once every summer he would announce at breakfast that this looked like a good day for a night on the mountain. Sleeping bags were rolled up, the big enamel coffee pot and its mugs, eggs, bacon, bread, and milk were packed into rucksacks and baskets, and finally the expedition set out across the harbor for the climb. There was stargazing, and moonrise to observe, and a great sing around the fire, and nobody slept much, although when James got up at dawn to build the fire, he moved among what looked like half a dozen mummies.

Sometimes less elaborate outdoor feasts were held at various favorite picnic spots on the island, or they might decide to sail right up Soames Sound, the nearest thing to a Norwegian fjord on the entire east coast of North America, and find a niche under the steep cliffs for a picnic of corned beef hash and cookies. Or they might decide on Baker's Island and picnic on rocks facing open sea.

The whole family was mad about acting and would dress up on the least occasion and make up a play to perform in the evening of a rainy day, even when the audience was composed only of Captain Philbrook, Snooker, Daisy, and cook. Sometimes they read a Shakespeare play aloud, taking turns at the "best parts." Jane at sixteen was a remarkable Lady Macbeth, I am told, coming down the stairs in her nightgown with a candle for the famous scene. And ever after there were jokes about "all the perfumes of Arabia."

The weather, always changing, provided drama, too. More than once, boats grounded in the fog, and strangers loomed up, grateful for light, warmth, and a hot meal, and for help in getting the boat afloat and tied up to the dock for the night.

Guests came and went, and many were family: the aunts of course . . . Aunt Susan, who had taken the Harvard Annex under her wing, and Aunt Viola, who had married a Norwegian cellist and came over for a whole summer whenever she could bear to part with him, or when he was off on a world tour. The Minnesota cousins, two handsome boys, came one summer and it was always supposed that Martha's heart was broken by one of them. (Marriage with a first cousin was taboo.) There were days when fourteen sat down to luncheon on the porch, friends sailed over from Northeast Harbor or from Southwest Harbor. But all these guests and the older girls' beaus seemed like an extension of family, and in Vyvian's case eventually became family. They were the same kind of people.

Yet with all the goings and comings, the picnics and expeditions, there was ample room for solitary exploration and for adventure by oneself. If anything was lacking, I have sometimes wondered whether it was not intimacy between parents and children. When there are so many involved, when was there time, where a place for a quiet heart-to-heart talk? This happened perhaps only in a crisis. So that role, the role of understander and confidante, fell to Snooker, as far as Jane and Alix at least were concerned. It was to Snooker they ran in tears when deprived of something dearly wanted, such as to be allowed to row alone to Northeast Harbor to see a friend. It was Snooker who insisted that a doctor must be fetched when Jane had a high fever and a pain in her side which turned out to be appendicitis, the operation taking place just in time. It was Snooker above all who listened to the anxieties and woes of adolescence, for one of the salient characteristics of Allegra was extreme reticence when it came to any problem that might be interpreted as sexual. In this family, as in most families of the period, such things were never talked about.

Snooker, always deferential toward her employers, had a mind of her own, and a fanatical devotion to her two girls. Without exactly criticizing their parents, she made it quite clear that she sometimes did not agree with a decision or rule. She was the refuge in time of trouble, the comforter in time of woe, and perhaps Snooker was at least partly responsible for Jane's flowering as she did. Mamma and Pappa may have been rather like gods, adored, but seen as always a little distant—partly because they were deeply in love, held themselves apart. They enjoyed their children mightily, however, of that there could never be any doubt.

What did it do in the deepest sense to be brought up in a

world like this? And how did the Jane Reid I knew emerge finally as herself from such a patterned background, in essence conventional? It did not happen as revolt, but as I put together the bits and pieces, I have come to believe it happened as simply an overflowing love of life that took her on adventures that stemmed from a vivid response to people and from pressures inside her to feel and experience everything possible. So she was drawn out of the family circle quite naturally without the need to break out, or to deny anything for the sake of something else. For example, she had a good ear and when she was fourteen was given a violin by her Aunt Susan, who had enjoyed hearing her sing, for I have omitted a very important gift in the preceding pages. Jane had a beautiful alto and burst into song whenever she was alone and whenever there was a chance within a group. At school this meant singing in the yearly Gilbert and Sullivan performances, where both her voice and her acting ability, and the fact that she was tall and loved taking men's parts, gave her the chance at big parts when she was still a child. She felt an instant rapport with her violin and played well enough to be in the school orchestra, but the problem was to find time to practice. How often between the ages of fourteen and sixteen she must have heard some teacher say, "You could do very well, Jane, if you would only concentrate!" But how concentrate when every day brought such an infinity of things one wanted to do? How choose?

At fourteen she was, one might say, simply a loving, warm young person, a kind of all-round person who might turn out to be one of a hundred things, including a wife. But there was, nevertheless, something that already set her apart from her sisters, something that Mr. Perkins had noted. It was in her eyes, in the way the soul leapt up through their blue, the spell they cast entirely unconsciously, for at fourteen she was far from being a beauty and was too aware of what beauty could be as she observed Edith and Viola. But "spell," it occurs to me, suggests a sexual attraction . . . it was not that at all. It was an amazing openness and power to be moved, a power that could be embarrassing, for it might carry her into an explosion of laughter, or a flood of tears, that seemed out of proportion in an adult world, and sometimes got her into trouble.

It was what delighted Maurice Hadley, a young lawyer who had been invited to dinner to meet Edith. The talk had turned to Sarah Bernhardt, who was playing in Boston, and Jane said, "I would give anything to see her. . . ." Maurice Hadley saw the blue flame in her eyes, met the intensity of it by chance across the table, and on an impulse said,

"I'll take you to the Saturday matinee . . . may I, Mrs. Reid? May I capture your daughter for an afternoon?"

There was a second's hesitation as Allegra and James queried each other in a glance.

"Oh, please, Mamma, Pappa!"

"I think it would be all right. Maurice can act as a kind of surrogate uncle," James said with a twinkle in his eye.

"It is awfully kind of you," Allegra assented.

It did seem a little strange that this handsome dark-eyed young man should choose Jane, a little girl, they all felt, but he seemed sincere in his wish to give her a pleasure she wanted desperately. And after all, why not? Snooker beamed.

"The only trouble is we'll be living with Sarah Bernhardt for at least a week after you come back," Edith teased. "Jane can mimic anyone, Maurice, even a great horned owl!"

"As long as it does not involve getting a leopard to live here," Viola added.

"Or a coffin to sleep in," Martha giggled.

"Don't tease me," Jane said, blushing furiously. And Maurice showed his tact by changing the subject to politics.

45

"Oh, Snooker, how can I ever wait till Saturday?" Jane asked when Snooker came to tuck her in that night.

"Dearie, try not to get overexcited. Remember, it's a little hard on Alix, this sudden interest in you. You've always done things together."

"Why didn't Maurice ask Alix, too?"

And how did one answer that, Snooker must have wondered. For it was quite clear that for the present it was Sarah Bernhardt and the thought of seeing the greatest actress in the world, not Maurice, that would keep Jane awake that night.

"You will have to figure that one out for yourself," she said, patting Jane's head. "Now try to sleep. You have a French test tomorrow, you know."

When Alix came in from her bath to go to bed in the other small iron bedstead opposite Jane's she whispered, "Do you think he's in love with you?"

"Of course not, don't be silly. It's not that at all," Jane said, alarmed, a little disconcerted.

At last Saturday came. Snooker had spent the day before letting down Jane's red velvet best dress, and washing and ironing the round lace collar. White stockings and black patent leather slippers were all prepared, and on Saturday morning she washed Jane's hair. The preparations seemed interminable, especially sitting in the rocker in the sun waiting and waiting for it to dry. Alix had gone to her best friend's for the day, for everyone in the family knew that this first departure from their entity, the inseparable "little ones," was difficult for her.

Finally, when Jane was all dressed before lunch Mamma came in with a little black velvet pouch. "You had better have something to put a handkerchief in," she said.

"Oh dear, thanks, I'm bound to cry," Jane said.

"Try not to, dearie, you don't want to embarrass Maurice."

"I can't help it, Mamma. She's going to die on the stage."

"Well, don't begin now," Snooker laughed at her.

At last it was half past one. Jane had not been able to eat and swallowed down a glass of milk only at Mamma's insistence. She was all ready in her blue coat with a fur collar and a dark blue velour hat with a wide brim; she had on Edith's white gloves when the doorbell tinkled.

"You look splendid," said Maurice. "What a splendid girl!"

Mamma and Pappa waved them off, and then Jane was alone with someone she hardly knew, in a hansom cab, a conveyance she had never experienced before. What an adventure!

It took an hour to go from Cambridge to the theater by cab, but for Jane the time simply flew. For once she was allowed to talk as much as she wanted to someone who seemed genuinely interested and amused. "Alix is the only person who ever listens to me," she said at one point, "so you must stop me if I go on too long." She had made Maurice laugh by describing her French teacher, who was able to make a whole dramatic scene out of a small incident which if spoken in English would have seemed negligible if not boring, and who wore Paris hats and a black velvet ribbon round her throat. In the heat of this piece of theater Jane took off her hat and swung it in the air, saying, *"Vive la France!"* And then, *"Ouf! Je suis bien mieux sans mon chapeau, n'est-ce pas, Oncle Maurice?"*

"Yes," he said, giving her a critical look, "you look like Alice in Wonderland." And so she did with her long fair hair, just slightly wavy from being plaited, and a dark-blue velvet ribbon holding it back.

She gave a sigh and leaned back against the leather seat. "Don't you love the smell of leather?"

"Mmm, yes."

"Especially when it's mixed with the smell of horse."

And for a second then Jane looked at him, really looked at him without shyness, because she felt they were friends. The mood changed, and she began asking him questions about himself, what it was like to be a lawyer and what exactly it meant and how it felt to sit at a desk all day poring over huge volumes, and Maurice found himself telling her things he didn't often talk about. "Anything worth doing has a lot of tedious work involved, but it's a little like a hunt. You always hope to find a precedent that will give you something to stand on, so it's worth all the digging. . . ."

And Jane was grateful because he was talking to her quite seriously without condescension.

"What do you dream of doing?" she asked.

"Do you really want to know?"

"Of course."

"It's not 'of course,' but I'll pretend you mean it."

"I don't say things I don't mean."

He turned to give her a piercing look. "No, I guess you don't. Most people do."

"Because of what Mamma calls the 'amenities.' When you grow up you have to lie a lot of the time."

"And you think you won't . . . when you're grown-up?"

"It depends on what I decide to do," Jane said. "I mean I'm not going to be like Viola and Edith, who are only interested in getting married."

"Bravo for you!" Maurice said, smiling at her. "But . . ."

"Oh, I know, people change. They can't help it. But right now I am who I am, and please tell me your dream."

Maurice's dream was to found a law firm which would be designed to help people who cannot afford a lawyer, who have learned the hard way that they don't have much of a chance.

"What do they do now?" Jane asked, her eyes wide.

"Pay up. Go to jail."

"That's awful," Jane said.

48

"Yes . . . well, it means getting the government interested. It would have to be financed, so I may have to go into politics first to get anything of the sort accomplished."

"Pappa would like to hear about that," Jane said.

But they were now in a throng of carriages on Charles Street, and life outside the cab was so interesting that they became absorbed in watching the drivers pull in and out and Jane became suddenly anxious that they might be late.

"Don't worry, they'll hold the curtain for such important people," Maurice told her.

And indeed they were settled in their seats, fifth row on the aisle, ten minutes before the curtain went up. "I can't believe it," Jane whispered, as the orchestra tuned up in the pit and launched into the prologue of *Traviata*. "Sarah Bernhardt in *Camille*." She was hugging herself with excitement, the bliss of it, leaning forward in her seat, as the lights dimmed and they waited for the immense red curtain to go up. And when it made that slight rustle as it glided upwards she turned to Maurice with a smile of pure joy. But after that, nothing existed for her except what was going on on the stage, except the slight figure in white and the strange haunting slightly nasal voice of Bernhardt. Every now and then Maurice glanced over at the uplifted face beside him, a person literally entranced, totally unaware that she was being observed. He had never before witnessed someone who could give herself up so completely. And he wondered how life would use this power . . . or abuse it, and what it really was.

In the intermission he asked if she would like to stretch her legs, but she shook her head, and as she clearly wished not to talk, he left her and went out to the foyer to have a smoke and be greeted by various acquaintances, including his Aunt Maude, a great gossip who asked, "Who is that pretty girl you have with you, Maurice?"

He explained that she was Jane Reid, "I am her surrogate uncle, this afternoon."

"Oh?" Aunt Maude lifted an eyebrow.

"She's just fourteen, Aunt Maude—now, come."

It is the instinct of society to spoil everything, he thought as he turned away. He would not brook teasing about Jane. He wanted to guard her and himself, to guard something precious that he did not even want to define. And when he slipped into his seat beside her, he felt at home. They did not have to talk, to make small talk. How much he enjoyed being with a girl who didn't have to flirt or ask some response from him to herself, a girl who could lose herself completely in an experience beyond them both.

But in the last act, the agonizing waiting for Armand and his arrival like a touch of warm wind at last, as he handed Jane a large white handkerchief, her mother's small one having been soaked, and saw the tears flowing down her cheeks, he wondered if all this was a little much for her.

"Oh Maurice," she whispered when the lights went on and the applause, rising in wave after wave, shattered the illusion and shocked Jane back into the theater, and made her cover her face with both hands.

"We'll stay a while," he whispered, "till they've left."

"I can't bear it to be over."

But it really wasn't over because they had the long drive back to Cambridge and could talk about it all, and remember each gesture and intonation. Jane, who had been, as she said herself, "a wreck" a half-hour before, was sparkling with all she wanted to share and discuss, and astonished Maurice with what she had taken in even while being so deeply moved. They agreed that the actor who played Armand was rather a bore and simply did not have the passion in him required by his part. "I think it's not easy to do," Jane said thoughtfully. "But I would have done some things differently myself."

"Like what?"

"I didn't feel he really looked at her at the end . . . looked into her face, *saw* that she was dying. . . ."

"Could you do that?"

Then she laughed, "Of course not. . . . I just like to imagine."

They sat then in a companionable silence for some time, until they were on Brattle Street and nearly home.

"I can't bear for it to be over," Jane said again.

"Well, Hampden is coming in *Cyrano de Bergerac* after Christmas. How would you like to see that?"

"Oh Maurice!"

It was dark when they drove up to the door. There on the doorsill, Jane flung her arms around Maurice and kissed his cheek, "Thank you," she said, just as Mamma opened the door.

"Come in, come in, Maurice . . . and tell us all about it."

But he made an excuse of work to do, paid the cabbie, and walked over to the Square. Somehow he wanted to keep the Jane he had taken to the theater to himself, not be present as she was swallowed up by the family.

Much later, when the tale had been told in every detail at supper, and when Snooker came to say goodnight to the girls, she asked, "What was he like, dearie?"

"Perfect, just perfect," Jane said. "He understands everything. He didn't make me go out in the intermission. He gave me a big handkerchief when I needed it terribly, and we sat in the theater till *everyone* had gone."

"Mmm," Snooker said solemnly, "it's a wholly characteristic definition of perfection, a young man who does everything *you* want."

51

"Oh," Jane said, blushing with the shame of it. "But Snooker, I think he understands me. We're friends. Can't you see?"

"I'm teasing, dearie. You're much too high up in the air to be teased right now."

"I'm happier than I've ever been, if that's what you mean."

Alix, sitting up in her bed, threw a pillow at her sister and the entity was re-established with a pillow fight that ended only when they were both out of breath, and Snooker turned out the light.

In the next year Edith entered the Annex at Harvard and Viola married Vyvian. Maurice was firmly entrenched as Jane's friend, a circumstance Jane took quite for granted, but that was unusual, for the older girls were not allowed out with their beaus without a chaperone. Maurice had been persuasive that his role was that of an uncle, so he was allowed to take Jane to the rink to skate, and four or five times a year to the theater. Those were the gala afternoons, of course. None more memorable than *Cyrano de Bergerac*, their second outing, when Maurice proved his perfection in an unforgettable way. Jane, of course, was dissolved at the end, and had used up two large linen handkerchiefs by the time the curtain went down. This time she was crying not only because it was so sad, but because it was over. "I can't bear it to be over, Maurice," she said. But then he felt in the inside pocket of his jacket and brought out two tickets for the matinee the following week.

"I knew we would have to see it again," he told her.

When Snooker was told about that, she shook her head. "I have to admit that that *is* perfection, dearie."

She did not add what she was no doubt thinking, that Jane had such abundance of life in her and responded so swiftly and at such depth to any event that she constantly took herself and everyone else by surprise.

At school she was always in demand for plays and singing, but did not do as well as Alix in her regular lessons, except in the reciting of poetry. Snooker had puzzled about this from the time she was teaching Jane to read. She was quite slow at learning, and very stubborn. She wanted to do things in her own way . . . once took the first reader out of Snooker's hands and went off into a corner with it, determined to work out the words by herself. Sometimes this trait irritated her teachers because Jane, determined to understand, continued to ask questions when the subject had been rather completely covered. In the ninth grade now, she had to write short papers, and they were always handed in late because she put off beginning in time, and then got in very deep, too late to do as good a job as she might have.

"Jane is very thorough and works hard, but seems a little slow," was the comment on one report. "Her emotions are ahead of her intellect at present. She is behind in math partly because she does not enjoy figures."

"It's not that I don't enjoy math," she said to Mamma when this report was explained to her. "I just can't get it through my head. When Miss Rogers explains I can feel my mind going blank right away. My head gets so hot, I think it's going to burst!"

"Miss Rogers is very violent," Alix came to the rescue. "She shouts at Jane . . . she treats any mistake as a *sin*, Mamma!"

"It appears to be a collision between two powerful forces," Pappa murmured from behind the *Boston Evening Transcript.* "I have an idea you're getting into your own way. Just pretend it isn't important."

"But it *is* important," Jane answered passionately. "I can't graduate without math."

Maurice came to the rescue and for three weeks spent two hours every Saturday afternoon helping Jane with algebra. He discovered that it was at least partly a matter of tempo. Jane simply could not be hurried, but if one had patience and she was allowed to make mistakes and flounder for a while, the light was apt to dawn.

"Oh Maurice, I've got it. I see what I did wrong . . . there!" And quite often she had to hug him with the relief of it.

This was a different girl from the one he took to the theater, one who seemed able to understand completely and to feel with things far beyond her age. It was also a different girl from the one with whom he waltzed at the rink and who had a wonderful flow and skill on skates, even though she was almost as tall as he and might have made him feel awkward. There was nothing awkward about her, and Maurice decided that that was because she seemed totally unselfconscious. He wondered sometimes if she was even aware that she was beautiful. Am I in love with her? Maurice sometimes asked himself. And decided that he was not, partly perhaps because he was very much aware that if he overstepped his role as surrogate uncle there would be hell to pay. And then their friendship was so unlike any other relationship he had ever had with a girl, he wanted to keep it as it was, innocent and deep.

He was asked to debutante parties as an eligible bachelor and enjoyed flirting and squeezing a girl's hand as much as any young man, enjoyed the sensation of holding a young woman in his arms in a waltz, the softness of a young woman. But somehow these feelings had never led him into a desire to go further, to capture one of these charming young ladies and make her his wife. And sometimes he worried about this. Would he ever fall in love? Twenty-eight seemed awfully old.

Jane was very sympathetic. "I can't understand anything about it," she told him. "I don't want to be touched. Maybe there's something frightfully wrong with both of us!" And at that they laughed, secure in all they shared, glad to shut out what everyone else did and everyone else felt.

But in the year Jane graduated, Allegra and James came to

the conclusion that now she was putting her hair up, Jane would have to stop seeing Maurice. Or only with a chaperone present. Maurice was asked to come for a little talk at eleven one Saturday morning while Jane, not told of this, was sent off to play tennis with Alix.

"I know you will understand, Maurice, that Jane is about to come out into society, and what was unusual even when she was only a child will now become impossible."

"Mrs. Reid, you must believe that I have never by a word or gesture gone beyond the limits of an uncle and a niece."

"Dear boy, I do believe you . . . your discretion and kindness have been impeccable. You have given Jane joys she will never forget. We are grateful." There was a slight pause while Allegra arranged the bow at her throat. "But . . . ."

Maurice observed this small firm person sitting very straight and wondered how on earth to deal with her conviction. "You don't know what you're doing!" he said passionately. "It's cruel!"

"Please don't make it harder for me than it is," she said with great dignity. "I have often wondered whether our decision to permit such a friendship was wise. You will make me regret it, Maurice, if you persist."

"Jane will never understand," he said, rocking back and forth as though in physical pain. "How can you do this to her?"

"You are making me very unhappy," Allegra said, but her glance did not yield. "I think you must promise me and my husband that you will not try to see Jane or communicate with her for a year. Give her a chance to meet other young men closer to her own age. I know you are fond of Jane, and I ask this for her sake."

Maurice was close to tears, and so ashamed of the intensity of his feelings that he got up with only one instinct, to get away as fast as possible. "You have my promise, Mrs. Reid."

"Thank you."

She gave him a firm, warm handshake. And then, with a characteristic gesture, slipped an arm through his as she escorted him to the door. It was so unexpected he felt quite undone.

"Good-bye, dear Maurice."

And then the door closed behind him. In the distance he could see a white dress, returning a serve, running, running to the net.

It was the first major crisis in Jane's life. No doubt she had been occasionally deprived of something she wanted very much to do, usually something that involved risk of one sort or another. But this attacked her inmost self, and seemed an invasion of her very being. It was so unlike Mamma, warm, loving Mamma, who often persuaded her husband to give her daughters a free rein, but when Jane had tried to argue her mother said, "The subject is closed," and left the room.

There were torrents of tears and many a night her pillow was soaked after Alix was safely asleep. Even Snooker was hard put to say anything comforting. This was a matter of honor and she could not take Jane's side against her mother.

"It's the price you pay for being who you are," she said.

"And who is that?" Jane cried out. "I'm not a criminal!"

"You are a beautiful young woman whom many a young man is going to want to marry, and . . ." here Snooker hesitated, but Jane might as well face reality while they were at it, "you will inherit considerable wealth someday."

"What's money if it makes you miserable and cuts you off from your best friend?"

"It seems hard, I know, dearie, but you'll get over it in time."

"I'll never get over it," Jane said quietly. "It's rocked my faith in everything."

As far as anyone could see, she did get over it in time, but what they could not know was that when the tears stopped flowing—no one cries forever—a determination was forming to do things her own way as far as that was possible. And the first visible sign of this new firmness and will was Jane's decision to go to Vassar. Who had ever heard of a Reid or Trueblood female not going to the Annex, Radcliffe College as it would soon become? Edith was there, doing brilliantly, and it had been taken for granted that Jane would live at home, and see young men, the brothers and friends of her schoolmates in the normal social life of Cambridge.

James Reid was violently opposed to her wish. The first time Jane spoke of Vassar he had flung his napkin down and left the room, a gesture of such unusual violence that it silenced the whole family. Jane had blushed to the roots of her hair, but held her head erect. And perhaps because Allegra had minded dismissing Maurice more than she let on, she decided there and then to back Jane. That night in bed she and James had a long talk about it. And she was able to persuade him that real harm could be done if Jane ceased to trust her parents to be fair. "In time she will understand about Maurice . . . but she won't understand if we force her in the matter of her education. And, truly, James, there is something to be said for leaving home to go to college. She will make friends on her own, people from other parts of the country."

"People from other parts of the country, as you put it, come to Harvard and Radcliffe. . . . after all, I, her father, did so, and you didn't meet me, my dear, by going to Vassar!" But the tone had changed and now they were laughing. Allegra knew it was going to be all right.

Vassar did seem very far away compared, for instance, to Smith, Wellesley, or Mount Holyoke . . . but Jane was adamant, and when she told her parents that two of her class at school were entering Vassar, they felt reassured.

There would be one more summer at the island before, as

Martha put it, "everything starts breaking apart." She had been thinking of the family, but what she could not know and none of them could know was that the guns of August would precipitate a world war that would radically change the safe, hopeful ethos of their childhood forever. For this was 1914.

I have chosen to dwell on Maurice and that friendship at some length because, as I think over Jane's life, it seems clear to me that it was of great importance in her growth as a human being, and perhaps the enforced parting set her on a course she would follow to the end of her life.

After the year of silence, Jane and Maurice did see each other again. Nothing changed their ability to meet and talk about everything, and when he volunteered for the ambulance corps and went to France he wrote Jane at Vassar long, confidential letters. She was one of the bridesmaids at his wedding, and godmother to his first child, a daughter named for her.

It is odd that, on the whole, novelists speak little of friendship between opposite sexes, and especially these days, when sexual encounters dominate everything else in most fictional characters. I am writing about a woman who had a genius for friendship with both sexes, and touched deeply an enormous number and variety of lives. Could she have done so to the same extent, and at the same depth, had she married? I think not. It is one of the questions I hope to be able to probe as I pursue my quarry.

I now come to a block, for although Jane always glowed with happiness whenever she talked of Vassar, we had so much else to talk about when I knew her as a grown-up person myself that only rarely did I glean some facts about that seminal time in her life. But one thing is certain. She met at Vassar a young woman, Lucy Goodspeed, who was to be woven into the rest of her life as her most intimate friend. Jane's nickname at Vassar was

Reedy, possibly a reference to her height, or simply a diminutive of her family name, but whenever I was with her and someone called her Reedy, I knew that person had been a classmate at Vassar.

When one saw Lucy and Jane together it was clear that Lucy had the greatest respect for her friend, that although she was herself head of a girls' school, she deferred to Reedy out of love and something like honor. She honored Jane, and was able to prove it in singular ways. For instance, for years she went over Jane's accounts (shades of dismal math days at school), which were apt to be in some confusion. Lucy was dark, with deepest brown eyes and a rather dark skin, and reminded me of a bird, a shy bird. My guess is that at Vassar she had entered Jane's orbit as one of a group who gravitated toward that immense vitality and sense of adventure, for Jane was an imaginer of every sort of fun, an instigator of every sort of adventure, from picnics by the lake to plays. I have hesitated to use the tarnished word "glamour," but there is no doubt that Jane Reid had it and that women as well as men were entranced by those extraordinary eyes, that women as well as men wanted to ally themselves with her in one way or another.

But then Jane herself had an instinct for devotion, an intense need to follow as well as to lead. She could be swept off her feet, and at Vassar she was, by a young instructor in the English department, Miss Frances Thompson. Miss Thompson was very tall, very thin, quite plain, but she was a great teacher who could tease her students, only a few years younger than she, as well as inspire them, and she had a contagious passion for education. Also she opened doors for Jane into a new world, for Miss Thompson came from Chicago and her father was the well-known head of a settlement house there. She had been brought up among the poor with a burning sense of the injustices done to immigrants, and the need to help was bred into her bones.

59

She brushed away Jane's somewhat Victorian ideas of poetry by reciting Carl Sandburg's "Chicago," its terse, vigorous language and its celebration not of the beautiful but of the tough and harsh. This is what Jane had been looking for when she decided to go to Vassar. Not the genteel world in which she had been brought up, but the real world, or what she thought of as "real." In the course of two years under Miss Thompson she came to the decision that teaching was what she wanted to do.

So it came as a blow but also as an opportunity when Frances told her one day in Jane's senior year that she was going back to Chicago to teach at the Parker School, and that if Jane would like to come along and get some training there, it might be arranged.

All the charming, seductive things about college life were still there, but as the war dragged on and became more terrible, the young men with whom Jane had danced were volunteering for the Canadian army or, as Maurice had done, for the ambulance corps. France, greatly beloved, became almost as dear as the United States, and the students sang the "Marseillaise" on their way to classes. Lucy and Anne dreamed of getting over somehow as soon as they graduated. Like everyone else, they knitted socks and sweaters and rolled bandages in their spare time.

As I ponder the very little I know about those years two images stand out above all others. The first I found out quite by accident, and it was illuminating. On my way to the island I had stopped to see a former classmate of Jane's to deliver a present to her from a mutual friend, and thought Jane would be happy to hear what Jewel was like now that they were each in their seventies. I learned then that Jane had never forgotten and would never forgive a practical joke played on her by Jewel a few days after she arrived at Vassar, terrified, homesick, and taking comfort in a family of Brownies, small plump figures covered in silk, which were her fetishes at that time. When she came back to her room after supper, the Brownies had disappeared, *stolen*. There was anger in her eyes when she told me this story fifty years later, and it was clear that Jewel would never be forgiven—although she did return the beloved Brownies a few days later. It has stuck in my mind because it is an example of the child who never died in Jane and also of the intensity of her feelings. The Brownies were still kept on her bureau at the island. And it was of course that child who came to life whenever Jane was with children, even into very old age. Though the unforgiving anger took me by surprise.

The other image which not only Jane herself but several of her friends always mentioned when the Vassar days were referred to was, I imagine, the greatest experience of all. Far more important than her being class president or getting an A on her final paper from Frances Thompson. She was chosen to play Cyrano in *Cyrano de Bergerac*. Those who saw this performance never forgot it—"She was simply great," they all agreed. Here her innate romanticism had full play in a role which she took into herself and made her own, that part of her that would have liked to be a man, swashbuckling, in love with language, with an irresistible power to woo . . . but doomed to failure because of an immense nose. In that role she could literally play out every romantic dream, every secret desire. And how she would have hated to have to play Roxane!

When I referred to the notes I made immediately after the funeral I found the phrase "She was never virginal," and I suppose what I meant was that she did not resemble anyone's idea of a spinster, dried up, afraid of life, locked away. On the contrary it may have been her riches as a personality, her openness, the depth of her feelings that made her what she was, not quite the marrying kind . . . a free spirit.

She was intensely romantic but it occurred to me that she had almost nothing of the narcissistic young woman whose romanticism has at least something to do with being admired. Jane wanted to admire, not so much to be admired, and she wanted to throw herself into some heroic act or life, as a follower, not a leader. The need to dominate which one sees rather often in powerful women was not in her.

Outside the college itself and all the life there and in the summers on the island, World War One created a highly emotional climate. Young men came to say good-bye, among them Quentin Blake, just graduating from Harvard and snatched by the army as he was about to enter law school. He managed to take a night train up and had two days in which to woo Jane, something he found quite frustrating, for the island had become an enterprise for raising food, and Jane met him in her gardening khaki pants and shirt, and as soon as he had changed she took him to the big cleared place where Martha and Alix and Pappa were hard at work hoeing between long rows of corn and cabbage for what seemed an eternal two hours before she relented, and allowed that they might go for a swim. At least for the walk down to the pool he had her to himself. He lost no time.

"Oh Jane," he said, "you're beautiful!"

"Don't," she pleaded, and he saw her blush.

"Don't what?"

"Don't say flattering things. Can't we be just as we always were? Remember when you chased me down to the dock and I fell in?"

"I wanted to kiss you then and I want to kiss you now. Please Jane, try to be human for a change." He felt quite cross. Jane didn't play the game, and how did one get hold of such an elusive person?

He had touched her to the quick and her response was slow in coming. They walked along side by side and he felt diminished in every way . . . even the fact that she was taller than he was a humiliation. Finally she looked at him, then looked down as she said, "Quentin, it's human not to want to kiss someone, isn't it? You're my dear friend, but I'm not ready to commit myself. Don't you see?"

"One kiss isn't that serious, is it?" he teased, blocking her way.

"It might not be for you—I suppose you've kissed a hundred girls," and her eyes flashed dark blue, close to anger, he could see.

"I don't understand you," he said bitterly, as she pushed past him. *"Belle dame sans merci* . . . the role doesn't suit you."

But this sally had the unexpected effect of making Jane, who had been so serious a second before, suddenly burst into laughter, and run down the path until he caught her by the hand.

"The *belle dame sans merci.*" She faced him, still laughing. "Oh Quentin, you are such an idiot!" But under the laughter she herself had to recognize that she simply did not like being wooed, if that was what Quentin was doing.

And it was quite a relief when the others joined them at the pool and she could swim in peace while Quentin, still disgruntled, sat at her mother's feet.

I am a little in love with him, she thought, floating on her back and looking up at the sky, watching a gull fly over, but something in her violently resisted being swept away into all sorts of feelings she was not ready to accept. No, she told herself, I want to find out first what I can do myself. She hated the pressure put upon her by his feeling as though she were a wild animal and he had a net in his hands. Why do I feel like this? she asked herself, startled by the force of the image that had come out of the blue. It did not help that Alix was in love already and that Edith seemed on the verge of marrying a young psychologist from Colorado. When Jane tried to talk to Alix, she was told, "Don't worry. You're just not in love. When you are there won't be any problem. You'll just *know.* . . . "

Quentin, Norris, Paul . . . Jane felt hedged around with young men who wanted something of her she could not quite give. And since she was not a *belle dame sans merci,* not a flirt by nature as Viola and even sweet Alix were, she could not enjoy this predicament. It seemed to get in the way of everything she did want, the dream of heroic action, of proving herself as every young man going off to war was about to do.

Most of what was happening came from far away to people at home, the horrible trench warfare which the men who were living it did not even talk about in letters, but in 1918 something did happen at home: an epidemic of influenza raced through the army camps. Two acquaintances of the Reids died in their tents, without ever getting to France. It seemed so useless and unbearable. James Reid had gone to Minnesota when a call went out for volunteer nurses for the Boston hospitals, packed with the ill and dying.

Jane, who had been reading the headlines by the fire in the Cambridge house, laid the paper down and glanced across at her mother. They exchanged a look of instant rapport and understanding.

"You want to volunteer. . . . I'll go with you. We'll do it together."

"Oh Mamma!"

Never since the episode of Maurice's dismissal had Jane felt the barriers go down between herself and her mother. There had always been constraint, but now she felt that she and her mother were truly united. Of course if James had been at home, he would never have allowed his wife to take such a risk. But fortunately he was away and would not be back for two or three weeks. There were business and family problems to be seen to in St. Paul after the death of one of his brothers.

So the next morning they took the trolley in to the Massachusetts Memorial Hospital, where one of Allegra's cousins was a doctor. They were whisked into white gowns and set to work making beds in a former office that was being turned into a ward; then Allegra was summoned to help in one ward feeding the very weak with a spoon while in another Jane went about with a basin of warm water washing faces and hands, throwing each small cloth she used on a patient into a pail and reaching for a fresh one. The fear of infection was everywhere. So many nurses were themselves sick that volunteers had to do many things without much help. The doctors looked close to exhaustion. Jane was startled when Cousin Philip's familiar voice behind her said, "Good heavens, Jane, what are you doing here?"

"Mamma is here, too . . . I don't know where. They asked for volunteers."

He seemed very upset and looked ill himself.

"But why should we be safe when everyone else is in danger?"

"As soon as you get home, wash thoroughly, take off everything you have worn, and see that it is washed," he said severely.

Just then, the old woman Jane had been washing threw up and there was no time for conversation. "I'm sorry," the old woman murmured.

"It's all right, just rest." Jane laid a hand on the burning forehead. Then, after a moment, when the crisis appeared to be over, she ran down the hall to the nurses' room to get a clean sheet and another basin. There, a nurse was in tears of frustration and exhaustion.

"There isn't a clean sheet," she said angrily. "You'll just have to do what you can. Three dead on this ward this morning. . . . It's becoming a morgue."

Jane stood there for a moment catching her breath and then went back to what seemed now a kind of war in itself. She was very very glad to be there, strong and alive and able to help.

However awful this was to witness, it was real. She was at last doing something needed. And she and her mother were very close during the month of long, exhausting days, so tired when they climbed onto the trolley for Cambridge after dark that Jane sometimes fell asleep. Allegra never did. She sat upright and could still manage a smile at a baby in a woman's arms. Jane had never had a chance until then to feel Allegra's strength, her unfailing spirit. So much, she realized, had been taken for granted, partly because they had been spared any ordeals such as serious illness. Terrible as it was, the war called out courage and endurance that were not tapped in "ordinary" life. That is what William James meant about "the moral equivalent of war," Jane thought, recognizing that she was finding strength in herself that she had not known she had, not only the physical endurance to be on her feet all day, but a well of compassion beyond tears. She who wept so easily at the beauty of a fish hawk's flight or a grand poem did not have tears in her eyes as she washed and ministered to the dying. She was strangely happy in the simple concentration of transfusing something like love, a love she could understand and could give.

Cousin Philip had stopped scolding her now for being there. "You are doing a good job, Jane. Even the nurses are grateful."

"There's so little one can do," she said pushing her hair back and standing straight for a second, a relief after all the stooping.

"You Reids have a lot of stamina. Your mother is quite amazing."

Three weeks before, praise from stern Cousin Philip would have delighted her. Now it didn't seem to matter. She was beyond anything as personal as that. How infinitely far away tennis parties and dances had become! Even the island seemed a little unreal. And when it was over Jane Reid knew that those things would remain precious, but she had to find a way to live that would involve and use the whole of her.

And when Pappa returned, dismayed to find his wife thinner and looking extremely tired, and Jane a little withdrawn and somehow older, they talked about it, "I can't see why you have to exhaust yourself to feel that life is real, life is earnest," he teased.

"Oh Papa, if you had seen how people struggle to live, even very old people—and then how at a certain moment they are ready to die. Something happens, and there is a look on their faces . . . perfect peace. I'll never be afraid of death again."

"Tell us about St. Paul, dear. . . ." Allegra, back to normal, deliberately changed the subject. Jane was becoming a little too intense, and besides, their experience had gone too deep to be discussed, she felt. They had done what they needed to, and now it was over. The hospital had been reorganized and qualified nurses brought in, but people were still dying like flies. Prayer seemed more appropriate to Allegra than talking about oneself, and this reaction was entirely characteristic. Jane went up to her room, feeling at a loose end. There she read and reread a letter from Lucy in Philadelphia. Lucy was working at the Red Cross but quite dissatisfied with her job of organizing volunteers to roll bandages and knit socks and sweaters and woolen caps: "I wish I could find some way to deal more directly with people, Reedy. Have you ever thought that when the war is over . . . and they say it can't be long now . . . there will be enormous need for people to help in the rebuilding, and to take care of children? There will be so many orphans! Don't you think we might go to France together and help somewhere, in an orphanage maybe?"

Jane sat in the little rocker for a long time with the letter in her hand. France! The word itself. France had been a lodestar for so long—but could she afford a year away, not begin her life as a teacher as planned? Of course she could. At last the door was opening to something she could do, like the nursing, something really needed, acutely needed. And to do it with Lucy, quiet, steadfast, imaginative Lucy whom she loved as much as anyone in her own family, her chosen friend. It seemed almost too good to be true. The only awful thing was that they would have to wait a year or more . . . God knows how long!

It would be a very long year of disasters, learned of through the newspapers and in letters from soldiers in France, a year in which President Wilson turned the United States from peace to war, and in doing so had to sabotage his own pleas for tolerance as the propaganda machine in Washington went into full gear and hatred of the Hun swept the country. Submarine warfare was sinking hundreds of thousands of tons of shipping and the holocaust in the trenches began to be nearly matched by the loss of men at sea. The world was to be made safe for democracy by the massacre of millions of young men, and among them Quentin, who was killed at Belleau Wood. Alix married and within a month went down to New York to say good-bye to Fredson, drafted and bound for Fort Bragg. Edith's fiancé joined the medical corps. Everything cherished was in peril, Jane thought.

And at the table Allegra's wish to keep things as calm and peaceable as possible often failed. For, as the full horror of the trench warfare trickled in, Martha asserted that she was a pacifist and that nothing could justify the slaughter, and Allegra reacted strongly to any emotional wholesale condemnations of Germany. Jane, ardent, fiercely partisan on France's and England's side, reciting poems by Rupert Brooke as the gospel, had been swept with millions of others into a passionate rejection of everything German.

"But, dearie, you can't just brush Goethe, Beethoven, and Wagner away," her mother would answer. "Hatred isn't the answer."

"They are murdering little children . . . innocent people

... they invaded Belgium, didn't they? This whole horrible war is the Germans' fault!"

"Let us have peace at our table," her mother said with unusual severity.

At this point Snooker, who was usually a silent witness, burst into tears, and left the room.

"I'm sorry," Jane said. "It's my fault."

But when she found Snooker in her room at the top of the house, there seemed no easy comfort. "Everything's breaking apart," Snooker sobbed. "When will it end?" Snooker, the controlled, the comforter, had, for once, really broken down, and this more than anything else brought Jane to her senses.

A small matter? But small matters can change people. Jane was much too passionate to be naturally tolerant as Martha seemed to be. For her, tolerance had to be learned, and learned through living out strong convictions and the inevitable collisions that take place when strong conviction is confronted by reality, when a person actually lives what he or she believes. It had been a shock when quiet, gentle Martha spoke with such force about pacifism. In her heart of hearts Jane had to admit that this sister who had always chosen to stay in the background had a strength she had not suspected. And of course she had been wrong to speak so hotly against the Germans. Now in her room she blushed to think of her mother's just reprimand.

And on an impulse she took out her violin, tuned it, and played a Beethoven violin sonata. It would always be Jane's instinct to do something active to solve problems.

I am now once more confronted by my ignorance and must treat only briefly what was certainly a major experience. For at the end of 1918, soon after the armistice had been signed, Reedy and Lucy did manage to get to France and spent some months in an orphanage on the Norman coast. It was run by the order of Saint Vincent de Paul, those nuns who wear a white coif starched so that it resembles great white wings, and a dark blue habit. "Les Miss," as they were immediately called, were welcomed into what I imagine as a dreadfully cold stone building to help take care of a hundred or more orphans, boys and girls, most of them under ten years old. No one was very well fed. It rained incessantly. No doubt "Les Miss" organized games and got the children outdoors as much as was permitted. They learned French willy-nilly, and created a good deal of laughter among the nuns with their sometimes ludicrous mistakes. Luckily they both had lively senses of humor, and Jane more obviously, Lucy more subtly, had a genius for lifting the spirits of both the overworked and exhausted sisters and the children.

Jane never told me anything about what it was like for a Unitarian to find herself in the middle of the Catholic mystique, nor whether "Les Miss" got up at four or five to join the nuns at Mass. I do know that her love of France and her intention to teach history to children led her to use any free time she and Lucy had in finding out everything she could about the life of medieval people and in immersing herself in the legends of Roland and Charlemagne. No doubt they made pilgrimages to such legendary places as Mont-Saint-Michel, the cathedral of Amiens, still in ruins from the war, and Jane with her power to imagine herself into the past surely felt all this on her pulse as a poet might rather than a scholar. She was never a "quick study," never facile or glib, but she took into herself what she cared about deeply and re-created it much as a novelist or poet does. When she came back with every intention of joining Frances Thompson at the Parker School in Chicago, fate intervened in a curious way.

But I must add one footnote to the little I know about the time in France. "Les Miss" did not abandon the children they had known the best and for the next forty years had a tradition of meeting at Thanksgiving time, busy though they each were, and taking out the large white copybook where the names and addresses were kept, the marriages, the children's names, and finally the grandchildren, and writing each one a Christmas letter. There were many summer vacations spent going back to see them, scattered in time and in different provinces.

Back from France I have an idea that the way in which fate intervened may have not been altogether to Jane's liking. It must have been rather a shock, when she was all set to adventure far from home in her first teaching job, to learn that Frances Thompson had been invited to head the Warren School and would herself be coming to Cambridge. She offered Jane a position teaching medieval history.

There was no doubt in Jane's mind that she wanted to teach under Frances Thompson, so that was that. But it meant living at home. Naturally her parents were delighted, as was Snooker, who, increasingly frail, remained with the Reids as a friend. Martha and Jane were the only children still at home; Allegra and James, still very much themselves, were in their sixties. There could be no question, Jane felt, of moving out. But staying meant that she was still a child, finding meals waiting for her when she came back from school, and her mother and father and Snooker eager for a report on the day. It meant that she was part of a society that expected something of Trueblood's granddaughter, and, overflowing with life as she was at twenty-five, young men were always inviting themselves to meals, or begging her to play a game of tennis, or to go to a concert or a dance. That was enjoyable up to a point.

But in her own mind at least she was first and foremost a teacher at the Warren School, and that, she soon discovered, was really a twenty-four-hour-a-day job. Her mother occasionally suggested that she was refusing too many invitations.

"Dearie, the Warren School is not a nunnery, after all!"

It might as well have been in demanding the whole life of its teachers, and at that time there were very few men on the faculty, and few married teachers. Jane was teaching the seventh grade, twelve girls and boys. She was the classroom teacher. She taught medieval history and English. Each year at Warren was built around a central subject. Themes sprang out of the material they were studying. It was quite usual for the students to write a play and perform it, inspired by something they were reading in history. And there were no textbooks, for the theory was that teachers must use primary sources as far as possible. Jane had thought she was well prepared after her year in France, but she soon found out that being prepared meant hours in the library, hours copying out texts and getting them mimeographed, hours planning each class, and, on weekends, hours thinking ahead as well as reading papers.

And that was only her own province. There were meetings after school, almost every afternoon, of one committee or another, and sometimes in the evening.

Frances Thompson was in her first year of a gruelling job and relied on Jane for advice and comfort . . . they had come to the school together, as outsiders, in a very close community, and that fact drew them together in a new way. Jane was no longer a student of Frances' but a powerful ally. The school was in a perpetual state of drama, self-criticism, and growth. Thirty teachers, most with strong personalities and often in violent disagreement about both theory and practice, had to be kept in balance.

But for Jane every single day was an adventure. She left home at eight with her eyes shining. Her children in the class delighted, fascinated, irritated, kept her on her mettle, and partly because she was so young she felt an instant rapport with them all. She felt she had been catapulted, quite unprepared, into the thick of life, a life she loved passionately.

Prologue, Part II

I had not realized how much I had absorbed of Jane Reid's childhood and youth until I began to write about them in these pages. So many small incidents and occasions welled up that it was almost as though I had been there on the island, at Vassar, in France, and finally of course at the Warren School, where I myself now enter the scene.

Here I am finding problems I do not know how to solve, and it has taken weeks to make a start. How much of my own life, for instance, will have to be revealed? It is not my intention to indulge in autobiography, and in fact I feel extremely reluctant to do so. But I am the narrator, and who I am—and was as a child—and what I have done with my life is, at times, going to be relevant. And that is troubling. I have never been a very open person; when I was teaching in college my students knew very little about me, for instance. As I think it all over and remember the years at the Warren School, where I first met Jane Reid as her pupil in the seventh grade, I see that I changed a great deal more than she did over the fifty or more years of our friendship. For she remained as passionate, as unselfconscious, as committed to life in every way as she had been as a child, and that was one of her charms.

But for reasons which will become clear later on, I did change, and by the time I was forty-five I was leading a secluded and settled life as a professor of history in a small college. And I had closed off some parts of me that Jane Reid had touched deeply when I was a child in her care. Perhaps that is why I have found it difficult to go back and unbury those years. The only way to do it is to become that child again. But the risk is very great.

Part II
The Growth of a Friendship

It all began in the seventh grade at the Warren School, when I was at last in Jane Reid's room. I had come to Warren in the sixth grade from a public school near where we lived on Raymond Street. I loved Warren at once; everything there was so interesting, such a challenge, after the pressures of being in a class of thirty under a rather tense spinster who always seemed to be on the verge of crossness and more interested in keeping order than in teaching us. Although my sixth-grade teacher at Warren scared me with her unexpected explosions and my life under her eye was made harder by the fact that I was not good at math, her subject, the atmosphere at Warren quickly won me over. The biggest change from the public school was that we laughed a lot, and for me at least that I made real friends, especially Faith Franklin, with whom I invented all sorts of jokes and finally a secret language which reduced us to helpless laughter whenever we spoke in it. I realize now that we must have been rather a handful for Miss Everett, and I can still hear her calling out, "Cam and Faith, keep down your nervous energy!"

The school was open-air at that time, and the schoolrooms

rather like barracks, low wooden buildings, walled-in windows which were kept open even in winter. We could not help being aware of Jane Reid's seventh-grade classroom next door to ours; the children always appeared to be having such a great time. And Miss Reid, tall and beautiful, was glamorous indeed compared to round, plain Miss Everett. So I looked forward to being elevated to the seventh grade as to some marvelous unknown country where wonderful things were going to happen.

Meanwhile it was exciting to find myself in a school which was as much a creation of the students as of the faculty, or so we children believed. I soon found out that Frances Thompson, the head, was open to suggestions and I could go in and talk to her almost any time. I liked her a lot. She treated me with respect, with a slight twinkle in her eye which I felt was not patronizing when, for instance, I complained that it was hard to write in mittens. In winter the classrooms were arctic, as a small pot-bellied stove in the front of each room near the teacher's desk was the only source of heat!

This Spartan atmosphere did cure me of a tendency to bronchitis, and in general colds were rather rare. Clothes never mattered. I loved dressing up in thick sweaters and heavy boots with thick socks inside, "woodsman's socks" they were called in the Sears Roebuck catalog. I had always been a tomboy; in those days, sixty years ago, blue jeans for girls did not exist, and in most schools a girl was expected to look like a girl and wear dresses, so Warren, with its unisex clothing, was just what I needed.

In the spring Miss Reid got a new convertible Dodge, one of the first where the roof could be raised and lowered automatically. I sometimes witnessed her arrival at school a little before eight, the top down, and the car filled with children she had picked up on her way. I wished I was not on a bicycle then, but on the other hand, it was two or three miles between our house and the school and it was easier on a bike to evade horrible little boys who threw stones and jeered, and safer, too, when crossing a kind of wild place near the Divinity School where I was sure danger lurked. As I look back I realize that at that time in my life, at age twelve, boys were a threat and a menace rather than anything else, a foreign tribe best kept at a distance.

That year in the seventh grade, studying Roman history and the start of the Middle Ages, was a very good year. I used to stay around after school to talk to Miss Reid about things. Sometimes she was sitting at her desk, going over papers, and didn't hear me come in. Then she lifted her head, "Oh Cam, it's you. I thought I heard a mouse."

"I wanted to ask you about my theme. . . ."

But that wasn't it, of course. I wanted the chance to talk about myself and life in general. It was a good year at school, but my father and mother were not getting on very well, and as an only child I felt very uneasy and somehow rootless as a result. Half the time my father was not home for supper, saying he had work to do. My mother confided in me, which was perhaps not a very good idea. There were times when I dreaded going home. I was being forced to grow up a little too fast that year, and Miss Reid with her rather childlike enthusiasm and sense of fun was a real help. Once when I didn't have my bike for some reason and had been hanging around after school she noticed and suddenly said, "Come on, Cam. I'll race you to the car and drive you home." With her long legs, she could run terribly fast.

Once I asked her in to see my dog, a Cairn I called Andrew, and I guess she saw that my mother was pretty upset and said, "Why don't I take Cam home for supper, Eleanor?"

"Isn't it too much? I mean, you've had a long day."

"I didn't know you knew my mother so well . . ." I said, a little envious of this intimacy I had not suspected.

"She's on the parents' committee on art," Miss Reid said, "didn't you know? Your mother is a tremendous asset on that committee. She's so imaginative and quick to see what could be done—what a marvelous person!"

It was quite a surprise to hear my mother praised out in the world. I took her so much for granted and my father never paid very much attention to what she said. But it was even more surprising to see Miss Reid at home and to meet her parents and sister, a very plain woman who seemed exceedingly shy.

They lived in a huge house full of old velvet furniture and knickknacks, comfortable and sedate, but somehow not at all like Miss Reid. I liked her mother and it was impressive to be waited on at table by a waitress in a white apron. I realized for the first time that Miss Reid must be very rich, although I had heard that she was the granddaughter of Benjamin Trueblood. So I figured it out and dared to ask Mrs. Reid if she was the daughter he had written a poem about.

"Yes, Cam, believe it or not, I am his daughter, referred to, as you remember, as 'radiant Allegra.'" And her eyes twinkled. But her face was very wrinkled and of course she was terribly old. She smiled at me then in such a warm way that I felt it was all right that I couldn't think of anything appropriate to say. Besides, I rather wanted to eat my creamed chicken in peace. And we had strawberry ice cream and brownies for dessert. An unforgettable day for me.

That night when mother came to say good night I said, "I didn't know you knew Miss Reid so well. She thinks you're a wonderful person."

I knew mother would be pleased. She hugged me and said, "Sweet dreams, Cam."

"Don't put out the light. I have to read Tacitus." I was proud of having to read Tacitus. Not just any old textbook.

In the middle of that year I had a disaster, and pride came

before a fall. The school had decided to experiment with something called the Dalton plan. The idea was to give a month's assignments ahead so that the students could go at their own pace. There was a big board on the wall with our twelve names on it and squares you checked off as an assignment was completed. There were various texts to be read, among them Shakespeare's *Julius Caesar*, which we were to compare with a contemporary text, and five written papers. One was to imagine the day of a centurion on the Scottish border. I was a quick reader and quite a good writer, so I plunged in and was crossing off squares like mad by the second week of the four and had done everything ahead of everyone else by the start of the fourth week. So for a week I could make maps and do anything I felt like, and I lorded it over the class, I'm afraid.

We were kept in suspense for a week after all the papers were in because Miss Reid had to go over them. Except in math, there were no grades at Warren, but you knew when you had done well, all right. Finally the day came when I expected an accolade. Joan, a quiet girl in glasses, and Peter, a brilliant kid who did everything well, got high praise, and almost everyone else had done pretty well, it seemed. I was the last to be commented upon and I was still hopeful. Maybe Miss Reid was keeping the best for last.

Then she explained that the purpose of the Dalton plan was to give a student the responsibility of planning his own work, and (here I remember she smiled), "speed is not really what it is all about. It is not a race, Cam. But that is how you took it. You did sloppy work fast and the results are far below your own standard."

At that I hid my face in my hands and groaned, which made the class laugh. But Miss Reid didn't like that at all. I guess it had been hard for her to be so severe, and she suggested that we have a little talk after class. Of course I dreaded that and stopped clowning right away. I felt terribly humiliated.

After class I sat at my desk and waited. I could hear the other kids shouting out in the playground. Finally Miss Reid came back and sat down beside me instead of at her desk. She sat with her long hands clasped. . . . I'll never forget that talk. She was solemn and unlike herself, a little stiff.

She didn't find the words easily, but what she said made a deep impression on me and was a piece of true education as I see it now. She made me see that my tendency to talk a lot in class sometimes prevented shyer students from contributing. She warned me that being very quick and bright had its dangers, and they had been proved in the superficial work I had just done. "You have great things in you, Cam, but you are letting yourself get away with gliding over the surface. You just have to go deeper and take more time," she said. And then finally she did smile and told me the fable of the tortoise and the hare. "So try to be a tortoise instead of a hare."

It became a joke between us, and when I handed in a good piece of work she sometimes wrote on it, "Good for tortoise-Cam!"

Another hard thing took place that year. I wanted terribly to play Nicolette in *Aucassin and Nicolette,* which our class was going to put on at assembly. But Deborah was chosen instead. It didn't seem fair. I knew I would have been better at it. Deborah was rather slow and too fat. Almost anyone would have been better than Deborah. So why did Miss Reid choose her? Finally one day I couldn't stand it any longer and burst out with it. "Why?"

Jane Reid flushed right to the roots of her hair and her eyes got that dark blue they did when she was upset or angry.

"Sometimes someone has to be given a chance," she said very quietly. "I think Deborah needs to have a good part. Maybe you could help her," she said tentatively.

"I don't like her," I said, furious with her and with myself.

"Cam, all your life you are going to have to get along with people you may not like, and if you are wise you'll come to see that half the trouble is with yourself."

"What's wrong with *me?*" I asked bitterly.

"You think I've been unfair. Is that the trouble?"

I nodded.

"You'll just have to take it on faith for a while that I try to be fair. Maybe you have to think of the class as a community of people helping each other. That's the thing you've still got to learn, Cam."

Well, I didn't quite understand then. But I liked her a lot, so I tried to believe she was right. And I had to admit that Deborah was really quite good in the part. She learned to speak out and not to mumble, for one thing. We all learned that at Warren because we often performed in assembly and could get on our feet and tell the school what we had been doing in science, for instance, and not be shy.

It is strange how vivid that whole year in the seventh grade remains nearly sixty years later. I had other good teachers, but what made the year exceptional was Jane Reid. At twelve, I was at the right age for her enthusiasm and the imaginative way she made things happen in the classroom. Everything from that year has stayed with me, and when Ruth and I took a trip to England and saw the Roman wall, it felt almost as though I had been a soldier guarding that wall in another life, although that other life was simply the seventh grade at Warren. I found myself remembering:

> My father's father saw it not
> And I belike shall never come
> to look on that so holy spot
> The very Rome.

And she taught me a great deal outside the actual subject matter in class. She seemed always to have time to look at things, a spider making its web across a windowpane, the first song sparrow. She stopped right in the middle of a sentence, I remember, and listened intently; then her face lit up. "It's the song sparrow," she announced. "Be quiet and let's listen." Best of all was her sense of humor. She could make a joke of almost anything and the class was often dissolved into a gale of laughter at nothing at all.

If she had a flaw it was her worship of self-control. She would never allow herself to show that she was angry, though we knew very well when she was by the quick flush, and then a kind of stiffness that made me, at least, uncomfortable. She would ask the offender to see her after class, and that "little talk" was painful in the extreme because she was so determined to reason something out that might have been settled at once and in a healthy way by an instant rebuke.

What she did do, and very effectively, was to demand that we respect each other. I could see that she went out of her way, for instance, to get Alice, a very shy girl, to have a chance, and tried not to let the talkers dominate. I was one of the articulate, eager to please and to respond at once to any question she might ask, so I was apt to be put down at least once a day. Occasionally I resented this, and once she must have caught my sullen silence for the rest of the period, for she stopped me as I was running out the door for recess and said, "Cam, you have a lot to say, but so do other people, don't you see?"

"I feel stifled," I answered because I was still cross, and determined not to give in.

"I'm sure you do," and her eyes twinkled, and suddenly she couldn't help laughing and I felt she liked me, so it was all right. At any rate, by the end of the year I knew that being quick and bright was not enough.

On quite another level I suppose, as I look back, that something else was happening to me at the Warren School. It is hard even now to put into words, but reading those ardent poems made me realize that we were being in some subtle way fertilized as sentient beings. A whole world of feeling had been opened up in me, and if at times that took absurd forms, it was essentially a door opening into womanhood, into what it might be to become a woman. Here both Frances Thompson and Jane Reid were inspiring role-models, and I understood why Jane Reid's eyes always shone whenever she spoke of Frances Thompson. These two extraordinary women never married, but each in her own way radiated a kind of influence which had very little to do with intellect.

Yet they were very different. For all her sensitivity and shyness Frances Thompson was an initiator and a leader in educational theory, a pioneer in what was then called "progressive education," and I suppose she was a spinster in a way Jane Reid never was. She was wholly dedicated to and absorbed in the school, perhaps because she was physically frail. Her power lay partly in her enormous empathy for any being suffering grief or malaise. Parents, children, teachers, all felt free to come to her with their problems. I never left her office without feeling restored to myself. But hers was a costly gift and Frances Thompson, I feel sure, was often near exhaustion. Whereas, at that time anyway, Jane Reid seemed able to handle a hundred relationships with ease, and what emanated from her, her influence if

85

you will, was a deep and rich sense of life, an inexhaustible *joie de vivre* that encompassed men, women, and children, her parents, her pupils, her friends, and her suitors.

The image that comes to my mind as I write is of the yearly garden party held at the Benjamin Trueblood house, where there was music and folk dancing all afternoon in a day in May. That year of the seventh grade brought me, amongst other things, my first friendship with a boy. Tommy Weston's parents, like my own, were separating, and although we almost never mentioned it, this family upheaval—divorces were rare at the Warren School—had drawn us together. And we had decided to go to the Trueblood fete together. Tommy was a good dancer and so was I, so we had a great time, until, out of breath, we sat down under a tree to watch, especially Jane Reid, who had on a white dress with a blue sash and looked smashing. They were dancing "goddesses," I remember, and she, tall and graceful and so light on her feet, seemed almost to be flying a little above the ground. It was rather special to think that Benjamin Trueblood's granddaughter was our teacher.

Afterwards, she saw us and came over and asked us to have some ice cream and cake with her, and that was so grand I was speechless for once.

"She's a great lady, isn't she?" said Tommy as we walked home under the flowering chestnut trees, and stopped now and then to peer into secret gardens, here a small blue lake of scillas, there daffodils, and an ornamental cherry surrounded by a snow of petals.

"A princess," I amended the remark. "Lady" didn't seem quite right for Jane Reid.

"It's going to be awful next year without her," Tommy said. "I wish we could stay in the seventh grade."

Hearing it uttered like that, I felt a sharp pang. How could I live through a new year in another room with a new teacher?

And I realized that something like love had happened to me. It had crystallized while we stood eating ice cream and Jane Reid's eyes had looked incredibly blue. I was not going to let her go.

Tommy had been right; the eighth grade was nothing like the seventh. Miss Chase, who taught us medieval history, was a true scholar and knew an awful lot, but she was very reserved, almost never laughed, and treated us with quiet authority, as though we were grown-ups. She would have been more comfortable with college students, and we, with the cruelty of children, disliked her and showed it by being uncooperative. Of course the trouble was that she was not Jane Reid; we had a standard she could not meet. All through October, while Cambridge became a gold and scarlet world and we scuffed leaves on the way to school, things got worse and worse. We passed notes and whispered in class, Miss Chase took no notice, preserving an icy calm. We were bored by the Venerable Bede, did not rise to the challenge of writing a medieval lyric. Nothing quite like this had ever happened at Warren before and I think Miss Thompson was nonplussed.

Then one day Miss Reid appeared in our class to be greeted by shouts of joy and loud applause. Miss Chase, she told us, had the flu. But Miss Reid did not seem like herself. She was clearly nervous and upset. She looked at us quite coldly and did not smile at the applause or recognize that it had taken place.

She said she was bitterly disappointed in us. She talked about Miss Chase and told us that we were missing a great experience, that this was a distinguished scholar whom we were very lucky to have teach us. Then she paused and thought before going on. Finally she said, and it was clearly difficult, that it was a poor kind of loyalty to someone else to close our eyes and ears to what was being so generously offered us every day. "You have been both rude and cruel," she ended. "Your behavior this month doesn't speak very well for me. You have made me ashamed."

We were absolutely silenced. No one dared to speak.

"Very well; you may write a theme in this period on anything you choose."

After she left we talked, of course. For once Alice spoke up right away, "She doesn't know," she said bluntly. "She has no idea what Miss Chase is like."

"It isn't fair," Faith chimed in.

But this was bravado and each of us in our heart of hearts knew we deserved the rebuke, and in the end maybe it did have some effect. Some of us made a real effort, but unfortunately Miss Chase never won our hearts.

The next year, my last at Warren, my mother was teaching art part time, and she and Jane Reid became friends, so I began to know her in a new way as someone called "Jane," not "Miss Reid."

In that last year I still used to stop by after school once in a while to have a talk or confide something that needed Jane Reid's counsel, and she chose me to play the angel in the Christmas play, so for a few weeks I was working with her every day. She took words very seriously and I must have gone over my part a hundred times to get it right.

Just before we graduated Miss Reid invited Faith and me to spend a night at an inn and have supper with her there. It was terribly exciting to dress in a blue dress and patent leather slippers, and to be going out with Miss Reid. Especially as the inn had been made famous in one of Benjamin Trueblood's novels, one I liked a lot. By then I was aware that my hero, Benjamin Trueblood, was not very popular with grown-ups any longer. He was considered "old hat" and Victorian. But Jane Reid made it all seem magic. She took us to the small barn where Belinda was frightened by a horse and first met Andrew, the groom with whom she fell in love. We saw the well where they used to hide messages. We went all around imagining how it must have been when people rode up in carriages and the ladies carried muffs and wore violets in the fur collars of their jackets. Of course it was warm, a May evening, but in the novel it was winter most of the time, so we could almost hear the sleigh bells. Miss Reid's eyes were shining, and I thought she must have been in love, the way she talked about Belinda and Andrew, but I didn't dare ask. Our bedroom, Faith's and mine, had a four-poster bed in it and underneath a trundle bed. It was like being in a play, and of course we giggled a lot when we were getting undressed and decided we would both sleep in the big bed rather than fight about who got it. We did have a pillow fight though and made rather a noise whooping it up. The inn was very silent except for us.

Miss Reid came in to say good night in a lovely blue wrapper, with her hair in a long pigtail, and whispered, "Other people may be trying to sleep, so maybe you could settle down, kids. I'll knock on your door at eight tomorrow morning . . . sleep well."

But of course we couldn't sleep. We lay awake and talked a long time, mostly about how awful it was going to be to leave Warren, to be parted because Faith was going to the Winsor School and I to the High and Latin in Cambridge.

After a while it began to rain. We could hear it on the roof and suddenly decided we had to get up and go out. There was something about the rain and the smell of wet grass that excited us. We sneaked downstairs, terrified by every creak. Then we realized we would get our nightgowns wet, so we just took them off and left them in the hall. The inn was all closed down, not a light anywhere, and we had to unlock the door to get out. But the grass felt delicious and cool on our bare feet and we did a dance we made up, until we got into a fit of giggles and ran back in, so wet the rain poured down from our soaking hair all over our faces.

I am struck as I remember this—and I do remember it in every detail—by how innocent and young we were at fourteen. We didn't even smoke cigarettes! We thought the jazz records our parents played were soupy, and folk dancing was the only kind of dancing we enjoyed.

I remember I felt a pang when Miss Reid told us, as we devoured a huge breakfast of pancakes and bacon, that she and Marian Chase were going to Europe for the summer, "to study" she said. "Marian is working on a book about guilds in the Middle Ages." It was clear that she felt it a privilege to be travelling with that sobersides, and it did seem odd to me that a person as full of life as Jane Reid could attach herself to someone like Marian Chase.

Anyway, it was a satisfaction to observe that she was treated with great respect by the manager of the inn when she paid the bill. I was dying to know how much it was—money had become very interesting lately, because my mother and I did not have much to live on. "It has been a pleasure to have Benjamin Trueblood's granddaughter with us, Miss Reid," the manager said. It dawned on me that Jane Reid might be called an American aristocrat. And I was proud to be with her. But it took many years before I knew what that meant in her case, how true it was, but not exactly in the way I envisioned such a person at fourteen.

As I was then, to be an aristocrat meant being beautiful and grand and having money, lots of it, and a blue convertible Dodge that made her seem like a princess. I figured out that the bill at the inn must have been about forty times what my allowance of a dollar a week amounted to. Whew!

*　　*　　*

Leaving Warren and going into the High and Latin school as sophomores added to our sense of being strangers from another planet. The freshmen had already made alliances, chosen clubs and sports, when we entered the following year, and we were really a little like addicts deprived of our drug, suffering withdrawal symptoms. If Warren had a flaw it was to be a world so exciting in its demands and rewards and so rare in its human quality that all of us who graduated from there felt—it sounds absurd but it is a fact—a little like exiles for the rest of our lives. Of course this was poignant for me because of my parents' divorce. Tommy, with whom I could have talked about that, had disappeared to Exeter. Of my best friends only Anne had gone on with me to the Cambridge High and Latin. In a way I suppose that first year there was a year of mourning.

It can't have been easy for Jane Reid, our lodestar, to manage an occasional visit as she did, although that year she was beginning the ordeal of arranging her grandfather's papers at the Trueblood House, and this, on top of her teaching, really devoured her life. My mother was quite firm with me at that time not to "run in" and try to see Jane at home. But when her father died I wrote her a letter and got one back in her clear, handsome writing, and it was an event because I felt I was being treated as a friend rather than a pupil: "It was good of you, dear Cam, to find time to write to me. The loss of one's father seems at the time like the worst thing that can ever happen. The house without Pappa feels terribly empty. For Mamma his sudden death has been a shock she was not prepared for, but she is her usual valiant and serene self. You must come and cheer us up."

Of course I did, the very next Sunday afternoon, and we went for a walk along the Charles on a cold November day. It was tremendously exciting for me because I realized that I had very rarely been alone with Jane, and never before, perhaps, had a real conversation in which I was treated as an equal. It would not be the last time that we argued about politics. Hoover had just been nominated by the Republicans and Jane Reid felt that he would make a good president because of the tremendous job he had done organizing war relief in 1919. I was passionately for Smith, "the happy warrior," even though he was a Catholic and I heard on all sides that he would be influenced by church dogma and not be able to act as a free man. I felt he was flexible and imaginative, and cared more for people. "Hoover cares about people—he has proved it." Jane Reid flushed as she said it, a little angry, I could sense.

"But Hoover is for big business, you can tell."

"Smith is for ending Prohibition," she answered hotly. Then we laughed, and I slipped an arm through hers as we trudged along. It was a great moment.

"I suppose you're a dyed-in-the-wool Republican," I teased, intoxicated by the subtle change in our relationship.

Then she became serious, and we stopped for a moment before turning back, stopped and looked at some rather miserable ducks at the frozen edge of the river. "I'm not a dyed-in-the-wool anything, I hope. And anyway the Republicans have not provided very well lately—Harding, Coolidge! No, I'll vote for the man not the party any time."

"So will I when I can."

It was amazing to be talking like this. It was my first experience of Jane Reid's way of being apart from school and family, the fact that she felt deeply about politics but wanted to be reasonable, not partisan, that she would think about this a lot. Somehow that surprised me. And I felt glad that the glamorous person, "the princess" I had adored, was turning into a different person, that the distance between us was diminishing, not because she had changed, but because I was growing up.

I suppose that I was forced to grow up by the situation at

home. My father was being mean about the divorce, giving mother the house and barely enough to live on. He wanted to marry someone else and build a house for her, Mother told me. She looked drained and strained, as though some vital fluid were being lost every day, and I'm afraid my reaction was to close myself off and stay away as much as I could because it had become too painful. Meanwhile my father gave me an English bike and a suede jacket for my birthday and asked me to lunch with him on Saturdays, which wrecked the day for me . . . and besides, I felt I was betraying Mother by enjoying it, if I did, which was rarely. It felt as though we were sitting among the ruins there in the comfortable Harvard Club eating some extravagant dessert—and it usually ended in a row about something, mostly politics. My father, a corporation lawyer, was cynical and, I felt, arrogant, pretending always to have inside information which transformed any idealistic statements I might come up with into sentimental foolishness. No doubt I judged him harshly, but listening to him talk did make me rather sceptical about the rich at an early age.

That is one of the reasons why Jane Reid haunted me, I suppose, for she was the only very rich person I have known who was wholly uncorrupted by her money, and the power it inevitably gave her. She was, in my mind, the great exception.

She used her power in very imaginative ways always, and that year when my mother was going though hell, Jane suddenly invited her to join three Vassar friends of hers, including Lucy of course, on a month's trip to France. What a marvelous gift it was! And actually it was a gift to me, also, as Faith's family invited me down to their summer place in Duxbury for that month, where we played baseball (Faith had three sisters) and swam, and Faith and I even resumed our secret language, a reprieve for me from the tension of home.

Mother came back more like herself than I had seen her for

a year, bursting with adventures, for I gather they behaved like schoolgirls, packed into a big open phaeton, singing everything from Bach to Gilbert and Sullivan, picnicking somewhere every day, landing in strange towns to find a hotel often after dark. And Jane was the leader in all the fun, set free from the constraints of Cambridge and school, making everything a lark. The only tension apparently was the daily one of finding the right place for their picnic, and dreaming of the perfect place sometimes lasted until nearly two o'clock, on damp stones under a bridge or in a prickly furze under a blazing sun, famished, because they had not been able to decide. Once they came at dusk to a closed chateau and Jane fired them to spend the night in the courtyard, scrambling together some supper out of what was left from the noon picnic. They had no sleeping bags with them, but managed to improvise with the car rugs and their coats and sweaters. They lay and looked up at the stars for a while, but before light a frightful thunderstorm blew up and they had to creep into the car soaking wet and wait for the dawn. Finally, as the sun was rising and its light dancing in the poplar leaves, they found a workmen's café open in the next town. There four boisterous women in wet clothes caused a sensation and the *patron* insisted they have a *fine*, on the house, with their coffee. Nothing, my mother said, had ever tasted as good as that *café au lait* with brandy.

None of the four had been in the Dordogne, where they were bound. Mother's eyes shone when she described the winding river with a fairy-tale castle around every bend, and the fortified towns, *bastides*, on the crests of hills, the Romanesque churches, the whole peace-inducing landscape. It had clearly been a kind of heaven. At night in the hotel they read history aloud and Jane, of course, acted everything out.

"She is such a romantic!" my mother said, "and lives in what she is seeing or reading in such an extraordinary way—oh what a marvelous time she gave me, Cam, the generosity of it!"

I could see what the trip had done for my mother, but in those weeks I too had been plunged into a new and electrifying experience that actually changed my life for the next ten years and that, for a time, made Jane Reid and her romantic ways distant from my own preoccupations. I was fifteen, and I think I guessed that in some ways I was already older than Jane Reid would ever be, or perhaps simply more vulnerable and more conflicted. Perhaps, too, I recognized that Jane and my mother had become intimate friends. Sometimes when I got back from school Jane was there for tea . . . she had a way of turning up when Mother was feeling lonely and anxious . . . and then I would sneak upstairs on the pretense that I had homework to do, and leave them alone.

I was learning about Jane then at one remove. From little things Mother let fall I gathered that Sam Dawson, active in the founding of the League of Nations, very much wanted to marry Jane and was pursuing her quite relentlessly. We talked about it over supper one evening. It made me feel very grown-up to be confided in.

"They share a great deal," Mother said thoughtfully. "Jane's idealism and her passionate interest in the League . . . but . . ."

"But what? Why doesn't she marry him?" I felt somehow cross at the thought that she might marry.

"I really don't know. I think she is sometimes tempted but then she is so involved in the school and in doing everything she can for Miss Thompson."

"Why couldn't she teach and marry too?"

Mother smiled, the smile, I thought, of someone involved in a secret world. "Warren devours its teachers. I don't think you have any idea how hard we work." I did often see how tired

Mother was when she got home, but she was older than Jane, and Jane had never seemed tired. "Besides," Mother went on, "she would be expected to give dinner parties and go out a lot, and, unless they were separated half the year, go over to Geneva."

"Do you think she could be happy being so social?" I asked. It was all appalling, impossible, not to be believed.

"Darling child, who knows?"

"You don't really think she'll marry him?"

Mother looked at me in that tender amused way she did when I knew she loved me a lot, "You don't want her to, do you?" Then she laughed, "And I don't know that I do myself."

"I want her to stay just as she is." I was amazed at the violence of my feelings. For after all why shouldn't she marry? That was the normal thing for a beautiful woman and an heiress, most people would think. What was it, then, that made marriage for Jane Reid seem preposterous? I couldn't have said.

"Well, that's all very well, but none of us stay as we once were . . . there is old age, loneliness. . . ."

"Oh Mother, don't be so dreary. . . ." I had said it in a sharp tone and saw at once that I had hurt her, so I went and hugged her, and after that we cleared the table.

What had happened in Boston in the month of August 1927, while Jane Reid and my mother were driving around in the Dordogne, was the execution of Sacco and Vanzetti. I don't know quite how or why I had become involved except that everywhere it was the cause of passionate belief on the one hand in the two men's innocence, and on the other an equally passionate fear of anarchism and, buttressed by the findings of a commission chaired by President Lowell of Harvard, the certainty that guilt had been proved, and the trial fair. The Franklins, with whom I was staying, did not want the issue discussed at table . . . they were firm in their trust in President Lowell. But Faith and I had become convinced through all we had read in the papers and through all the people we admired who were involved, especially the poet Edna St. Vincent Millay, that two such simple and poetic characters could not be guilty of murder. We walked the beach at Duxbury talking about it, wondering how President Lowell could have betrayed the two men, what a stuffed shirt he must be, and so on. We became experts in arguing about anarchism and what it really was . . . if Warren had taught us anything it was to go to sources and find out facts. We argued with our friends on the beach, and with Faith's older sister Joan until we were all in tears of rage and frustration. And meanwhile the only hope now was that Governor Fuller would pardon the two men. We wrote letters to him as thousands of other people did, and finally, on the night of August twenty-second, we joined the vigil on the Common, having been expressly forbidden to do so by Mr. Franklin. Edna St. Vincent Millay was there. We caught a glimpse of her with a blue beret pulled down over her hair . . . at least we were sure the slight figure must be hers, and no doubt it was.

The execution was to take place at 10:00 P.M., and up to the last minute everyone felt there was hope that Governor Fuller would be persuaded to pardon. The last ten minutes were excruciating. There was total silence. We hardly breathed, but when a clock struck ten the hundreds of people there gave a groan of such despair, such united grief and pain, that I shall never forget it.

.That night and the sense it gave me of some kind of commitment to "the people," the people there, the people who were not cynical like my father but could believe that innocence existed, and could believe that anarchism was not a crime in itself—that night radicalized me, I suppose. From then on through college I identified myself with the unions battling for reasonable wages in the textile industry, in steel, and especially in the automobile industry, and by the time I was in college I called myself a radical and a socialist. The Depression when it came two years later only intensified my belief that something was very wrong with capitalism.

And I was reading not only Marx but also Ibsen's plays, and Alfred North Whitehead's *Aims of Education,* which added fuel to my fire in my wars with some of the teachers at the High and Latin. It was a heady brew and led to some pretty hot discussions with Jane Reid. Once I went over to the Reid house when I had been told by my English teacher that I could not write a final paper on Ibsen "because Ibsen is immoral." Even now I find it hard to believe, but it is true. Miss Pheasant had no doubt been brought up in a parochial school, and was rigid in her views. That evening in early spring, Jane herself opened the door and asked me in. She explained that she had to go over a batch of papers before the next morning, but she would love to hear my news first. I didn't barge in that often and she must have guessed that I needed to talk. We sat in the billiard room to the right of the front door because Martha and her mother were sitting by the fire in the parlor. I was grateful for Jane's making our talk private.

It all spilled out then, my hatred of Miss Pheasant, "my mortal enemy," I said passionately. "She doesn't care about anything except grammar." This made Jane laugh; she couldn't help it, I could see. "It's not funny," I said.

"But, dearie, after all her job is at least partly to teach the structure of language and how to use it, isn't it?" And since I didn't answer, she said, "I laughed because if you never have an enemy worse than one who tries to teach you grammar you'll be a lucky person, Cam-the-Absolute."

I was not mollified, "But that's not it, Jane." Once in a while

I dared to call her Jane now. "It's that she is so narrow and bigoted she won't let me write a paper on Ibsen!"

"You are rather advanced for your age, perhaps. . . ."

"It's not that. She called Ibsen 'immoral'!" I let the full horror of this sink in.

Jane sighed. Everything she didn't choose to say in words was always there in her eyes, and what I saw in them, that deep look as if you could actually see the soul come up into them, always demanded honesty.

"I guess I'm pretty intransigent. But Ibsen is not immoral, you have to admit that."

"I doubt if you can change her mind, Cam, so maybe you just have to accept her as she is."

"I won't! I won't let Ibsen be so misunderstood."

"But perhaps it's really not up to you. Maybe Ibsen will survive without your help."

"Oh dear, you're just teasing me, making me into a child."

"I admire your fighting spirit, Cam, always have. The trouble is, you are so sure you are right. I feel rather sorry for Miss Pheasant."

"*She* has the power!" I said. I was nearly in tears, tears of frustration.

"Maybe. But she has to face St. George out to kill the dragon every day in class . . . and that can't be much fun."

"I don't fight every day," I murmured, "only when some outrageous thing happens. Then I go to Mr. Cleveland."

"You do?" Jane lifted an eyebrow. "And what does Mr. Cleveland say?"

"He usually says I have a point. He is very gentle about everything, you know. Then he says to calm down and try to see Miss Pheasant's point of view . . . something like that."

"I doubt if there are many school heads who would let you come in and talk like that."

"I am rather violent, I guess."

"And awfully sure of yourself, Cam."

"The trouble is because of you, because of Warren, we're way ahead of the other kids."

"And you feel superior."

It was said lightly but it brought me up short, for I saw at once that Jane was right, and I took it to heart. If I really believed all my own talk about the goodness and rightness of "the people," if I were honest, I had to admit that my attitude at the High School was pretty bad. "I guess I'm pretty arrogant. I rush at things like a bull in a china shop without thinking them out."

"You're so quick, Cam, such a blaze of brilliance—and impatience! Sometimes you don't give other people a chance." She turned away then and poked at the fire with a long poker. "I guess one of the hardest things to face is our limitations, but how else is one to grow?"

"Why does it make for growth to recognize what one is *not?*" I was thinking aloud and knowing in my heart that one of the best things about Jane was that she wouldn't let me get away with just quickness and what she called brilliance. My motto at that time, as I suddenly remember, was *toujours l'audace.* "It's so hard to believe in oneself at all!"

"Yes," Jane agreed, "I know."

"How can you know?" I asked passionately. "You have no doubts. You know you're wonderful."

At this Jane laughed. "Little do you know, dear Cam. At school I'm being forced to learn my limitations every day . . . and one of them is I can't do anything fast. So I'm afraid I have to go upstairs now and tackle papers."

I thought she was just being gentle with me about her own limitations, but I felt a lot better anyway.

100

There is always a discrepancy between what we see of a person, especially one at a certain distance, and what has been actually happening to that person. I have painted a picture of Jane Reid as I saw her as a child in her class, and as a young woman in high school. Only many years later did I come to realize how much harsh reality, how much conflict and even rejection, she was experiencing during those years when she seemed chiefly a lover of life, a great life-enhancer, a glamorous, beloved teacher, running off to Europe in the summers, safe in the bosom of her family, always available as counsellor and friend wherever there was need, and communicating such joyous, inexhaustible response both to people and to nature that the image perceived was that of that rare person, a truly happy one.

Many years later I learned by chance that the summer in London with Marian Chase had been a disaster. What feelings were involved on both sides, what irritations, what disillusionment I cannot know, I can only guess. I do know that Jane Reid held Marian Chase in the greatest esteem and had imagined that taking her to London and thus giving her a chance at doing some research she badly wanted to do was a privilege. Children usually are not wrong in their instinctive estimate of people, and the class's dislike of Miss Chase was based, I think, on a sense that she was not a giver, that something withheld got in the way of any real exchange between her and the children she taught. She was discriminating and learned . . . these are not traits that appeal to thirteen-year-olds, but they had immense appeal, no doubt, for Jane. There was also something else, a breath of passion that took me by surprise when I read her letters—letters that Jane Reid had privately printed in two volumes after Marian's death—and I saw what intense feeling Marian could show toward those she loved. But she did not love Jane in that way, and that was clear also in the published letters.

Was it perhaps in part that Jane Reid's mind did not interest

101

her? Did she resent Jane's wealth, feel uncomfortable as the recipient of her generosity just because she could not reciprocate the love Jane undoubtedly felt for her? Did she close herself off because to an ultra-sensitive like Marian not giving love where it was needed creates almost unbearable guilt? Whatever went on between those two will never be known and perhaps should not be, but Jane told my mother that after a month Marian had closed the door against her completely, and refused even to speak at meals or when they met for tea after a day's work at the British Museum. Jane spent night after night weeping . . . and she herself never understood what went wrong.

I have come to see that Jane's attitude toward women was chivalrous (there she was always romantic), toward men humorously maternal, never taking them quite seriously, perhaps, and toward children childlike, for part of her immense charm was no doubt that the child she had been on the island never grew up. Jane's attitude toward Marian did not change, and they stayed friends until Marian died; whatever pain had been involved was buried. But perhaps because of this rejection, I have a hunch that in the next year, my last at high school, when Marian had left Warren and was working on her book, Jane must have seriously contemplated marriage. Sam Dawson was no doubt a determined suitor. She was a perfect match for him, and he was not going to give up easily. But he, like others before him, came up against the one rival hardest to overcome, the Warren School. Invitations to theater or a concert had too often to be refused because of a meeting, a rehearsal, or papers to read, and he must have sensed that time with him was snatched from something that always tugged at her, those twelve boys and girls in the seventh grade, and Frances Thompson. On his side he could try to persuade her that she would be helping him with the League of Nations, a matter of world importance, that he needed her more than the children did. Besides, he must have asked, didn't she want children of her own?

Didn't she? I ask myself as I write this. Strangely enough I cannot imagine her as a mother. She was the marvelous *friend*. She must have thought hard and no doubt had long talks about it with Lucy before she turned Sam Dawson down. Within a year he had married a handsome, rich Bostonian, and that was that. But Jane must have been aware that her decision was radical. If she did not marry Sam Dawson, she would not marry.

What did she know or guess about herself that informed the decision? Partly perhaps that she was attracted to Sam but not passionately attracted, partly that marriage would mean giving up her freedom—every woman, especially these days, recognizes this and has to come to terms with it. For the rest of her life, Jane, as I observed her, entered into families as a kind of fairy godmother whisking an exhausted mother away for a weekend, inviting a whole family of seven children and their parents to the island for a week, so that the mother could have a real rest. Possibly she sensed that her way of being a mother would turn out to be mothering the mothers.

In the middle of that year Allegra Reid, Jane's mother, died, quite suddenly, of a heart attack in her sleep. She had seemed to me ever since I was first invited to the house one of the happiest people I had ever known. The word that best describes her is "benign." I could not imagine her angry or weepy or anything but cheerful as a robin, and much of the time quietly amused by the life around her, and immensely curious to the end so she drew one out not out of courtesy alone but with great enjoyment.

I went to the funeral with my mother. The Unitarian Church was thronged with friends and relatives, some from considerable distances. Part of the Trueblood clan still lived in Portland, Maine, where Jane's great-grandfather had been born. I was chiefly fascinated to see the five daughters, for once together, in the front pews, Edith with her husband and little boy (she had married a doctor); Viola in a purple toque with her handsome husband, Vyvian, and their two children, a boy and a girl; Alix and her husband, Fredson, and Martha and Jane, the two unmarried ones. They were very different one from another, those five women, but as I observed them, I was struck by the family resemblance. They had all inherited their mother's long chin, they were all tall, all blue-eyed. They wore Trueblood on them like a signature.

I was thinking about all this during the service, but when it was over and they came down the aisle, I turned away from Jane's grief. She was unable to hide the tears flowing down her cheeks, unable to nod at a friend here or there as her sisters were doing. I closed my eyes. What would it be like now in that ark of a house alone with Martha? Martha, a little stooped now, an aging heron with a plain, wrinkled face? Would Jane really stay on there forever?

Mother and I went back to the house after the funeral to join the family and friends for tea and cake. There for an hour or so Allegra's presence was far more tangible than her absence. Everyone had some delightful story to tell about her humor and love of life, and the words "Mamma" and "Pappa" made of it all a litany of rejoicing rather than grief, a litany, too, of a family life that seemed relatively cloudless.

In the midst of all this Jane came to sit on the arm of Mother's chair and put an arm around her. "You know, you and Cam must come to the island this summer—could you? Would you?" There was an urgency to her request that I attributed to her need to have friends of her own there now that Allegra Reid would not be there, she who had created the atmosphere and set the standards for so long. As in a royal family, Martha would now be the power, the true inheritor of the island life, and its queen. "Of course I must ask Martha," Jane added almost as an afterthought.

I look back on that first visit to the island as the last great holiday, the end of childhood, and it seems quite miraculous in retrospect. I was coming from a painful week with my father on the Cape at an expensive hotel in Barnstable. I think he was as bored as I was. Our long walks on the beach, swims, and miserable games of tennis, in which he always beat me, were amicable enough, but my fervent socialism infuriated him, and he kept throwing at me that going to Vassar was going to cost him too much and I should have settled for Radcliffe and living at home. I was as prickly as a porcupine and deeply resentful of his wife-to-be. It had been anything but a happy time.

So the relief of being with my mother, who had given me Shaw's *Intelligent Woman's Guide to Socialism* for my seventeenth birthday, was bliss, and then the island! Because it is an island, the sense of being sheltered, of entering a magic world, makes itself felt already at the dock in Southwest Harbor. There we left the car and waited for Captain Philbrook to meet us in *West Wind,* an elegant motor launch with an awning to protect passengers from the wind, and an air of rather sedate luxury about it. Jane was on board lifting her long arms in wide waves as soon as she saw us, exuberant, beautiful in a bright-blue cotton dress, and so unlike the person I had seen bereft at her mother's funeral that it was immensely reassuring.

Happiness flooded in as, once the luggage had been stowed, we glided off. I felt sorry for the people on the dock, who were staying on the mainland, wondering no doubt who these people might be, bound for what unknown pleasures. I enjoyed the sense of privilege. Who is not occasionally a snob?

The island was quite close to the mainland and once we had left the Coast Guard and the harbor we could see it clearly. I had imagined it way out to sea. But in a half-hour we had chugged past the great open field which had been a golf course in James Reid's day, past the farmhouse and the farmhouse dock, past the swimming pool. We could now glimpse a house with blue-green shutters through the trees, but Jane explained that it was not *the* house, but her sister Alix's. She and Fredson would be coming in August, Jane explained. Much to my dismay she said, as though she were giving us a special treat, that Marian Chase would be with us still for a few days.

"That little boy waving on the dock is Matthew, Viola's youngest. He's with us this summer while his parents are abroad."

Something in Jane's tone made me think Matthew might be a problem, but she had a twinkle in her eye when she said that Viola hardly ever came to the island. "She has built herself a French château on the North Shore . . . and Matthew is sent to us now and then, to be tamed."

"Is he wild?" I asked.

"Oh dear no," Jane said, chuckling, "I guess 'tamed' was not the right word." And she left it at that.

He was a fat little boy and seemed amiable enough as he caught the rope Captain Philbrook threw to him and tied us up. The luggage was put on a wheelbarrow and we set off up a mossy path to the big house still hidden among tall pines. The smell was salty and piny and delicious, and I was much too excited to do anything but breathe it in.

"Dearie, you run ahead," Jane said. I was sure she knew I wanted to come upon everything freshly by myself. She always knew things like that.

I don't know exactly what I had expected, but it was quite amazing to push open the big door on the encircling wide porch and find myself in a huge living room where nothing had been changed since it was built in the 1890's and where no doubt nothing would ever be changed. The living room had a fireplace at each end, and in front of each a bear rug, one black, and one brown. In spite of a huge window to the second floor and a staircase at one side and a window seat there, the room was dark because of the wide porch that faced the bay, wide enough to contain the long table where we would eat all our meals, and the wicker chairs and hanging lounge where we would have tea every day, watching the sails go by.

During the week we were there I had a chance to look at everything, the long Japanese painting of a carp in the dining room, the enlarged photographs of classical scenes that hung on the landing, the paintings of trees and ocean by an aunt long dead, the fascinating photographs of the family, one of which still haunts me. It showed men in white flannels and straw hats and women in long skirts walking single file across a field on the way to a picnic, several carrying baskets. Somehow it conveyed the essence of family life on an island and had something of the intimate charm of a painting by Vuillard. The dining room was dominated by a small photograph of James and Allegra on the mantel. They are sitting on a rock, exchanging a look of such sweetness and intimacy, such delight in each other, that a whole marriage is communicated in their glance. I noticed that Martha always had a small bouquet of pansies or nasturtiums there, and when I think of the island, that photograph stands out. Those two had created the life there and their presence was ubiquitous.

I suppose all this penetrated more deeply because of my own parents' divorce. We had no home where the past and present could flow together as it did here. As an only child I had felt a kind of emptiness in the air around me . . . and that was partly why the Warren School, a big extended family, had meant so much. On the island Mother and I shared a room at the back, for Marian Chase of course had the best guest room, with a balcony where she could lie out in the sun and read. The luxury was in the bathroom for each guest room. But it was otherwise fairly Spartan, as there was no electricity and we went to bed each carrying a candle. I discovered that reading by candlelight had its drawbacks and also that my bed was rather lumpy and hard. But it was fun to be with my mother, and we often talked for an hour or so in the dark about the day and all that had happened.

It is strange how when one looks back on a scene years later, the emphasis changes. Small details remain indelible. A large inner world may simply be forgotten. I spent the mornings, till it was time for the ritual late-morning swim, writing pages and pages to Faith, making all kinds of resolutions about college and what my aims would be there, demanding to know everything about her attraction to an English boy she had met that summer, and hanging around on the porch steps when Captain Philbrook arrived with the groceries and the mail pouch every morning, hoping for a letter. Sometimes there were ten pages in her little cramped handwriting, and I went away into the woods to read them. But it is not those letters and all my feelings, so acute and sometimes painful, that have stayed by me. It is the shelter and peace of the island that week for me and my mother, for she had arrived exhausted and, I sensed, depressed.

If I had heard that Marian Chase would be among us with less than enthusiasm, I now began to see, in spite of myself, what it was about her that fascinated Jane. She was extremely delicate; even her features had a delicacy, an elusiveness, that I had not appreciated when I was younger and in her class. She had the beauty of a pencil drawing of an eighteenth-century lady. She was shy, extremely reserved, but she had a delightful sense of humor and a way of seeing things and saying things that was highly original. I think Jane enjoyed her language as much as anything. It was the language of a poet, exact, and therefore often made Jane smile with recognition, savoring the words, as when Marian spoke of the "creaking of tulips." They do creak on their brittle stems, but who but Marian would have said that? The other thing was her passionate love of poetry. She knew hundreds of poems by heart, and one of the games we played by the fire after supper was to see how many each of us could remember and recite. Marian always won, though Jane came in a close second.

Toward Marian, Jane's attitude was one of deference. She seemed sometimes almost hesitant in suggesting a walk or a swim and was always protective. Because of what I knew about the hard time in London, I marveled at her capacity to resolve the pain, or so it appeared, for the sake of what had obviously remained precious to her in the relationship. It suggested a kind of generosity that I recognized as rare.

With Matthew, on the other hand, Jane was positive and commanding, though she sometimes seemed on the point of laughter, for his clumsiness could be disastrous, and his love of food ever-present. Occasionally the cookie jar was found to be empty. Jane could be sharp when he whined as he had a way of doing (I found him rather repulsive, I must admit), but she never stopped treating him with hope, drawing him out, getting him to look at things, helping him collect moss and tiny trees for a Japanese dish garden. How did she find time for all she did, for all she gave? She was the center of activity and yet at the same time managed to make each guest feel cherished in a special way. She always had time to drop whatever she might be doing, and listen.

Among other things she listened to the cook's complaints and teased the waitress, new that summer and very shy. I came upon her one day when I was hanging around waiting for the mail, having a cup of coffee with them in the enormous kitchen, trying to get Cathy, the new one, to understand about the kitchen stove, an ancient coal range. Apparently it had twice been allowed to go out in the night because the damper had not been adjusted properly. But what might have been a cause of some irritation on both sides ended in gales of laughter. When Jane saw me standing in the doorway, she got up, still laughing, and said, "Come on, Cam, let's waltz." How she loved to dance! I was swept along while she hummed "The Blue Danube." Jane could lead very well, I discovered.

The others had already gone down to the pool, except for Marian, who was writing letters, so I had the luck to walk down alone with Jane. Lately I had seen her only with my mother, but the dancing had set me at ease, and it was easy to talk about real things. For she asked me at once about my mother. "It's been such a hard year for her; I have been really anxious; she has looked so tired these last months."

"She feels depressed . . . I think it's my father marrying again."

"It's too bad you'll be away this year. . . ." No doubt she didn't mean it as an accusation, but I reacted hotly.

"I have to go, Jane. I couldn't bear Radcliffe."

"I know; at your age I felt the same way . . . and my family couldn't understand." She laid an arm around my shoulder for a moment. "So . . ."

"I have to go to Vassar for one reason."

"And what is that?"

"To study under Miss Lockwood and really learn about socialism. I have to be prepared, you see. Somehow I want to work with labor, with the workers, the real people." I think I wanted to get a rise, and I did.

"By your definition then Miss Lockwood isn't real!"

"Oh Jane, you know what I mean." I wanted to talk about it.

"Ever since the Sacco-Vanzetti horror I have somehow had to put them, their innocent dear letters, beside President Lowell —I feel strongly that they were real in a way maybe he is not. They were not cushioned by wealth and position. They were so pure."

"Yes . . ." Jane murmured. "They certainly seemed so—"

"It was a dirty business!"

"Oh Cam, we don't really know that, do we? We have been guessing. But President Lowell reviewed the whole case. . . . It's too easy," she said, flushing, "to attack someone simply because they are well off and come from a great family. That seems to me just as crude as blaming someone because he is a poor immigrant."

She was right, of course.

"I guess the trouble is that when it comes to politics everyone oversimplifies . . . and being passionately convinced is narrower than being moderate, I suppose. But Jane, nothing would get done without passionate conviction!"

It is strange that now, fifty years later, I remember that conversation and how deprived I felt when we got to the pool because we had only just begun to explore things of the utmost importance to me and to my whole life ahead. Jane was swept away by Matthew's shout, "You said you'd teach me to dive this summer!"

Marian Chase left on a rainy day. I had meant to go down to the dock and see her off as everyone was apt to do when a guest had to go back to the mainland, but I was upstairs reading Shaw and making notes, and forgot the time. I was sorry because I had certainly come to understand in these few days that I had misjudged her and to understand, too, her elusive charm.

Perhaps to get over the parting and fill in the absence, Jane asked Martha at supper the next night whether she might have Captain Philbrook and *West Wind* and plan a climb and picnic on the small mountain just opposite the island, one of the smaller mountains below Cadillac. "Matthew and I have a secret," she said, a twinkle in her eye.

"Don't tell, Aunt Jane!" he said, his mouth full of apple pie.

"Well," Martha said in her gentle voice, "I had thought to go over to the mainland and pay a call on old Mrs. Charles. . . ." It seemed a little awkward suddenly. I saw Jane flush and pretend to be absorbed in her own dessert. "I suppose I could put that off. Then there's the picnic. . . ."

"Oh, we'll do that," Jane broke in swiftly.

"It will be a lot to carry . . . how many will you be?"

"Cam, Eleanor, Matthew, and I. But all we'll need is a thermos of milk, one of coffee, and some sandwiches. I'm sure we can manage." But her tone, for once, was uncertain, and she waited for Martha to assent.

"There are brownies," Martha said, so apparently she had come to her decision. "Very well, if it looks like a good day."

"It can't rain forever," I said.

"Oh," and Martha gave one of her rare smiles, "it has been known to do so."

But the gods were with us and it turned out to be a just-about-perfect island day, a taste of autumn in the air, all the outlines sharp as we crossed the bay toward the humpback mountain we were going to climb. It looked quite formidable as we came in to dock, but I remember looking forward to the exercise.

Jane Reid's passion for this place, her awareness of every lichen-covered stone and bunchberry leaf, her acute ear for any bird, a towhee scratching in the underbrush, was contagious. I found myself looking at everything around us with intense interest. Then, after scrambling over the rocky path, to stop and take in the view over the island toward other islands, the grand perimeter, gave us a whole other dimension. None of us, except Jane, were avid climbers. Matthew, who had started out by running ahead shouting, "I'm going to find the place!" soon tired and dragged his feet.

Jane teased him gently about the fact that one can't take a mountain by storm. "You've run out of steam, dearie, and we're only a quarter of the way up . . . the thing is to pace yourself and take it slowly."

"Tortoises win," I reminded her as we rested for a moment and took off our knapsacks.

Jane laughed aloud. "To think of your remembering that!"

"I'll never forget it."

"Dear Cam, I was hard on you, wasn't I?"

"You taught me a lot—about tortoises and other things."

"My feet hurt," Matthew said crossly. "I'm tired of climbing."

"You can go back if you like . . . and wait for us down at the dock," Jane said quite coldly.

"But I want to find the place," he whined.

"All right then, let's get there," Jane said.

"What place?" Mother asked. "Is it a secret?"

"Shall we tell them?" Jane asked Matthew.

"They'll see," Matthew said, his interest aroused once more.

So Jane and he proceeded, keeping a little ahead of Mother and me. We took our time, savoring the climb, and Mother, I feel sure, was glad to take it slowly. The bay began to seem far below us now, the water appearing to be like wrinkled silk through which the wake of motorboats drew long V's. After a while a schooner in full sail came around the island—a glorious sight. We heard Matthew shout, "Hey, Aunt Jane, look at that boat!"

When we caught up with them a little later, they were standing under a small cliff, the granite cracked here and there with tufts of grass and moss, even a few tiny fir trees rooting them-

113

selves in the crannies. Jane and Matthew were facing it and appeared to be searching for something.

"What are you looking for?" Mother asked.

"Shall we tell them now?" Jane asked Matthew solemnly, and took a little leather pouch out of her pocket.

"We're going to hide a treasure," he said. "We have to find a little pocket that we can put it in and then close it with a rock."

"And it must have some clue in it, so someone could find it again," Jane explained.

"A million years from now," Matthew said, his eyes shining, "some boy will find it."

"It could be a girl, you know."

"No," Matthew said rather crossly, "not a girl."

"We might find it ourselves in twenty years. . . ." Jane mused. She was standing on tiptoe, feeling along a crevice with her long, sensitive hands.

"That's too high," Matthew said, doing the same thing further down. "Look, Aunt Jane, there's a white line here through the rock. That could be the clue, if I can only find a little place." And suddenly there it was, a fairly large stone in his hands and a small, perfect cave where it had been stowed.

"Good for you, Matthew! That's great!"

There was quite a ceremony as Jane gave Matthew the pouch and he emptied it and showed us with a beatific smile a twenty-dollar gold piece and two ten-dollar gold pieces. "The treasure," he said in a whisper. "Don't tell anybody, will you?"

After that memorable first visit to the island, Mother and I talked about Jane, of course, in her happy island incarnation and decided that she was probably a person who was more herself outdoors than indoors. But we agreed that living under an older sister's rule both at home and on the holidays could not be altogether easy. She must have thought a lot about it, about herself and her own life now that she had evidently decided not to marry. But it was only four years later, after I had graduated from Vassar and come home to get an M.A. in modern history from Radcliffe, that Jane made up her mind to take a major step and build a house. She was thirty-eight years old.

It was in early May when she came to see us at teatime in a great state of excitement. "Eleanor, I'm going to build myself a house," she announced in much the tone of voice, that tone of surprise and delight, in which one might say, "I'm getting married."

"Good for you," my mother responded at once. "It's time you had your own place."

"Where?" I asked, "Where is it going to be?"

"You'll see! In fact," Jane added with a radiant smile, "why don't you and your mother come and have a picnic on my land —Sunday, how about that? The day after tomorrow." I heard the ring in her voice as she uttered the words "my land." There was such excitement in it, a declaration of independence, I felt it was. Yes, a little as though she were getting married, leaving home, becoming her own woman.

Mother insisted that we bring the picnic, knowing very well how Martha might react, so Jane picked us up in her Dodge with the top down, on a perfect May day.

"The land" was further away than I had imagined, about forty-five minutes away, rather a long commute, it occurred to me. But when we arrived, I could see why Jane had fallen in love with it, why it had become such a dream to her, for it was a just about perfect exemplar of what a New Englander might consider as essential in a landscape. The house would stand, she told us, on a gentle knoll, backed by white-pine woods, and to its right a half circle of meadow dotted with juniper bushes, a

115

kind of amphitheater. Below, an open field led to a brook. "Yes, even a brook!" Jane said leading us down.

"It's like a Robert Frost poem," my mother said, stooping down to pick a violet from the grassy slope. "It's yours," she said presenting it to Jane. "Your honest-to-God own violet, Jane."

"Oh, it's so amazing," Jane cried out, after slipping the violet into a buttonhole, "to own land ... I mean, it doesn't seem right, does it? Imagine owning a tree!" And as though she were already lavish in the gifts from her land, she suggested we go up the hill and fill our picnic basket with pinecones to take home. "I'm starving, aren't you?"

She spread a rug then right where the house would stand eventually, but the soft grass was so warm to sit on in the sun we ended by using the rug as a tablecloth and settled ourselves around it. There was a moment's silence after Mother's chicken-salad sandwiches had been unwrapped and cups of hot consommé poured. We sat and soaked in the warm sun, and the silence.

"Mmm, what a great sandwich," Jane murmured. "How did you make it taste so good?"

"A little lemon juice in the mayonnaise, maybe."

"There are brownies, too," I announced, having just discovered them in a tin box.

Jane sighed a long, happy sigh. "Martha doesn't approve." She turned to my mother with a mischievous look.

"Why not?"

"Firstly, it seems extravagant, I expect, wildly extravagant when there is plenty of room for me in Cambridge. . . . Secondly, she thinks it's too long a ride back and forth from school."

"I expect the real reason is that she minds your moving away," Mother said.

"Yes. But if I'm ever to have a life of my own, it has to be soon. I'm thirty-eight, after all."

"It wouldn't seem strange if you were getting married," I said. "It doesn't seem fair."

"Well," Jane chuckled, "Martha is worried that I'm getting into something I know very little about," and she laughed aloud. "She's absolutely right. A little lemon in the mayonnaise. You know that would never have occurred to me!"

At that time in my own life domesticity was the last thing that interested me. But I was interested in the house. Jane would not feel comfortable in a modern house, I surmised. So what then? An imitation old one? That seemed so suburban. She was eager to tell us what the plans were, and to talk a little about Caleb Smith, her architect, "Oh such a dear," she said. "He thinks we can build the house using the remains of an old one he has found that we can buy and tear down, using the exquisite eighteenth-century fireplace mantels and paneling. Then we have invented a screened-in porch with bunks in it for children and a big fireplace so we can cook there sometimes. It has a lovely design with oval doors so it doesn't look like a porch but more like a wing of the house."

We listened and enjoyed all the plans, but I could not help wondering what it would all cost and feeling that Martha's doubts about that were understandable. But I could tell too that Jane's dream was to create an open house and fill it with children and friends in a way she could not do at home, fill it with *her* life. No wonder her eyes were shining, no wonder they looked bluer than ever on that day.

Jane reached over and just touched my hair. "You and Eleanor are going to be an important part of all this, I hope." Then she confided: "One of my dreams is that Marian will come for long visits—she needs the quiet and the peace, and since

117

I'll be at school all day, she would feel quite free and alone."

So, after all, I thought, Jane was not building a house only to escape. She was building it to be a haven.

"You're trying to put a halter on a unicorn," Mother said gently, "Marian is elusive. . . ."

"The whole thing is an enormous risk," Jane murmured, half to herself. "But what an adventure!"

During the next two years, while Jane's house was being built, I hardly saw her or my mother either. . . . I was absorbed in a mixture of volunteer work, the writing of my thesis on the Fabians, and endless discussions over politics with Tom Weston, who was in law school at Harvard, and his friends and my friends in the Square. Roosevelt had taken over and we all felt the relief of someone who could and did take hold and do something about the Depression and the unemployed, whom one could not avoid seeing, as they were everywhere, selling apples. "Brother, Can You Spare a Dime?" and "Who's Afraid of the Big Bad Wolf?" were the songs. As a convinced socialist one side of me rejoiced that capitalism, as we had known it, anyway, seemed to be proving to be impossible if one thought in terms of human beings. Frankfurter was our hero, or one of them. The word *fascist* was beginning to have a sinister ring as Hitler came to power in Germany. At twenty-three I felt that the world was coming apart. Only in Russia did there seem to be any real hope.

What was I going to do with my life? I envied Tom, who had it all clear in his mind that he would work for the Civil Liberties Union when he graduated. I worried because I was not in love . . . after all, at twenty-three should one not be? I felt full of fervor without any specific endeavor or person to invest it in, rather at a loose end in fact. And sometimes I envied Faith, who had married and was expecting a baby. Sometimes I dropped in on her and her husband, Bill Goodman, a very tall, thin man who was teaching (of all things, I thought then) at the Harvard Business School. Faith seemed so incapable of even putting together a decent meal that I wondered how she would cope with a baby, but strangely enough, she seemed beatifically happy, unconcerned, and in a sort of dream of motherhood which had little to do with reality.

I am gliding over a great deal because this novel is not about me, yet I am present in it as narrator. So I have to exist as myself as I write, and this is proving awfully hard to do. I have often thought since I began to write that it is a crazy project for an old historian to attempt.

It is also painful, of course, to go back ... who would want to live her life over again? I simply can't do it and don't intend to. But when I did know exactly what I wanted to do, then there are two scenes that seem relevant. One was a devastating talk with my father at the Harvard Club in the autumn of 1936, when I knew that the war against Franco in Spain was the one place where fascism could be and must be stopped. Hitler was sending planes and pilots by then; the European powers and the United States had come out for nonintervention though everyone sensed that was a farce. I had been helping to raise money for an ambulance, standing in the Square rattling a box, and that seemed pretty frustrating at times. I got more arguments than I did quarters and dimes. And then I got tired of all the talk and began to feel that the only thing to do was to get over there and help. At the very least I could drive a truck or an ambulance. And maybe I could get some word back as to what was really happenning ... *was* Hitler sending planes? *Was* Russia coming in on our side? The newspapers were filled with rumors.

I soon found out, of course, that American citizens could not get a passport for Spain, and my attempts to get sent as a corre-

119

spondent by *The Atlantic Monthly* and *The Boston Evening Transcript* were abject failures. "They just treated me like a crazy kid," I told my mother.

"Darling one, it is a little crazy, isn't it?" She looked at me in that quizzical way she had.

"Only because I'm a girl. Plenty of men are volunteering. Mother, this war is going to decide the history of Western civilization for years and years to come. It's the one chance, maybe, to stop the fascists, don't you see?"

"I do see," she said gravely, "but the question is what you can really do if you do manage to sneak in somehow or whether you might not be an added problem in some unit. I don't know, of course . . . nobody knows."

"Luckily I took Spanish in college . . . I was thinking of South America then."

"Cam, you'll need to be self-supporting. How do you think you can finance this? I wish I could help, but I just squeeze through these days. Warren is not famous for paying teachers very well, and in these Depression years we have to carry more students than ever. Parents are losing their jobs. . . ."

It was immensely generous of my mother to be as supportive as she was. Faith's mother would have had a nervous breakdown if she had wanted to do such a mad thing. It was mad; I knew that in my heart. But at the same time I felt so strongly about the war, felt also, I suppose a great unused fervor and belief inside me that the tug was irresistible to go, to be part of it. I sensed that I would end up teaching history and here was a chance to help make it. How could I stay home studying and writing papers forever, when I could have helped prevent what I looked on then as a disaster for the civilized world?

So I decided to ask my father to stake me to a year. I figured that I could manage on one hundred dollars a month plus the fare on a ship to Bordeaux. From there I could get in touch with socialists in France, who were already organizing help of various kinds. He agreed to take me to lunch at the Harvard Club, which was not too far from his office. After we were seated he started on his usual tack of putting me down. But I was determined not to get angry this time.

"You look like a tramp," he said. "Why can't you dress like the young woman you are?"

I had on a khaki army shirt I had bought at a second-hand place in the Square, and a black skirt. "Oh Daddy, you never appreciate what I do. Look at my slippers. I took off an old pair of sneakers and put these on just for you."

"Well, what's all this about?" he asked after we had ordered scrod and Prohibition beer.

"I need to go to Spain for my work," I said. It had just occurred to me that I could after all incorporate the war in Spain into my thesis by doing some juggling. I would meet with English Fabians who were volunteering. And Spain now was a test tube.

"I really don't follow you." he said, eating, as he always did, so fast that he had half finished what was on his plate before I had done more than taste. "If the club does one thing well it's hash-brown potatoes."

"Daddy, please listen to me."

"I'm listening." Half listening, I thought. Half his mind was always on some case he was working on.

"I cannot see," he said after I had tried to explain why the war was so crucial, "why a civil war in Spain is any of your business. And I cannot see why I should help support a lot of commies, either . . . and that's what you'll be doing, you know. I do read the papers, strange as it may seem to you, and it's clear that Russia is getting involved."

"So is Hitler."

"Exactly."

"Exactly what?"

"What is a crazy young woman going to do in that crossfire! You won't be fighting windmills, Cam. You'll be fighting tanks. I'm sorry, but as your father I feel it would be totally irresponsible to aid and abet this mad scheme of yours. You might get killed!"

"You'll never understand," I said gritting my teeth. I was near to tears, tears of frustration.

"I'm quite willing to be called names to save my daughter's life," he said, trying to ease the tension now. And then he really did look at me. "I bet it'll be all over before you can possibly get there. In fact, I'll make a deal with you. If it's not over by summer I'll see what I can do."

"Wow!" I was so relieved I could hardly believe it. "Do you really mean that? You're not just teasing me?"

It was like my father to do what he did. He would put up a big fight about something like my going to Vassar and then suddenly, perhaps just to get on with things and get away, capitulate. He was a very impatient man. And I was, as usual, grateful, but wondering why I could not love him more for what he gave and realizing when he asked about my mother that I could not because of her and never would be able to until she died. Then many years later we did become friends.

"Mother is awfully tired," I answered. "She works too hard at school, and she is always worried about money." I wished at once that I hadn't said it. I saw his face go red with anger.

"I'm not a millionaire," he said. "I have two households to support now and things are very tight."

What was there to say? We each might have been screaming in a high wind. And so, as usual, we parted both feeling sore.

In that autumn, the autumn while I worked away at my thesis and devoured every bit of news I could get about Spain, Jane's house was at last nearly ready to be occupied. And in late October there was to be a housewarming. Marian Chase would be there, Mother said. She and I would bring Faith and little Edward. Martha had promised to come too, so it was quite a gathering, in Jane's mind, no doubt, the first of many such gatherings to be, the plunge into a life of her own at last.

It turned out to be a brilliant day, warm for the season, and we were all excited and happy, helping to bring things into the "shed," as Jane called the big closed-in porch. There was already a wood fire burning in the fireplace and a delicious smell of wood smoke, and Martha and Marian chose to sit there and mind Edward in his playpen, as they had already seen the house earlier that morning. For the rest of us it was a thrill to go and explore as Jane suggested we do while she unpacked picnic things.

It was quite strange, I felt, to walk around in this absolutely immaculate house, the floors shining, the small-paned windows shining, but the furnishings still rather spare. It was beautiful, but a little cold. I couldn't help trying to visualize Jane here alone. How would she manage cooking a meal when she finally got home from school after seven? Had she any idea what shopping for food, cleaning a house, keeping things in order would mean in time and energy? How would she fill the empty space? I had never really thought before what it is that makes a house come alive. . . . that was my mother's great gift: a bunch of flowers on a table, a sense of the color and texture of things. And the two small mirrors she had painted for Jane with brilliant blue-and-green frames for the coat cupboard downstairs and the bathroom upstairs had just that signature which seemed a little lacking in the house so far. We did admire the brown-and-white star-patterned quilt on Jane's four-poster double bed, a present, we learned, from Lucy in Philadelphia. Martha had come through with lovely sheets and blankets, yellow and blue.

And in fact the house was the occasion for a whole lot of what seemed like wedding presents for Jane, who was marrying solitude.

Had she imagined what living alone would be like? I asked myself, standing for a moment in her bedroom window looking out over the gentle pasture.

"What are you thinking about?" Faith, who had followed me upstairs, asked. She slipped an arm through mine and we stood there a moment, silent, before I answered.

"I wonder what will happen here . . . I mean inside Jane," I said.

"It's a big adventure, isn't it?" And then Faith laughed. "It's so terribly neat, it scares me."

But then we were summoned to lunch to settle down in the shed for the festivities. There was much laughter and congratulating and a bottle of cider Mother and I had brought in which to toast the house and all the life beginning there. If I had doubts a moment earlier, one look—Jane's shining look, brimming with the joy and the triumph of it all—dispelled them. She seemed, except for Edward, the youngest of us all. There was a moment when the bright pieces of talk and activity around eating our lunch coalesced as we drank our coffee, as Marian, who had been rather silent, spoke in her gentle, contemplative way about living alone and what it might be like. It made quite an impression on me, for I realized then that she brought something to Jane that no one else could, a way of looking at life that was unique.

"You will hear the birds as you never have before," she said, "and be conscious of the shadow of wings as they fly. Small sounds, a mouse in the wainscot, become momentous, and also light, touching the back of a chair, swashing down a wall. You will slowly find your places, the places where you sit to think." This, I remember, brought a smile as Jane interrupted,

"I never have time to think." And the answer, "You will."

"The house," Marian went on, still looking at the fire, "will become a presence in itself. It will shelter and enfold you. It will come alive in the silence—ah, the silence," she ended.

At that moment Edward, who had been as good as gold, sucking the ears of his teddy bear, suddenly let out a wail, and we all laughed.

"I hope there'll be human voices"—Jane smiled across at Marian—"like yours and Edward's"—while Faith picked Edward up and held him on her lap—"as well as bird voices."

"No doubt there will," Marian said. She got up then and announced that she thought she would go for a little walk.

"I'll come with you," Jane said instantly.

"But I would like to get the feel of it, alone. . . ."

There it was again, the way Marian had of absenting herself just at the moment of almost intimacy. Perhaps fortunately, as we watched Marian walk down the pasture toward the brook, Caleb Smith, the architect, and his wife, Jenny, arrived to join in the celebrations. I had not met him before and was surprised to see a white-haired man, but it was evident in the way they greeted each other that he and Jane had become real friends, and now she pulled him out to "sit on the front stoop, Caleb!" The two large granite steps had been one of the last things to fit into the puzzle and had only arrived that week. He walked slowly and was slow of speech, and I sensed that their tempo was alike as they settled themselves and chuckled and laughed as they remembered various extremities they had weathered together while the house was being built.

Meanwhile, Jenny, a stout woman with something warm and tempestuous under her reserved exterior, had gotten into a conversation with my mother about gardening, and they went off to measure a place way down the field where Jane was planning to have a vegetable garden.

125

I lay on my back in the grass by the steps half listening, half watching clouds move over. What was missing, I decided, was an animal, and I sat up then to ask Jane whether she might not want a dog.

"Caleb wants me to have a dog," she answered, her eyes twinkling, "and I'm sure my class would love me to have one, but somehow the idea of a dog remains in the back of my mind."

"Why in the back of your mind?"

"Welllll." Jane had a way of extending a word and that "well" became a rather long vocable. "I feel quite safe here as it is." Then she swallowed a smile as though it were a joke on herself and said, "Have I time for a dog?"

"Nobody expects you to work yourself to death," Caleb teased.

"No . . . but . . . well, I do have things to do that take me away a lot."

I was curious to know what they were (she could have taken the imaginary dog to school, of course). And I was glad that Caleb dared to press her on this. So she explained, rather as though she were adding it up for herself as well as for him, all those responsibilities I had hardly known existed until then. She had to go to New York periodically for the International Refugee Committee she was on, she said, "and that gets more important all the time." She wanted to see Lucy and that meant Philadelphia. And to Texas to see her sister Edith. I learned then, or later, that Edith and Jim had a retarded boy, Russell, and had bought a sheep ranch so that he could stay at home and be safe and have things to do that he could do. "Besides all that," Jane mused, "I don't mean to give up going back to France now and then, to visit the children. So you see . . ."

"It does appear to be rather a full life for a gentleman farmer," Caleb smiled. "and all this time I thought I was build-

ing a house for a woman who wanted to be a rock and a root
—to stay put, in fact!"

"It will be a traveling rock, I guess." But if there was conflict,
Jane refused to acknowledge it. I could tell that she believed
that her dream of the house could be realized, even so. And I
wondered. . . .

"About dogs," Caleb intervened. "What you need is a housekeeper to look out for things when you are away, and have a hot
supper ready for you when you get back from school on a cold
winter night. A dog would keep the housekeeper company."

By now Jenny and my mother had joined us and Martha had
brought a deck chair out. She had not said a word and I wondered if she had fallen asleep, but now she had something to say.
"I'm afraid it would not be easy to get help way out here," she
murmured.

"I just want to live here for a while," Jane said, "feel my way,
not make decisions."

Marian wandered back with a pine cone in her hand, "to light
the fire tonight," she said, giving it to Jane like a treasure.

I was glad when we all got up then, to gather ourselves together, that Jane would not be alone on this first night in her
new home, and especially that the person staying with her was
someone she truly loved.

On the way home we talked, Edward fast asleep on Faith's
lap beside me, Mother in the back seat.

"It's wonderful," she said leaning forward, "to see Jane so
happy, isn't it? And even Martha appears to be reconciled."

"Well, you know," Faith said, "it's odd but it doesn't feel quite
real to me. It feels a little like a playhouse designed for a child
who imagined she would live there and then found it wasn't
after all a real house."

"Faith!" I was shocked. "What an awful thing to say."

"Well, that's extreme, but something is missing."

"What makes a house a real house?" I asked. "You know," I said, turning to my mother.

"I don't know. Not necessarily a family, children, which is what comes to mind first. But something that can't be willed, some life going on inside the house which can be felt when one walks in. It's too new, Jane's house I mean . . . she's only just beginning to imagine her life there, let alone live it. So we have to wait and see . . . oh, I hope it will be all she dreamed—and more!"

"A lot depends on whether Marian Chase wants to come often and stay," I ventured.

"All I can say is I never imagined when I married Bill how much time and energy I was going to spend just dragging in toilet paper and food!" Faith said and of course we laughed. "At least Jane won't be dragging in tons of diapers!"

As I think back on it now I see that Jane did that first year very consciously put down roots, and the dream began to be fleshed out. Very early on she began to drop in on Mrs. Cole, a near neighbor whose husband had a dairy farm and kept cows in the big barn attached to the small white house. He had died the year before and Mrs. Cole now lived there alone, sitting in a sun porch at the side where she kept geraniums, somewhat crippled by arthritis and always welcoming a visit. That was a real root, and another was Jane's first experience of Town Meeting in March. But it can't have been easy to drive back long after dark on school days and walk in to turn on lights and put up the furnace, and find herself in a silent house, having to get her supper. Once in a while, in a blizzard, she stayed with us for supper and the night, but I think she felt like a homing pigeon, tugged back to Sudbury, to her nest, and little by little she *was* thinking of it as her nest.

* * *

In the summer of 1938 I did go to Spain. When my father, not unexpectedly, reneged on his half promise, I spent a weekend in Sudbury at a point when I was nearly in despair and poured out my rage against him and at the same time why I felt it imperative that I get there, that I be in some way part of what was going on. Jane listened. I sensed that she was not entirely in accord, that she felt I was rushing into something I could not really know very much about, without needed skills. "You are not a nurse, Cam, after all, and who knows whether a woman will be allowed to drive an ambulance?" she asked at some point.

"Women went to the Civil War here," I said at once, "without any skills, and nursed and rescued wounded after the battles."

"Yes," she said, "but they were in their own country, after all. They were rescuing their brothers."

"Anyone fighting Franco is my brother," I answered in the fervor of my commitment. The argument went on and on.

"Cam, the hare," she murmured at one point, trying to break the tension.

"Maybe so, but the tortoise wouldn't get there in time . . . it's touch and go, Jane. Everyone who cares at all must get there fast, now. Madrid is being encircled . . ." and so it went on and on.

That day whatever Jane had planned to do was put aside. We did finally go for a walk in the rain, just to get out, and after tea by the fire when we got back, Jane went upstairs to work on school papers and I paced the floor and felt caged, until I remembered that mother had given me a box of brownie mix and a little can of walnut halves and suggested I make brownies. Jane loved chocolate almost as much as I did, as I well knew.

She came down the stairs saying, "What is that delicious smell of chocolate?"

"Want to lick the bowl?" I said.

129

"Do I!" She sat right down at the kitchen table and fell to with zest.

"I'm sorry I talked so much," I ventured.

"Dear Cam, I need to know," she answered, apparently wholly absorbed in getting the last smidgeon of chocolate scraped off the side of the bowl. "This time," she said then, to my utter astonishment and even for a moment disbelief, "I'm betting on the hare. I would like to help you, Cam. And I think perhaps I can. Did you say one hundred a month plus the boat over?"

"Wait. I must put the brownies in. . . ." I had almost forgotten them. Then I sat down opposite her. "Do you really mean it?"

"Well, I was thinking about you, Cam, and your fiery spirit. Sometimes one has to trust a person to know what is right, even when it feels a perilous venture. While I was upstairs I had a little talk with Lucy—Lucy is a very realistic person, you know." Jane chuckled. "I found myself taking your side, Cam, as we talked," and the chuckle turned to laughter. "So I had to realize that I was hooked, in spite of myself."

"It's unbelievable," I said, "I never thought . . ."

"I know you didn't."

Then I laughed too, "I feel as if I had been running for months and have just fallen flat on my face!"

Jane looked at me thoughtfully, "There is only one possible obstacle—we must have your mother's consent."

"You know Mother has always believed that I must do what I need to do—about going to Vassar, for instance."

"Yes, but . . ."

"But what?"

"You did not risk your life by going to Vassar. You will surely be in danger of freezing, of being wounded or even killed. It makes me ache just to think of you in a war. A frightful war, as you say yourself."

"Mother is with me," I answered. "I know she is."

I am still amazed now nearly fifty years later when I think that Jane did what she did for me. But it was like her, it was a perfect example of her wish and ability to help people realize a dream even when the dream was outside her ken. Hers was a life devoted to people, not to causes. Theoretically, perhaps, she was not convinced that the war in Spain was crucial, but she saw that it was crucial for the person I had become.

I learned then also what a team Jane and Lucy were. For Jane could see the need and had the means to help, but it was Lucy who came up with a lot of practical suggestions, Lucy who took the time and trouble to find out what the absolute necessities would be to take along, what medicines, what shots I should get. For years I kept her letters to me, and the two twenty-dollar pieces to sew into my belt in case of emergency. That was Lucy.

I was in Spain from September 1938 to the final debacle in 1939, and I learned all about the mixture of terror, horror, and boredom that war means. I was an ardent twenty-six-year-old when I managed to crawl over the Pyrenees with a small group of French and English volunteers, over the green mountains to the other side, barren, burned, hot as hell. I was in some ways an old woman when I disembarked from a freighter in the late summer of 1939. I have never been able to talk about what happened in that year, not even to Ruth, and I do not intend to do so here. I grew to hate the glamorous reporters who came back with books to write, all except Orwell, who was there as a soldier, and wrote the only good book, *Homage to Catalonia.*

Many of the men and women I knew were killed. I was not even wounded. But I came back with something gone from me that I would never get back, the fervor that had persuaded Jane Reid to help me go. I saw what seemed from a distance the one pure war turn into a war in which Russia and Germany used the

Spanish people as guinea pigs, and I came back with the political idealism I had felt burned out of me. Never again would I
be as committed, even in the war against Hitler. It took me
years to get sorted out and able to function.

I was at first in a state simply of sterile exhaustion. I couldn't
cry. I couldn't talk about the experience—partly, I suppose,
because I had seen so much brutality on our side, and felt it
would be a sort of betrayal to speak of it. I found it difficult to
eat because my stomach fluttered constantly. That at least
seemed a specific enough symptom for Mother to insist that I
see a doctor. Unfortunately, this specialist proved to be an
angry man, furious with me after a painful examination of the
colon because there was nothing wrong! He never inquired
about me. Apparently the stomach was all that interested him.
And when he found no tumor he scolded me roundly for not
taking care of myself better, said I should rest in the afternoon,
which I had been doing since my return, and made me feel
altogether like a fool or a worm.

It was then that my mother intervened. She said, "We are
simply going to tell people that the doctor ordered you a complete rest for three months. Darling one, rest is what you need."

"Limbo"—but how could I rest at home? I couldn't let
Mother, who worked so hard every day at Warren, attend to
meals and all the rest of it. How could I justify being a total
dependent? I went up to my room and lay down, staring at the
ceiling.

Apparently, while I was up there, Jane dropped by for a cup
of tea before going home, as she often did in those days, and
persuaded Mother that it would be a positive boon if I would
consent to go and rest and recuperate in Sudbury. She had just
hired a couple, refugees from Hitler, to be general caretakers
and to cook for her, and it was not proving to be an altogether
happy arrangement because Jane herself was so rarely there,

getting home for dinner sometimes at after eight, leaving the house at seven in the morning. Of course for me it was the perfect solution, and Jane picked me up late the next day to take me out to Sudbury.

On the way, on that September evening in the dusk, she suggested that I would find a surprise, and it was clear that she looked forward as much as I did to my discovering what it was. She told me a little about the Rosenfelds and I gathered that there were problems, partly because of the language. So maybe my rusty German would be of use, I thought, while I heard that Hans, who was supposed to do odd jobs around the place was totally unsuited to any such work. He had been a brilliant lawyer in Berlin, but he had been so starved and ill-used in three months' detention in a camp (not a concentration camp—they had escaped that) that he would never perhaps be able to resume an intellectual life. So everything depended on Thea, a huge woman with immense vitality who loved to cook . . . here Jane paused in her tale and seemed a little hesitant.

"The trouble is, I don't really want huge meals. I have dinner at school, you know, but Thea launches into pies and cakes and stews, and sometimes I just can't eat enough to justify all that, so . . ." she turned to me with a twinkle, "Cam, I hope you'll have a good appetite!"

How could I say that I had no appetite at all? But as we got nearer to the house I began to feel dread. "Will it be all right if I just sleep a lot?" I asked. I felt totally incapable of making a connection with anyone at that point.

While Jane was taking my suitcase out of the car and singing "Men of Harlech" as she did so, I was suddenly nearly knocked over by a huge Newfoundland puppy whose enthusiasm was immense. "That's Nana," Jane said, and in the gentlest of voices, which had no effect at all, "Down, Nana."

"Oh, so that's the surprise!" I couldn't help laughing, as my face had now been thoroughly licked. "Well, Nana, how are you? Are we going to be friends?" The trouble was that I felt incapable of dealing with anything as exuberant as Nana, and was quite glad to go upstairs to my room and unpack right away.

Everything felt a little strange and difficult at first. There was something stark about the house, and why I felt that when I had been sleeping often on the ground or on straw in a barn or in a shelled-out farmhouse seems strange. But I did. There was no cosy chair or sofa where one could curl up, I soon discovered. But if there was no warmth in the furniture there was great warmth in Thea. I felt it in the way she shook my hand when we were first introduced and it sustained me through that long autumn of convalescence.

I who had read omniverously found it impossible to concentrate for more than a half-hour, and anyway there were not many books around. I was amazed to discover that I could lie out in a deck chair with a steamer rug over my knees for hours, half dozing, aware of a bird flying past or a cloud going over, and not thinking about anything that might tear at the wound I was trying to heal. I did think a lot about Jane, as she was being revealed to me, not as the goddess of the seventh grade but on a far deeper level of reality. Those months knit together forever a friendship that was to last until her death.

One of the things I learned about Jane was her particular way of touching people she loved. Before she left for school at seven every morning, she never failed to come and lay a hand on my shoulder. It was a light touch, without pressure, as though aware of the weight it might lay on me of possessiveness, of a demanding warmth. I've never known another human being whose touch was as light and as comforting as hers.

After she had gone, the house would have felt cold and empty, except for the fact that Nana at that time of day was obviously longing for someone to throw a stick for her and I often obliged her for a half-hour or so before setting up my deck chair and settling in for a long doze, the dog at last lying beside me, her nose on her paws. Sometimes I was startled when Thea brought my lunch out on a tray . . . where had the morning gone? If it rained I had lunch with the Rosenfelds in the kitchen. They were eager to talk, but the language was a formidable barrier and our attempts often ended simply in laughter because we could not communicate anything well enough for our talk to be called a conversation. Hans anyway was silent more often than not. I sensed that, sheltered now, safe at last, the safety was something of a prison. Without a car, what could they do? Very occasionally they went for a walk. And I was in such a state of passive limbo that I could not put my mind on their problems.

After lunch I went upstairs to my room and slept sometimes for two hours. Then I took Nana for a walk and once in a while stopped in on my way to visit with Elizabeth Cole, Jane's only near neighbor, a tiny, frail woman, who was always there, sitting in her rocker on the porch or tending the geraniums in the window.

"Well," she always said, as if totally surprised to see me, "I never. Come in, Cam." She must have been close to eighty, but she seemed to manage all right. After I had dropped in several times she surprised me with some rather dramatic news.

"How is my friend Jane?" she asked that afternoon as she always did. Perhaps because Elizabeth Cole was outside Jane's life except as a neighbor, Jane confided in her, and I sensed this.

"She works too hard. She comes home absolutely white sometimes and then after supper corrects papers till God knows when."

"I know," Elizabeth Cole sighed. "She'll work herself to death. She used to stop in to see me often when the house was going up, but since then, with the Rosenfelds there and all, I don't see her." She was rocking now slowly and looking out the window. But she came back to me and asked what had evidently been on her mind. "That man," she said then. "Have you seen him around?"

"What man?"

"That rich man, Breckenridge, has the big place just across the road when you come out on route one seventeen."

Jane had never spoken about him. "Well, you don't know about that, I guess." She gave me a piercing look. "Maybe I had better hold my tongue." Then she added with a half smile, "But I guess it's too late, and besides, since you are living there, you had better know. She was upset when he bought that place, I can tell you."

"What is this all about?" Jane had always seemed so completely in control of her own life, it was hard for me to imagine any such drama going on. "Why did Jane mind his coming here?"

Elizabeth Cole looked me straight in the eye. "He's madly in love with her, that's why. She thinks he moved here just to pester her, wouldn't take no for an answer, you see."

"He's not dangerous, is he?"

"Well, before the Rosenfelds came—and I was relieved when they did, I can tell you—he used to wander around the house with a gun and peer in the windows at her. He spied on her, and you know she never pulls the shades."

"I can hardly believe it," I murmured. The whole thing struck me as preposterous. "Is he crazy, or what?"

"He has time on his hands, in spite of those expensive horses, time on his hands and Jane on his mind. It's not good."

"Can't she go to the police?"

"There is such a thing as harassment, but I can't see Jane going to law about such a personal matter, can you? She never talks about herself . . . only that one day she did. I've often wondered why. I suggested she get a gun and she laughed at the idea and said she did not think a shoot-out was the answer." Elizabeth Cole chuckled, "Still," she said, "I can't help worrying sometimes."

"Why do you suppose she never married?" It was a question I had had on my mind the past weeks. I had been witnessing how much Jane gave out all the time to life. What nourished her? Marian was in England that year. There was a kind of emptiness at the heart of the house, I felt.

"Well, I've thought about that some. But I never knew a woman just like Jane so I can't figure it out. Can you?"

"She came close to marrying a few years ago, I think, a fellow high up in international affairs, but she finally turned him down and he married someone else. At school when I was a kid we imagined the man she loved was killed in World War I. But maybe it was just a rumor. Kids are pretty romantic."

"She loves that school, doesn't she? That's when her eyes light up, when she talks about a play she is putting on."

"She is a marvelous teacher—the best I ever had until I went to college." And because in the last few minutes Elizabeth Cole and I had become friends, I could say aloud what I had been thinking. "I can understand someone being madly in love with Jane; she's so much more alive than most people, so free . . . and yet, there is a wall, I think. There is something she always holds in reserve. And if you were in love, it might drive you to do crazy things."

"Well, now that the Rosenfelds are there, she's safe. And we can forget about Breckenridge . . . I've talked more than I should have, Cam. Bury all this, will you?"

I realized that it was not something I could ever mention to Jane and said so.

"Want a cookie? I made some of those ginger ones you liked last time. Take a few home for Jane, too."

And so that remarkable conversation ended. Nana and I walked back to the house in the crisp autumn air, watching the leaves fall one by one. I wondered whether the whole fantastic tale could be true, but Elizabeth Cole was a realistic woman and a wise one. She would not have invented such a tale, so I had to believe it. What it did was to bring into sharp focus for me, as I thought about Jane, her extraordinary glamour. What was it that could make a Breckenridge behave like a lunatic? What had made me and Faith and even Tom fall in love with Jane and want to follow her to the ends of the earth, and weep floods of tears when we left Warren to go out into the world? Lying in my deck chair the next morning I thought about it—men, women, children, all came under her spell. But she herself was absolutely unselfconscious and unaware . . . or so it seemed . . . of the aura around her. None of her sisters had this quality, unless possibly the oldest one, who, I had heard, was worldly and sophisticated, but whom I had never set eyes on.

What was it then? An unusual capacity for enjoying life to the limit married to a great sense of responsibility? Jane was not at all self-indulgent. A single piece of chocolate was savored with the delight of a child. But she would deny herself a second. Nothing glamorous about that New England denial of the excessive! Was it the sheer exuberance? Maybe the thing about glamour is that it cannot be defined. A beautiful woman may not have it; an ugly woman can. So I finally came to the conclusion that it had to do in Jane's case anyway with something mysterious which I reluctantly (what an academic I have become) called soul. And it was visible in those extraordinary eyes through which joy, grief, wisdom, even anger flowed. "Pallas Athene" I had used to call her when I was in the seventh grade. The mystery was something held in reserve, something I now believed no one would ever touch and reach. And perhaps glamour always has to do with the distant, the unattainable, *la princesse lointaine.*

The day never seemed long until around six, when I began to wait for Jane to come home for supper. Then I allowed myself a Scotch from a bottle brought at some time by her brother-in-law, Alix's husband, for Jane never bought liquor. Then I usually read something for an hour or two, often not really taking in so much as a page. My mind wandered. It was time to turn on lights and put another log on the fire. Where was she? Sometimes I knew she stopped in to see my mother. Sometimes it was eight when Nana let out a volley of barks and we both ran out to help carry packages in, and life came back to the house where we had all been in limbo, waiting.

Jane always went in first to greet the Rosenfelds, then ran upstairs to wash and change into slippers, and finally came and sat down for a half-hour by the fire before our supper was served. The Jane I talked with then about what had been happening all day out in the world was not the glamorous Jane I had sometimes been thinking about. She was often dead-tired, and it showed. But still she recounted some hilarious thing that had happened that day at school and I drank it in, while Nana, beside herself with joy, tried to get into Jane's lap. So it always ended in laughter while Jane put on a big apron and let the dog climb all over her.

I couldn't help being amused by her lack of capacity to deal with a large, friendly animal. And it reminded me of school days, when the inability to show anger or speak sharply had sometimes seemed a little strange. A sharp command, which is what children as well as dogs need at times, must have seemed to Jane a fascist approach to life. One must treat every living thing with respect and never impose one's will.

"Get down, Nana," Jane would say gently, but the tender

tone had the opposite effect of that intended and made Nana indulge in an orgy of licks, till finally Jane had to push her off and put her outdoors. More than once I laughed aloud, as we went in to supper. "What's funny?" Jane asked, quite at sea.

"You're not cut out to be a *Gauleiter*," I teased.

"I should hope not! You think Nana needs a *Gauleiter?*"

"Dogs must be taught to obey and are happier when they learn to." But I know I never convinced Jane of this truth.

After dinner more often than not the phone rang and there would be long talks full of laughter with Lucy in Philadelphia, with Edith in Texas, or with one or another of the dozens of friends in Jane's life. I was beginning to understand the breadth and depth of the relationships she kept going.

"How do you do it?" I asked once. "You never seem hurried, although you say you have papers to correct every night. You are always available to everyone who calls."

Jane gave me a quizzical look. "Good heavens!" she said, "Would it were true! But there is so much I don't get done . . . answering letters, for instance. Half the time I simply fail to do what I want to do, what I know needs doing."

"How could you? Warren takes so much energy and time." These days I sometimes resented Warren a little.

"Do you suppose everyone lives with a sense of failure?" Jane had been standing at the door ready to go upstairs and work, but now she came and sat down in the snowshoe chair and seemed to want to talk. "Sometimes these days I feel so inadequate at school."

I held my breath. Jane had never confided in me before, but I knew from what Mother had said that she had a difficult class this year. Now she turned to me. "Why can't I reach those kids?"

"You certainly reached us. . . ."

"You were a marvelous class."

"How we adored you!"

Jane laughed. "I don't want to be adored, Cam. But I sure would love to be allowed to teach without constant rebellion and brouhaha." She said it still smiling, but I could feel the hurt underneath.

"Mother told me there's one awful boy. . . ."

"I go and talk to your mother when I'm at the end of my tether—what a comfort she is!" Jane looked thoughtful, a little tense. "Ned is not awful, but he does react from the gut, one might say . . . yesterday he took the wastebasket and emptied it all over the room."

"Why?" It was very hard for me to imagine such a thing happening in Jane's class.

"No reason. He was bored, I expect. It is quite clear that I bore him almost to death."

"What did you do?"

"Asked him to pick up the rubbish he had strewn around."

"Did he?"

"No, he went out to have a talk with Miss Thompson. He has her permission to go and have a talk with her whenever the spirit moves."

I sensed by Jane's tone what she felt about that. "That doesn't seem quite fair—to you, I mean."

"Fairness isn't the point." I felt she was reminding herself. "If this sort of freedom is going to help Ned, that is the point."

"But does it help him?"

Jane gave me a searching look. Perhaps she felt she shouldn't have said anything about this prickly subject. She smiled a kind of secret smile. "I guess it's almost as hard for Frances to admit failure as it is for me." Then she got up, once more on the way

141

upstairs to work, but at the door she stopped and said, "A school maybe is a microcosm of the world. If Ned's father were not so famous, things might be easier for us all."

Whatever did she mean by that? It made me feel very uncomfortable. Of course Ned's father was a Nobel laureate in physics, and I felt the school's prestige might be involved, but how could a whole class, and Miss Reid too, be sacrificed to pride? I hated the humiliation for Jane. But I also wondered what was going wrong for her as a teacher . . . how could a child in Jane's class be bored? Could her kind of imaginative resourceful teaching ever become old-fashioned? I still don't know the answer to that question. But even then I was aware that children were far more sophisticated ten years later than they had been in my day. Probably none of those in her present class would have read Trueblood, for instance. They would have been reading *The Hobbit*. And because Jane was a slow reader she could not keep up with all that was going on. And did her marvelous sense of fun get dampened by the negative atmosphere? No doubt it must have. She must have felt on trial that year, yet with her hands tied because of Frances Thompson's attitude and demands. It hurt to think of Jane not being loved by her class, questioning her own value as a teacher and woman.

I had been in Sudbury for a month—going for walks and, after two weeks of doing almost nothing but sleep and eat and wait for Jane to come home, setting myself a daily stint of uprooting sedge grass, which was taking over the lovely open hillside and pasture—I had been there all that time before Spain was mentioned. Jane must have sensed that I was not ready. But she had helped me go, after all, and at some point I knew I must try to reassure her, or at least share with her some of what I had been through. But to do that I had to come to terms with what felt inside me still like an ocean in tumult, in which I could drown if I allowed myself to go down into it, as, sooner or later, I knew I had to if I was ever to get out of this limbo of not feeling and hardly being alive. Even if I could have spoken, Jane was too preoccupied with the school for it to seem fair to lay this burden on her.

And then one day she came home with a bad cold and decided to take a day off and stay in bed. It was lovely for me to be able to take her breakfast up and make a little bunch of wild asters and bayberries for her room, and then to let her sleep for once, as she did for most of that day while we crept around downstairs. The house had been made of pieces of a very old house, but unfortunately the walls were thin and it was the most trans-audible house I have ever been in. And I have sometimes wondered whether that explained why Marian never did come for a long stay as Jane so wished she would. And why the house itself gave the illusion of being an old house but never felt quite real, as a house where generations have lived and died does. To *feel* lived in, after all, a house has to *be* lived in. And Jane was simply not there enough.

But on that day, lying in bed, dozing and waking, perhaps she did reach a center in herself . . . it may have been the only time where she could watch the light change from morning to evening. And by tea time, when I tapped gently on the door, she was ready for life to pour in again. I had brought tea on a tray, so although she may have been ready to get up, we had it there. I sat in a chair first, but after a while I climbed up on the bed and lay there at the foot of it, curled up. The atmosphere was so relaxed that it seemed the most natural thing in the world to talk.

"What have these long, empty days been like for you?" she asked gently. "You do look less like a ghost, dearie, so I hope you are beginning to feel rested. . . ."

I felt terribly frightened suddenly as though I was standing

over an abyss and would fall in if I moved. "I don't know . . .
I can't . . ." and suddenly tears began to rain down my cheeks,
tears I could not stop. I blew my nose, and waited.

"You don't have to, Cam."

"Oh, but I want to . . . it's only . . ." and again I was choked
up. "It seems like the end of everything I believed in. I don't
know where to go from here, you see. Or who I am. So much
died there, Jane, I mean, not only people."

"Yes," Jane sighed, "the awful waste." And I knew she must
be thinking of World War I, when millions died.

"It's different from the world war—I know millions died then,
but the vision didn't die."

"I wonder . . ."

"It was clear at least who was right."

"Maybe. But the peace got all muddled up. There was nothing clear about that." Jane had her hands behind her head and
was staring at the ceiling.

"I almost envy John Cornford, Julian Bell, and so many
others."

"They were your friends?" Jane asked.

"Oh no, they were English poets . . . I never saw them. But
I think about them because they died believing in something.
They must rest easy in their graves."

"Oh Cam!" There was just a slight irony in her voice as
though to imply I could be exaggerating. That made me angry,
and I guess anger was what I needed to break through the fog
and begin to exist again.

"You don't know. You can't know!" I got off the bed and
paced up and down.

"It would help me if you would try to tell me all you can," she
said.

"Well, I saw anarchists, who are supposed to believe man is
so good he doesn't need governments, line people against a wall

and shoot them with machine guns—women and children, Jane
—only because they suspected the village of belonging to another faction. I saw a whole village blasted off the face of the
earth by Messerschmitts. No one seemed to know what was
really happening. . . . The communists were absolutely cynical.
On the one hand all of Spain was a kind of bloody playing field
for Russia and Germany to experiment with . . . on the other
hand the anarchists and communists were really at war with
each other . . . it was just a rotten bloody mess. So many of us
went believing it was the last chance against fascism, you see
. . . so many of us *believed!*"

"I wish you could tell me a little of where you were and what
you were doing, Cam."

"But I can't talk about it." I stood shaking my head as though
trying to disentangle myself from a twisted rope. The generalities were easy. But the abyss was still there. "What was I doing?
Getting drunk on cheap wine, stealing bread out of bombed-out
farms, if you must know. I wandered, Jane, for months I attached myself to anyone who had a jeep, crisscrossed between
the lines. I was in Madrid for a while. I must have had a concus-
sion when the house next door was hit. For a while I guess I was
a little crazy and sick. But finally I joined the Friends' ambulance corps. We moved with the International Brigades defend-
ing Madrid, pushed back, putting up our tents and then having
to flee."

"You were nursing?"

"Not exactly. I did the dirty work nurses had no time for, got
water to the thirsty, dirty water, we never had any distilled
water. It had to be boiled for the surgeons and I got very good
at doing that."

"How brave you were."

"No. Glad to be with friends. And to have found a niche
where I could be useful. I got so a little sleep was the only thing

145

that mattered, sleep anywhere, my head on my backpack, sleep for a half-hour, till we were ordered to strike the tents, leave the dying . . . that was the worst." I wasn't crying now. It felt more like vomiting. "Dr. Herman had been operating for twenty-four hours . . . we were running out of bandages. People tore up shirts. And then . . ."

Jane was sitting on the bed in her wrapper now, and she made me sit down beside her, and laid a cool hand on my forehead just as though I had been vomiting. "You don't need to go on," she said quietly.

"I have to. Let me go." Long ago that is what I had said and she had helped me go. Now it was different. I drew away. "Dr. Herman—his head was blown off by a grenade. I was right there. I was covered with blood."

"Oh Cam!"

But now it was said, I felt absolutely cold. No tears. No vomiting. Rage. "The filthy bastards."

"You had a Red Cross on the tent, I suppose?"

"Of course."

It should by all the rules have been relieving to utter what I had held back for so long, to let it out, once and for all. But it did the exact opposite of what it should have done. What I felt was an immense distance from Jane, and from everyone I knew, as though talking about what happened in Spain—it seemed an eternity ago in another time, another life—was bound to be only betrayal. In the first place it could not be put into words. Words had never seemed to me so futile, so inexpressive.

"I sometimes thought they used the Red Cross as a target. It would be no waste of ammunition, as a direct hit would be certain to kill doctors and wounded all in one go."

Jane was silent. What could she say, after all?

"I shouldn't say all this."

"Yes, you have to. And I and lots of other people have to

know, Cam." Then, as I did not respond, she took my hand. I was standing by the bed, turned away. "Do you think you might be able to write some of this down, make a record?"

"And throw it in the wastebasket!"

"Why?"

"I got so fed up with the correspondents, the Hemingways, coming in for a few weeks with plenty of liquor stashed away and plenty of money, just to watch people getting killed. It made me sick."

"They were not important. The people you believed in, that surgeon, were important. You persuaded me that the war itself was crucial. . . ."

"The more fool I."

"You don't feel that now?"

"I don't know what I feel," I said. "So I had better shut up." How could I tell Jane that I had come back convinced . . . I had witnessed it . . . that Spain had become simply a wounded bull in the arena being gradually driven mad before the kill. The Russian communists and the Nazi and Italian fascists didn't give a hoot for Spain. It had become simply a playing field for testing weapons and murdering hundreds of innocent people so when it came to a real war they would be able to do it better. Guernica was just a successful experiment.

"Dearie, I am going to get dressed now," Jane said. "Let's go on talking by the fire."

She was right. Jane, who always allied herself with a moderate view, winced visibly before these intensities. And sometimes I found this irritating, but that day I sensed that she was wise. I had shot my bolt. I went and lay down on my bed, wishing my heart didn't pound inside me like some imprisoned animal.

Not that day, but perhaps a week later, we talked again after supper on a Saturday night, when, for once, she did not have to run upstairs to do schoolwork. I had begun to feel restless,

took Nana on longer walks. Some mornings now there was frost
on the grass, and the leaves, except for a few oaks, had about
fallen. My sedge-grass digging went on, though. It was the one
thing, the one positive thing, I was engaged in doing.

"I feel as though something has gone out of me and I can't get
it back," I said while Nana for once snoozed on the hearth.

"You have to give yourself time, Cam."

"I've been here six weeks . . . just sleeping, doing nothing."

"Would you like to go home now? Maybe you need to see
Tom and Faith. Tom graduates from law school this year. . . .
" She was feeling her way. Perhaps she was suggesting that
where she had failed, friends my own age might succeed. But
I felt empty, too empty still for that sort of excited talk.

"No," I said without explaining. "It's better here."

"That's good news, for me, as you must know, Cam. It's been
wonderful to come home every night to a dear person."

"I feel such a dud."

"What you feel, I suppose, is only loss and pain. But what I
see, dearie, is someone battling very hard things with a lot of
courage."

"If only I could imagine something ahead!"

"Do you still sometimes think of teaching history as a possibility?"

"I don't know. I feel as though I had no skin. The very thought
of an interview makes me go into a sweat."

"But you could perhaps write some letters, send out a résumé
. . . it wouldn't mean facing an interview for quite a while. After
all, it's the middle of the academic year!"

"Tortoises hibernate," I said. "That's what I am, I guess, a
hibernating tortoise." And we laughed because that was easier
than trying to go deeper.

Maybe I could get a job as an instructor in some small college,
I thought, but how could anyone teach who had lost some vi-

sion, some certainty that it seemed to me a teacher must have? That is what had been burned out of me in Spain. What would I be teaching from? I said it aloud: "A teacher has to have some belief. . . . I seem to have lost mine, Jane. What was so wonderful at Warren was that we really thought we were part of some great ongoing hope, that we could help make things better. . . ."

"Yes, we did, and I still do . . . but it's very slow, Cam. After the World War we really believed it was the war to end all wars. We thought the League of Nations would lead the way to lasting peace."

"So we now know there is no such thing as a war to end all wars, or a war to free people as in Spain. What's left?"

"What's left is to go on trying to educate people that war is not the answer, that we have to find better ways to make radical change."

"But radical change is never achieved by moderate means. . . ."

"Maybe not now." I felt the tears start in my eyes, the prick of deep feeling brought alive. I wanted to bury my head in her, to hug her fast. But Jane was not someone one could easily embrace. I learned in those two months that people teach mostly by what they are. Quite unconsciously she was helping me knit myself together.

How did she see herself? Some people have a sense of destiny, of something "meant" about their lives. People with a specific talent have it. But I haven't a clue as to what Jane thought of herself. She lived as fully as possible—this person who loved picnics, who loved children, who loved history and loved teaching it—but did not apparently think much about her role or roles, except—and perhaps this is the clue—she did have an ingrained, unselfconscious belief in noblesse oblige, that a fortune such as hers must be used, that her own gifts were to be

149

used, spent, in a constant outward flow, that more was asked of her because of her heritage than could be asked of those less fortunate.

Jane hesitated to spend money on herself. Building her house was the one great extravagance. When I lived there she sometimes laughed at herself because she was wearing the sweater she had worn for days. "Lucy," she said with a twinkle in her eye, "would not approve. She always goes with me to buy clothes and her ideas are much grander than mine." Then she looked down at herself. "Oh my dear, there's a button gone!" Then she smiled. "Who cares?" Nevertheless she let me sew it on for her and changed into a dress. And as she went off, a bulging briefcase in one hand, she waved and called back, "Now I'm respectable, if not beautiful!"

"Very respectable." But I wanted to say, "Very beautiful." At forty-five she still was. My mother, who observed such things, always said, "She has the profile of Nefertiti," and it was true. The long chin, and something in the way she held her head, had that air of a queen about them. An Egyptian queen with very blue eyes!

It did not surprise me that she was being pursued by that neighbor, although I never did catch a glimpse of him and Jane never mentioned that he existed.

Here I am writing a book about Jane Reid and I keep discovering that I know nothing about her, about the inner person.

But I did know by the end of the two months that we were friends for life. Something fluid between us, partly her instinctive withdrawal before my exaggerated feelings as an adoring pupil, had solidified into a real and deep affection.

And at the end of those months fate intervened and I was handed a temporary job teaching American history at a girls' school in Concord, a position left open by the sudden loss of a teacher because of a heart attack. In a way it was an accidental start to a career; providential, as it swung me back into life and kept me too busy to question what I was doing or where it was taking me. Almost by accident, then, I became a history teacher, and finally moved into college teaching after World War Two. There at a small college south of Boston I met Ruth Arbor, with whom I lived until her death ten years ago.

Jane was forty-five in 1941. As I now—from my own perspective at seventy—think back over her long life, it becomes clear that those middle years between forty-five and fifty-five were the hardest. Within the immediate family there was illness. Her younger sister Alix's husband had a severe heart attack and had to take a leave of absence from his job as President Conant's assistant at Harvard. During his convalescence he came more than once to Sudbury, and Jane must have been happy to see the house become the haven that she had envisioned it might be, and that it had been recently for me. Fredson's death a few years later left Alix terribly bereft and Jane saw more of her then than in the years before. Then Edith, who, as they grew up, had become the closest to Jane of the four, had to face inoperable cancer and months of decline. That year Jane managed to go out to Texas on every holiday and help plan what would happen to the retarded boy Russell, around whom life on the Texas ranch had been planned.

Meanwhile, a most astonishing thing took place in Cambridge. Martha, a true old maid, and the last person one would have imagined to do such a thing, decided to take in an English family of three children, nine, ten, and twelve years old, a boy and two girls—Jonathan, Alice, and Sally. This was the year of the bombing of Britain, and Americans had been asked to take in as many children as possible for the duration.

Of course Martha could not have managed this without Sarah, who was librarian at Warren, where Martha also worked part

time in the office, and who had come to live in the big
house in Cambridge. Sarah, a natural-born leader on expeditions, taught the children to ski, took them on tramps and picnics, and in the summers taught them to sail. Nevertheless it
was a stunning decision for the retiring, shy Martha to have
made. And it must have taken Jane by surprise . . . for there
suddenly was her sister with a family to bring up! And the house
in Cambridge, which had seemed to be chiefly a receptacle of
the past and of family traditions, suddenly came very much
alive in the present.

I find that I have been reluctant to take up what must surely
have been the most difficult period in Jane's life, that period
during the forties when I myself hardly saw her, as I was carrying a heavy load at the college. What I know about it comes
from what my mother told me, and then, the other day, my
unearthing a few letters from Faith, who had decided to become an apprentice at Warren and go into teaching herself. She
was assigned to Jane's class in 1941–42 and for a while we wrote
each other long letters again, because we were each involved
in experiences that needed an ear to help us sort out, she rather
excruciatingly aware that Jane was not any longer as able to
communicate with children, I because I was in love with Ruth
and at that time, forty years ago, such a relationship raised all
sorts of questions and heart-searchings. I shall copy out some
parts of Faith's letters because they tell better than I can what
was going on.

September 1941
My duck, it is great fun of course to be working with
Jane, and seeing Warren now from a teacher's point of
view. But I am a little concerned about Jane. She doesn't
seem like the free spirit we knew and adored; she seems

—it is so awful to say this even—somehow beaten down, and looks so tired sometimes that it hurts. She spends an unholy amount of time preparing each class and brings in wonderful material. There is no textbook, you know . . . wow, I am learning what that asks of the teachers! And sometimes I can help by going to the library myself and coming up with things. Jane, I have discovered, is a slow reader . . . that means that it takes her longer than it should even to correct papers. Luckily she is still very good at getting the kids to dramatize and act things out. We are working on an assembly about Roland and Oliver, and I can see that it's going to be good. I'm just hoping Jane will have a real success and feel taken back into Miss Thompson's fold. It is simply exruciating to sense that somehow Jane is no longer, as she was when we were at school, Miss Thompson's right-hand man. She has been dropped from several committees this year. I know all this, my duck, of course, but can't say a word. It would be too humiliating, I feel. And of course Jane never says a word of criticism of Miss T. There are rumors, by the way, that Miss T. herself is thinking of resigning, and that might be the best thing that could happen for Jane.

February 20th

Oh duck, Jane has been out with the flu, so I have been in command. It's really quite thrilling, but also a little troubling because I get on better with the kids than she does, and have no problems keeping the class on an even keel. I have discovered that I can be quite sharp and definite when I have to . . . can you imagine it? But why can't Jane do this? It's as though she censors herself just when she should let go. What is so awful is that the wonderful sheen she had when we were here has gone. It can't be just that she is middle-aged now, can it? I mean, Miss Stout must be much older, and her classes

153

are absolutely quiet and attentive, just the way we used
to be. And Edward adores his teacher, who is not young,
either. I wish I could talk about it with with F. Thompson,
but she is so driven herself, I hesitate to ask for time . . .
and then what would I say? I mean, anything would be a
betrayal.

March 1st

Well, I did have a talk with F.T. I just felt I had to. She
was honest with me and clearly disturbed herself, perhaps
even glad to talk with someone who knows the whole
situation and loves Jane. She agrees that Jane should get
out of teaching but apparently she feels she can't ask
her to leave. But how can anyone else do it? She's the
head, after all. I must admit, duck, that I felt she lacks
courage—but then we don't know the whole story.
There's no doubt in my mind that Jane has been an immense support all these years, financially, and as a friend.
You must be tired of hearing all this . . . but I know you
care. I keep remembering how Jane defended Marian
Chase to us that time and scolded us for behaving so
badly. There is no one to do that for Jane now. I can't, obviously, since she is my boss and in command. But I get
very upset. It is hard to see such a great person humiliated and baffled . . . she herself does not know what the
matter is. And children even in a school like this can be
very cruel. One of Jane's strengths as a teacher is her love
of words and belief in precise use of language—you
remember, duck! We used sometimes to think she was
pernickety. But the other day one boy answered a
query about the use of a word with "Fuck you!" I saw Jane
flush to the roots of her hair, but she didn't have the foggiest idea how to handle this "dare," for that is what it was,
of course. Jack was sent out of the room, I'm afraid, as a
sort of hero.

April 20th

With spring here at last everything is a lot easier. I went home to tea with your mother the other day, haven't seen her for ages. She looks washed out, but don't we all? In some ways this school is a dragon that devours its teachers! Anyway, your mother feels she has to have things out with Jane. Someone has to.

May 4th

I decided to take Jane out to dinner last week. Mostly I wanted to thank her for all she has taught me this year; the breadth and depth of what she brings in to a class every day is just amazing, and the way she dramatizes and makes things come alive. There have been good days, duck, and I haven't said enough about them, I fear. Anyway, Jane had on a lovely blue dress when I picked her up at Martha's. You can hear her voice, the lilt in it, "How festive this is!" as we sat down in one of those booths in that place on Church Street where you and I have talked for hours. When am I going to see you? I ordered a glass of wine, though you know she does no more than take a sip, but it seemed appropriate.

At first she asked all about you, how you are faring down there, whether I had ever met Ruth, what she is like. And I told her all I could, and that you are happy. She's awfully fond of you, you know. Then she asked me how I had felt about being an apprentice. I tried to tell her something of what I had learned, and she listened with that wonderful look in her eyes of total listening. How rare it is!

"Well, dearie, I'm glad someone learned in my class, for I'm afraid the children did not."

"That's not true,' I said quickly. "They'll never forget Roland and Oliver!"

"Maybe not altogether true," she said with a smile, "but

155

true enough so that I think the time has come for me to leave Warren."

But not, I gathered, right away. What she has in mind is to stay on after Miss Thompson leaves and help bridge the transition when the new head (who has not yet been found, so it may be a year or two still) takes over. In some ways I wish she were going to leave now. It's a compromise of sorts . . . she talked about maybe working as a tutor with children who need reading skills, not being a class teacher any longer.

Never once did she show me any of the pain or humiliation back of this decision. Really, duck, what a super human being she is!

Reading those letters made me feel depressed, made me miss Faith acutely, and Ruth—both dead now. I seem to be a survivor. I suddenly wanted to touch base with someone who had known Jane well and admired her. I wondered if in these last pages I had exposed her as too flawed, and overemphasized the struggle. Two people came to mind whom I might be able to talk things over with.

Why wait another day? I reached over for the telephone and called Laurel Whitman. She had been at Vassar with Jane, one of the group of intimates who went off to Europe together, now and then. All this flashed through my mind while the phone was ringing. Finally a surprisingly young-sounding voice answered.

"Is this Mrs. Whitman?"

"Which Mrs. Whitman? I am May. Perhaps you wish to speak with my mother?"

"Yes, I do. Tell her this is Cam Arnold—she may remember me."

After quite a wait, a frail voice came through. "Cam? Of course I remember you, Reedy's friend. What can I do for you?"

"May I pay a brief call today or tomorrow, whenever is good for you?" and I explained why I wanted to see her.

"Oh Cam, I'd love it! But you must be prepared for a very old lady who forgets things." And she added, "Better come over today so I'll remember you are coming. Teatime would be best." She was laughing at herself, I could tell. "At least the past remains quite vivid . . . so I can tell you quite a lot about Reedy, though I shall forget your name."

I knew I would like her, and at four o'clock, walking over to Raymond Street, I was excited by the prospect of being able to talk about Jane, to enter a dialogue after being isolated for so long as I struggled to write day after day, to try to make Jane come alive for someone who could not have known her. I had been stuck for days, and when I reread what I had set down so far, I had terrible doubts.

Autumn is fine in Cambridge, and at the gate to the Whitman House one maple was still glorious, a mass of gold that would have made Jane Reid cry out at its splendor. Carroll Whitman, I remembered, had been a professor of history at Harvard and had died some time ago. Evidently the daughter, unmarried I presumed, had moved in with her mother. It was a large house with a mansard roof and I felt comfortable with all that I saw, even to a wheelbarrow with bags of tulips and fertilizer in it. Then I rang the bell.

"Come in, Miss Arnold, Mother is expecting you." May Whitman took my coat and hung it up. "If you'll excuse me, I'll go out and get those tulips in before the light fades. Just go right into the drawing room, on your right."

Mrs. Whitman was sitting by a wood fire with a cane beside her chair, a round, pink-cheeked, blue-eyed old woman who raised a hand in greeting. "Sit there where I can hear you," she commanded. I drew the small armchair even closer as I sat down.

"May will bring in tea later on. I wanted to talk in peace."
Then she gave me a penetrating look and burst into laughter.
"How can you be so old, Cam? One thing I cannot get used to
is everyone being so old, myself included. Good heavens, child,
I think of you as a seventh-grader in Reedy's class!"

"That was almost sixty years ago." I laughed, too. "Can you
believe it?"

"No. And what have you been doing with yourself since then?
Did Reedy tell me you were a brilliant professor of history
somewhere or other?"

"Not brilliant, alas. And I retired a few years ago."

"I can't keep up with it all." And again she chuckled. "I'm still
twenty myself a lot of the time, still at Vassar, I'm afraid. It is
very odd indeed to be told I am ninety. The thing is, when you
get to be that age, the present seems to fade away. . . . I never
can remember where I put my glasses . . . but the past becomes
extremely vivid."

"Tell me about Jane."

"What do you want to know?" She sounded a little anxious,
as though being pinned down frightened her.

"Anything, everything . . . what you think of first when you
think of her."

Laurel Whitman considered this for a long moment. "First?
What I think of first? What fun she was . . . I have never known
anyone in all my life who made everything seem such an adventure . . . because, you see, to her it *was* an adventure! Why,
walking down to the Square with Reedy was an adventure. An
ice cream cone was pure heaven! Some part of her never grew
up, you know, maybe that is why she enjoyed teaching children.
And then, unlike a lot of people, she had a marvelous childhood
—she may be that rather unlikely person who actually would
have loved to be a child again. Maybe nothing later on quite
came up to that life on the island, especially on the island." Mrs.

Whitman was clearly enjoying herself and I did not want to interrupt this happy current. "And then she was completely unselfconscious, you know, bursting into song in the middle of Harvard Square! Acting things out all the time—did you ever see her be a mating great horned owl?"

"No, but I wish I had!"

"It was hilarious. Of course she was a born actress. . . ."

"I have heard that her Cyrano at Vassar was quite a performance."

Laurel Whitman gave a small hoot. "That's putting it mildly. She had the whole college at her feet—it was glorious! Cam, she was the most glamorous young woman you can imagine in those days—not excepting Vincent."

"Vincent?"

"Millay. We all called her Vincent, you know." And again the old woman fell into thought, looking into the fire as if she could find Jane there in the flames. "She was adored, yet—and this is odd—she was not at all narcissistic, as Vincent certainly was. You know, Cam, as I think about Jane it comes to me that deep down she was a very humble person, and what she really wanted was not so much to be a leader herself as to follow someone great."

"Frances Thompson," I uttered.

"Of course. What really happened to Reedy at Vassar was Frances Thompson . . . and from there the Warren School."

"Was she a brilliant student, I mean at Vassar?"

"Not really. She did well enough, you know, she worked hard. What she did best was write papers for Frances Thompson. And even that didn't seem quite as important as acting, and going off on picnics with her circle of friends—Lucy and I and three or four others."

"She must have had beaus," I ventured.

"Of course . . . several young men—she could have been quite a catch—but we were pretty enclosed in those days. And somehow I see her as happiest in the world of women."

"I wonder why."

That phrase brought Laurel Whitman back to me with a jolt. "Why should I tell you?" she said, half laughing, with just a shade of antagonism. "I don't know myself."

"She never really fell in love, did she? Never head over heels in love."

"She was in love with life. That I can say. Head over heels in love with it."

I felt it was an evasion, but this was not the moment to press on, or to probe into what clearly was proving a little bothersome to Laurel Whitman. "But not the marrying kind, as they say?"

At this Laurel turned directly to me. "Cam, whatever made you embark on this project? And what is it really, a biography, or what? And why are you doing it? Is that too blunt a question?"

"First, it's a novel, not a biography." It was a great relief to be talking about it at last, to have an ear at least, a kindly ear, "But the main problem is that I'm not a novelist—don't laugh! I mean, it's so crazy, isn't it? At seventy to embark on such a project. I feel sometimes like a person who never learned to swim and is trying to swim across the channel, floundering about and nearly drowning on the way!"

"You're a historian by profession . . . why not a biography?"

"Cowardice. I didn't want to be tied down to all the dates and facts. I wanted to be free to imagine just because in some areas I really don't know enough. Oh dear, nobody is going to like it, I'm afraid."

"Cam, you amaze me," she said then. "You're so brave."

"Foolhardy, I suppose. But you see what interests me is the essence, not what happened in September 1939 precisely, but what was happening to the essential person. I'm tired of card indexes."

"How far along have you got?" Laurel asked. I knew I had not satisfied her.

"Well, Jane is forty-five and is about to resign from Warren."

"Oh. Yes. That was a bad time. It really was, you know. It seemed at the time like an earthquake that could destroy the foundations. I got quite anxious about her. We all did." Then Laurel turned to me and laid a hand on my knee, "Between you and me, Cam, that dream house in Sudbury never quite worked out. Too far away. And the people she wanted most to come there never came."

"Marian Chase, for one."

"You do know quite a lot, don't you?"

I sensed not unexpectedly a trace of resentment. "Tell me about Marian Chase. I saw her of course, more than once after I was grown-up, but when we had her in the eighth grade we didn't like her at all."

"I'm not surprised. Marian was for grown-ups, not for children."

"Jane always came alive when Marian was around. That I did see . . . and the enormous respect."

"Well, of course Marian was a scholar, a distinguished one. Reedy admired that in her, for she herself was not a scholar, not at all. She was a romantic." Here Laurel paused, whether hesitating to go on, or not knowing what she wanted to say. "You know there was a chivalrous side to Reedy, a side that wanted to protect her women friends, wanted to help them in any way she could to do whatever they most needed or wanted to do. Sometimes it didn't work. That summer she spent in London with Marian was a disaster."

"Yes, I know."

"How do you know?"

"Jane confided in my mother . . . all through that time."

"Hmph." Laurel gave me a penetrating look. "At some point Marian balked. People do that, you know, and for different reasons—when it came to marriage, Reedy balked, herself, but she never understood why Marian did."

"Why did she?"

"It's really none of our business, is it?"

"But I have to try to get at the truth."

"What cause are you serving?" Laurel asked. We had come to an explosive moment and I knew it had to come. "Why do it? Why expose the dead to your delving around?"

"Oh dear," I murmured, "those are the questions I ask myself every day."

"But you keep on."

Now I lifted my head and looked right into the old eyes. "Yes, I keep on. You see, Mrs. Whitman, in fifty years no one will exist who remembers Jane Reid. I want to celebrate her. I want to make her come alive for those who never knew her."

"Millions of exceptional people die and are forgotten. It is an endless stream, generation to generation. You want to dam the stream. Can it be done?"

"Probably not, but I'm going to have a try." It was my turn to feel a little prickly now.

And sensing it, the old woman softened. "Very well, ask me another question."

There were a hundred in my mind. I opted for one I had wondered about often. "What made her as different from her sisters as she seemed to be? Or am I wrong? They were all tall, they all had that long, recognizable Trueblood chin. They all had blue eyes. Yet Jane really seemed to be of a different breed. What was it in her that made the difference?"

For a moment Laurel was silent, even closed her eyes, and I

wondered whether I was tiring her. Then she lifted her head and said quite loudly, "Jane was passionate!"

The answer took me by surprise and I thought about it for a second.

"The others were all at heart conservative . . . in every sense of the word, politically, where matters of money were concerned, and houses, and how one behaved . . . you know what I mean. They gave money to Radcliffe College, to the Unitarian Church, that sort of thing. Jane adopted French orphans, invested in the black settlement house in Cambridge, in refugee organizations . . . you know all this. They were all five charming women, reserved, well-behaved, preoccupied with family matters. Jane just never could be contained in that frame . . . though you must never forget, Cam, how she venerated her grandfather!"

"I don't forget it. Was she passionate about old Trueblood?"

"In a way she was. At least she took on a lot of responsibility about the House when it was made a national monument . . . think how she worked on those papers!"

"I haven't come to that yet. . . ."

"But you will. She was passionate about Trueblood because she felt that he was being put down and disregarded by the academic community. It was fashionable at one time to sneer at his novels. Thank goodness she lived long enough to see him reinstated."

"Passionate." I had come back to that word. "Yet she never married, never, as far as I know, had a love affair. It seems odd."

"Odd, yes," Laurel murmured. Then she gave me a rather penetrating look. "Take sexuality out of passion and you may have a clue."

At this notion I had to smile. "Is that possible?"

"Nothing about Jane was possible, really . . . that's what made her so interesting, so captivating." But having said so much she now withdrew. "I think I'm getting a little tired . . . haven't had such an interesting afternoon for years, but . . ."

And as though summoned by telepathy her daughter now came in, flushed, her hands dirty, and apologized for having completely forgotten about tea. And I took my leave. "I can't thank you enough."

"Nonsense, Cam, I feel rejuvenated. Come again . . . anytime."

My conversation with Laurel Whitman had done what I hoped, given me a fresh start, as though talking with her had pushed a button and set going a fountain of memories and insights. And gave me the courage, too, to see if Tom Weston would have the time for a talk. I hadn't seen him for years, since the twenty-fifth reunion of our class, in fact, and I hardly dared add up how long ago that was. It was strange to imagine that he must be a grandfather and perhaps even retired, though that was hard to believe, he was such a live wire. And whether retired or not I felt sure he must still be active in the Civil Liberties Union, and still a pillar of the parents' association at Warren, where his two sons and daughter had gone. He had headed the committee that managed to raise a million dollars for the school in the sixties. But I myself was not living in Cambridge at the time Jane resigned from Warren, after Frances Thompson did. Tom might be able to tell me more about that, for one thing.

I knew that he and Adele had moved out to Lincoln some years back, and found their number in the phone book and was invited out to Sunday dinner.

"I'm not the cook Adele was, but I can put a roast in the oven."

I told him I would bring dessert, and then, though overcome with shyness, not knowing how to ask, I murmured, "Adele?"

"She died last year, Cam."

"Oh, how awful."

"It's strange how I can't get used to it."

"I know. Ruth, my friend, died ten years ago."

"So we're both bereft. It will be good to see you, Cam. But to what exactly do I owe this pleasure? Raising money, maybe?" I could hear that he was smiling.

"Heavens, no! I'm writing a novel about Jane Reid."

"You are?" Astonishment raced across the wire.

"Yes, crazy, I expect. I'll tell you more about it on Sunday," and I added, "try to remember all you can."

"Right on. I'll do my homework and expect you at twelve. Scotch okay?"

It was a cold November day, and that, perhaps, added to the rather desolate air of the living room in spite of the wood fire burning at one end. But no flowers... I remembered that Adele had loved flowers. Piles of magazines and books everywhere and the smell of dank tobacco. A widower's house.

"Cam, you're just the same," Tom announced when we sat down with Scotch.

"Preserved in amber like all retired professors!"

"Come now. People preserved in amber don't write novels. . . ."

"Not a first novel at seventy, anyway!" I didn't say it, of course, but Tom had changed. I couldn't get used to his face with a shock of white hair above it, although his eyes were very bright under thick gray eyebrows.

"It's strange, isn't it, what an indelible mark Warren left on all of us in that class ... in that class, so I must believe that Jane Reid was at least partly responsible." After a slight pause he asked, "What are you after, Cam?"

Almost without thinking I uttered it. " 'I think continually of those who were truly great.' "

"Yes, I see. Yes, she was. I grant you that. An extraordinary woman."

"I'm bogged down in all that went wrong in the middle years. Sometimes it feels like betrayal to be writing about it."

"You have your problems, honey."

"One of them is that I know so little about the last years at school. I was immersed in teaching, not living in Cambridge."

"Maybe I can help. My children were in school when Starbuck took over after the war, and Frances Thompson had gone off to Germany. I think maybe it was a good thing that Jane stayed on through the transition. She was one of the few of the old guard still teaching and she helped Starbuck—though of course he had taught in the school for a couple of years before he went off to the war." Tom stopped and looked across at me. "May I just think aloud for a moment?"

"Please do." It was comforting to be with someone from our class, to feel Tom's quiet strength again, and conviction. Especially as he was clearly enjoying this journey into the past.

"Frances Thompson was a different breed, terribly intense. Her whole life was the school. And in a strange way what had been the strongest bond, between her and Jane, got pretty frayed at the end."

"Because Jane was losing her grip as a teacher?"

"Yes," Tom sighed. "My children didn't get on with Jane at all. I couldn't understand it. I blamed them, but Adele was a help in making me understand, I guess. She said Jane was out in the wilderness when Frances no longer asked her advice about crucial matters . . . and being out in the wilderness she lost her nerve."

"Oh Tom, do you really believe that?"

"I don't know what to say. . . ." He shook it off then and went on more cheerfully, "Starbuck was very good for Jane. She gave up being a class teacher and worked for a while with remedial reading. And she was good at that. Her tempo and her endless patience were right for that. Hey, I had better think about cooking some vegetables. Come out to the kitchen and we'll have a second while we get things together."

Out in the kitchen he and I were both more relaxed. I learned a great deal that I had not known. As a lawyer, Tom had been drawn into a painful episode, and he and Jane became friends as a result. During that time he was invited to a dance at Jane's eldest sister's château, and he told me all about that. I could feel the novelist in me coming to life again, and I knew that much of what I learned must come to life if I handled it as a novelist and that I intended to do in the next part, which I think of as "The Giving Years." At the end, when we were again sitting by the fire with our coffee, Tom chuckled and told me a story.

It seems that when they were raising money for Warren one of the new parents, whose husband had come to Harvard from California, had been assigned to do some interviews. Apparently, as Tom explained, the new method is to find out what people have in the bank by one means or another, and then to name a specific sum that might be offered.

Lenore, the Californian, when it was suggested that she visit Jane Reid, who had retired by then, had sold the Sudbury house, and was living in a small apartment over the barn, back of the family house in Cambridge, said, "How can we ask Jane Reid for *money?*" Jane indeed lived so frugally that if one were not a New Englander it would appear preposterous to do any such thing. She was told to ask for one hundred thousand.

"Whew!"

"I must admit that even I felt it a bit much. Anyway, Lenore of course could hardly bring herself to say the words. Jane was sitting on a dilapidated old velvet sofa in the tiny living room, which was also the dining room. Lenore said she finally uttered the words, 'We had thought you might give a hundred thousand.' Apparently Jane did almost gasp, then smiled that secret smile she swallowed when she was amused by something and said, 'No, I'm afraid I can't quite do that. But I think I can give seventy-five thousand.' "

We both laughed with the pleasure of it, and Lenore's absolute astonishment. "I was afraid," she told Tom later, "that I would burst into tears."

I felt I must race home and plunge into part three of the novel as quickly as possible. I felt so warmly toward Tom, and I guess he did too, that we hugged each other when we said good-bye.

"You must come back, Cam! I am very interested in this resurrection."

Prologue, Part III

When I reread what I had managed to put down so far it became clear that I was allowing the historian—and a rather dull one at that—to take over from the novelist, and that now I must plunge in and turn all that Tom had told me into an imaginary reconstruction. I never had realized before how hard this is to do. I have sat here at my desk for an hour unable to get things into sharp enough focus. What finally did it was when the house without the Rosenfelds came alive in my mind. They had left after two years because they felt too lonely and were now happily ensconced in a small, idealistic boarding school in Vermont where Mrs. Rosenfeld could mother a hundred boys and girls and Mr. Rosenfeld could escape to the nearby town for an occasional beer. I was happy for them, and for the great galumphing Nana, too, for she had gone with them. It was now Jane and her house alone.

Part III
The Giving Years

The extraordinary thing for Jane was to wake in Sudbury in the silent house, before light, start out of a deep sleep thinking she must get up and go to school, then look at the clock and realize she could have another snooze, and not hurry at all. In some ways every day felt like a holiday, although once she was up, had had her breakfast, and had put out seed for the birds, she did still feel pounced upon by all there was to be done before nightfall. Jane woke herself up by singing as she went about the chores, and if the house was trans-audible, as Marian complained it was ("elephants appear to be thundering up and down the stairs"), Jane's voice soared out in a very satisfactory way as she made the bed singing "Over the Sea to Skye" and "Men of Harlech" as she washed the dishes.

When she stopped singing, the house did seem very silent, a shell that needed human voices to come alive, and she did also miss Nana and those eager barks. By the time she was dressed, however, the pressure to get going and be off to Cambridge for a session on the Trueblood papers with Jay Appleton was growing—and what would Nana have done without her all day?

On the drive Jane prepared herself for some rather taxing

hours. Jay was exactly her age—they had grown up together, acted in plays together on the island, but they had never worked together, and that, Jane was discovering, was a very different kettle of fish compared with the fancy-dress parties and dancing of their youth or the tennis matches which Jane always managed to win.

It was now a rather prickly relationship. Jay Appleton had been for years ensconced in the back of the Trueblood House as caretaker. He was a student of the theater and rather an expert on Russian theater, had written several books but had no teaching position or other regular job, and unlike Jane and her sisters had not inherited a fortune. He was a warm, affectionate man who for some reason seemed perpetually flustered, disorganized, and on the defensive. For years he had been expecting to get at the Trueblood papers but had never gotten around to it. Now that he was being pinned down, it made him nervous and irritable.

He was a grandson of the writer, just as Jane was, but because he had published books himself, he did not feel that Jane was equipped for the job they were doing and occasionally showed it.

All this was in Jane's mind as she drove from Sudbury to Cambridge. Some of it she understood all too well—getting down to things was sometimes hard for her, too. But she was determined to get the Trueblood papers in order because the pressure from students of literature, scholars, professors, and especially the young man who was writing Trueblood's biography, was clamorous, and once she had taken on the enormous task, she wanted very much to get it done. In some ways it seemed an obstacle to all that she most wanted to do now with her life.

What they did share, she reminded herself, was a deep respect for the material itself and for the man who had written

174

all those letters and journals. If the pace sometimes seemed frightfully slow, it was partly because they sometimes became too involved in what they were sorting out. Then there were perpetual differences of opinion over what should be destroyed and what opened to the public. Trueblood's first wife had suffered from melancholia and committed suicide before she was twenty-five. How much of this should be kept? There was a poignant journal, in which she told of two miscarriages and how inadequate she felt as a wife. . . .

Thinking about this, Jane stopped at Martha's, two doors down from the Trueblood House, to have a cup of coffee with her sister. Luckily Martha was not going to work that day, and the sisters sat by the fire for a half-hour in quiet conversation.

"I sometimes think we'll *never* get it done, Muff . . . it's awfully hard for Jay to buckle down."

"Poor man," Martha said gently—she was always the peacemaker—"he does make things hard for himself." Jay was family, after all, and one did not criticize family.

"Oh dear, you make me feel guilty," Jane sighed. "I try to be patient!"

"Take it a day at a time, Jane. You can't change Jay now . . . it's too late."

At this Jane suddenly laughed. "I'm not trying to change the leopard's spots, just hoping he'll be out of bed by the time I go over!"

"Of course he works half the night . . . you have to remember that."

"And his eyes are tight shut in the morning."

"Why don't you work in the afternoon?" This gentle suggestion was, Jane felt, so exactly like Muff that she had to smile.

"I never thought of that . . . and it's a very good idea." Then she added, "But he falls asleep at any time of day or night . . . he took me to see Gielgud in *Hamlet* and we sat in the front row. Gielgud uttered the first words with tears straming down his cheeks, 'A little more than kin and less than kind,' and at that second Jay gave a loud snore and woke up. I wanted to disappear, it was so embarrassing."

"He can't help it, you know . . . I sometimes wonder whether he has narcolepsy."

"Heavens, Muff!"

"Well, it's not quite normal, is it?"

Jane made no answer to this. Something even more troubling was in the back of her mind. "Well, Muff," she said briskly, brushing that thought away, "I'm off. Thanks for the coffee. It's been a rousing start to the day!"

Whatever was going to happen, Jane never entered Jay's study without feeling excited, a large room with four or five tables covered with boxes of letters and Jay's own work standing about, two old revolving chairs where they would work, and a charming window seat in one of the long windows. She never walked in, either, without a delighted glance at the ceiling, which was covered in Japanese fans, glued on in a casual design.

Jay was apparently not up when she arrived, so she set herself to going through one box open on the desk. These were easy to go through as they concerned Benjamin Trueblood's first trip to Europe after he became famous, the year he took his daughter Allegra, Jane's mother, along with him and met so many English aristocrats. It was great fun reading these, but Jane forced herself to proceed without pausing to savor. What riches the young biographer would find! She was so concentrated that she didn't hear the door open until she heard Jay's voice.

"Good morning," he said in sepulchral tones.

"Oh there you are," but as she lifted her head she saw an unusually rumpled figure in an old seersucker wrapper over pajamas. He looked quite a wreck, she thought. "Are you all right, Jay?"

"No," he said. "No, I'm not."

"Would you like to take the day off? You don't look well."

He shook his head. Jane could not get used to someone her own age looking so old. Jay had deep lines carved into his face, his hair was rough and gray and tousled at the moment, but he always seemed in some strange way a very young person to her nevertheless—and that is why his "old" look shocked.

"I have to fling myself upon your mercy," he said so dramatically that Jane had to suppress laughter. But she then perceived that he was weeping, and said, "Well, old dear, you are in a bad way. What is it?" It was hard not to be impatient . . . there the work lay and must be pursued, willy-nilly. "But whatever it is, don't you think we might talk about it later? We really must get on with things, Jay."

"You are such a governess," he growled, "pitiless. But this is real, Jane," he said soberly. "You *have* to help me."

Jane found something stiff-necked rise up in her. She found that she resisted hearing whatever it was. She wanted to be left in peace this morning, and above all not to be disturbed by an emotional outburst from a man her age . . . it was disconcerting. So she was not able to control the slight coldness with which she said, "Well, Jay, come and sit down. I'll help, of course, in any way I can."

"Will you? Will you really?" He sat down then in the other chair and pulled it closer to hers. "It will mean going to the police," he burst out.

"What happened? Did you fall asleep at the wheel?"

"Oh, Jane," he groaned, "it's much worse than that." He covered his face with his hands.

Jane waited what seemed an eternity. Finally Jay clasped his hands and bowed his head in a curiously touching gesture of desolation. "I was caught propositioning a boy in Central Square last night."

Jane had of course heard rumors about Jay's escapades . . . her mind instinctively took shelter with that "safe" word from a less kind one. But she had refused to believe the rumors, or chose not to.

"I suppose you think I'm a monster." He raised his head now and looked her straight in the eye. "But I'm not."

"Of course you're not," Jane said vehemently. "What I find a little hard to understand is that you would take such a risk, Jay. Can you talk a little about it? Can you help me?" For Jane felt as though a dark well had opened at their feet. She felt dread. Jay did not need to tell her that from the point of view of the world, of the police, anyway, he had performed a criminal act, or had been caught, she corrected herself, with the intention of performing one.

His confession made, Jay was pulling himself together. "You know, Jane, you are quite extraordinary," he said humbly. "I'm overwhelmed."

"I can't see why. . . ."

"Your question, can you help me? *Me?* It shows such an open heart where most people close theirs against men like me . . . and," he added, "there are a lot more of us than most people know. That's what's so hard . . . feeling always that you have to hide what you are. Punished for what is deepest in one, that need. . . ."

"Have you ever had a friend, I mean a lasting encounter of this kind?" Jane asked gently. She felt if she could get hold of one positive element in all this it would be easier to cope with her instinctive distaste, and even revulsion.

"Don't you remember David?"

"David?" Her eyes opened wide. "That beautiful young man who helped with your last book . . . of course I remember him."

"We were lovers for two years."

In this house, Jane thought, where the presence of Benjamin

Trueblood in all his genius, charm, and authority still lived? It came as quite a shock.

Jay went on unburdening himself. "Then he graduated and went home to Oregon . . . he's married now, I believe."

"That must have been awfully hard," Jane murmured.

"One has to accept what the gods give and take away," Jay said and Jane realized that he really meant it. It was not just more dramatic words. And she honored him for it.

"How much pain goes into learning just a little wisdom," she said. "I feel for you, Jay."

Jay sighed. "Now I'm an old man. Old and finished. Left in the desert to roam around, hungry and desperate."

"No," Jane said. Self-pity had come in now to ruin what had sounded so dignified a moment ago. "What most people see is a distinguished scholar and lover of the arts, a grandson of Benjamin Trueblood. Self-pity is not going to get you anywhere. We can't have it, Jay."

"Oh, very well, have it your way." Then he gave her a keen look. "I don't suppose you have ever been in love . . . you are above all that, like the student in *The Cherry Orchard.* You're as cold and smug as all the Reids are. The Truebloods have the passion . . . to love and to create."

"I'm as much a Trueblood as you are." Jane had flushed under this attack. "Love?" She paused then, hesitant to give herself away. "Of course I have loved. Even governesses fall in love." And she smiled her teasing smile.

"Happily?" he asked.

"No, not happily," Jane answered, opening her long hands in a gesture as though letting a bird fly out which had been held tightly . . . Maurice, Quentin, Marian . . . Frances . . . she was shaken by the truth of it. None happily. But more she could not, would not yield. "Jay, what must I do now? What is involved with the police exactly? Do you need a lawyer?"

"Well, unless it can be quashed, it will come up in court."

"You could go to jail?"

"I don't think so. I might be put on probation. But the danger is the papers, a scandal. The family . . . oh Jane!"

She was being asked then, Jane realized, to use power, "pull," behind the scenes, to keep Jay safe from the law. How could she do that when people without influence had no chance? "We'll have to talk to Tom Weston," she said. "We must have legal advice."

"He's so young."

"Jay," Jane said sharply, "I trust him. He's a friend. It's got to be someone we know well."

Jay put his head in his hands. "It's so humiliating," he said. "To think I should do this to you."

"Well, I'm awfully glad you felt you could talk with me about it, Jay." Jane had recovered her equanimity, and was determined to get going and do quickly whatever could be done. No more bemoaning, she thought. And so she went downstairs and called Tom Weston.

He was able to help entirely behind the scenes. He guessed, accurately enough, that Jane's presence, her dignity, her sense of who she was, would be the best plea, and that it was she who must see the judge and get the whole thing settled and taken out of the hands of the police.

But that took some persuading on Tom's part. She was loathe to use "pull." Why should her family be able to protect itself when a poor family with no great name would have to go through with it and "face the music," as she asked him? What right had she really to protect Jay?

Here they got into a brief argument. Tom's generation was already more aware of the problems of the homosexual than hers had been. They had learned a little more than Henry James had been willing to face in *The Bostonians*. It became clear that it was the sexual element here, and especially one involved in "corrupting youth," as the phrase was at the time, that Jane could not accept.

"I can see it, Tom, where real love is involved . . . but picking someone up on the street! After all!"

"No one thinks twice about a heterosexual man going to a prostitute . . . what's the difference?"

Jane was blushing, Tom noted. "Well, you know about these things and I don't," she said. Then she looked at Tom with a pained and embarrassed look. "I shall keep this to myself," she said. "I shall not tell Muff. It would upset her terribly. She is so fond of Jay. Let's keep this between you and me, Tom. You have been simply wonderful about it."

Neither of them ever mentioned that episode again. And the only time Tom saw Jay afterward was under wholly benign circumstances at a party given by Viola, Jane's eldest sister, whom Adele knew because they had been on some committee to do with the Museum of Fine Arts that year. The party was held, of course, in the French château Viola and her husband had built on the North Shore, which was mentioned by the family, if at all, with something like chagrin. But Tom loved the luxury of it, the glittering chandeliers in the huge salon, the ubiquitous servants who really should have been in livery, the champagne and the orchestra. This was in 1947, the first big party there since the war. "The flowers alone," hundreds of white roses, often reflected in mirrors, "must have cost a fortune," he whispered to Adele.

"Oh good, there's Jane," she said, and pulled him over to where Jane was standing with Jay. He, in white tie and tails, gave Tom a curious look, then launched into talk.

"Cousin Viola is doing us proud," he said, every inch a Trueblood, Tom thought. "Isn't she?"

Tom thought Jane looked very distinguished in a dark-blue

evening dress with a wide lace collar that showed off her long throat, and her eyes were shining with amusement and pleasure.

"Splendiferous! All those roses! I must say, it's quite a bash!"

At that moment Viola herself joined the group and was introduced to Tom by Adele.

"It is good of you to join us, Mr. Weston," she said. "Adele has told me how hard you work, how terribly involved you are in making it a better world." Perhaps there was a trace of irony?

"We're understaffed. . . ."

"Come with me," Viola said, taking his hand and pulling him away, "you must meet Professor Tucker—you know, of course, how involved he has been with MacArthur, bringing civil liberties to Japan?"

"But," Tom murmured, "Adele . . ."

"I believe in separating married couples," Viola said firmly, "otherwise everyone huddles together and nothing happens. Come along. . . . I'll see that Adele isn't lost; besides, every man in the room wants to dance with her!" She laughed then. "Don't look so wary, I won't bite." With that she let Tom's hand go.

It was not wariness that explained Tom's look, but amazement at the contrast between Viola and Jane. Amazing that they could be sisters! Viola was dressed in white, a long dress embroidered in spirals of white beads, with a large diamond pin at her throat. She had the Reid blue eyes, but hers were scintillating. What a sheen of money and power there was about her! Tom felt helpless against it. But Tucker, an old gentleman with white hair and an immensely warm and enthusiastic personality, was not at all what Tom had expected, and they got along famously. So for a half-hour Tom forgot all about Adele—after all, she was with Jane.

But when the orchestra launched into a waltz he tried to extricate himself, which was not easy to do. Their group had now been joined by several other men and Tucker was being quizzed about MacArthur, who was not, Tom gathered, popular in this particular world.

"He is, whatever you may think, very aware of what is civilized about Japan—the austerity and purity of Japanese art," Tucker was saying. "Has it crossed your mind how strange it is, that perfect taste, the sobriety and elegance of it, and the violence under the surface? MacArthur is quite good about that."

"You might say the same about Germany," someone ventured.

"They can't be compared," Tucker was vehement. "Look at German architecture, so heavy and pretentious."

"I really must find my wife," Tom murmured and made his escape.

Adele, he found, was dancing with someone who turned out to be their host, Vyvian Porter. Where was Jane? There, he discovered, in a corner talking with a very old gentleman, and Tom went to the rescue. "May I have this dance?"

"I'd love to," Jane said. "I haven't waltzed in ages."

If Tom felt shy at first because he was not quite tall enough as a partner, they were soon whirling away, and he forgot everything but the pleasure of it, for Jane was so light on her feet he was hardly aware of leading her.

"Vyvian has made off with Adele," she whispered as they floated past. "He was a great tennis player, you know."

Tom didn't know. What he saw now was a rather stout man, still handsome, and tall enough to look down at Adele. "What does Vyvian do?"

"Insurance. I'm told he's a wizard."

"I suppose they travel a lot?"

"Oh yes. I never know where Viola is. And then there are all those houses to open and close . . . Palm Beach, the Adirondacks, Pebble Beach. They are here only in the spring and fall."

"I can't put you two together as sisters."

"Oh, she is very grand indeed," Jane said, swallowing a smile in the way she did when she was not saying all she was thinking.

"But so are you!" Tom protested.

"Grand? Dearie, my sister thinks of me as an old-maid schoolteacher, an ex–old maid schoolteacher, at that. Once in a while she invites me to one of her parties. . . ."

"And when you come she is immensely flattered," said the ubiquitous Viola, who had overheard Jane's last remark as the music stopped. "Jane is so busy I hardly ever see her." And turning on Tom her glittering smile she added, "Jane has the most interesting friends—I caught a glimpse of her the other day at the Faculty Club with a handsome black man. Who was that, Jane?"

"John Jackson . . . we're on the board of the Cambridge Community Center together. He's a professor of anthropology."

"You see!" Viola said triumphantly, "Jane moves in the most distinguished circles!"

Jane gave Tom a wink as Jay broke in to ask Viola for the next dance. She accepted gracefully, though, Tom discerned, with little enthusiasm. He noticed that before long Jay was led to one of the tables for a glass of champagne, as he proved to be an awkward though voluble dancer.

"How mysterious families are," Tom said as he watched them go. "Who could believe you are sisters?"

"But we all have the same frame," Jane said. "We really are all variations on a theme, tall, blue-eyed," and she laughed, "all with big mouths. Anyone would recognize a family resemblance I think, a race of herons!" Then, as though perhaps she had seemed earlier critical of this sister, Jane said, "I admire Viola, you know. She broke right out into this world about as far as one could get from that of our parents. It took courage."

"Of a sort."

"I suppose it is what Mr. Frost says, 'We love the things we love for what they are.' "

Tom felt they were suddenly back in Jane's world and knew how precious it had become to him. "How do you interpret that exactly?"

Jane hesitated. She did not think aloud easily, "Well, we love what is, not what might have been or even what ought to have been. In her way Viola is very fine."

"And what is her way, then?"

"We just saw it—making an ugly duckling into a swan . . . carrying social grace to a high level. You saw her building me up just now!"

"You value that. . . ."

"I value something done supremely well." Then she suddenly laughed. "Of course it made me feel quite ludicrous, Tom." And then, "Let's go and join Jay. He looks a little lost."

Tom finally did get to dance with Adele, just before Jane and Jay left at precisely eleven. And they soon followed and had great fun on the drive home talking the whole affair over.

"I just hope Jay was sober enough to drive," Adele said.

"My guess is that Jane will drive. He's apt to fall asleep, you know."

Jay and Jane were now pushing harder than ever on the Trueblood papers because Austin Richards was breathing down their necks. "I have to have the letters and journals to do with his first marriage," he had told Jay. "I simply can't wait. I have been stopped short."

Partly because the unfortunate episode with the police had drawn them together, partly because Jay was on his mettle now, the work was going well. It led them into serious discussions about the responsibility of any biographer.

"I think we have to have a talk with Austin," Jane said. "I think we have to have some idea about what he is after."

So on a fine June day they had agreed to meet with him in the front parlor downstairs. On Mondays the house was not open to visitors. A large marble bust of Trueblood and a painting of him surrounded by his daughters hung on the wall behind the sofa where Austin had chosen to sit. It was rather a cold room, cold partly because nothing had been changed in it for years and years and the Victorian furniture and tables covered with heavy green cloths were really not beautiful. It had the atmosphere of a museum rather than a lived-in house and lacked the warmth and charm of Jay's study with its Japanese fans on the ceiling. Jay and Jane sat on either side in stiff Victorian armchairs.

"What am I after?" Austin said in answer to Jane's question.

"Jane means that we feel we have to have some idea of the trend of your thought about Benjamin Trueblood. We can't expose his intimate papers to someone who, for instance, has the attitude of patronizing contempt that appears to be fashionable these days, at least in academic circles."

"I see your point," Austin said.

"What made you want to write this biography?" Jane asked, for this was after all, the point, she felt.

"I am being interrogated, then," Austin said, looking a little uncomfortable.

At this Jay chuckled. "We are not Russian commissars, Austin."

There was a short pause, in which Austin glanced up at the marble bust of Trueblood, looking down at them from the end of the room. "I think I can best say what I have in mind by directing your attention to that marble portrait over there. I want to bring Benjamin Trueblood to life, restore him, resurrect him if you will. At present he is encased in pious legends, a serene old bore, if you will forgive me, an eminence like something on a tomb!"

"Yes, I can see that," Jane said gently. "George Washington had to be rescued from the cherry tree."

"Exactly. I want to come at the human being, the complex and in some ways mortally wounded man."

"Mortally wounded?" Jane asked, mystified.

"Well, surely the suicide of his first wife must have been traumatic!"

"I don't see that exposing such a painful matter is relevant," Jay broke in. He was flushed. "I mean, of course it has to be told, but why delve into it?"

"Because it may have had a lasting influence on the view of life communicated by the novels. That's why."

"The novels would have been different if she had lived?" Jane asked. "Well, that may be true, Jay, after all."

"Works of art are not usually created by perfectly serene, untroubled minds," Austin said, gathering steam. "What made Trueblood produce as much as he did? Through what disasters and anguish did he go to become the legendary affable old man we see in the paintings? He went to Europe, you remember, he fled Cambridge."

"There you are," Jane pounced. "Now you are reading his travels in your own way, and that is what is dangerous."

"Every cultivated New Englander made the grand tour, Austin," Jay added.

"Of course. But Trueblood made it rather differently, as a form of therapy, perhaps."

"That may be your view. . . ."

"And I am writing the biography, Miss Reid. Surely a biographer has a right to a point of view?"

"Yes, of course," Jane said, but she felt uncomfortable just the same and at a loss to say exactly why. "Let me be frank with you. Biographers today seem often to be more interested in the warts on a face than on the face itself. Trueblood has been neglected for years. Do you want to 'bring him to life,' as you put it, only to diminish his greatness? To create pity and perhaps even contempt rather than admiration?"

"That is our fear," Jay put in for himself. "Don't you see that we, the family, have a certain responsibility?"

"Oh indeed, I do see that. You might decide to close the intimate papers to any examination by any scholar. I can't but feel that would be to serve your grandfather ill. Besides, sooner or later they will become available unless you choose to destroy them. So why not let me be the one to have first look in depth? What is wrong with me?"

"Because we aren't sure what your motives are," Jane said. She felt they were going round and round the bush and things must be clarified once and for all.

"My motives?" Austin seemed genuinely at a loss.

"Are you out for blood because that would make your name, because scandal pays off, to put it crudely," Jay said quite impatiently.

"Crudely is exact." It was Austin's turn to flush. "I hope I am a scholar and a gentleman. I'm not out for blood, I'm out for understanding. I'll admit that when I first thought of this biography I had no idea what a great influence Trueblood was, what cross-fertilization he represented between European and American literature, nor was I aware of his generosity, of how hard he worked at translating from the French and Italian. Far from denigrating your grandfather my intention is to give him his full due. He was an astounding man, and an immensely influential one."

"But was he, do you believe, a great *writer* as well?" Jay asked.

"In some ways yes. There are books that have had and still do have great influence without being great works of art—*Uncle Tom's Cabin,* for example."

"But Benjamin Trueblood had no axe to grind, did he?" Jane was pondering this. "He was simply, I suppose, the most loved author of his generation."

"Widely read then, a household word, then . . . but not now," Austin said gently. "A teller of tales."

"And what is wrong with that?" Jay asked.

"Nothing's wrong with it. But I would like to show that he was something more interesting than merely successful . . . and one of the things that interests me is what great fame did for him, in what ways he was changed or not changed by it, and what a tremendously happy marriage and large family did to heal the wound but perhaps slacken a little the tension in the bow, if I may use Philoctetes as an image."

Jane, who could not remember what the myth of Philoctetes was all about, glanced over at Jay. " 'The Wound and the Bow.' Edmund Wilson has made a whole theory of literature on that, in a famous essay," Jay explained.

"Oh," said Jane.

Austin, perhaps feeling that he was on safer ground at last, dared to ask, "Are you feeling a little better about the biography? Have I persuaded you that I am not out for blood after all? And may I see the letters and journals that concern Jennifer?"

Jane and Jay exchanged a look and Jane nodded.

"There's nothing for it but to let you go ahead," Jay said then. "Just don't let Freud and your own imagination go wild."

At this Austin laughed for the first time. "I'll keep them both on a tight leash," he promised.

And so they parted. And Jane and Jay went back upstairs, having agreed to give Austin a look at the papers the following week.

"Oh dear," Jane said with a sigh, "it's awfully painful, making these decisions, Jay. Are we doing the right thing?"

"I think we are, Jane, I think we are. But heaven knows no biography ever tells the whole truth. It is truth filtered through someone's mind . . . someone of another generation, often, as in this case—the whole ethos has changed. So it is going to be Trueblood seen through twentieth-century glasses, and we can't do anything about that."

"How glad I am that no one will ever write my biography!" Jane laughed.

"Or mine," Jay assented, with a quiver at the very idea.

"Of course Grandfather was used to being in the public eye." She was smiling now with the relief of something settled. "It's only that Austin seems so young and so sure of himself. I don't really like him, do you?"

"One doesn't see the wound in him, only the bow." Jay grew thoughtful. "But he seems to be learning something from Trueblood himself. He has changed his view. Do you remember how detached and smug he seemed the first time we met?"

"Yes, I do. And you and I have changed, too, since then, haven't we?"

"In what way, Jane?" Jay looked surprised.

"We know a lot more about Grandfather than we did. We, too, have come closer to the truth. It is exhilarating. When people are alive how little we ever know about them, the complexity . . . and after they die very rarely are we given a chance to know what we know about Benjamin Trueblood."

Then they set to work, but after an hour and some conferring about the date on one folder that Jay was setting into order,

Jane, who had been thinking, said, "In spite of what I said just now, I am troubled, I must confess. Is one of the responsibilities, no, that is not the word—obligations—to society of the very famous that everything in the life be open to public scrutiny? I mean, is that right? What would Grandfather himself say?"

"None of their damn business is what he would say . . . that is my guess."

"Maybe. . . ." She lifted her head to look out of the window at the tulip tree outside, just coming into leaf. "But the older I get the less sure I seem to be about what is right and wrong. If the anguished Jennifer played such an important part in Trueblood's eventual great work, shouldn't that be known . . . for her sake as well as his? You know Mamma never spoke of her . . . never that I can remember. I suppose that is why it has been rather a shock to know what we now know, Jay."

"There is that letter to Lowell where Trueblood speaks of going to Mount Auburn to take flowers to her grave, as apparently he did every year on the anniversary of her suicide. He speaks of the lilacs being in bloom . . . is nothing sacred then? Is everything to be exposed?" Jay had tears in his eyes.

"Austin says yes, everything."

"And we have agreed, you and I, to the rifling of a tomb."

"Have we?" Jane said with a twinkle in her eye. "Strong words, Jay."

"I never realized till now what a prickly subject biography is."

"I come back to the difficult problem that if you are a writer and make your work public, and as a result become in a way the possession of the public—at least they may think so—maybe the doors into the intimate life are going to be forced open, sooner or later."

"It's a high price to pay for fame."

"Think of poor Keats!" Jane said.

Jay smiled, "And think of lucky Shakespeare, about whom little or nothing is known . . . although that has not prevented scholars from digging around and making guesses."

"At least whatever Austin finds will be authentic. The man himself speaking to his friends."

"But not, curiously enough, to himself . . . he never mentions Jennifer in the journals, does he?"

"Only several times in the year after, a note: 'A lonely day,' or 'Very depressed.' "

"We have to remember that he could have destroyed her journals and letters, but instead they were carefully preserved, tied with a lavender ribbon in an inlaid box."

"Oh, I am glad you remembered that . . . after all, what is not destroyed is perhaps deliberately left to be discovered in time."

"We must hope so."

This insight took some of the burden of responsibility off their shoulders, Jane felt. At any rate they had promised Austin and it was useless to go on worrying about it. There was work to be done.

She looked forward now to working with Jay. He was, once he got down to it, far quicker than she would ever be. Only it took him a few hours to achieve momentum, so he often worked late into the night, long after she had driven back to Sudbury with aching eyes.

A lot of things besides the Trueblood papers were on Jane's mind. And one of them was the Cambridge Community Center for the black community just east of Harvard Square. Her considerable gifts to the Center over the years made it natural for her to be asked to become a member of the board, but Jane was not one to attend quarterly meetings and then go her way. She spent hours at the Center, doing odd jobs, helping in any way she could, from taking curtains out to be cleaned to going out to get a sandwich for Ellen Ford, the head.

Ellen and she had hit it off from the start, and Jane treasured this friendship with the first black person she had ever known as an equal. Ellen, thirty years old when she came to the Center and educated at New York University, had great charm . . . for one thing, she was apt to burst into laughter when someone else might have shown anger. They had to improvise all the time, as there was never enough money, and the problem was always that new furniture or anything brought in was apt to be rather quickly broken down or destroyed. This year she and Jane were determined to get an annex built that would provide a gym that could be used also as an entertainment center for dances, plays, and meetings of all kinds.

"Even if we never manage to get it funded, the project has served to bring the community together," Ellen said one day. "It's not a cohesive group, as you know as well as I do."

Over and over again, in the two years Ellen Ford had been there, opportunities had been offered. For instance, a Harvard boy had tried to do a production of Obey's *Noah*, but half the time the actors failed to show up for rehearsals.

"Why don't they come to rehearsals?" Jane had asked.

"They just don't see it as their thing, I guess," Ellen answered gently. "We're up against years and years of indifference, you know, indifference and resentment. After all, Harvard's just next door . . . all those rich boys in their sports cars! Do they even know we exist . . . right down the street? So when one isolated young man shows interest he pays for all the others who couldn't care less."

The community house was indeed three blocks from the college, but it might as well have been on the moon. When Jane mustered the courage to try to raise the large sums necessary for the new building, and went to family friends on the Hill in Boston or even friends living within a mile of the black pocket, they often seemed astonished that it existed.

"Why, I had no idea there was a sizable black community in Cambridge," a professor's wife had said. The Episcopal church had black members, but they were not the poor, and they did not live in the slum where many of the services were curtailed, garbage collection for one. There were no black police to be seen on the streets. The Irish still dominated the police and judiciary, and this was long before the civil rights activists, before "Black is beautiful" became a slogan.

Very occasionally there was a fracas and then public reaction was strong. Jane was amazed to see at once the fear it aroused, as though the blacks were an enemy army about to pillage and rape and destroy.

"The thing is, you see, that we have such high visibility. When I walk down the street in the Square I know that the first thing that is noticed about me is my color. Even for a liberal white person that is true."

It had never occurred to Jane that this was so. But she saw it at once. When they lunched together in the Square, her own visibility was heightened because she was with Ellen. People stared. How really awful it was! What would ever change it?

During the time that she was immersed in the Trueblood papers, it was nourishing to go down to the Center and feel that she was part of a going concern, and even, in a small way (for she had no illusions), helping to make things happen in the present.

After one especially frustrating meeting, she and Ellen decided to walk to the Square and have lunch.

"And cool off," Ellen said. "I was pretty mad inside, I can tell you."

"A boiling kettle with the lid on?" Jane laughed, and Ellen smiled her discreet smile.

"Exactly."

At lunch Ellen's bitterness came out and Jane listened, and devoured her mushroom omelette and roll. Meetings always made her ravenous, for some reason.

"You're the only one who ever comes and finds out what we are doing, the only one who has any idea what I'm up against day by day."

"I'm the only one without a full-time job, you know."

"They could take an hour a month, Jane. Florida, for instance, is in Cambridge quite often."

"I get the feeling that she doesn't really care very much . . . and she's awfully busy, as she made clear."

"Why accept the job then?"

"Maybe she doesn't look at it as a job. . . ."

"Prestige? Something she can say she's doing. . . . I'm sick and tired of blacks who think only of themselves."

"It's hardly racial," Jane said gently. "I can't say that many of my acquaintance move out beyond the Warren School . . . granted that the school asks a lot of parents and teachers, and granted that the school is concerned and imaginative on the racial question. But still . . ."

"Oh well," Ellen sighed. Then she looked up and gave Jane a warm smile. "If only there were more people like you. You really are amazing . . . do you know that?"

"Am I?" Jane was genuinely surprised. "But you see I have no children, no husband, to look after. I think it's natural that I have time and energy to get involved."

"You know what's amazing about you . . . among other things?"

"What?"

"You never use money as power. I'll tell you something, Jane.

When we first met I thought you were just another Lady Bountiful, a do-gooder."

At this Jane laughed. "And maybe that's just what I am!"

"No, you're not. And the reason is that you give yourself. You spend yourself in a wildly extravagant way."

"My grandfather would turn in his grave, if he heard that. He was against extravagance . . . but to go back to what you said, I don't think of money as power."

"But it is, Jane."

"I think of it as responsibility, as a requirement to serve life."

"Well, you are unique!" It was Ellen's turn to laugh.

"The problem is that one has to make choices . . . there are so many people and organizations I want to help. That's the rub, as far as I am concerned. I get overwhelmed sometimes by all that I would like to do, so I sometimes feel awfully frustrated." Even as she admitted this to Ellen, Jane realized that this was one of the very few people with whom she ever discussed such things. Almost never with anyone in the family. Jane surmised that they might feel she was going a bit far. Better in their view to give a million to Radcliffe, as her aunt had done, a solid contribution that was memorialized in the Trueblood building on the campus, than to give continually to civil rights organizations and refugee organizations, where whatever she gave was swallowed up, drained off, with little to show for it.

"Yes," Ellen assented, "choices. . . ." She thought about it for a moment and then said with her characteristic practical sense of things, "You know, people do what they want to do. That is what I see every day. I see it at the Center, where one person is simply no good at working with a group but then turns out to be an excellent accountant. I came to Cambridge because I wanted to . . . but my friends in New York thought I was crazy to do it. I had been offered a much more important job, but it would have meant a lot of administrative work and less contact with people."

"I wish I could find a job where I was doing more, not just giving money," Jane said and Ellen caught the look of uncertainty, of being at a loss, in the tone. "That's what I want to do. I'm too old to be of use to you really."

"On the board you are very useful, you know," Ellen said quietly.

"Maybe, but I'm an outsider there and always will be. You know that as well as I do. And besides," Jane added quickly, "I want to be able to work, not just help make decisions."

"You'll find a way," Ellen said, smiling her warm smile. "I know you will."

But after they had parted, Jane wandered around for a while in the Square unable to shake off the feeling she had that she was not living her real life and had not been since she had resigned from the school. She was surely busy enough, off at the end of the week to New York for a meeting of the Refugee Association and then to Philadelphia to take Russell out for lunch somewhere and see how he was getting on at the new school. She would have a chance at least to catch up on everything with Lucy and maybe shake off this feeling of uncertainty, of being adrift.

Jane pushed the dark thoughts away as she boarded the train for New York three days later. There was something about a journey that lifted the spirits and the Merchants Limited to New York, a fast, comfortable train, took just five hours. Jane, who considered lunch in the diner an extravagance, carried a sandwich and a thermos of milk in her bulging briefcase and settled in to read first a lot of papers from the Refugee Association that she had laid aside for weeks, then *The Atlantic Monthly* and a novel by Sylvia Townsend Warner.

But as the train swung along by the shore, she drank in the scene, and felt the mounting excitement of New York City and her wonderfully beautiful and interesting nieces, Angela and Ruth, who would be meeting the train and would sweep her off to dinner and the theater, or a concert. It was restful to have these hours of just sitting and thinking or reading. At noon she ate her sandwich, drank her milk, and had a little nap, and suddenly she found they were stopping at 125th Street and she had better get herself together. What fun!

And there they were, the dear things, running down the platform to meet her, Angela in a red coat and plaid skirt and Ruth in an old trench coat, her fair hair flying.

"Is that all the luggage you have?" Angela said, taking her bag from her.

"Well, I'm only away for three nights," Jane said, laughing. "I suppose you expected more!"

"Let me take the briefcase," Ruth said.

And before she knew it Jane was being whisked off in a taxi while they talked and laughed as always. Neither of the girls looked like their mother, but they sounded like her and Jane drank their voices in like an elixir, Angela so buoyant and full of her new job with the New York Symphony, and Ruth quiet and humorous. They were enjoying New York, clearly. They who had seemed before the war permanent exiles rooted in Italy, in love with Florence . . . and perhaps one of them, Ruth, in love with someone there whom she could not marry.

"You're looking so well, Aunt Reedy," Ruth said when they had settled down in her apartment in the village, on East Tenth Street.

"She looks ten years younger," Angela agreed. "It's not teaching, isn't it?"

"I bet it's great to be free," Ruth said. "So what about a glass of champagne before we go out to dinner? It's an occasion, after all."

Jane laughed, "You know me ... I can't take more than a sip. So is it worth opening a bottle?"

"Of course it's worth it—and besides, it's only a half bottle. There won't be more than a sip."

Jane was greatly amused always by the extravagance these two had been brought up to ... that was their father's legacy.

There was so much to talk about that the time flew and they had finally to run to the restaurant just around the corner, because they were going uptown afterward to see Katharine Cornell in Chekhov's *The Three Sisters*.

"Let me order, Aunt Reedy. . . ." Ruth said.

"That will prevent her from ordering the least expensive thing on the menu," Angela agreed at once.

"When it comes to food, Aunt Reedy, you are a little child," Ruth said quite tenderly, "so I'm going to order *Chateaubriand* with braised endive, carrot soup first maybe, and those wonderful chocolate meringues for dessert . . . is that all right?"

"Splendid! But isn't it awfully expensive?"

"Aunt Reedy, I'm making a good salary these days . . . not to worry."

Soon they dived into talk, about Russell first of all.

"He seems quite happy in that school," Ruth said. "It was a good decision, after all."

"Lucy has been wonderful about going out to see him," Jane assented, "and she feels it is the right place. It's not easy because he is so big now and looks so grown-up." They all knew that Russell would never be more than four years old inside, and sometimes had violent rages. That was all very well when he was six or seven, but now that he was twenty-five he could hurt someone.

"He's a handsome young man," Ruth said. And no one said what they were all three thinking, that it was a cruel stroke of fate that Edith had died, for while she lived Russell could be taken care of on the ranch, and even do small tasks like feeding the dogs.

These thoughts were blown away by the arrival of the *Chateaubriand*.

"Mmmmm—what a feast!" Jane said after tasting a first mouthful.

"I bet you don't eat properly out there in Sudbury," Ruth said, "Do you really cook for yourself now?"

"Well," Jane said, "I've learned to cook scrambled eggs in a double boiler . . . it's great."

At this the two girls exchanged a look and burst into laughter. "I suppose you have that every night?" Angela teased.

"Not every night," Jane said. "I have hamburger quite often, and all those frozen vegetables are so easy."

"You are going to fade away," Ruth said.

"Not likely," Jane answered. "And that reminds me of Jacob. . . ." Jacob was the other brother, just graduating from Yale. As he was the youngest of the four, their mother's death had been hardest on him.

"Why does it remind you of Jacob?"

Jane felt a little shy suddenly. "Oh, because when he comes to Sudbury he always brings steaks and all sorts of extravagant things because I know he fears starvation!"

"Jacob looks out for himself," Angela said, smiling without malice. "When he comes to see us on weekends he orders the most expensive thing on the menu without batting an eye."

"I bet he does. . . ." The laughter was indulgent. Jane asked, "What is he planning for the future? Have you any idea?"

"He wants to start a publishing house . . . that's his last idea."

Jane really could not get used to everyone growing up, and

she could not imagine dear Jacob, so vague and dreamy, being a publisher. "How would he finance such a project? He seems awfully young for such responsibility."

"He's a slow learner," Ruth said, "that's for sure. He just gets through by the skin of his teeth."

"And with the help of a very good tutor," Angela said. "He's raised money, though. I really think he can be persuasive."

"But that's starting at the top. . . ." Jane felt suddenly irritated and didn't conceal that. "Shouldn't he go through some sort of apprenticeship first?"

"He says the Yale Press will take him as an editorial assistant."

"Oh well, then, he's all set," Jane conceded. Still, it bothered her. What would Edith have thought about this? All these children thought in large terms. The world had always been their oyster, and maybe, she thought being brought up in Texas had something to do with this, brought up on the ranch, a small kingdom in itself. Their genial father too had had large dreams, and the fact that the ranch never made money, only cost money, did not affect him at all. "What troubles me a little," she said out of these thoughts, "is that Jacob seems to have rather grandiose ideas as to what life is all about."

"We were not brought up in the Puritan tradition, that's for sure," Ruth said.

"Was I, do you think?" Jane said quite humbly.

"Well," Angela exchanged a look with her sister, "in a way I suppose you were. You're really quite rich, you know."

"What has that go to do with it?"

"Yet you never spend money on yourself."

At this Jane laughed, it seemed so preposterous a view. "Don't I? After all, I built the house in Sudbury and that was not a small expense, and I did it for myself. Why, it seems to me I'm quite extravagant. . . . I go to Europe. And then the island . . ." But this was an easy way for Jane to change the subject, as she was eager to do. "By the way, are you planning on the island this summer? Muff will need to know fairly soon."

"I would like to come," Ruth said at once," and maybe bring a few friends." Their mother's house had not been used much for years and so had been given to various friends.

"Splendid! Muff will be so happy to hear that. She pines when the family can't come. She so wants it to be a place of family times . . . as it used to be when Mamma and Pappa were alive."

"She's quite feudal about it, isn't she?" Ruth said.

"Well, it's an enormous job for her, organizing it all, and without Sarah she could never do it. Especially now that the English children are grown up . . . their family comes over, you know. I think Muff would welcome some help."

"Tell her I'll come this summer," Ruth said, looking at her watch. "Hey, we'd better get going!"

"Just one more mouthful of heavenly dessert," Jane said.

"I'll settle up," Ruth said. "Angela, see if you can get a cab."

Jane basked in all this expert organizing by her nieces. She was rarely not "in charge" these days and it was a positive pleasure to have everything done for her in such an efficient and loving way. How precious family is, she was thinking! But in the cab, because she was feeling happy and at ease, she finally answered Angela's question about teaching. "You think I'm enjoying my freedom, you dears, but I feel quite at a loss about my life these days."

"Oh Jane," Angela said passionately, resorting to "Jane" instead of "Aunt Reedy." "You've earned a rest."

"And to have some fun," Ruth said. "You used to look so worn out."

"Did I?" Jane didn't want to be reminded of that. "But I'm not sixty even. I'm not ready to retire!" And she laid a hand on Ruth's knee in an unusual gesture of intimacy for her. "What I want is to go to Germany with Frances Thompson and work there with the Unitarian Service Committee."

"Good heavens, Jane. To *Germany?*"

"Why not Germany? We have to help rebuild what was destroyed. The trouble is whether they'll have me, whether I can be of use."

"Do you know the language?" Ruth asked.

"I'll learn it."

"What courage you have!" Angela said. "I can't imagine wanting to go to Germany now . . . like going into hell."

"Somehow we have to remake the world. . . . Of course I would never have the courage to do it alone, but Frances has gone over and comes back glowing about the seminars the Unitarian Service Committee has been organizing. There are some extraordinary German women involved . . . women who have been buried alive, she says, and can now come out and be heard."

"It sounds pretty Utopian to me," Ruth said. But there could be no argument, as they had arrived at the theater, and solemn as Jane had been a moment before, she was now swept into eager excitement. A theater . . . since childhood she had been in love with the theater—since Cyrano, and long before. And she never entered a theater without remembering the magic occasions when Maurice had picked her up and taken her off in a cab to Boston to see a play. If going to Germany had seemed to be life as she longed for it to be for herself a moment before, life was now sitting in the dark, waiting for the curtain to rise, with a dear niece sitting on each side of her.

"Isn't it thrilling?" she whispered.

Part IV
Waging Peace

It was spring before Jane's dream of going to Germany with the Unitarian Service Committee began to seem a real possibility, but by then her sister Alix was seriously ill. Jane stayed at Muff's, went to the hospital every day, and studied German with a tutor three times a week.

At that time I had lunch with her more than once. I sensed that she felt rather at a loss, suffering from self-doubt about Germany, and perhaps about her life in general. The roots that had been so deeply planted in the Warren School were still dangling.

"They are awfully high-powered people," she told me, "the group Frances is working with."

"What's wrong with that?"

"Nothing," she smiled across at me, "only I wonder whether I should go if I am asked—and I haven't been asked yet," she added.

"Alix?" I ventured.

"Oh, I won't leave her . . . but the talk is for August, and . . ." She didn't finish the sentence, but I gathered that Alix would probably not live that long. "Frances is over there now for one of the seminars. When she comes back, she told me, she'll have a better idea of what is hatching and where I might be fitted in."

It seemed preposterous that Jane should be so humble about this, and I didn't like it. After all, she was who she was and they had better remember that.

"What is wrong with Alix?" I asked.

"She had pneumonia and a spot on the lung doesn't heal," Jane said. "But that's not it," she added, giving me a quick glance as though deciding what she could say. "She has lost the will to live. Even the doctors have come to that conclusion." Jane's eyes had filled with tears. "I feel so helpless, Cam. I go and sit with her but it is as though she wasn't there, as though she had closed herself off. She and I were the little ones, you know, set apart because we were a few years younger than our sisters. So Alix and I had a life of our own within the family. It seems so strange, so hard, not to be in touch with her now . . . to watch her moving so far away."

"She took Fredson's death very hard, you told me."

"Yes . . . her children are married, and Alix is first of all a family person like Muff. I think when Fredson died she felt abandoned, though she never talks about it. She is such a reserved person, Cam. I feel I have failed her, that I should have been more aware." Then she gave a quick sigh and looked up at me. "That's enough about miseries, isn't it?"

She wanted to hear all about Ruth and how my work was going while she ate chocolate mousse, small spoonful by spoonful "to make it last longer."

Even when what we talked about was depressing, I could not be with Jane for an hour without feeling more alive, in some indefinable way understood and blest.

But we were not through with the miseries that day, because over coffee Jane surprised me by expressing anxiety about my mother. "Please try to get her to see a doctor, Cam. I can't make any headway there."

It was my turn to feel abashed, as I had been unaware that anything was wrong. These days Mother and I were each busy —in the summer holidays she always got back to painting—and we did not see each other often.

Jane and I had talked for over an hour and the restaurant was emptying. It was time to go, especially as I now needed to drop in at my mother's before going home.

"We've just about covered everything, Cam, haven't we?" Jane slipped the check into her purse.

"Now see here, I invited you to lunch," I protested.

"You've invited me to lunch often enough," she said firmly.

"Very well. But next time, Miss Reid, you won't get away with this!"

Alix died in a nursing home in June. I find it hard to write about this major event in Jane's life because I hardly knew her sister, did not go to the funeral, and was preoccupied by my mother's illness, which had by then been diagnosed as a rare form of cancer, and in those days before chemotherapy there was little that could be done. I moved back to Cambridge to be with her and arranged for a leave of absence for the autumn term, should she still be alive by then, but the doctors had been frank with me and suggested she had at most six months of life ahead, if what she was suffering could be called life.

It seemed suddenly as if everything were going to pieces around me . . . is one ever prepared for the death of one's parents? I certainly was taken by surprise, and when I heard that Jane would leave for Germany in August I must say I felt cross. How could she just walk out on everything at home, go to Germany, that hell? What made her so determined to do it? In my heart of hearts, of course, I did know why—she needed a big job to do. One day on an impulse I dropped in on Muff to talk things over.

"Well, Cam!" she said. She was sitting by the fire sewing the hem on an evening dress for one of the English girls, and there was something comforting about her being there as she nearly always was, comforting to walk into that house where nothing changed, except that Mary, the maid, had grown very old, and Snooker did not come downstairs anymore. She must have been well over ninety. But Muff looked exactly the same. Because she had never seemed young, she now did not seem old. "A cup of tea?" she asked at once. "Mary would be happy to get it for you."

"Don't bother. I can only stay a moment."

"Sit down then and tell me the news," she said gently.

"Mother's dying, you know," I blurted out.

"Yes, Jane told me. It must be awfully hard for you, Cam. When my mother died I felt the world had come to an end," she smiled her wry smile, "but it hadn't."

"And Jane is off to Germany!" I guess there was a shade of anger in my voice, for Muff came at once to her sister's defense.

"It will be good for her, however strange it may seem to us." So, she was admitting that it did seem strange.

"Germany of all places!"

"But that's it, that's the point, isn't it?" Muff said, laying down her sewing. "Jane is such an idealist . . . you don't remember World War I and how little we did then to help rebuild a defeated people. Jane feels we must do better this time."

"And so prevent another Hitler, I suppose?"

"She sees a great need. . . ." Muff was silent for a moment before she added, "And then she has always been enormously influenced by Frances Thompson. She wants, I think, to be part of this new endeavor, part of what Frances sees as of primary importance."

"Mother feels that Frances treated Jane badly about resigning."

"Some people may have thought so," Muff said, "but rather characteristically Jane blames only herself."

"She's such a great person," I murmured.

"I'm glad someone is aware of that!" Muff said in, for her, quite a vehement tone of voice, then picked up her sewing again. "She spends herself so lavishly—is that greatness? I wonder whether I would use that word about Jane myself." And this retreat from any tendency toward exaggeration was typical.

"I would," I said firmly.

Muff smiled. "You were in the seventh grade once at a time when you were perhaps like one of those goslings who gets an imprint—Konrad Lorenz has written about it, as you no doubt remember—and then follows whomever takes care of it."

At this I laughed aloud. "And so I have become a great goose, Muff!"

"A faithful goose, Cam," she amended, smiling.

"I used to think of her as a princess then, and I expect I still do." It came to me that Jane must have missed that glow that surrounded her when I was a child at the school. Would she perhaps recapture it in Germany? Was she in search of a role that would give her back that sense of herself? "I just hope she won't be disappointed. It seems such a risk!"

"Jane couldn't live without risk."

"It seems awfully Christian, too—love your enemy and all that."

"She doesn't analyze herself, Cam, you know that as well as I do. Jane does what she wants to do."

And there the conversation ended. It gave me a lot to think about.

* * *

211

Jane knew that when she left for Germany she would not see Mother again, and that made her almost daily visits have an intensity I sometimes felt may have been too much for Mother, who made a great effort while Jane was there at her side to be herself again but was often exhausted after she left.

"But it's worth it, Cam," she whispered to me when I suggested that we might ask Jane to limit her visits. "It's the essence now—I'm not turning my back yet on life."

Jane's relation to my mother was rather different from any other that I knew about in her life. Jane was the rock and haven for so many friends of all ages, but in this case my mother had often been the rock and haven for Jane, especially during the hard time at the Warren School. So I sensed that Jane was determined to make these last times memorable in any way she could. Once when I tiptoed in she was reciting "I have been one acquainted with the night." Another time she had put on a Mozart flute concerto and they were listening to it in silence. More than once I saw the tears in Jane's eyes as I met her on the stairs.

Perhaps, in the end, it was a relief for Mother, too, when we all knew this would be the final farewell.

I did see Jane myself once more before she took off, saw her at Muff's house up in her bedroom, where she was packing. It was like her to be able to sit down and have a real talk in the midst of suitcases and piles of clothes, to set all that aside for a half-hour.

We talked about death and dying and Jane told me a little about Marian and how hard it had been for her to accept that death, to accept that Marian must die so young, at just forty-six. "I found it unbearable," Jane said, "because she was such a genius at living. Why, of all people, should she go, she who could use every moment to its fullest?"

I had no answer for that.

"People vanish," she murmured, "and that's why I gathered

Marian's letters together and published them . . . and it was a way, I suppose, in that year after her death, of still being with her, of keeping her alive."

"And perhaps a hundred years from now, they will be discovered."

"Perhaps."

I suspected that Jane must have suffered because none of Marian's letters to her had shown the intimacy and the kind of passionate ecstasy of appreciation she had been able to give to other friends. I myself had been astonished that the scholarly Marian Chase had been capable of such intensity of feeling. They had explained to me why Jane had loved her so deeply—and had been so hurt by Marian's aloof bearing where she herself was concerned.

"Why am I talking about this, Cam?" she asked, giving me a deep look of pain and astonishment.

"Death is with us today."

"Yes." She paused to think. "Perhaps I have been moved to talk about Marian and her death because somehow I do not have that agonizing sense of the incomplete where your mother is concerned, of a promise unfulfilled. Your mother has achieved a remarkably complete life—that is not quite right," she amended. "But Eleanor is ready to go . . . because in some strange way she has come to fruition. Oh, how I have felt that these last weeks!"

"Dear Jane," I managed to utter, "she shines when you are there, but it's a hard death just the same. Awfully hard." I knew if I tried to say more I would dissolve in tears.

"I wish I didn't have to leave you, leave you carrying the weight." She had, until now, not been thinking about me, I realized and I saw that as a compliment.

"I just feel totally inadequate," I said. "The loneliness . . . dying is such a lonely business."

"What matters is your being there, Cam."

"But I can't sit beside her as you did—I'm afraid I'll begin to cry and then I could never stop."

"Cam, dear," Jane said gently, "we do what we can. I think your mother understands. I'm sure she does."

But this time I was not comforted.

I did not see Jane again, but for those last weeks she managed to write often from Germany and it was a tremendous help for me to be able to tell her what was happening almost day by day. That she was able to keep closely in touch and to infuse courage from so far away is amazing.

Mother refused to see my father because I think she knew he didn't want to come. He did come through with some help when I had to get a night nurse in the last two weeks. But when I tried to tell him about symptoms and how awful it was for me to watch her wasting away, he simply would not or could not listen. So, added to what I was suffering as I watched my mother die was rage, a rage that could not be healed. After Mother's death I saw my father very rarely. So in a way I was losing both parents.

Without Ruth I do not know what I would have done. She came on weekends, did all kinds of practical things like bringing splits of champagne, which, near the end, was almost the only thing Mother could swallow. But more importantly, Ruth could sit with my mother because she was not torn apart and could control both compassion and grief.

At last, in November, death, which had become a friend, death we longed for as deliverance, came. Mother died in her sleep a few hours after I had kissed her good night.

During the Christmas holidays Ruth helped me close the house and empty it. And when that was done, and the new term started, I went gladly back to teaching.

Much as I had loved my mother, I had not been fully aware of what she had meant to innumerable people who took the trouble to write to me. Teachers and students, too, from the Warren School, fellow artists, friends who went back to her college days had felt the imprint of a remarkable human being. Was that what Jane meant when she told me she felt Mother had led a fulfilled life? The statement had startled me at the time because I knew too well how deprived my mother had been in her marriage, how much love and imagination had not been used or wilfully ignored by my father. So the letters brought me a kind of peace, for they helped me to see that whatever she had not experienced as fulfillment in the usual sense of the word, she had created herself, through her own gifts as painter and teacher, and by touching so many lives. In the academic world we are apt to judge people by achievement, by whether their Ph.D. dissertation was worthy of publication, by honorary doctorates, by position in the world. None of that applied to my mother, or mattered to her. She was a lavish spender of the life in her, never counting the cost.

Ruth and I talked a lot about it that winter and spring, and of the wonderful way she had welcomed Ruth into the family when we decided to live together. "She has left us a trust fund," I said once, laughing about it as I spoke, and I meant a fund of personal integrity which we must draw on as long as we lived.

At this point in my tale I bogged down in a state of dismay and discouragement. How was I ever to deal with the German experience, so important in Jane's life, when I knew next to nothing about it? I had a few letters but they became less frequent after Mother's death. And once more I almost gave up.

Then one spring day when I had wandered down to the Square with the idea of lunching there alone and reading *The New York Times*, I ran into Sarah, who knew everything about

Jane in her last years, for had they lived together in the barn after Muff's death and the sale of the big house.

"Oh Sarah!" I said with such pleasure in my voice and face that she looked a little startled. "you are God-sent!"

At this Sarah laughed. "What is on your mind, Cam?"

"Come and have lunch with me and I'll tell you."

Sarah was one of those ageless women who had not changed in any way that I could see for the last twenty years. And although she had lived first in the shadow of Martha and then after Muff's death in the shadow of Jane, she was very much her own person. I had always been at ease with her and when I first conceived the idea of this book tried to get in touch with her, but after Jane's death she had vanished, was traveling in England, I heard. So it was fortuitous indeed to run into her that crucial day when we sat in a booth in the restaurant where I had sat so often with Jane.

It was not easy to broach my subject. What if Sarah did not approve? What if she questioned my ability as I did so often myself? Sarah had known me as an historian, not a novelist. At seventy I was daring something even a young person might hesitate to undertake. But I was soon launched and very much relieved by Sarah's immediate interest and assent.

"This is very good news," she said, smiling across at me. She did far more than approve; she offered to let me read Jane's letters to Lucy over all the years of their friendship, and including of course the voluminous correspondence during the years in Germany. I could hardly believe this stroke of luck. "You may keep them until the book is finished, Cam."

"If it ever is," I murmured.

"Of course it will be!" Then she startled me by quoting Shakespeare, a passage I had often heard in Jane's voice, as it had been a favorite of hers,

"I see you stand like greyhounds in the slips . . .
straining upon the start. Follow your spirit!"

"I'm a pretty old greyhound, Sarah, and it's Jane's spirit I have
to try to follow."

"Yes," she said thoughtfully, "but any work of art has to do
with both the interpreter and her subject, surely? You can't
keep yourself out of it, can you?"

I had not thought of it like that. I had seen myself simply as
an observer, a recorder, but I saw at once that she had hit the
nail on the head.

"You're right, of course. Oh dear, you should be doing it
yourself."

"I couldn't possibly," she said firmly. "I wouldn't have the
courage."

"Oh, it's not courage, you know—some kind of wild impulse
seized on me after the funeral. I couldn't bear to think that soon
no one will remember Jane Reid. And then, it has given me
something to work at. Without Ruth life has been too empty for
words."

Sarah had always been a listener and she listened then with
the greatest sympathy as I told her something of my life alone
since Ruth's death. Finally we agreed that she would bring the
letters over the next morning.

Reading the letters from Germany was enthralling, for it became clear at once that Jane used Lucy as a sounding board, a
way of finding out what was happening to her. And Lucy, so far
away in Philadelphia, shared in it all in an extraordinary way,
often with a small, practical response. When the first letters
were penciled because Jane's trunk had not arrived, a pen flies
over by magic in the next post!

After reading for a week and thinking about how to use the letters I came to the conclusion that the only valid way was to quote Jane directly, let her in this instance tell her own tale.

But there is something, I felt when I finished reading, that the letters do not say in so many words and that concerns the relationship itself. Jane was in the position of a pupil with both Frances Thompson (after all, she had been her student at Vassar) and in a different way with the elusive and scholarly Marian. For Lucy, Jane was the star, and one might dare to paraphrase the Twenty-third Psalm to suggest what Jane must have known, "Goodness and Lucy will follow me all the days of my life." With Lucy, Jane flowered.

Thirty-two years earlier, when Jane and Lucy had landed in France, they were together and could laugh about all the impossible things they had to face, but now, in August of 1950, Jane was alone and plunged into the German language, an ocean where she found it difficult to keep her head above water. She had to travel here and there to get the necessary permit that would take her from the American zone to Bremen, in the English zone, but after forty-eight hours, she was at last on a comfortable military train, flying through the night toward the destination she had imagined for so many months—the much-bombed city of Bremen, on the North Sea.

And there, at 7:30 A.M., she took a taxi to the Hotel Bremen, where the Unitarian Service Committee was billeted, to be met by Joan Plummer, head of the USC in Europe, and launched immediately into a day of meeting people and getting an idea of the city itself. For Jane it was a day of surprises. She had been prepared for the ruins, the powdery smell of smashed brick and dust, the desolation, but she was not prepared for the atmosphere of hope and vitality she sensed all around them. And in those first days of getting her bearings it was astounding to meet such friendliness from the German people. Remembering the

resentment the French had felt under the German occupation,
she had half expected that same sullen silence or obsequious-
ness toward Americans, but there was none. Everyone to whom
they spoke smiled in the friendliest way. And the city felt busy
and alive . . . people whizzing past on their bikes, talking and
laughing.

The hotel was comfortable; Lucy's fears that Jane would not
be well-nourished proved entirely false. Here they were billeted in an old, rich part of the city which had not been as badly
bombed as the dock area. In its tree-lined streets, life seemed
almost normal again.

But those first two days were gone almost too quickly, and
then she, Joan, and Erika Housman, the moving spirit of the
Unitarian Service Committee, were en route to Lundersen for
Jane's first experience of the *Arbeiter Wohlfahrt* seminars.

There, in an old castle on a hill above the town looking out
over fields and farms, thirty social workers had gathered for the
seminar and Jane was able to watch Frances Thompson at work
and the kind of response she elicited, and to write Lucy long,
enthusiastic letters about what she saw happening. In some
ways it was very much like a faculty meeting at the Warren
School. Here again Jane was aware of how Frances operated,
never didactic, rather challenging the German women to express themselves and their own views, so that discussion was
always intense after she had spoken. Luckily there were several
people who could translate for Jane when, especially at the end
of a long morning, she found herself at sea.

Her letters to Lucy recounted it all vividly, and especially in
a few vignettes, such as this, after Frances had given a talk on
basic human needs:

After this talk the discussion was fascinating, especially
an example one of the women social workers described,

which happened in a home for disturbed children. One night a bunch of boys twelve to fourteen years old stole food and blankets and ran away and lived in the woods until their food was gone. Then they had to go back to the home, where the head was in doubt as to how to treat the matter.

The music teacher asked to be allowed to handle it himself. His solution was to write an opera on running away and to make it known that he needed some boys with inside knowledge. So he got the boys acting out the whole thing, the whispering over the plan, the stealing of food and of blankets, the creeping out in the night, and the adventure of camping in the woods. He himself wrote the music. The children performed it many times, each time differently, and somehow the antisocial act was transformed into a work of art and brought success and satisfaction instead of guilt and shame.

At times like this, when her attention was fully engaged, it was terribly frustrating for Jane that she could not speak herself, but at least she found that her understanding grew with every session and her admiration for what the social workers achieved, often in isolated homes and very much alone. She writes:

> One day there was a lively discussion about their own needs, how desperately they wanted an opportunity to talk over personal problems and to be able to lead some sort of personal life . . . and how hard that was when the staff was so small and a day off extremely rare. No wonder they all agreed that there should be someone to whom each individual could talk and so get relief, encouragement, and perspective, especially the head, who must manage both the children and the staff and often deal as well with opposition from the outside world.

In the evening, after supper, in long talks between Joan, Frances, and Erika, Jane could participate because they spoke English. What a relief! The idea of the neighborhood house was beginning to be hammered out, and the complicated means to get it going. It would have to be supported by the Unitarian Service Committee, HICOG (American HQ), the *Arbeiter Wohlfahrt*, and the city of Bremen, a tall order, since all these organizations had to be persuaded of the need for a neighborhood house in the first place and then persuaded to help fund it. Now at last Jane began to see where she would fit in and be working, assisted by a German social worker, who would eventually take over.

She writes to Lucy:

> Bremen is a Hanse city with its own senate and representative to Bonn. That representative is a most lovely man, Herr Uhland. He and his wife are devoted to Erika and very fond of Joan and Frances, and they have put time and labor into helping get the neighborhood house started. We are going there tonight to meet with a group of social workers whose support is needed, and the problem will be to try to get them to understand the neighborhood house purpose as we see it. They are accustomed to day care centers with someone in charge who makes a program and puts it through. For that you can calculate pretty clearly in advance the space needed. Our thinking is a house that will start small and grow as the neighborhood is built up and be flexible enough to meet the needs of the people around it—whether for small-child care, or youth groups, or a parent center, or all three. This is something to which they are not accustomed. Much in the plan has to be left open and that seems to them rather vague as if we didn't know our own minds. All this communicating and interpretation would be impossible without Erika.

Erika had been born in Germany, although she was an American citizen and had been a social worker in New York. She more than anyone in the group had the ability to make bridges, partly because she was at ease in the language and partly because she had a genius for human relations and the ability to handle even fierce disagreements with tact. Jane's letters are full of her praises.

Jane accompanied Erika to endless committee meetings with the city officials and social workers in Bremen, but since she did not bear the burden of responsibility yet, it was all rather like a holiday. It was marvelous to be able to sleep until after eight, to be able to read and write letters in her room at the hotel, which had become home by then. There were books by her bed and often flowers on the table, for she was learning that in Germany the giving of flowers accompanies every visit and how delightful a custom that is. In fact her fears that she might not cotton to the Germans had been unfounded. She was finding an immediate warmth of welcome that bowled her over.

In November Erika and Frances went off on a holiday to Italy. Erika had now been in Germany for over two years and desperately needed a rest, so Jane was left to hold the fort with the help of Lisa, a young woman who spoke English and could interpret when needed. In December she herself went on holiday to Paris to visit some of the French families and the mother superior, now very old, of the order for which she and Lucy had worked in 1918.

She came back in February to bad news—there would be no funds from Frankfurt (the McCloy Fund). This was a blow, as the negotiating had been going on for months and Jane knew that their chief there, a colonel in the army, had been keen on it. That decision threw the whole responsibility back to the German board in Bremen. They couldn't afford to build, so they were considering taking over an army barrack as a temporary center. There was by now a lot of pressure to get things going somehow, and they waited impatiently for Erika to come back from her holiday.

Beyond the organization itself, what had to be negotiated little by little in endless meetings and discussions with the board was the philosophy of a neighborhood house. The idea of training young people by giving them responsibility, by letting them plan their own activities and run their own clubs, was a radical departure from German mores, in which training had been ingrained always to obey a leader whose word was law. But of course that change toward democracy was what the plan was all about.

The seminars under Frances played an important part in this reshaping of an ethos, but they lasted at most a few weeks. After that Jane went back to Bremen to struggle on, hoping to get things moving forward inch by inch. She was the anchor. And no doubt, in all those months of waiting, hoping, and making strategic moves, it was an asset that her own tempo was slow. She did not lose her patience, her nerve, or her faith that the dream could and would be accomplished.

But she had been in Bremen nearly a year, and she had to make a decision herself, as the time she had contracted for was nearly at an end, and the neighborhood house still had no director who would take over after she left.

During this period Jane's letters to Lucy, who was planning to come over for the summer months, are full of uncertainty and self-questioning. She says:

About the possibility of staying over—this is the way it begins to look to me. I have been a learner ever since I have been here, and really not much else, and pretty much at government expense too! I have watched and listened and tried to understand what was going on, and have had time to read and sleep as well. Now at last the job we had hoped to get started is beginning to stir. The essence of it is, of course, the working together with other social agencies, and the attempt to bring together the people of our neighborhood. For there is an awful separateness here between religions, political parties, departments of the city government, etc. These invisible things take a long while to grasp and even longer when you don't understand the lingo. So I feel that I have all this time been an apprentice and am only now beginning to pull my weight in the boat.

While Jane came to her own decision about staying on she was also weighing Lucy's longing to join her, not only for that summer, but possibly to come again in the autumn as a working member of the group. For Lucy the prospect was clearly irresistible, although it would mean finding a substitute head for her school, and perhaps even retiring. Jane's letters are full of these considerations. "When I left Warren," she says, "nothing was at stake except my own future, and yet I felt almost overwhelmed by the uncertainty of how I should manage without being a member of the school."

Thinking about Lucy's hope to come over for more than a brief visit, she says:

I didn't dream that you were turning over in your mind the possibility of coming over for some autumn months, my dear. I have found the language business so slow and hard, and my own timidity so increased by it, that I am slow to advise a short period from the point of view of what one can give to a job in that time, though it certainly can be rich in learning and observing. This whole set-up is so different from the French undertaking, largely, I suppose, because of our own ages. That all seems, at least from this distance, fairly uncomplicated and we could act with a great sense of assurance. Here there are layers and layers of things to be aware of every time one acts, and that plus increasing lethargy makes one often hesitate about acting at all! I have always had the feeling, though, of being glad to be here, to know some Germans close to, and I think it is a blessing for them to know some Americans who care.

Reading the letters and coming to see how long-drawn-out the negotiations had to be, the endless delays, the hopes that failed to materialize, I can understand very well what Jane's presence must have meant, her quick response to each person's needs and doubts, and her ability to "wait and see." This must have irritated some quick movers, those who wanted to leap in and get things done, but Jane's resilience and sense of fun, her absolute integrity and wish to serve, must surely in the end have set a remarkable example. For things did get done, little by little. And in August they were finally able to move into the barrack, a year after Jane's arrival in Germany. Of course Lucy's practical nature was invaluable during all the planning of the rooms, the furniture to be bought and curtains hung, the endless details to be attended to before the opening.

"How can I ever thank you," Jane says, "for making the great trek, my dear, and for the countless thoughtful things, great and small, you managed to do to help me. When I opened my drawer and saw all my clothes washed and folded, with new stocking and slips I nearly wept."

By August nineteenth Jane could be telling Lucy of the harvest of all the work:

> These two weeks have flown and our team is working very well together. Frau Biendorf is a tower of strength and practical know-how and it is lovely to see her with the boys in the workshop—in fact her enthusiasm and friendliness with all ages is fine.
>
> The rooms look really lovely and the shop is in constant

use. Some big boys who have no work have come in to read and have asked to bring their radio. A few fathers have come, but after the first day no mothers to use the three beautiful sewing machines. School starts for the children tomorrow, and it may be then that the mothers will be free to come.

We have had a great many visitors who had heard about the house and wanted to see it. That takes so much time that I have hardly worked with the children at all, nor am I any too good with them yet, I find. My discipline is not quick enough, with the result that they fool with me just as our French boys did.

So far the boys in the shop have made towel racks for the *Haus* and key racks and all sorts of things for themselves, boats, a nice stool, a picture frame, etc. Now Frau Biendorf wants to give them training in using tools and have them all make one thing—lanterns. This is the season when the children march around after dark carrying lighted paper lanterns and singing. A few little girls have sewed on the towels for the kitchen and toilet and some have made dolls' clothes under my expert guidance!

Meanwhile we bristle with interviews re our various accounts—thank goodness Lisa has a clear head!

These first days are really great fun!

The time for "reading and sleeping" was clearly over, and when Lucy did come over in November it was to take part in a going concern, and to move into a housekeeping flat with Jane, and share a small rented car. From November till March, when she had to go back to her school, there are no letters. But during that time the new *Haus* was finally under construction and delicate connections were being established between groups that had not worked together before. The tact and wisdom demanded become clear in a letter dated in late March of 1952:

The great thing of the week has been Elsa Brock's visit. She is a wonderful person and has tried her best to help us Americans to see the necessity of allying ourselves with a group and giving the *Nachbarhaus* a *Gesicht* (face), i.e., that we stand for what the *Arbeiter Wohlfahrt* stands for. She says there is a deep sense of class struggle here, that the workers suffered so during the *Hitlerzeit* and were so looked down on that their long struggle for recognition was set back, and their mistrust of all other groups intensified. She feels we must take a stand that we believe in the working class and stand with them, and then gradually work with individuals from other groups whom we feel have similar values—like the *Lutherhaus* people. If we were an American organization we could act as we would at home and our actions would then be considered the *Dummheit* of foreigners who don't understand the German scene. But if the work is to be carried on by Germans (as it must be) it must proceed in full recognition of the existing feelings and patterns. We asked all sorts of questions and she took endless pains to explain. The workers, she told us, are almost like blacks in America, or like poor people in India—so strong a caste feeling exists separating workers and professional people.

The letter ends, "Today was an orgy of curtains." It gave me the best idea I had yet been given of the complexity of what Jane was handling, from the most minute housekeeping details to the intricate realities of a culture. How could she ever have imagined all that she would be asked to do and to understand?

It must have been a relief at times to concentrate on her own contribution to the new *Haus*, a map of the world which she was making on a big table. This as least she could create without having to ask anyone's advice or deal with a committee, although several boys and other members of the community helped.

You should see our room now, a regular workshop. Frau Preis kindly let me take our dining-room table, and I have put in two leaves, so it stretches almost from the lamp to the washbasin and makes a perfect place to work on the map. I have done very little this week, but this evening got in Arabia, India, and Australia. I'm leaving Africa for black-haired Hans, who has started it and wants to finish.

In this second year in Germany the atmosphere has changed. Jane is using German words a lot in the letters and talks about many people she knows as friends and fellow workers. And her letter on her birthday to Lucy is full of joy, the joy of being loved for herself:

What a day this has been! When I got up München's door was already open and there was a vase of glorious flowers from her awaiting me, and two packages. We decided to eat breakfast first and when we went downstairs Frau Barth was waiting to *gratulieren*—on the table were flowers from Frau Preis, who came in and made a birthday speech. I flew over to Lisa's to tell her about the good peasant chairs I saw yesterday and was presented with a darling little bowl filled with forget-me-nots and prim-roses. She came back with me and as we started off I found hanging on the door of the car a garland of spring flowers with bells and chocolate eggs, the gayest thing you ever saw. I thought it must have come from the police force, but it turned out that Anna Uhland had come all the way to the garage, found the car gone, tracked it to *Oberdeich,* hung the garland, and taken the trolley all the way back to the 10:00 A.M. meeting. Can you beat that?

At the barrack there was a round of festivities. All the *Kindergarten* children came in and sang a song and pre-sented me with a plate of moss, flowers, a chocolate rabbit, and eggs—such darling solemn faces!

After lunch I came back and finally ordered the whole

bunch of curtains and did some other jobs. Then home, to find the most marvelous cake with a chocolate shield bringing me *Glückwunsche* and a gold-tied sack of chocolates full enough to last till you get back! München came home by seven and we went to Fletts for a good meal, and home for dessert—yum! I shall take the rest to the barrack tomorrow so all can enjoy a piece. What a delicious cake!

As spring came into full bloom, work was rising to a crescendo for the great move from the barrack. Jane writes:

A dazzle of spring glory: all the first fruit trees are out, the chestnuts are towers of green, sailboats on the river, children bathing, birds singing, and everyone expansive. The house has dried out so fast that the linoleum is down —furniture goes in this week. And three of our staff plan to move in this week. Frances and Erika will arrive tomorrow night, Joan Plummer the day after. The hope is to close the barrack on the twenty-seventh, pack things together on Monday the twenty-eighth, and move them over on Tuesday, the twenty-ninth to their new abode with horse and buggy.

On April twenty-fifth she tells Lucy:

I've just come in from our last evening in the barrack, and we couldn't believe that almost a year had come around since we first started coming in that door. It was a nice evening. München made a little speech to tell the children that they were at the heart of the doings at the barrack and would be in the new *Haus,* and that we counted on their help to make it the kind of place it should be. Tonight München is sleeping in her new room. On Monday we hope to pack up the barrack things and on Tuesday move them over. There are three teams, six men each, of *Jugendliche* who have volunteered to move the stuff, and we may get a horse and cart as well. The big things, office stuff, will go over in the VW bus.

And at last The Day arrived, and Jane's letter of April twenty-ninth is exuberant:

> The great *Umzug* from barrack to *Haus* was accomplished today. Tables and chairs were piled on the horsecart to an unbelievable height. On the second trip they attached the sign from our gate up over the driver's head. Two little boys marched ahead carrying brooms with colored streamers. Wolfgang rode behind on his bike and a great stream of children and young people danced along on either side of the slow procession.
>
> The unloading went like lightning but all in good order, and at the end they all went out on the terrace and had a drink of Coca Cola all round.

By May fourth, "Lilacs, hawthorn, and chestnuts are in flower. Bremen is a garden." And on that day, "Herr Uhland brought the wording for a bronze plaque that will tell that it has been a joint effort of Germans and Americans and what the purpose of the *Haus* is, 'a place where all can learn and experience living together in a truly democratic fellowship.'"

On May twenty-second the map is set in place, and on May twenty-fifth Jane can say:

> The first two housewarming parties are over and really a fine success. The *Jugendliche* just couldn't have been nicer. Everyone came looking so washed and combed and pleased to be there, and they all did their stuff carefully and with pride in doing it well. And then the dance was delightful. Herr Uhland came to the party and we danced the first waltz together, and he was as jubilant as I.

As I read over the letters, feeling my way into what did prove to be the fruitful adventure Jane had so hoped it could be, to see how useful her presence had been and what it had meant to have Lucy at her side for two long visits, I felt an immense relief that she had, after the hard time at the end at the Warren School, found the resilience and power to make her own renewal through such a difficult and demanding project. But I wondered sometimes whether the Holocaust had ever been mentioned or talked about. How could one be in Germany in the fifties and appear to ignore it? And to be with so many liberal Germans like Herr Uhland, and never have it surface? So I was happy to come upon a letter written in the midst of the rejoicing about the move to the *Haus* which had this to recount on May eighteenth:

> Today was distinguished by an amazingly moving ceremony at the Jewish graveyard, where their chapel, destroyed by Bremen citizens, was rededicated. Their rabbi, who had emigrated to the United States, flew over for the service, and his speech honoring the friends who had been faithful unto death—nine hundred fifteen Jews from the Bremen synagogue—was unforgettable. Many of us stood outside the chapel in the sun among the peaceful graves with their Hebrew inscriptions, and I could hardly believe that the things he told of had happened only five years ago. Then we all walked to the new monument and the *Bürgermeister* spoke. He was so deeply moved by what had been said that at first he could hardly speak. Then gradually the words poured out of him, the terrible weight of shame before such brutality done in our time by German hands. However to atone for it, how to go forward and rebuild a civilization that could have sunk so low? We must all together teach our children to respect one another and to value and protect individual freedoms. Germany seeks to be respected by the world and this can happen only if she respects and cares for all her citizens regardless of race or color. At the end he said, "I take this memorial under

the protection of the city of Bremen and bow in homage to the men and women to whom it is dedicated."

It must have meant much to the group of Jewish families, mostly old people, who were there from Bremen, Lübeck, and Kiel. It certainly meant much to the rabbi, for he and the *Bürgermeister* were old friends who had stood by each other through the days when both, for different reasons, were suspect. The *Bürgermeister* recalled those days with a final tribute.

Part V
Homecoming

If Jane in some moments of homesickness had thought of home-coming as coming back to a changeless world in Cambridge and Sudbury, what she had to meet was radical change in her own surroundings, the planning and taking hold of a new pattern. I think she found first of all, as she had suggested in a letter to Lucy from Germany, that she did not need to go back to Warren, that the German experience had in some way cut the cord that had held her for many years so tightly. And I think she rather enjoyed her relation to the new head, Julian Starbuck, whom she had known well in the years when he had been a teacher at the school, enjoyed being an elder statesman, for Julian held her in high esteem and liked having her ear now and then when he needed to talk over problems. He asked her, for instance, to come and talk to the apprentice teachers about her German experience.

We met again just before that event at our usual restaurant, "for auld lang syne," as she put it on the telephone. She had been at the island all summer and I had not seen her, but there she was, looking younger than before she had taken off three years before, full of laughter, eager to be filled in on what had been going on in my life. I must admit I was put off at first by her repeated *"Ja"* at every pause, as she had no doubt been used to doing in Germany. It seemed incongruous, but when I said so, she just smiled and said, "Oh, what a relief to be back in English again!" Our conversation that day pivoted on her upcoming talk to the apprentices.

"It's marvelous that I have to pull myself away from all the things here, and take a look at what we achieved in Germany . . . sort it all out and see inside myself what really happened."

"I can't believe you were there for nearly three years!"

"Well, I could never have done it without Lucy . . . and of course I went off on some great trips, so it was not continuous. But I did get embedded!" she added, smiling at some memory that rose up as she spoke.

"It's hard for me to imagine," I ventured. "I simply cannot love the Germans."

"I don't see how you could have helped it, Cam, if you had been there."

"But all those ghosts . . . six million . . . I feel I would have seen a ghost behind every face. Did anyone ever talk about that? About the Holocaust?"

Jane took a moment to find an answer while I wondered if I had been wrong to bring it up; but I couldn't help it. *"Ja,"* she said then slowly (again that irritating *Ja*). "But you have to remember that the city of Bremen was anti-Nazi from the start. Two of my best friends, Herr Uhland and his wife, had taken great risks. Over there I could see what courage that must have meant! But I have to admit that the Germans are used to a strong leadership, and one of the things we had to try to do at the neighborhood house was to tame the instinct for rigid rules and the wish to organize everyone for efficiency's sake."

"How did you do that?"

"Well, Frances is a genius at getting people to come back to fundamentals and to talk things over. Her intensity brought walls down at every seminar. There I could sense the resistance sometimes, but also a slow, gentle change in a way of thinking. It was thrilling to watch Frances at work! It reminded me of the early days at Warren, for there, too, we were what you would call radicalizing a point of view about education. And there, too, she was dealing with strong individuals."

"And you?"

"Well, at first the language was a real problem, as you can imagine. Whatever I did for the first year was minimal . . . perhaps I was some sort of listening presence. At least they came to know an American who wanted to learn. But, oh Cam, there was so much sheer detail, so much maneuvering before any decision could be made! There were times, I must confess, when I wondered if we would ever get to where we could start, even, before there would ever *be* a house, and we could begin to show what we were after instead of just endlessly hashing it out! So many organizations were involved, you see. Without the Ford Foundation, which did come in at a crucial time, with sorely needed money, I wonder whether we could have made it."

"I gather that Frances came and went but that you were the one to stay there and deal with the day-to-day problems? You were the tortoise and she was the hare?"

"Dear Cam, will you ever forget that episode? It seems to have made an indelible impression!"

"It did. And the proof is that lately I have become a tortoise myself."

Jane chuckled. "What sort of tortoise? I can't quite see it."

"Oh, the hare, I guess, died in Spain. Life in an academic community demands a very long view."

"But you do love teaching?" And as I didn't answer she looked at me quizzically. "Or don't you?"

"I get all revved up in the summer, working on my book on the trade routes, and then I bog down. The students devour me. Maybe that is the way it should be, but . . ." And then I asked, "Did you ever want to get out from under teaching?"

"No, I guess that is what I wanted most to do . . . but I was not working on a book at the same time. I can see how you sometimes long for clear time." She really looked at me, then, as though she was suddenly seeing me as I am now, not quite the Cam she had known as a wild, passionate child. "And Ruth? She must be a comfort."

"She is. She was absolutely wonderful while Mother was dying. I could not have managed without her. She is such a reserved person, but then she was able to give in ways I couldn't because I was too upset."

I found I didn't want to talk about this . . . so it was I who changed the subject. "Will you go back to Warren part time? What are your plans, Jane?"

"I really don't have any yet. Sudbury is rented to a young Mormon couple who are here for a few years while he gets his doctorate. It was a real blessing to find two such dears to take over while I was away and I can't exactly put them out, so I'm living at Muff's for the time being, catching up. I don't think I'll go back to school . . . we'll see—but I do look forward to talking with the apprentices day after tomorrow."

"We have gotten away from that. And that's still what I most want to hear about . . . why it is, for instance, that you seem so at peace with yourself, and a lot younger than when you left. It was, clearly, worth doing."

"Yes, it was. Although I still remember the awful pang it was to leave your mother and you at that time . . . but I had to go."

"Of course. And in the last weeks, Jane, no one could do very much for Mother. That was what was so hard."

"You, too, have been doing a lot of growing."

"If growth is shutting some things out, yes."

Inside I was appalled at how limited and sedate my life had become. But I didn't say it then. I wanted to hear Jane's answer to my question. "But you haven't shut anything out, have you?"

"I've taken a lot *in,* " she smiled. "I don't feel exactly younger, Cam. But I suppose I needed to be useful again. And I think I came to see that my slow tempo, which used to irritate you sometimes in the seventh grade, had its advantages in this experience in Germany. We did pull it off in the end!"

"Something solidly achieved. One rarely experiences that in teaching."

"No . . . the achievement, I suppose, is not clear until students go on into their own lives, and one is rarely there to see that. How lucky I am to be able to feel that the *Nachbarhaus* is a going concern! And that Americans and Germans did it together. Was that the real achievement that I would like to communicate to the apprentices? Was that it?"

"The miseries and triumphs of bringing two such different cultures together in a positive statement, a real 'going concern'? Yes, I can see."

"Bless you, dear Cam. How you do help me!"

So it was, as I had so hoped it might be, a real exchange. But when had it not been between Jane and me?

"I'm worried about Muff," she said out of the new found intimacy.

"She isn't well?"

"She seems rather—how to say it?—not exactly diminished but not quite herself. Without Sarah to help with the island and the English girls—you know the boy has gone back to England, but they are in college here—without Sarah I don't know what Muff would do these days."

"Has she seen a doctor?"

"She is reluctant to . . . but I must persuade her to get some diagnosis soon. She seems so weak, eats next to nothing."

On that note of anxiety we parted.

For the first time I felt a little envious. It occurred to me that Jane's life had opened out just in the years when mine was closing in. She was still extraordinarily youthful, capable of great enthusiasm and what I felt was a faith which I entirely lacked. It had been very good to see her and to renew what now had become intimacy. I suppose my mother's death had had something to do with it. I could never supplant what my mother had been for Jane in the last years, but I felt a tender regard in Jane's eyes when she looked at me that I had not seen before. There was certainly no one in my life quite like her.

But I wondered whether she would be happy without teaching or at least some part-time work at the school. Jane needed to be with children, to draw on her sense of fun and imagination, in a way perhaps to become a child again herself, I thought on the drive home. I have never liked children very much myself. I was far happier teaching at college age than I could have been in a lower school. I wanted a battle of wits and intelligence. I wanted to be with young minds that could catch fire. Jane perhaps still loved to make magic, and in a way to *be* magic, as she could be with children, as she could be by becoming a child again herself. What was life going to do about that, I wondered? Even her nieces and nephews were grown-up now, and none, so far, had children.

I was soon engrossed in college affairs and it was after Christmas when I went up to Cambridge to do some research and dropped in at Brattle Street to see Jane again. I sensed at once by the way Mary, the old servant, whispered at the door, "I'll just get Miss Jane" that there was a sinister hush in the house. And when Jane came she hugged me and I saw tears in her eyes.

"What's going on? I've come at a bad time. . . ."

"Oh dearie, I'm glad to see you. Come and sit down."

It looked as though the parlor was not being used.

"It's Muff," I ventured when we had sat down by the cold hearth where I always saw Muff, sewing or reading, the presiding presence. The room felt dead, filled with absence.

"Yes," Jane said quietly, "Muff is dying. One of us, Sarah or I, is with her all the time, so I can't stay long."

"The dear thing," I murmured. Muff had always been in the shadow, the one who could be turned to when no one else was around, the one who was always there. It struck me with great force that she was or had been in the last years the foundation of all the life here, and of course for the English children a mother and friend of supreme gentle authority. "Oh Jane . . ." We exchanged a silent look.

"I wish I hadn't been away so long . . . but I couldn't leave that job half-finished."

"No, you mustn't be sorry about that. . . ." I felt awkward, unable really to help.

"We did have a wonderful Christmas, with the English girls and Sarah, of course, and Sarah's sister came for a few days. Muff came down twice and saw the tree lit." After a moment Jane said, "I think she would like to see you. Let me just go and ask."

So I was there in the strangely empty room alone. Does the furniture itself die when people die? I wondered. And it all came back in a rush how we had emptied Mother's house, Ruth and I, and just wanted to get rid of things because the life had gone out of them. This house had been lived in for nearly a hundred years. Five girls had grown up here with their mother and father, Muff the last to live on in the unchanged surroundings, keeping something alive that would die now with her. I felt astonished at my own grief, for it was real. When Jane came down and whispered, "Do come up," I was ready.

I had never been upstairs in that part of the house before and found Muff, a tiny wizened face, almost smothered in small pillows, lying in a huge bed. I went over and sat in a red velvet chair close to her, and took one of her transparent hands in mine. It was very cold.

"Cam, I'm glad to catch a glimpse of you," she whispered and added with the ghost of a smile, "You have such warm hands." There was a small vase with three pink roses placed where Muff could see it on a small table.

"What beautiful roses," I said, searching for something peaceable to utter.

"Sarah," Muff whispered, "she says autumn roses are the most beautiful . . . and I can see that they are."

"Sarah has a genius for bringing Muff little bouquets," Jane said. "Isn't that perfection?"

But Muff, who had been present for a few moments, had closed her eyes, and at a signal from Jane, we tiptoed out.

"Dear Cam, thanks for coming," Jane said, escorting me to the door. "You understand I must be with her. Is everything all right with you?" She put a hand on my shoulder in a gesture I loved, for it was so like her.

"Everything's fine," I assured her, but I suddenly felt tears on my cheeks. And blundered away then, hardly able to see. Too many deaths. Too many.

I had my first class on the day of the funeral and so did not go. I really did not want to go. I wanted to see Jane alone, and to be as supportive as I could after it was all over. Ruth welcomed my suggestion that we ask her to come down for a weekend as soon as she felt she could.

"It might help her to get right away from it all, all the decisions," I said. But I was not at all sure that she would come. She had never come down to us before. So I was happy when she accepted with joy and we set a date for three weeks later, in

October. There were great confabulations about what to have to eat. We settled finally on roast chicken and a *ratatouille*, with apple pie for dessert. Jane, I reminded Ruth, was quite childlike about food . . . anything like liver or kidneys repelled her. I remember once ordering calves' brains when I was with her in a restaurant and felt she could hardly bear to look at what I was eating.

I placed a bunch of orange and deep-gold chrysanthemums in her room and put *The Oxford Book of English Verse* (shades of Marian) by her bed, and, just as a joke, *Peter Rabbit* and *Squirrel Nutkin*, as well as *The Manchester Guardian Weekly* and *The New Statesman*, to which I subscribed. It was wonderful to be getting ready to receive Jane in my own home, and if I had been feeling rather sedate, I was suddenly as excited as a child at the prospect of her arrival.

Buying the house had been quite an adventure for Ruth and me . . . it didn't seem possible that we had lived in it, then, for five years. In that time Ruth, who was the gardener, had created a charming three-sided group of flower beds, and we had planted dogwood and one or two tree peonies under them, our greatest pride. The house itself was a rather ordinary nineteenth-century one with a small porch at the back which we had added on after two years, and there we lived all summer.

Inside there were one or two eighteenth-century pieces, a corner cupboard in the small dining room, a bureau in the living room from Ruth's family, and a small, rather elegant sofa from Mother's house with one of her paintings of flowers above it. Ruth and I each had a study downstairs. Upstairs there were two bedrooms, ours and the guest room. I like to think that the house gave an impression of light, flowery and elegant.

And Jane caught this at once. "It's so like your mother," she exclaimed. "It's so airy and comfortable . . . oh my dears!" We sat down by the fire to have tea, and all the time she was noticing little things.

"What a perfect guest, Ruth, isn't she?"

"Am I?"

"Nobody ever notices anything . . . but you do. Imagine your noticing that mouse on the mantel!" And we laughed with the pleasure of it.

"It seems incredible that I have never managed to come for all these years! To see you and Ruth at home."

"After tea you must walk round the garden. That is Ruth's domain."

"I shall, I shall."

But over tea and shortbread, much appreciated too, we were soon talking about Muff, of course, and Jane's mood changed. "Of us all only Viola and I are left—it seems so strange. But I must tell you, upstairs in my room I delved right into *The Oxford Book,* and you know what it opened to? See if I can say it, and of course I hear it in Marian's voice," and she recited:

"Very old are the woods;
And the buds that break
Out of the brier's boughs,
When March winds wake,
So old with their beauty are—
Oh, no man knows
Through what wild centuries
Roves back the rose."

"Is it de la Mare?" I asked. "I seem to remember. . . ."

"Of course." I saw her eyes were bright with tears. "Why does it make me think of Muff? But it does."

"She was an ancient person."

Jane laughed then, her whoop of sudden laughter. "Ancient?"

"I mean she was in some odd way ancient from the beginning . . . that is what I always felt."

"Oh." Then she grew thoughtful, "Yes, I see . . . yes."

"You were young from the start and she was ancient . . . does that make any sense? I fear not."

"I am always surprised by Cam," Ruth said, smiling. "She does think of the most extraordinary things."

"But Jane," I wanted to get at what was to happen now. "What is going to happen about the house? About Sarah . . . where will she go?"

"Another cup of tea might help me try to tell you," Jane said, passing her cup, then setting it down and looking into the fire.

"You don't need to," I said. Perhaps she was not ready for that kind of planning. Perhaps she needed time.

"Oh, I must," she said quickly. "It's all in my head, you know, has been for two weeks. We are selling the house." (Who was "we," I wondered?) "Mary will go over to the Trueblood house to help out there—that was one of my chief concerns now that Snooker is dead. What to do about Mary. She has been with us for thirty years." Then Jane paused. "I'm keeping Sudbury for a while . . . the Mormon couple want to stay on and I'm not ready, really, to give it up."

It all sounded to me like an earthquake going on . . . so much that had seemed would last forever breaking up. "Surely not," I said. "You can't be thinking of that!"

"Well . . ." Jane sipped her tea and looked thoughtful. "You know Muff always felt it was too far away, too hard to go back and forth to. I see now that she was right."

"But that was it, to get right away, to have a sanctuary. . . . I'll never forget those months I spent there after Spain!"

"Yes, that was a great time, wasn't it?" she said gladly. "But you see, Cam, you are a person with a lot of solitude to draw on in you. . . . I guess I need people, and the trouble with Sudbury

245

is that it's not a place where people can drop in, you know. It would be different if I had a Ruth to share it with. Ever since I walked into this house an hour ago I have felt the sweetness of your life together."

Ruth and I exchanged a look. I felt too keenly the admission this was to make a comment. For the first time I faced in myself that Jane would never have what we had. Her most intense affections had not been wholly returned. Or was she, whatever she said, a solitary who could not cope with the kind of intimacy Ruth and I shared? I couldn't know then and still do not know.

"What I am considering, but it's not a sure thing, is when we sell the house to arrange, if possible, to keep the barn and the apartment above it." Here she paused, hesitated, leaned back in her chair and looked up at the ceiling. "For years and years it has been rented to the Hausmers . . . but dear Mrs. Hausmer has had to go to a nursing home and there is really no reason why I can't have it, I think. I am hoping to persuade Sarah to share it with me. There are two bedrooms."

I took this in in silence. Was Jane ready to take Sarah on? Would Sarah, who had been Muff's intimate friend, want to move in with Jane?

"You have your doubts?" Jane said with a twinkle in her eye. "And so do I, my dear."

"It sounds like a good plan," Ruth said, perhaps because I was still silent, thinking about all that might be involved.

"Sarah has built herself into the family. She has been an absolute trump about the English children. Muff could never have managed the island without her. She fits in so perfectly. She is a very powerful woman, Cam, under the shyness and self-effacement."

"That I can't know, of course." I did feel an indefinable malaise, as though something free in Jane were about to be caught and tamed.

"She'll be away at school—you know she is librarian there—so we shall hardly be in each other's hair, as they say," and she added quickly, "Sarah will have to make the decision. God knows we have our work cut out for us to empty the house when and if it is sold, and maybe that will show us whether we can work happily together. We'll just have to take it day by day."

I felt anxious to move into less troubling waters and pounced on the island. "Of course you will now be the one to run things at the island . . . that's going to be fun, isn't it, Jane?"

"Yes." Her eyes sparkled. "Let's plan right away. Will you and Ruth come for a week or ten days next summer? I expect I shall soon have a calendar and begin to write friends in. Oh yes, it will be fun! And there, Cam, Sarah will be the best right-hand man imaginable—oh, I hope she will want to come! She knows the ropes in a way I do not. She will be the most immense help in making the transition."

"It's rather like a puzzle, isn't it? Things fall into place. I begin to understand about Sarah. You are right. The French might call it a marriage of convenience," I ventured.

"A friendship of convenience," Ruth amended.

"And why not?" Jane seized on this idea with amusement. "Why not?" she asked again.

"Oh dear, we've talked so long it's too dark for the garden!"

"And it's time I started our supper." Ruth disappeared into the kitchen. I had set the table in the dining room before Jane arrived, so we had a little time alone together. And she was eager now to hear how we organized life.

"Ruth's the cook, is she?"

"Cook and gardener. I clean the house, make the beds, take out rubbish, and am, I suppose, what could be called the handyman. I cut the grass."

"Did it take long to work it out?"

"Not really. We each did what we felt like doing . . . I cook sometimes when Ruth has a long day."

"Does she have a lot of patients? It must be exhausting sometimes, listening to so many problems." I sensed that Jane was rather at a loss about therapy. Everything in her resisted the idea, I suspected, although her brother-in-law, Edith's husband, had been a psychiatrist, at least until they moved to the ranch for Russell's sake.

"She looks drained when she gets home sometimes. But then she has a drink while I get supper, listens to some Mozart. Ruth is a very balanced person, as you can see." And at that moment she came in with a martini for me and a glass of sherry for Jane. "We're talking about you," I said.

"Oh?"

"Your ears must be burning."

"Can't you join us?"

"In a minute. . . ."

"Mmmm," Jane said, "there is an aroma of roast chicken floating in here. . . ."

Ruth did fetch her martini then and sat down with us for a moment.

"Now," Jane said "you must tell me about McCarthy and that horrible committee of his. Is he as dangerous as he sounded when I was in Bremen? How can he be stopped?"

"It's a very bad situation," Ruth said, "because what he taps is that ingrained fear of communism which Americans seem to suffer like an addiction. He's already succeeded in getting the China experts fired from the State Department—Lattimore, for one—and the reason for that is that the experts all foresaw that the communists would take over in China . . . and were accused of being pro-communist as a result. It's all a little crazy."

"Worse because it's all like upside-down logic," I interrupted. "When Tydings' committee investigated McCarthy's charges about the State Department they called them a 'fraud and a hoax' . . . and what happened? McCarthy charged *them* with being soft on communism! And Tydings was defeated for ree-lection . . . all the rightist organizations ganged up to 'get him,' and they did."

"And you mustn't forget Madame Chiang Kai-shek's ma-chinations . . . and how she has wrapped everyone around her little finger, even Wellesley College, where she was a student, you may remember." Ruth was vehement and flushed.

"It's scary." Jane took a sip of her sherry and put it down. "I feel it, I guess, more than I would have before Germany. One can't forget that Hitler's trump card was always anti-commu-nism. It *could* happen here."

"At present every liberal person is labelled. It happens where one could not have dreamed it could happen . . . imagine this, Jane: The other day the local head of the Civil Liberties Union, after the last meeting, actually asked me if I had been a member of the party! I mean, there, in that context, it did seem preposterous."

"Cam was awfully upset when she got home that night," Ruth said. "I had quite a time trying to calm her down."

"When I said I wasn't a commie, Fred backed down . . . but he mentioned that I had been in Spain."

"That is called being a premature anti-fascist," Ruth said, "but we had better have our supper and forget that mess for a while." Ruth always sensed when the tensions rose too high.

"It's awfully good to be able to talk about it," Jane said, as we went into the dining room.

It was a real pleasure for me to see Jane enjoying her supper as she did, to be for once a hostess for her as well as a friend. In some way it set a seal on our long relationship. I felt very grown-up that evening. So grown-up that I didn't argue when Jane talked admiringly of Eisenhower. I even resisted the temptation to remind her that he had shaken hands with McCarthy in Chicago before the election. Jane had always teased me about being absolute and she was right. When I saw that newspaper photograph I was through with Eisenhower—trimming his sails to get elected.

After supper we listened to a Mozart quartet and went early to bed. Jane, with her leap of response to everything, never showed fatigue, but I knew she must be tired after the last weeks of grief and the endless decisions and chores that always accompany a death, and that in her case meant such upheaval on every side.

"Sleep well, you two," she said as we stood at the foot of the stairs. And she reached out and put an arm around each of us in a gesture of great tenderness that touched me.

"You, too, sleep well," I said. "And sleep as long as you can. We'll have breakfast anytime."

"What luxury!" But at the top of the stairs she turned to look back at us. "Sure you don't want help with the dishes? I feel rather guilty about that!"

"Three's a crowd in our kitchen," Ruth said quickly. "Not to worry."

"I'm just going to bask in being here, then. Bless you both and good night."

Later, when Ruth and I finally got to bed, we talked about Jane, of course. There were so many things I had wanted to ask, whether she would be going down to Philadelphia soon, for one.

"She's really alone now," I whispered. "I wish it were Lucy who would share that apartment with her. I can't help wondering about Sarah. Jane is so very different from Muff . . . will they get along?"

"Sarah is needed, that's for sure," Ruth murmured, "especially on the island."

"I just can't imagine it yet . . . except at Warren in the last years, Jane has controlled her own life. This seems like such a radical change."

"She is a realist, Cam. And I imagine she is thinking about the future. She's nearing sixty, you said."

"Yes, it must be lonely without a central person, Lucy so far away, Marian dead. Oh Ruth," I murmured, "how lucky we are!"

Over breakfast I did get a chance to ask about a lot of things. Lucy, for one. She had come to Muff's funeral but couldn't stay because she was needed at the school, but Jane would be going down as usual at Thanksgiving to see Russell, "and really catch up with Lucy, which I sorely need to do. Of course she'll come to the island this summer."

The island, I sensed, was going to loom large in the years to come, would even, perhaps, become the root endeavor and delight as Jane grew older. I asked about the Cambridge Center. There things had changed, too, and Jane no longer felt as closely involved as she had been when Ellen was the head, although she was still on the board, I gathered, and had no intention of resigning. My last question concerned the Trueblood biography, which had come out while Jane was in Germany.

"Oh dear," she answered, looking very guilty. "I haven't managed to read it yet, have you?"

"No, but the reviews were good. I really think that young man has succeeded in reviving interest in Trueblood."

"So I am told," said Jane. It was clear that she felt some resistance about the book, didn't really want to read it, and when I asked her why, she answered so characteristically, "Any biography these days seems an invasion of privacy. Something in me rebels against that. I can't help it."

"The dead are at the mercy of the living?" Ruth asked, pouring us second cups of coffee. "Another pancake, anyone?" No one could manage a fourth.

"That's it," Jane answered, her eyes bright. "By what right must we demand to know *everything* about a person for one reason or another in the public realm?"

"I suppose it is the wish to bring someone down from a pedestal into the human family . . . yes, perhaps to humanize the myth," Ruth answered.

"We went through hell, Jay and I, making decisions, but we finally decided that Austin must have all the journals, letters, everything."

"Surely you were right," I ventured.

"I'm not sure. I'll never be sure." Then she looked at her watch. "Good heavens, dears, it's nearly ten and I must get back to Cambridge. The real estate agent is coming at noon with someone who may want to buy. . . ."

"You must just walk around the garden!"

"Of course there's time for that. . . . I'll just pack my valise and come right down."

It had been such a good, a memorable visit that I hated to see her go. And when she drove off, a long arm waving good-bye from the window until we were out of sight, I felt a pang.

"It's lonely for her, Ruth, awfully lonely."

"Well, I'm not so sure about that. Jane has made choices all her life from what you tell me. She has gone her own way."

"Yes, with a hundred delicate threads binding a hundred lives to hers . . . you're right. I shouldn't mourn." But I did mourn. I couldn't help it. She was always driving off somewhere alone.

We did not see Jane again till after Christmas, although we talked occasionally on the telephone and I was aware that she must be going through a period of very hard work, emptying the big house, getting the flat over the barn repainted and shipshape. Whenever we talked Jane glowed with praise at all Sarah was proving to be: "She is such a good organizer, keeps things listed for me . . . oh, it has been such a multitudinous trial by *things,*" and she laughed. "How does anyone accumulate as much as Muff did? Of course she inherited most of it, piles and piles of dishes and silver, and God knows what! Sarah is a great preserver of the past . . . she loved that house passionately, has not wanted things to be sold, you see. . . ." And then she insisted that we make a date to come for tea as soon as they had settled in "because I hope you will like what we have chosen for you and Ruth."

So on a bright, cold January Sunday we set out, eager to see Jane settled in and to catch up on everything. It was strange to go right by the big house and out to the barn at the back. The house was not yet inhabited, but Jane had spoken with enthusiasm of the fact that it had been sold to a young architect and his wife and family, old acquaintances; and they, I gathered, were going to make some radical changes inside to modernize it. That work had not yet been begun.

It was exciting to stand by the small door to the right of the barn door, open to show it was now the garage and Jane's car safely inside, and ring the bell. It was Sarah who opened it for us, smiling warmly. "Come in. The stairs are a little steep."

"Sarah, this is my friend Ruth Arbor."

"Welcome! You are our first guests."

Jane met us at the head of the stairs, looking very tall under the low ceiling. "Oh, what fun!" she exclaimed. "The kettle's on, and I'm dying to show you our domain!"

In the cozy living room a large window, reaching the ceiling in a rather beautiful oriel at the top, gave an illusion of space and height. A big armchair, a small blue velvet sofa, and in the window a table piled high with books and magazines. At the end of the room near the kitchen the dining-room table was squeezed in by an upright piano. Over the sofa there hung a realistic painting of woods, perhaps on the island—Jane's taste in art remained conservative. I suddenly realized I had never before seen her in such a small space.

"It's amazing how homelike it feels already," I said.

"Wait till you see my bedroom!" That was back down the hall where we had come in. "Don't look to the right," Jane admonished us, "that is the dump at present. Total chaos!" But we then found ourselves in the very low-ceilinged room to the left. "It's a nest, isn't it? I feel just like a bird in a nest when I go to bed." And indeed her big bed was set under the eaves, the Brownies on the pillow. I glimpsed a row of photographs on a shelf to the left of it, among them one of my mother. A small table served as a dressing table and that was all.

The tiny apartment, I sensed at once, had a quality of hominess which Sudbury had lacked. Sudbury had been too pure, too beautiful, a little self-consciously so. Here, in a fine clutter, the accumulations of a lifetime, the atmosphere breathed.

"I love it!" I said. "It's just right, isn't it?"

"Tea's ready!" Sarah called and we settled down around the low table in front of the sofa.

If I had had fears about Sarah and Jane as companions, they were being set at rest, partly by Jane's constant use of "we": "We decided not to have curtains . . . the window is so beautiful —and see, it looks out on that great tulip tree. When we lived in the big house I never really noticed it. Now it's a constant joy. Rare to see one this far north." She turned to Sarah. "Will you pour?" It was a tiny but unmistakable sign that Jane was the mistress of the establishment. And I was glad to note it.

"What a triumph to be settled in," Ruth said.

"Well," Sarah smiled, "it's a little helter-skelter, but we do live here."

"And have our being," Jane added. "It's wonderful, you know, to be in Cambridge . . . I mean, people can drop in. Maybe I had better warn you that Maurice's grandchildren may interrupt us. They are coming to get the croquet set, and my tennis racket."

"And if Portia wants it, that Meissen soup tureen," Sarah reminded her.

"Oh mercy, I'd forgotten that altogether! Where is it, Sarah? Do you have the foggiest idea?"

"In the barn all wrapped up in that big box."

"Good girl. I should never have remembered."

There was a moment of silence as we sipped our tea and were passed a plate of very thin, elegant cookies.

"Mary made them—wasn't it dear of her?" Then Jane, munching on a cookie, looked at us, all three, and sighed, "It is wonderful to be sitting down with friends."

"We've hardly sat down for days," Sarah said.

"I've fallen asleep over the newspaper every night," Jane said. "I'm way behind . . . but I'm told that awful things are happening: Dulles backing down to McCarthy and forcing resignations in the State Department right and left. Poor Leonard, that star expert on China, has had to go."

"Yes," I said. Even here one could not get away from the disasters in Washington. "Leonard foretold that the communists would win. It's outrageous. I mean, you know the facts but if the facts don't agree with what Dulles and Eisenhower want them to be, you are punished. It's absolutely preposterous!"

Jane smiled, "I thought you said you had become sedate, Cam!"

Ruth laughed, "Cam imagines she is sedate, says she doesn't want to get involved, but . . ."

"I still care about the country, I'm still a citizen, after all. Dean Acheson is being called a traitor!"

"Where are we going? Where will it end?" Jane asked.

"God knows. At the moment Roy Cohn is in Europe visiting American libraries to make sure 'subversive' writers like Thoreau, Dos Passos, and Hemingway are removed from the shelves."

"How strange . . . meanwhile in Germany books banned under Hitler are being put back and avidly read!"

In the small room full of life we could not quite get away from the shadow of events, from fear. But there was some comfort at least in talking about it. Whatever had happened in Germany, Jane, I felt, had come back more politically minded, more aware than she had ever been. It made a new and precious bond between us.

But we never finished that conversation because the doorbell buzzed and we heard children's voices outside calling, "Aunt Reedy! Aunt Reedy!" Then some loud, deep barks. Jane excused herself and we heard her voice in a moment, after she ran downstairs to welcome them.

"Come in, you splendid people!"

"Can we bring Jumbo?"

Hearing this Sarah got up. "Jumbo is a huge Labrador. Maybe I'd better go down and take him for a little walk. That tail, you know—I'm afraid our teacups might not survive." We couldn't help laughing.

"Sarah does look after Jane, doesn't she?" I whispered.

Then two little girls in sneakers and jeans and their stout, smiling mother erupted into the living room where we sat, and we were introduced all round.

"Can we have a cookie?" Nancy, the younger of the two asked at once, seeing the plate still half full.

"You really should wait to be offered one," Portia, their mother, said gently.

"Aunt Reedy always has cookies for us," was the answer.

"Maybe you could pass them around," Jane said with a twinkle in her eye.

While they munched they looked around like squirrels, Prudence picking up the world atlas from the table by the window, Nancy going over to the piano and playing a few notes. She whirled around the piano stool. "How can you ever fit so many people in?" she asked. "It's such a tiny place . . . is this where you eat?" for now she was facing the round dining-room table.

"It feels very cozy and settled-in." Portia came to the rescue.

"Yes." Prudence set the atlas down, "Squirrel Nutkin would like it."

"Do you still go to bed with *Squirrel Nutkin* under your pillow?" Jane asked.

"That was ages ago," Prudence said, with scorn. "It's *The Hobbit* now."

"I am behind the times, I see."

"I like it here," Nancy announced. "I like it very much. Only, where are the Brownies?"

"In my bedroom . . . if you go down the hall and turn left you'll find them." And off Nancy went.

"I think we'd better rescue Sarah," Portia said then.

"Yes, let's all go down and find the croquet set . . . do you really think you can use it?" Jane asked Portia.

"We have a perfect place, a flat place behind the house."

"Good." Jane turned to Ruth and me and added, "You stay here and I'll be back in a trice." Then, "Come along, kids. We'd better get going."

Nancy's wish to take the Brownies down with them—she had them in her arms when she came back—was gently quelled. "They are very old," Jane said. "They mightn't like being bounced around."

"All right . . . as long as I know they're there," Nancy agreed. And then there was thunderous noise on the stairs, and loud calls from below. "Jumbo, where are you?"

"You see how she is with children," I said to Ruth. It was good to be left alone and to sink back into our chairs in peace. And then I added, "She took the Brownies to Vassar, you know. They go way back."

"That's the good feeling here, isn't it?" Ruth said, "that everything goes back and has been built-in somehow. She hasn't left the child in her behind."

"Yet she keeps on growing."

So we talked for a while, then looked at our watches. It was really time for us to be leaving ... but Jane, wholly given to the moment, had very little sense of time, as I remembered. It must have been a good half-hour before we heard the car door slam and "Good-bye, Aunt Reedy ... Good-bye" floating up to where we sat.

When Sarah and Jane came back, Jane was apologetic. "I've been away too long. But it was that Meissen tureen; we had to find a way to pack it in with Jumbo and the kids and to keep it safe. Portia seemed very happy to have it, I'm glad to say."

"We really must get going," I said with a glance at Ruth.

"Oh, don't go yet! Stay a moment," Sarah intervened then, offering to get the things set aside for us while we talked. "That will save time."

Jane smiled. "I'm afraid I spend time as though I were a millionaire throwing money away—but it's lovely to *have* time now." She stretched out her legs, sitting as she was on the low velvet sofa, and leaned back, looking up at the ceiling. "I just can't believe Maurice is a grandfather! That's the thing, isn't it? As one gets older one simply cannot believe that anyone else is getting old! It was quite a shock the other day to see that Maurice has snow-white hair, very becoming in a judge, I must admit, but for me he will always be an elegant young man who took me to see Sarah Bernhardt in a carriage which had a wonderful leathery smell. . . ." Then she laughed. "And now two little girls come and see me, his grandchildren."

Ruth and I got up when Sarah came back carrying a pile of plates which she laid on the table for us to see.

"Oh, I do hope you will love them, as I do," Jane said, taking one in her hands and holding it up to take a last look. "They're Bavarian . . . some have been broken and mended because Lucy found a man who is an expert. Will you mind that they are mended?"

"They're charming," I said, and indeed they were, brilliant flowers painted on them in small garlands—light pink, green, full of gaiety.

"Pink ice cream and cake will look splendid on them," Jane said. "Sarah really didn't want them to go, but when I told her you would be the recipients she melted."

"The trouble is," Sarah admitted without shame, "I can't bear for anything to go. But I know Muff would want you to have them, so I'm happy about it. I really am."

It amazed me to realize that with the hundreds of objects they must have listed and decided to give this friend or that, this niece or nephew or that, the English girls too, there was still a pang at letting each go. Sarah was clearly the one who minded most.

We talked about that, Ruth and I, on the way home, I holding the plates carefully on my lap while she drove. "I didn't think we'd ever get them wrapped, did you?" For each had to be carefully wrapped in newspaper after we had looked at them.

"It is like Jane to make this breaking-up of the house into a kind of festival, isn't it?" Ruth said.

"She never lets herself get bogged down. There's always new life to be met at the door." Then I added, "I wonder why Sarah seems so much more attached to the things . . . after all, it's not her family."

"What is her family like?"

"I have no idea, really. I just make a guess that her mother, a remarkable, very inward person, Jane once told me, was not at all domestic. Maybe Sarah basked in the taken-for-granted order and ease of the big house, maybe she hungered for that kind of security. But then," I added, "think of what she did to help Muff with the English children! Taking them off skiing, teaching them to sail!"

"It will be interesting to see how it all comes out," Ruth said.

"You mean Jane and Sarah."

"Yes."

For the rest of the way home we were silent, the kind of intimate silence we always enjoyed when we were together, each thinking our own thoughts; but because we were together and had shared the same experience, our thoughts had a keener edge—at least so I always felt—than if we had been alone.

The plates found their way onto shelves in our kitchen, exemplars of a life different from ours, treasured as honored guests. Our taste went to plain, modern pottery, so it was always a bit strange to take the bright-flowered ones out on special occasions, strange and touching. A little touch of Jane Reid and Muff, to be used with respect.

Sometimes a big transition in a life happens quite casually and suddenly. As I think over the big move to the apartment and the start of the companionship with Sarah there, I have come to see that it marked an immense transition for Jane. She, the most undomestic person imaginable, found herself the housekeeper. That was natural enough since Sarah was away at school all day. But it can't have been altogether easy. For the first time in her life since college Jane had no job, but for that reason her life seemed fuller than ever. Old friends, former students, family, all felt she was there and would welcome a visit, so hardly a day passed without someone "dropping in" and whatever she had been doing had to be laid aside. I, who guarded my time and was simply not available to my students except by appointment, never ceased to be astonished by Jane's capacity to drop everything and welcome me, as though it was the best possible thing in the world to be interrupted, to make tea, to sit down for an hour, open to anything and everything I might have on my mind.

And of course all those threads and interests she had held in her hands still pulled her to the Community Center in Cambridge, to New York for the Refugee Association—extremely active as the Russians took over one country after another in the north, Estonia, Latvia; pulled her to Philadelphia to see Lucy and be sure all was well with Russell; pulled her to the island plans for the summer months, not only juggling the calendar to fit everyone in, but going up at least twice a year to arrange about the summer jobs, the opening of houses, the endless things to be attended to: boats, the vegetable garden, the bedding plants for Muff's garden. Added to all this was Jane's passionate interest in what was going on in the world.

How she loved to tease me about my saying I was through with politics when it was clear that I was actually very much involved again. When it came to the Stevenson presidential candidacy, we were in total agreement. I remember Jane saying with her eyes very bright, "Isn't it wonderful to be voting *for* someone for a change instead of *against* someone?" I had organized a kind of Stevenson brigade in the college and of course she was eager to hear about that. The only thing I remember disagreeing with her about during those years was that I was also active in trying to get a teachers' union started. There Jane balked.

"Oh Cam," she said. "I feel that teaching is a vocation rather than a profession. It doesn't seem right to me to go about getting fair salaries that way."

"We've tried every other way," I reminded her. "There must be something wrong when the janitors and groundsmen are paid more than assistant professors . . . and they are because they have a union."

"But don't you lose something in gaining that?"

"What do we lose?"

"Dignity. Pride." She caught my quick denial. "Oh, I am probably wrong, but . . ."

I had to smile. "But you are not going to change your mind, dear Jane."

"Must I?" she teased, and then more seriously, "I don't think I can."

For her, I realized, teaching had never been a job. It had indeed been a vocation, and for her it was a little as though a priest or nun demanded a salary increase. But then Jane had not depended on her salary.

"Noblesse oblige just doesn't work in the everyday world, Jane."

"I can't imagine any teacher at Warren feeling as you do."

"Warren is special. No one would teach there who wasn't willing to work for next to nothing. God knows Mother did."

At this Jane blushed and I felt I had perhaps hit too near the mark, so I quickly siad, "Lots of profs at the college feel as you do. But I must say they are the ones with tenure and the best paid among us."

"For such a sedate person you do seem to be in the thick of it," she laughed again. "I'm all for it."

"Why? Why, since you don't approve of what I'm in the thick of?"

"Because you were standing outside, because you had been disillusioned. It wasn't your real self, Cam."

And of course she was right. For all my willed detachment I

was happier than I had been for years making war in a small college. When it came to the human situation Jane was nearly always right on target.

Was it about then or much later? I am bad about remembering dates these days. But it must have been in the autumn of 1957 that a great dinner was planned to celebrate the fiftieth anniversary of the Warren School. I suppose I was asked to be the one to say a few words about Jane Reid as a teacher of history because history was my own field. At first I was terrified and wondered whether I should be able to find the words at all. I must have written a dozen drafts, and I was very nervous that night.

But of course we were all lifted up by the occasion itself. It was held in a Cambridge hotel, a rather formal place for the Warren gang. But being formal, the men in black tie and the women in long dresses, added to the sense of importance, even solemnity, in spite of all the laughter. So many people of all ages rushing to shake hands and exclaim and all the teachers surrounded by men and women they had known as children. "Not Bob!" I heard Miss Everett, our excitable math teacher, exclaim as she recognized a tall, bearded man. "I never thought I'd see Bob Bernstein in a beard!"

Jane looked beautiful in a soft green dress, surrounded by former students, including Faith, so I joined them. It seemed years since I had seen Faith and of course we shouted with joy and dashed off into a corner to catch up with all that had been happening, for a few moments speaking in our secret language just for the fun of it.

"Look," Faith said, "isn't that Mr. O'Neil, the janitor?"

"It must be. He looks just the same but he must be a hundred years old!"

Of course we had to go over and speak to him. "Ah," he said, beaming, "it's Cam! Faith!"

"Do you remember us?" Faith asked. "That's amazing!"

He chuckled. "Of course I remember you. . . . Cam was always in trouble, you know, sent out of the room by Miss Everett."

"And you used to give me an apple. You didn't take my being sent out seriously, so I felt better."

"Did you now? I guess I was a subversive. But I like kids with spirit," he added.

We had to break off, for there was Frances Thompson arriving to a great brouhaha of people wanting to greet her, and Faith and I happily among them. She was accompanied by Tom Weston, so we were soon talking about those days in the sixth and seventh grades, Frances apparently delighted to be for a moment with us who had been at the school when she was new at the job. Tom, I realized suddenly, was now head of the board of trustees.

I had always liked Tom. We got to be friends because both our parents were getting a divorce. It had made a rather special bond. Now he introduced us to his wife, Adele, with whom he left us rather abruptly as he was to escort Frances to the head table.

"What seems so extraordinary," Faith was saying to Adele, "is that we have all grown so old and all these teachers, and even Mr. O'Neil, the janitor, all look exactly the same! I can't figure it out."

"I know," Adele said—she seemed to be an awfully nice woman. "My children are just about the age you were, I think, when Tom was in your class."

"Do they still think it's the best school in the world, as we did?"

"Of course," and she laughed. "I feel quite deprived because I was not a Warren child."

And finally, after an hour of talk and drinks, we found ourselves at round tables, where whoever did the logistics had made masterly lists, so contemporaries found themselves together with one of their old teachers. I was disappointed not to be at Jane's table, but we had quietly humorous Miss Ford with her bouffant reddish hair, the best science teacher I can imagine. And Faith was by my side. By then I was feeling rather nervous and surreptitiously looked over my notes.

I had been told that I would follow Tom who was to speak about Miss Ford. Of course he was quite a public person now and had all the ease and grace achieved by many an after-dinner speech. My heart sank. It was a long wait, but at last my turn came. From the podium I looked around to find Jane and there she was, giving me a most uncharacteristic wink, for she must have guessed that she would be my subject. It was a great help.

So I started off: "I come to praise Jane Reid. How rare and dear an opportunity it is to praise a great teacher after one has grown up, for isn't it true that with each decade we become more, not less, aware of what we learned between the ages of six and fourteen or fifteen and how incredibly lucky we were to have had teachers like Jane Reid! History happens in small rooms. It is thirty-five years since I sat in Jane Reid's seventh grade, but the happening goes on and on. How fresh, joyful, and deeply moving were the hours we spent with her. As I look back I get the sense that every day opened to some grand adventure, for we did not so much study history as become history ourselves. We were Bernard de Clairvaux; we were that centurion walking Hadrian's wall and dreaming of Rome; we were the early settlers of the eastern seaboard driven by the voice 'as bad as conscience' to climb over the Appalachian ranges to find 'something lost behind the ranges, lost and waiting for you—go.'

"Like them, we did not ever move very fast. We experienced

265

the slowness, the humanness, the struggle very keenly. So if I were to name the two qualities which could sum up Jane Reid's genius, they would be first, the sense of adventure, and secondly, the insistence that truth is hard-won. How carefully she taught us to read, to speak, to *savor* language—and life itself.

"Alas, a seventh grade report card reminds me that 'Cam has very interesting things to say, but she must give others a chance to talk too.' "

The laughter and applause came, such a fulfilling wonderful sound to celebrate Jane! I didn't dare look at her, but Frances caught my hand on my way back to the table and pressed it hard. "Well done, Cam!" And she whispered, "Richly deserved."

Well, it was not nearly good enough. But I was awfully glad to have been given the chance to say my say in praise of Jane to all those people. It occurs to me, however, that I would do it differently and, I hope, better now. I was so pleased when I found the scrap of yellow paper in the pages of an old journal, found what I did say so many years ago, that I wanted to place it here in this book. It is at least not "made-up," but authentic.

Faith and I went to the Square for a beer afterwards because we had to talk it all over. Bill was at home with the children so she didn't have to rush back. The Hofbrauhaus was noisy and jammed but we shut it all out.

When we had settled into a booth she said, "I feel sort of bereft; I don't know why!"

"I know why I do," I answered quickly, "but it can't be your reason. I felt a little jealous of Tom and Adele, so many of the people there married, with children at the school, involved still in a way I can't be. In a way you still are."

"But Cam, you didn't want all that, did you?"

"No, I didn't. I like my life the way it is."

"So?"

"Oh, feeling like an outsider, I suppose."

"But Cam, almost all the teachers celebrated tonight never married, after all. And surely they didn't feel like outsiders. Jane didn't."

"I sometimes wonder . . . she is the universal friend, but in a way she is always an outsider . . . except at the island."

"It must be wonderful to see her there now, in command. Did you and Ruth have a great time last summer? Oh, it's such ages since we have met, you and I! Where does time go?"

"Like water off a duck's back . . . time, I mean," and we laughed. "There are a lot of married teachers at Warren now . . . that's certainly a change."

"But I don't honestly know how they do it," Faith said, frowning. "That's why I felt bereft, I guess. I just couldn't make it as a teacher, you know. I wanted to, but the conflict was too agonizing between family and school. And I felt Bill was carrying too much of the load. . . ."

"I remember how relieved you were when you gave up the sixth grade. Do you really regret that decision?"

"I do and I don't. Oh, the awful choices . . . it's all very well to mind not having a family, but I can assure you it's a hell of a lot easier to live as you do."

"But," I defended myself, "I am just as conflicted—between teaching and trying to be a scholar. I live in a perpetual state of guilt."

"You do? Well," Faith said, "that does make me feel better." Our eyes met in a moment of sheer communion and then laughter.

"What idiots we are!" I said. "Yes," I added, "to go back a bit, the summer was marvelous—we were there ten days. It's like being a child all over again, so sheltered, so much fun, and Jane's voice singing on the stairs . . . why do you suppose that although she is, after all, a spinster she is not and never will seem like an old maid?"

"She's not at all sexual, is she?" Faith asked, thinking this over.

"Ruth thinks she is but it is all sublimated . . . and that is what gives her a kind of glamour."

"A pretty old-fashioned view."

"Glamour or sublimation?"

"Both, I guess. But, Cam, Jane *is* different from the others—Miss Everett, Miss Ford, even Frances Thompson. They are recognizable old maids, wouldn't you agree?"

"It's hard for me to talk about it . . . but it's true, adolescents would never write ardent poems to any of them, but I did, to Jane, and all of us who went on to high school together did. What was it that made us fall in love with her? That's the key, maybe, I mean we did really fall in love."

Faith looked alarmed. "But—you didn't want to touch her, I mean, did you?"

"How puritanical you sound!" I felt quite cross suddenly. "Let's drop it."

"Just when we are getting close to some reality outside my ken . . . don't leave me there."

But at that time I was not ready to go farther. I could only fumble. "I suppose to us then she was like a goddess. I know that sounds ridiculous."

"Not to me."

"But men did fall in love with her, you know, and probably women too . . . so there must have been sexuality. I mean, you can't really imagine a man falling in love with Miss Ford, can you?"

"Too pure, too single-minded, and, well, asexual, let's face it."

"It does occur to me that it has not been as easy as it looks to be Jane Reid."

And we left it at that as we walked through the Square, arm in arm, to where I had parked my car, and then I drove Faith home. How we hated to say good-bye!

I had much to think about on the way home. It had come to me as Faith and I talked that we were like twins and she was leading a life I might have led as I was leading a life she might have led. She was a brilliant student and, from all I heard from Jane and the others, a far better teacher than I would ever be. I don't wonder that she envied me at times, perhaps felt in a strange way muffled, swamped in family life. But did she understand that I too felt muffled at times in university life?

I had to think also about the fact that I could never have talked with Jane in the way Faith and I had talked, and why that was. Not, I decided, a gap in our ages, but something withheld in Jane, a deep reserve. Hers was certainly not the confessional style that perhaps the coming of therapy had partly permitted and even encouraged. She never said so, but I sensed that she didn't like it, that "telling your troubles" even to a psychiatrist seemed to her a failure of self-reliance and courage. And that stance may have partly explained her waning influence at Warren under Frances Thompson. For at that time many of the parents and many of the children were getting help in understanding themselves from a therapist. "I know, but I do not approve, and I am not resigned"—that line of Millay's came to my mind, although she was talking actually about death. But I felt it did say something Jane might recognize.

I decided that I must have a talk with Ruth about sublimation.

I have, I see, found that the best way to handle these years of Jane's late middle age is through my own meetings with her. I have no letters to Lucy from that period and am not a good enough novelist to invent episodes that never really happened, or that I can only imagine as having happened. That I think I shall attempt when I come to the final chapter. When I began this adventure in novel-writing, the only thing I was sure of was that it must begin and end at the island. For that reason I am loathe to bring life on the island under Jane's aegis into this section on the late middle years of her life. Yet the island was the continuity of our relationship. For ten years or more Ruth and I spent ten days or so there every summer. And after Ruth died I went alone. So I am at present in a dilemma, again take long walks, talk with my cat, Snoozle, put a record on and take it off, wake up in the middle of the night in a fit of extreme anxiety as I did two years ago, at the beginning. I must discover a way to proceed.

Let memory come to my rescue. For memory does bring back moments of unforgettable intensity as I look back, moments shared with Jane, for one reason or another, during the years from 1960 to 1970.

One of them is that snowy January day when Jack Kennedy and Lyndon Johnson were inaugurated. I had come up to Cambridge for a meeting of the Civil Liberties Union and invited myself to supper. I had said I would bring dessert and picked up chocolate ice cream and macaroons at Sage's on my way. On that cold, gray day, a light snow falling, and such hope and excitement in the air, it was wonderful to climb the steep stairs and find myself enclosed in the warmth of the tiny apartment, hugged by Jane, her eyes overflowing with love and joy.

"What a grand day!" Jane said at once. "And we must be sure to look at the news at seven, so we had better have supper first —it's all ready, the chicken's in the oven."

"And just time for a glass of sherry," Sarah added.

"And a toast to our young president. Hurrah!" I had not seen Jane so lit up for ages. And I basked in her fire, although I myself was not completely convinced, as she seemed to be, that Kennedy would be wise and strong enough at this time of trou-

ble everywhere, rumors that we were going to send more advis-
ers to Vietnam, increasing troubles and violence in the South.

But I soon realized as we sipped our sherry, Sarah and I, while
Jane disappeared into the kitchen, where she could hear what
we were saying and to some extent participate, that one of the
reasons for her enthusiasm was not as much our new president
but, as she said from the kitchen, "Great stuff to ask Mr. Frost
to be part of the inauguration!"

And later, she came back to it. "It's a landmark, isn't it? My
grandfather would approve. And while I was dishing out the
peas I remembered 'Poets are the unacknowledged legislators
of the world'—but who said it? Do you remember, Cam?"

I didn't so of course off she went to get *Bartlett's Quotations*
and look it up. "Well, I never! Shelley said it!"

"Jane, we really must eat," Sarah reminded her.

"Shall we have a silent grace?" And after that moment of
silence, Jane carved the chicken, remarking, as of some treasure, "It's from Sage's."

"That's where I got the ice cream," I said, laughing. "What
would we do without Sage's?"

"In this household at least," Sarah smiled, "we could hardly
manage at all."

"There have been major changes here since we discovered
what Sage's can provide!" Jane said. It was evidently something
of a joke between her and Sarah.

We put the dessert off until after the news, as it was nearly
seven, and sat ourselves down before the TV set, a small one,
sitting close together on the sofa to watch. And we were riveted
to the screen after that. Of course we did not get the whole
address. "Too bad they cut out so much," Jane said. But we did
get a sense of something stirring, fresh, inspiring in Kennedy's
delivery and his bare head in the cold wind, the youth of his
stance, the hope and triumph in his voice. When it came to Mr.

Frost (Jane always called him Mr. Frost, as she always called Trueblood Mr. Trueblood), oh dear, the papers blew out of his hands, he fumbled, and his voice was not clear. He looked a little bewildered, a very old man.

"Poor dear, he's having quite a time," Sarah said.

"It doesn't matter," Jane said with a lift of her chin. "Everyone will read that wonderful poem again."

"Why don't we?" I asked when the news left Washington, and we had turned it off.

"Let's read it. Of course we'll read it," Jane answered. "But where is it, Sarah?"

"I'll have a look."

"While Sarah's looking, tell me about Ruth, about you, Cam."

"Ruth is awfully tired. I'm worried about her. She says it's just her heavy load of patients these days. She often works at night now as well as all day, sometimes from six o'clock on. I wish I could get her to slow down, but how can she when so many people need help?"

"Yes," Jane said, "it must be next to impossible to turn people away."

Sarah came back empty-handed. "I can't lay my hands on it, although I'm sure I saw it somewhere last week."

"Well, let's see what I can remember," Jane said easily, rubbing her eyes with both hands as though to find the words behind them. Then she managed three lines:

> "Something we were withholding made us weak
> Until we found it was ourselves
> We were withholding from our land of living."

But that's all I can catch hold of, I'm afraid." And she repeated the lines again.

"That's pretty good," I said. "That's really what Kennedy was saying, isn't it? 'Ask not what your country can do for you, ask what you can do for your country.' Maybe Frost said it even better," I added.

That is what I remember of that evening, the hope in the air and Jane lit up by the joy of it. That and the rather scary drive home through the driving snow. They asked me to spend the night, but I was determined to get home to Ruth and be sure she had a hot drink after her long day.

As I looked up at the big, lighted window just before brushing the snow off the windshield, I saw Jane waving good-bye, a big wave of her long arm like a blessing.

It was a time of deaths and assassinations, of confrontation with the Soviet Union, of the CIA bungle at the Bay of Pigs, of increasing violence against the passive resistance in the South under Martin Luther King's inspiring leadership, so it is not surprising that my vivid memories of Jane are tied to disaster in those years. In November of 1963 Ruth and I had hoped that Jane would come down and share our Thanksgiving dinner with us, but she was going to Philadelphia to be with Lucy and to see Russell as she had done for many years. So she suggested that she come down overnight on November twenty-second instead and we could then have a pre-Thanksgiving celebration.

Her imminent arrival lifted us out of a doldrum. Ruth made her special cranberry sauce and I stuffed the small turkey with a mushroom-and-onion stuffing my mother used to make, all these happy makings and doings going on the night before, of course. Ruth made a darling bunch of chrysanthemums and one late rose from the garden for Jane's room and managed to change a late appointment so she could be home by six. I was just getting the Bavarian plates out for the "pink ice cream and cake" Jane had suggested would suit them when Ruth arrived, in a state of extreme distress, I could see at once.

"Cam," she managed to say, "Kennedy has been shot."

"How do you know? Are you sure it's true?"

"When I came out of my office, I stopped to speak to the janitor about something. He is a very gentle man, but he was suddenly furious. 'What is the matter, John?' I asked and then he blurted it out. 'Don't you know? Kennedy has been shot.' What I saw on his face was black rage. And then all the way home, Cam, people were standing by their cars listening to the radio. I saw a woman crying. And when I turned on my radio in the car I got it, the whole story."

"But who did it? Why?"

"They shot him in Dallas in an open car—Connally is badly hurt but they think will live."

We stood there in the kitchen in a state of shock, tears pouring down our faces.

But it was comforting to know Jane would soon be with us. It seemed to me suddenly a huge, lonely country we were in, with what I felt then was a stranger for president.

She came, bearing a bottle of sherry, and looking so expectant and happy to be with us, it was awful to hear the lilt in her voice as she hugged us each and said, "What a splendid Thanksgiving before Thanksgiving it is, dearies!"

But then she looked at us and saw that something was very wrong.

"Kennedy—he's been shot. He's dead."

"Oh . . ." She stood there, I remember, still holding the bottle of sherry, looking at me, then away as her eyes filled with tears.

"We'd better sit down," Ruth said. "Open the sherry. We're pretty shook up."

"I'm so glad you're here, Jane. I'm so glad we can be together tonight," I managed.

"I should call Sarah," Jane said. "She'll come home alone to this news. It's so very bad."

274

Ruth took Jane's coat and lit the fire in the living room while I found glasses and a tray, all these usual gestures suddenly hard to make. I felt as though my arms had turned to lead.

"Dallas," I said bitterly when we had settled by the fire. "Apparently they even had car stickers saying 'Get Kennedy' or something like that on them."

"Don't. . . ." Jane said gently.

"Anger is so close to grief," Ruth said in her wisdom. And she told Jane about John, the janitor.

"Who did it? Do they know?" Jane asked then.

Ruth looked at her watch. "It's nearly 6:30 . . . we can look at the TV. They must know something by now."

I felt paralyzed and let Ruth take over, turn the oven down, hold up supper, as we would surely not want to interrupt whatever news could be gleaned. It seemed unbelievable that we could see it all now, the open cars, the blur of Kennedy falling forward, as though we were there. The somber hall in the hospital, Jackie in her blood-stained suit. We watched it all in silence.

"Some madman," Jane said at one point. "It is quite unbearable." She turned to me with a helpless gesture lifting her hands in a kind of despair and letting them fall.

At nearly eight we finally sat down to supper. Ruth lit the candles while I carved. And then I asked Jane to say grace. It was not something Ruth and I did, but I felt it fitting to ask Jane. She took a moment to think, then most unexpectedly said:

> "Brightness falls from the air,
> Kings have died young and fair,
> Lord have mercy on us."

"That's perfect," Ruth said.
"You changed it around a little," I added.

"Marian used to say it, but I couldn't quite remember the whole stanza." And suddenly we were smiling for the first time in two hours. And suddenly I, at least, was ravenous.

"Grief may be close to anger, but it seems also to be close to hunger," I said, diving into my turkey.

And suddenly all the things we had each been thinking poured out, the sense of something horribly unfinished, the promise savagely broken. And we talked about violence and the fragility of human beings. And we somehow seemed to be growing together as we talked.

"It's very different from Roosevelt's death," Jane said. "Then it seemed we had to go on without him, but he had had time to show the way, as though a father had died, I suppose. Now it is the shock of the unfinished, the undone, and we are unprepared."

"I can't help resenting Johnson," I confessed. "He must be torn because after all he is president now, and that is something he could hardly have dreamed of . . . yet he is president in the midst of tragedy, so he can't exactly rejoice, can he?"

"We'll just have to see," Ruth said.

"Those little children," Jane murmured.

When it came to bring out the Bavarian plates, Jane remembered Sarah and impulsively went out to the telephone. "May I call her?" We could not help hearing what she said and I was touched at how imaginative she was, for her first words were, "It must have been a very hard day at school—oh, that was a good idea, so the children could be together and everyone feel part of it. Try to get a night's sleep. I'll be home tomorrow."

She came into the kitchen while I served the ice cream. "Sarah says they had an assembly before the children went home. She said they sang "The Battle Hymn of the Republic" and that, I expect, did everyone good."

Over dessert we talked about how children can be helped or

approached about death, a death in the family, for that, we agreed, was how this assassination made us all feel.

Jane remembered as a small child on the island finding a dead bird. "It seemed so meek," she said, "the way the head flopped over when I picked it up, and the dead eyes. I'll never forget it. I suppose that was the first time I faced the fact that a life, even a bird's life, has limits. Of course I took it to Snooker and she helped me bury it in the moss drawing room in the woods. She always knew what to do."

Ruth then told us of her father's death, how sudden it had been, and because she was far away at school, she had for years felt responsible, as though she could have saved him if she had been there. He died of a heart attack while mowing the lawn. "You see he had been saying all summer that he felt so tired, so terribly tired, and we all just told him he worked too hard and he ought to slow down. But nobody did anything!"

It flashed through my mind that Ruth lately had complained often of being overtired . . . but I shied away from facing that.

"We have been on a long journey this evening," Jane said after a silence. "And maybe it is time to turn in, blessed people. How much we have shared. . . ."

How did Jane keep her freshness, that spring of elation and responsiveness so near the surface during those years? Anyone else would have been overwhelmed by the sheer day-to-day demands. When Jay died she had the whole responsibility for running the Trueblood House, finding the right caretakers, not as easy as it sounded, for although they had a beautiful apartment to live in they had to be available on the two days a week when the house was open to the public. None stayed more than a year or so, so it was all to do again. Things that had been pushed aside in her active years were now accumulating in the "dump," that small room opposite her bedroom. The French families, who now had grandchildren as well as children, expected at least a yearly letter from Jane and Lucy. And Jane's own good health was not matched by that of many of her friends. One of her oldest Vassar friends went into a serious depression and had to be sent to McLean for a month. That meant visits to the institution where so many Bostonians went into retreat. Muff's interest in the Unitarian Church must be carried on, Jane felt. One of the last things Muff had done was to help financially in rebuilding the spire and painting the whole huge building. And there were still odds and ends to be tied up before the Trueblood papers went over to Harvard University. But none of these preoccupations ever blurred the moments of happiness with friends, the instant response to the suggestion of a picnic or a family gathering, a birthday or an anniversary where her presence would give delight, and she herself be brimming with joy and expectation about the occasion.

I gathered that Portia and her children had become a new part of her immense "extended family" and ran in and out several times a week. Jane had kept a lien on the tennis court and the children came over to play. Through Sarah, Jane was also in touch with Warren, and several teachers depended on her advice and wisdom, and dropped in for tea on their way home, as Jane had used to do when my mother was alive. And under all these comings and goings, she was deeply concerned about politics. By 1965 Johnson's "Great Society" had been swamped in the increasing anxiety and vast expense of the war in Vietnam. Student demonstrations were becoming more violent, draft cards were burned, at least one of her friends had a son in hiding in Canada. Whenever I saw her, which was not often except in the summer on the island, we talked about that.

Jane instinctively withdrew from conflict. She did not like the violence of the students, and we had at least one rather hot argument about what was right about it, for I, by then, was strongly committed to ending the war by any means possible. But when Martin Luther King was assassinated in the spring of 1968, Jane was the one person I needed to talk with. And for once I remember she was in a state of such acute distress that she could hardly utter a word. "I just feel so ashamed, ashamed of us," she kept saying. "What is happening to this country? When will it end?"

It was hard not to be with her, to talk only on the telephone. I felt it was the worst day of my life, worse than Spain. "Thank goodness you were there," I remember saying. "I needed to touch base so badly, Jane." And when I put the receiver down I understood in a new way that Jane was "base" for more people than I knew or could imagine.

When Ruth came home late that evening, looking white and drained, and we sat by the fire for an hour before going to bed, we talked about it.

"Where does she get that spring in her? That source we all turn to?"

"God knows," Ruth said, and I thought she was too exhausted to talk about it, but in fact she was thinking, and after a considerable silence she talked about it. "It is what is lacking in many of my patients—'burned-out' by an unhappy love affair, a failed marriage, agonizing self-doubt—what is lacking is what you call the source or spring, something that cannot be polluted, that can withstand whatever happens to throw one off balance, that is there, a foundation that sometimes seems to me below the personal. It is what the artist, the poet, draws on."

"But for an ordinary person, what is it? How do you help someone to find it who has lost it or never had it?"

Ruth sighed. Then she looked across at me and smiled. "But Jane, whatever she may be, is not an ordinary person."

"I know." And I ventured, "With Jane it is love, don't you

279

agree? The source, I mean, not personal love, not the way most people feel it . . . as I feel it for you."

"Maybe. But the burned-out people I see don't have any love inside them, nothing left over to give. They cannibalize themselves, I sometimes think, live on grief and resentment."

"You once said that Jane had sublimated her sexuality. Is that part of it? If sublimation means learning to surpass the self. I'm not really sure what it does mean."

"Converting one kind of energy into another."

"King never doubted that he was serving something greater than himself, did he?" I was up against it now. "He did apparently have no doubt at all that he was serving God. But does Jane believe in that way? I doubt that somehow. She never talks about religion."

"I know," Ruth said. "Jane is not a preacher, after all. Thank God for that!" And we laughed then, at last.

"She knows who she is. But how does she know it?"

"Well, as you've often told me, she has faith in a code of honor, in something deeply rooted in her by her mother and father, by her sense of family."

"Is that enough?" And I had to add, "Besides she has grown way beyond her family and all they stand for, it seems to me."

"Darling, I am beyond any more talk," Ruth said then. "We'll have to sleep on it."

If the last pages have in essence spoken of the bonding between Jane and me after her return from Germany, a bonding that had much to do with the terrible events in this country in the sixties, I come now to something private that for a time swept everything public out of my consciousness.

For months I had been aware that Ruth was overtired and caught in the responsibilities of a profession and the acute needs of her patients that precluded rest. I had begged her to see a doctor, but she always put it off, and often said that a few hours in the garden would do the trick and that was all she needed. In April of 1969 we had a big snowstorm that buried the daffodils, many broken off by the weight, but some, we felt, would survive if we could brush off the snow. In a way it was beautiful, but when we went out, booted and gloved in the high wind, we found many of the small bushes and trees near to breaking and it was more of a job than we had foreseen from inside the house. I remember how beautiful Ruth looked in her red parka, snow on her eyelashes, battling away among the trees, and the exhilaration of seeing one branch after another spring back, released.

"Oh, isn't this fun?" I shouted while I rescued daffodils.

"Glorious!"

It was early in the morning. We had rushed out before breakfast, in a strange twilight of snow. But after a half-hour the sun rose and everything sparkled. "That's enough," I called. "I'll go and put the coffee on!"

We had forgotten the time in our excitement, and when Ruth came in and looked at the clock, she had time only to take off her parka and put on a coat.

"You must have a cup of coffee," I begged.

"No time . . . I'll get one at the office." I heard the garage door going up. Then silence. Was she having trouble starting the car? I waited a few moments, and decided I had better go and see if I could help. She was sitting in the car, ashen.

"You're ill," I said. "Come back. Come in."

"Bring me some coffee," she managed to say, "quickly, Cam."

I poured a cup as fast as I could, put a shot of brandy in it, and ran back, feeling lead in my feet, as though everything had slowed down, as if I could never get there, get to Ruth through centuries of time.

She did manage to take a sip as I lifted the cup. "There," I murmured, "that will help." But she threw it up almost at once.

"Shall I call an ambulance? Get you to emergency at the hospital?"

"Don't leave me," she whispered.

I got into the car then and held her close to me.

"Good," she managed to utter, "it'll be all right." Then, "So stupid . . ."

I was holding her against my breast and could feel the fast, shuddering heartbeat, but was it mine or hers? I wonder how long it was before I realized that it was mine. Then I took one of her hands and rubbed it hard. All I could think of to get the circulation back. But there was no response. The weight against me had suddenly become a dead weight. There was no lift and fall of breath. Death? It couldn't be. What to do? I didn't want to leave her. But what if . . . ? Time was everything now. It was hard to extricate myself, unbelievably hard. But I managed to shift her over so she was half lying across the two seats, and ran, ran as fast as I could, to the telephone. Thank God we had an emergency number in clear view.

The ambulance was there in fifteen minutes. I stood at the garage waiting what seemed an eternity. Tears of relief poured out. They were quick and efficient, and within a trice Ruth was strapped to a stretcher and we were off, oxygen being administered by a male nurse.

"We'll have a try," he said, "you never know."

But I did know.

"Death by coronary occlusion" was the verdict at the hospital.

If I had felt numb for the past half-hour, I now became so speeded up I could not sit still. They had taken me to a private room and a nurse was with me. "Take it easy," she said. "Let me get you some coffee."

But I couldn't drink. I kept saying to myself, What do I do now? Where does Ruth go? I have to make decisions. But it seemed as though I couldn't move although my mind was racing. Other people, a doctor, came in and talked to me. Someone had called a funeral home for me and there the body would be taken, I was told. The nurse wrote the address on a piece of paper and I put it in my pocket.

"Is there someone you could call who could go home with you?" I heard someone ask.

Suddenly I remembered the patients. "I have to go right away," I said. "Her patients . . . they'll wonder what has happened."

"She was a doctor?"

"A therapist. I must go right away."

"Is there someone we could call for you?" the doctor, a very young man, asked. "You should spare yourself."

They did call the agency where Ruth worked, and one of her fellow workers promised to go over right away and deal with the patients.

And in the end I persuaded them to let me go home alone. They called a taxi for me. I wanted to see Ruth again. But that was not possible. Things happen so fast. No doubt the body had already been wheeled out, on its way to the nightmare of a funeral home. What was I doing here? I must be where Ruth was, I felt. But in the taxi I changed my mind. Home first. People to call. My mind was racing again. No time for grief. People to call. When we got there I found I had no money on me, of course.

"Wait a minute, I have to go in to get my purse."

In a way it was good to have to rush in with such a factual matter on my mind and rush out again. It would have been even harder to go in after the taxi drove off, to go in to that silence. . . .

What I had seen was Ruth's red parka thrown on a chair in the living room. And that was what I went home to, pressing it against me and suddenly crying like an abandoned child. But the motor in my mind would not stop saying, "People to call."

Ruth had a sister older than she, married and living in New York. They had not been close, but she must be notified. I stood with the phone in my hands and her number before me, but the number I rang, the only person I needed to reach, was Jane's, and by the grace of God Jane answered.

"Oh dearie, I'll come right away . . . just hang on. I'll be there in under two hours."

"Thanks."

It never even occurred to me that it might be hard to get through. But the sun would melt the snow. And Jane, I knew, would make it somehow.

What I could not know was that those two hours would be my only time alone for days. What I could not know was that death brings with it a thousand errands and responsibilities, and the bereaved are too busy to mourn or even to think. I had just sat down in the living room, trying to take in what had happened, when the phone rang. It was the funeral home. Would the funeral be in a church? Would I want an open coffin? Was I the next of kin? Would there be visiting hours at the home? Flowers? I did not have the slightest idea how to answer any of these questions. I just managed to say, "I'll come this afternoon. I'll make decisions then." Jane would be with me. Jane would know what to do.

Until she arrived I sat there, not even thinking, suspended in a sort of trance. Not grief. I have heard that when people are dying their whole life passes through their minds, and that in a way was what was happening to me. Floods of memories poured through me as though I could keep Ruth alive, keep her with me, by remembering. I saw her face so clearly, the deep line across her forehead, the rather stern mouth that opened in a smile in such a beautiful way. The dark eyes. Her strong, wise hands. And I could hear her warm voice. "Glorious!" she had called out to me only a few hours ago among the daffodils in the snow.

Death—I remembered Jane speaking of the small dead bird, so frail, its head falling to the side, the weakness of it. Ruth, Ruth, Ruth, Ruth.

Finally I pulled myself together and wandered into the kitchen, for Jane, after all, would need some lunch. There was soup Ruth had made in the refrigerator and I got that out into a double boiler and some French bread. There was plenty of coffee since no one had had any breakfast. I set the table. Everything seemed almost insuperably difficult. Would a brandy help? No, I didn't dare. I felt I was holding myself together and even one drink might bring all control tumbling down.

And at last I heard the bell ring and dashed out to find Jane carrying a small suitcase and what looked like a hamper. I took these from her and for a long moment we hugged each other. The perfectly unselfconscious tears I felt on my neck did me good. I couldn't cry.

The hamper proved to have in it a cooked chicken from Sage's, a pie, and Earl Grey tea. "It seems absurd," Jane said, rather shyly, "to bring food, but you'll have to eat, dearie, and it's so hard to think of cooking." And when we had put the things away she said, "Come, let's sit down and talk about things."

Of course she saw the red parka on the chair and knew it was Ruth's. "Shall I hang this up?"

"Don't," I managed to say. "It's what she was wearing when we tried to rescue the daffodils . . . it's . . ." But I could not explain really that it was my security blanket and what I wanted to do was bury myself in it.

"We'll just leave it there, then," Jane said and sat down by the cold hearth.

"Cam," she said then, "do you think it would be a good idea to make a list of what has to be done right away?"

"I feel so bewildered."

"Of course you do. But I can help with all those decisions."

I went out to my study and got a pad and pencil. "First, the family. It would be wonderful if you could call Ruth's sister and her mother, Jane. Neither of them has been close to us. They disapproved of me, I guess."

"Well, I'd better call them. But it would be better perhaps to wait until I can tell them when the funeral is to be."

"Will you come with me to the funeral parlor after lunch? Could we wait till then for the family?"

I don't know what I would have done without Jane. And I realized that she had had to face all this many times in the last few years. She knew the ropes about death. And even before we sat down to lunch she had called my department at the college and asked them to post a notice that I could not meet my classes till Monday. It was Thursday. She had gone over Ruth's history and roughed out a short piece for the newspapers. Strange how all these definite, factual matters took my mind off Ruth herself. I even laughed at doing what sounded like a résumé, "as though one had to submit a résumé one last time before being allowed into heaven!"

But then I thought of Ruth's patients. What would become of them? How awful to lose a therapist when it was perhaps her hands that kept one from drowning.

"Jane, what can I do about the patients? Oh, how terrible it is for them!"

"Surely the institute will make arrangements. I wouldn't worry about that, Cam. Though it's like you, dearie, to think of them."

For a few hours we were free of phone calls. And while we drank our soup, under Jane's gentle probing I told the whole story of the morning. It all poured out, every detail of it, as though I had made a record while it was happening and now must play it over and over.

"I should have made her see a doctor. I could have prevented this . . . I could have," I said drily. For now guilt had simply occluded grief. "It's my fault."

"I don't think that is quite true, Cam. Ruth made that decision herself, and all you could do you did, which was to beg her to see a doctor. We can't force people to do what seems right, can we?" Then she looked down, then up at me. "We all have guilt when someone dies, you know. It is the human thing. I wasn't there when Edith died. That haunts me. But one has to accept it, the guilt. Come to a sense of proportion. I finally came to see it was a kind of egotism in me that made the guilt."

"Thank you for telling me."

"May I make a suggestion?"

"Of course."

"When I call Ruth's family I wonder whether it might not be a good idea to put them up in a hotel. It will be hard for you to have them here, and I'll be in the guest room."

That meant that Jane could stay.

"I intend to stay as long as you need me, dearie. Of course I will," she assured me.

And then, with sunlight streaming through the windows suddenly and lighting up the bunch of daffodils on the table, and before we cleared away, we talked about Ruth. Until then there had been too many things in the way. Her death had taken over her life.

"We had twenty years, Jane. That's a lot. I was lucky."

"Yes," Jane said, "you were. I always felt when I was with you that you had a rare understanding. And," she went on thoughtfully, "I do believe that every good, fruitful relationship is a sort of beacon, a lighthouse. It must have comforted a lot of people to see you and Ruth together. You shed light."

This was a new idea to me and I felt it deep down, so I couldn't find a word to say. "Ruth was such a wise, honest person," I said after a moment. "Much wiser than I could ever be."

"Maybe . . . but less brilliant."

"I'm not brilliant, at best adequate as a professor of history, a little better as a scholar, I suppose."

Jane looked amused. "I wasn't really thinking about professional life. I was thinking of you as a person, that flame in you."

"Oh well," I laughed then, "the mad hare." But I wanted to talk about Ruth now. I wanted to bring her into this room alive. "What Ruth had was an amazing capacity to get inside people, to unknot their problems, to know when to be silent and when to open things up with a word. I envied her patients sometimes. . . ."

"Yes, I can imagine."

"Because, you see, they got something from her that I rarely saw . . . only when Mother died, I learned so much from Ruth. She could be a blessed presence without saying a word. That is what she did for Mother at the end . . . she could sit there by the bed and just *be* a help. Oh Jane, I couldn't do that."

"Love can get in the way," Jane said gently. "It did between me and Marian. I know." This was such a gift, Jane's saying that to me, that it really got to me only long afterwards. She looked at her watch. "Dearie, I think we had better go to the funeral home." She reached across the table and held my hand in hers for a second. Then we quickly cleared off and were on our way.

There we found what seemed endless stumbling blocks. I knew that Ruth wanted cremation. So I was not prepared for the pressure the rather stern, kindly man we talked with put on me about the coffin. Here Jane's help was invaluable, and her natural authority. She could insist that we wanted the cheapest possible coffin, and do it without the shame I would have felt at seeming to haggle. That small, pale-gray box we chose seemed to me so unreal, the fact that Ruth would be placed in it so unreal, the fire to come so unreal . . . death itself so unreal that I felt icily calm. Neither of us went to church, so I was at a total loss when it came to the funeral.

"No funeral?" Jane murmured when I suggested that. "You know, Ruth's friends and family, and her patients, may really want to make a farewell. I think you should not deprive them. It is, in my view," she added quickly, "a meaningful ceremony."

"I could ask the Unitarian minister, Jack Fulbright." He had come to mind because he and I had worked together on civil rights matters and I knew Ruth liked him. It ended by my calling him there and then, and he promised to come and talk over the service with me the next day. The funeral could be on Saturday at eleven in the small chapel.

We finally got home again at four. "How shall we ever get through all that has to be done?"

"I must call the family right away. Why don't you lie down for a half-hour, dearie? I'll let you know when I've done that, and the newspapers."

"I guess that's a good idea." I felt suddenly exhausted, and as though everything ahead, including my life, were an interminable journey. But when I lay down I was wide awake, strung up, sleep out of the question. All I could think of was that I had put off writing out a final exam and there were still senior theses to read. How would I ever do it? Go on . . . how? I must have finally dozed off, for I woke to the phone ringing, and staggered up from a nightmare about trying to rescue Ruth from an oncoming train. It was really better to be awake.

Jane had managed to reach both Alice, Ruth's sister, and her mother, and they would come to the funeral and spend the night before at the hotel. Arrangements about a room had been made. Jane would meet them at the local airport. She had even found out that there was a plane that would make the connection from Boston.

"Her mother asked about the will," Jane said. "It seemed a little odd."

"Oh God, where is it?" I stammered.

"There's time," Jane said quickly.

"She left everything to me. I know that," I said, "as I did in my will if I had died first."

Three people had called. One, my chairman, two, a colleague of Ruth's, and the third, a young assistant professor at college who had been a patient for a few months the year before. Jane had told them about the funeral.

"People will come to the house afterwards," she said. "We had better have coffee and sandwiches ready." I had had a rest but Jane's face showed me that she was the one now to be given an hour's relief, and I forced her to go upstairs.

"We have all day tomorrow, Jane. We'll manage." But how could I tell her what it meant to be able to say "we"?

By late that evening I was learning about death and the way it is handled in our society. Four friends had come by with casseroles, a salad, a chocolate cake, and a bottle of Scotch! While Jane rested I was glad that I had something to do. I was glad to play the record of Ruth's dying over and over as though reciting it would eventually make it real. I found myself forgetting and talking about her in the present. But I was also touched especially by young Myra's grief and the way she said, "I know she was your family," and then, "You must comfort yourself that she was the one to go first, and not you. You are bearing the burden for her, you see. I mean, it would be worse for her the other way." It made me want to howl like an animal, howl my grief, but I managed not even to cry. From now until after the funeral I knew I had to maintain icy control.

"Thanks for coming, dear Myra."

The chairman of the department offered to give me two weeks off, but I knew that was not possible, not at the end of the term. "Oh no," I said at once. "I shall need to get back into harness. It's the only salvation."

And when people asked how I was managing I could say, "Jane Reid is here," although some of them had no idea who she was.

Jane Reid was there. She was there in a hundred ways, when she came down to put supper on the table while I talked with someone, to answer the telephone, and, when at last we sat down, to talk with me about what might be said, what music played at the funeral.

That was the real test, far more nourishing than lying down, to get down to essence and for half an hour forget about all the lists and things to do. I knew Jane felt it too by the way her own tempo slowed down and she said, "Let's put our minds on it quietly," and she added quickly, "Of course it's your privilege, not mine. I'm just here to listen, dearie."

In the back of my mind was a poem written ages ago by a friend of mine, but all I could remember was one line: "Now the long lucid listening is done." Mary had written it after the sudden death of her psychiatrist, but I had no copy I could lay hands on.

I said the line twice. "Jane, that is what ought to be said somehow," and I explained about its source.

"I wonder," Jane said, leaning her cheek on her hand. "That line says so much so well. Could it be read, and then music perhaps? Perhaps even repeated several times during the service?"

"Oh, what a good idea!" And it came to me in this atmosphere of peace that Ruth would have liked Patience, another friend of ours, to play the organ. So I called her, hard because she didn't know about Ruth, I discovered, and at first was overcome. But she would love to do it, she said, and I told her the line we would build the short service around. She suggested Albinoni, that lovely slow movement. "Yes, yes . . . and could you end with Bach's Toccata and Fugue?" Patience would come over the next day and suggested we meet at the church at Jack Fulbright's convenience. Patience said she would call him and call us back, "to save you at least that," and she added in a low voice, "I am so sorry, Cam. It shouldn't have happened. Please know I am with you."

Memory is a strange thing. Most of that poem had dropped out of my mind, but I suddenly drew out of the magic box the last lines.

"Listen to this, Jane. I've just caught the last lines of that poem. I'm changing the 'he' to 'she,' but Mary would not mind, would she? Here it is:

"Because she cared, she heard; because she heard
She lifted, shared, and healed without a word."

"That sounds excellent," Jane said at once, and I experienced again that deep look she had when it seemed as though the soul was there at the surface from deep down. For a moment we considered, then Jane asked rather tentatively, "You don't want anything from the Bible, Cam?"

I was troubled and didn't know how to answer that because partly I wasn't sure how Ruth would have felt. "She was not a believer in the usual sense, you know, so why pretend that she was?"

"Yes," Jane murmured, "I see . . . but that caring life was rooted, just the same," and she lifted her head and recited, " 'For I am persuaded that neither death, nor life, nor angels, nor principalities, nor powers, nor things present, nor things to come, nor height, nor depth, nor any other creature, shall be able to separate us from the love of God!' "

I let the words sink in. "Well, that would be all right. Ruth and I could go along with that." For a second I felt Ruth was there with us, she seemed so close. Oh, not in a believer's sense, but the way Jane and I were talking brought her very close. That half-hour had been a saving grace.

So little by little the lists got crossed off. Myra offered to make sandwiches for after the funeral. Jane and I got in sherry. Everything got arranged with Jack Fulbright.

In those days that seemed like years, they were so long and so exhausting, Jane had been the pillar of strength, so wise and so able to deal with the practical matters at the same time. But her greatest gift to me was something she did quite unselfconsciously after the funeral. I myself was moving through it all now like an actress on a stage. A funeral is after all a ritual that takes place in the theater of a church. We had spent over an hour arranging the flowers, there were so many. I couldn't believe how many there were, how many people Ruth's life, so private as far as I was concerned, had touched. And during the funeral itself I was detached like a producer, listening and wondering how it would all fit together. Many people cried, but I held myself tight, only relieved that our plan did seem to work, the words and the music. But when Fulbright came to the part of Romans that Jane had recited, it all cracked open and tears poured down.

Jane left me afterwards to find Ruth's mother and Alice as she would bring them to the house. And that was where she showed her sovereign gift. I felt at once that she had managed to say something to Mrs. Arbor, must have done so, because when I met them at the door, Mrs. Arbor kissed me. And Alice, so prim always, managed to say, much to my astonishment, "Thank you, Cam, for all you did for Ruth."

In fact, it was quite unbelievable to find myself sitting between them drinking coffee in the first natural and amicable meeting we had ever experienced.

"Jane Reid seems to be a remarkable woman," Mrs. Arbor said. "She has been very kind."

"She was my teacher in school," I said.

"Really?" Mrs. Arbor was obviously confused by this. "She seems such a lady—no, that isn't the word . . . rather grand in a way."

"Oh well," I tossed off, "she's a granddaughter of Benjamin Trueblood after all."

"Oh, that explains it, then. They must be very rich." Ruth always said her mother was the greatest materialist alive.

"Maybe," I said. "I wouldn't know about that."

"She thinks the world of you . . . and Ruth."

At this Alice broke in, for once rather shyly, "She said she honors you. 'Exemplary lives,' she said. I never thought of that before . . . I mean, two women living together."

So that is what Jane had been up to! I had to smile.

We had reached a prickly subject and I was rather glad to be interrupted then by an old friend of ours from New York whom I got up to hug. "Daisy, you angel!"

Of course later on Mrs. Arbor made some objections to the will, telling the lawyers I was surely not next of kin, but since the will was legal there was nothing she could do. We corresponded briefly about some things, a ring and a valuable small desk which she wanted back, and of course I was glad to oblige.

Jane stayed another day and then had to leave, and I was alone in the empty house. But that long game of solitaire which has finally "come out," I suppose, in my endeavor to write this book does not belong in it. I buried myself in work. I managed to survive. And finally, after I retired, I moved back to Cambridge with my cat, Snoozle.

Prologue, Part VI

I must now for the last time become a novelist and hope to suggest the quality of a whole life as it was lived in a month on the magic island. For there everything that made Jane remarkable was gathered together in the last years as each summer brought together friends from all her lives—tradition and the explosions of new life that flowed in and out with the tides, brought together in a seamless whole—while Jane herself came into her own as the moving spirit and reigning queen of the kingdom her father had founded and her sister had ruled for so long.

Once when Ruth and I were there we amused ourselves on a rainy day by looking over the old guest books and comparing them with the one started in the last few years. In Muff's day the names were almost all names of members of the family as well, of course, as the English children and their parents, who came over several times. Aunts, nieces, nephews, sisters made a goodly company. But the new book opened up new worlds as all Jane's lives brought friends from Germany, Canada, Ireland, God knows where, as well as young teachers and their families from Warren, black friends from the neighborhood house in

Cambridge, her architect and his wife, Ruth and me, an Italian contessa her nieces had worked for in Florence. We were amazed at the range of people of all ages who had suddenly, after Muff's death, been invited to paradise for several days or a month. The sheer logistics of opening several houses and getting them ready again and again for new arrivals staggered our imaginations.

How much, as I look back now, we took for granted! How much planning went into daily life that seemed to saunter along unplanned! Somewhere Jung has noted: "We must not forget that only a very few people are artists in life; that the art of life is the most distinguished and rarest of all the arts. Who ever succeeded in draining the whole cup with grace?"

So let me open the door now to a month on the island when Jane Reid was in her seventies and her life itself had become a "house of gathering."

Part VI
The House of Gathering

On a foggy morning in late June, Jane lay in her mother's bed luxuriating in the fact that it was just after six and she did not have to get up for an hour. Before she turned over for a last snooze she looked over at Lucy burrowed into the other bed and still fast asleep. Even asleep, a blessed presence to wake up to, Jane was thinking. In this gray light the wallpaper with its small sprigs of blue flowers on a white background had a sprightly charm, and as always when Jane woke in this room that had been her parents' she thought of them. The wallpaper must have been chosen by her mother and brought back memories of those summer dresses she wore, freshly starched and smelling of lavender. There was happiness in the very air of this room, and Jane felt it every morning and on this one could hardly separate dreaming from memory as she turned over with a sigh of contentment and went back to sleep.

An hour later Lucy was the one to get up and go out on the balcony to taste the air, and peer out into a landscape almost blotted out by fog, a single fir looming up here or there. When she came in again, shivering, she was smiling as she looked around for something to wake Reedy up with and, on an impulse, picked the Brownies up from their place on the high bureau and tickled Jane's cheek with a Brownie hand.

"Oh!" Jane opened her eyes and seized the Brownie with a delighted smile. "So you are telling me it's time to get up. The Brownies are wide awake, I see."

"No hurry," Lucy said gently. "You have five minutes while I brush my teeth."

"What shall we do with the lazy sailor?" Jane was singing as she pulled on her stockings when Lucy came out. And so the day began. By the time Jane was dressed and had done her hair and tied her sneakers, Lucy had disappeared. And when she went down breakfast was nearly ready in the cozy kitchen and there was a delicious smell of bacon in the air.

"Isn't it great to be here alone for a few days?" Jane said. "Time opens out. There's no hurry."

On a foggy day the kitchen was certainly the place to be, warmed as it was by the huge coal stove, which was kept going all night and which Jane now replenished from the coal scuttle. "I love that roar," she said as the coal clattered in.

When they had settled with their breakfast and large cups of hot coffee, Lucy looked across at Jane and smiled her mischievous smile. "No hurry, Reedy? We only have to make six beds up, mend the sheets that are torn, get out towels, go over to the small house with blankets, check the bathhouse . . ." and she was suffused with laughter.

"But somehow here it all gets done . . . although without you and those wonderful lists I doubt whether it would or could!" And Jane added after savoring a sip of hot coffee, "I only meant that somehow time is different on the island. It opens out instead of closing down. And we have three whole days before anyone comes."

"And that, dear Reedy, is a century, no doubt."

"Look, the titmouse is back—hunting for crumbs!" There was

a bird feeder just outside the window where they sat and crumbs from their supper had been waiting for a customer. "There's a purple finch, too!"

So breakfast turned into a bird-watching breakfast and time did stand still for a half-hour. Then Jane brought out the big calendar where the names of guests were fitted in and jotted down during the winter, and they looked over once more the list of those who would arrive in the first week of July.

"It's such a big job, Jane. Who will take over eventually?" Lucy was the one to think ahead.

"Well," Jane laughed, "that we can't know today. But Frances and Erika are due on the third. I am just dying to see them, so maybe we could get those rooms ready first.

So the two women went upstairs and had in an hour of concerted work made up four beds, shaken out rugs, swept, and dusted. Frances of course would have the best room, with a balcony looking out over the sound. "Amazing how these spreads have lasted," Lucy said as they flung the old Indian cotton spreads out. "They must be fifty years old!"

"Mamma loved them. See how the colors are still brilliant, the tree of life. . . ." And for a moment Jane paused as she smoothed out one spread on the bed, paused to savor this rite, then, just to touch base, went over to the mantel and chuckled as she took the ancient photo of her cousin Jay, in an eighteenth-century costume with Edith also in fancy dress beside him, and dusted it off. "Jay in his glory," she said, laughing. "Poor dear . . . he did so love dressing up."

Lucy meanwhile was sweeping out the bathroom. "I can't understand why there's so little dust," she announced.

"It's so still all winter long, nowhere for dust to blow in from," Jane said. "I'll get the towels. Muff was a great investor in towels, as you may remember."

So the morning sped away, and by noon the sun was out and

the gray, muffled world began to twinkle and shine as the drops of water on every twig and frond caught the gleam.

"We simply must go out and take the air," Jane said. "Lunch can wait, and don't you love the expression 'take the air'? Swallow it in all its freshness like a glass of champagne?"

"Let's," Lucy agreed. "Lunch? I can scramble eggs and it won't take a minute."

"We'll walk down to the bathhouse and have a look around. I want to be sure there's a rowboat out for the Speedwell kids."

It was rather like a perpetual getting-ready for a series of festivals, Jane was thinking, even as she noted that she must remember to plant nasturtium seeds along the path, to climb two great boulders later on.

"Ah," she sighed, "smell the smells!"

The fog had brought in a strong smell of salt water and in this sort of weather the spruce and fir were pungent.

"Think how many feet will be going down this path all summer!" Lucy said.

The point of a walk, they agreed, was to take it slowly; there was so much to recognize and savor. And as always when she was happy, Jane was soon singing, this time "How Lovely Is Thy Dwelling Place, O Lord of Hosts" from the Brahms Requiem. But this burst into song stopped midway through because it was interrupted by the white-throated sparrow and they had to listen to that three-note song repeat itself like a litany.

"Alix could imitate it perfectly," Jane said as they walked on. Then she smiled. "Marian, however, said it was the most boring of bird songs . . . and I expect she was right." Marian's name brought with it a shadow, at least for Lucy, and she did not respond.

Anyway, they had reached the formal garden now, a little thin early in the summer, when the bedding plants had only just been put in. "I do hope the salpiglossis will do well this year—they look rather spindly, don't they?"

The croquet set, which would soon be the scene of such fierce battles, had not been set out. They walked on across the great open field that had been a golf course in Jane's father's day and was still kept going in a rather rough way. At least the nine greens were kept cut, although all except their trimmed circles had been allowed to grow wild. Here they stopped for a moment to look out on the elegant outline of the hills across the bay with swirls of fog still caught here and there, "like dragon tails," Jane said, taking a deep breath of the salty air and straightening up, perhaps aware of Lucy's glance in her direction, for Lucy sometimes reminded her that in her seventies she was developing a slight stoop, a hunch in her shoulders. Jane's response the first time Lucy mentioned this was to stand tall and then smile. "After all, Lucy, we are bending toward the earth now . . . it's natural, my dear."

"But not for you," Lucy had protested, "you are still so young —and so beautiful to look at," she added warmly. And Jane, always a little embarrassed by a compliment, had laughed.

"Well, then, hold me to the mark! But as for being beautiful, I gave up any idea of that years ago!"

"I can believe it," Lucy smiled, "since you almost never look in a mirror except when you are doing your hair."

They had now reached the boathouse, the scene not only of a lot of work getting the boats painted and shipshape in the spring, but all summer long of little boys making toy boats out of odd pieces of driftwood or leftover lumber. It was quite a large room, the door at the back framing the view of Southwest Harbor.

"Bobbie will be down here in a trice as soon as the Speedwells have landed," Jane was saying, "to see whether his bird houses are safe. See, they are . . . a little crooked, I must say, but no doubt birds will not pay attention to that!"

"Time to go back and have lunch," Lucy announced. "The island always makes me ravenous."

"But we haven't seen the bathhouses," Jane said. "and whether the swallows have nested again in mine!"

"It's after one," Lucy said. "We can come down before supper."

"Very well, ravenous one." This time propelled by hunger, they walked fast along the lumber road through the woods, noting on the way a patch of bunchberries still in starry flower, and they picked a few to put in a little vase on the mantel in the dining room, in front of the photograph of Jane's parents.

"Lunch is ready," Lucy called from the kitchen.

"Splendid. We'll look at the mail pouch after we've eaten." Captain Fuller had left the huge, worn leather pouch on the dining-room table while they were gone. "Maybe there'll be a note from Erika. I do want to know when they plan to arrive."

"All in good time. Scrambled eggs must be eaten hot."

"Yum," Jane said after a first bite."

Then they were silent for a while, finishing off with applesauce and gingerbread Lucy had brought with her.

"Perfect peace," Jane murmured. "Sometimes I wish no one were coming at all."

"It's rather nice while it lasts," Lucy agreed. "But I love getting ready for all the people."

"It's great fun, isn't it?" Jane yawned. "Oh, I am sleepy! Let's have a snooze, Lucy."

"You go right up. I'll wash up, it won't take a moment and you might wake up if you hung around."

"No, no, I'm going to help." And what Jane really meant was that she didn't want to leave Lucy. "Besides, we can talk while we do it."

Dishwashing took place in the pantry, in an ancient copper

sink that was green with verdigris. On all sides were shelves and shelves of Italian and English plates and elegant demitasse cups and saucers and glasses. While Lucy washed Jane wiped and put away, and while they did this they settled a lot of things they might do and Lucy got the arrivals straight: Sarah and Annie, the cook, in two days, the Speedwells in three days, and maybe Frances and Erika at the end of the week.

"Tonight we'll have a fire," Jane murmured, when they had settled into their beds and pulled blankets up, "and read something aloud. . . ."

"We forgot all about the mail pouch" were Lucy's last words. But Jane did not hear this, as she was fast asleep.

An hour later she was awake, looking up at the ceiling with her arms crossed under her head to stretch her back. She looked over at Lucy and saw that her eyes, too, were open.

"I've been thinking about old age," she said. "Do you feel old, Lucy? I mean, after all, we are in our mid-seventies, aren't we? But when I wake up I just don't believe it, do you?"

"No. I never imagined for a moment that the time would come when I could remember things seventy years ago. It's quite preposterous."

"It's only when someone I am with thinks of World War One as far back somewhere in a history book. Then I feel like Rip Van Winkle. It all is so vivid still . . . that time in France . . . only yesterday."

"The smell of wet wool clothing, the awful chilblains, and the hot *café au lait* after Mass. . . ."

"What a lot we have shared, you and I," Jane said. Then, coming to into the present, she sat up. "Do you think the new head at your school is doing a good job? I keep meaning to ask, but then we get so absorbed in things to be achieved. . . . Good heavens, Lucy, is it nearly half-past three?"

"Yes, we had better have a cup of tea to wake us up and then get going at the little house."

And while Jane put the water on to boil, Lucy began to put new candles in the seven or eight candlesticks guests would take to bed.

"My practical dear, come and have your tea."

Over tea Lucy did talk a little about her school and the problem it was that the parents still turned to her in any emergency and simply could not accept the new head, a young man whom they all liked, she said, "but they just are so used to me!"

"He has a lot to learn," Jane said. "I don't blame them for going right to the source."

"Thanks, but he's way ahead of me in some ways, braver about tackling political matters. After Kent State he organized two assemblies about the Vietnam War and why conscientious objectors were growing in numbers and why we all felt so bitterly about what happened there."

"But those kids are awfully young, it seems to me, for that."

"They grow up so fast now, Jane. Even in the sixth grade they were terribly upset, you know."

"So talking about it did make sense." But Jane was not convinced. "I wish they could stay children longer."

"Oh my dear, things have changed. About a third of the children have divorced parents. They talk about things we would never have dreamed of at ten or twelve years old. They *know* things we could not have imagined."

"But is that good? I mean, after all, they may talk about sex but they can't really *know.*"

Lucy smiled. "I'm rather glad I don't have to deal with it any longer. Let Frank plunge in where angels fear to tread."

The discussion went on while they gathered sheets, flashlights, towels, candles for the little house, and it was late in the afternoon when they finally got back.

"I don't really know how it all gets done," Lucy said when they were finally sitting out on the porch to catch their breath and watch the sails go by out in the sound, in the evening light.

Jane laughed, "I haven't the foggiest idea . . . but it does . . . thanks to you."

"Thanks to Sarah, and a good thing she arrives tomorrow with Annie!"

"It's marvelous that Annie agreed to come this summer. And of course she never would without Sarah."

They talked a little, then, about that rare friendship which had begun when Muff was still alive. Sarah had been to Ireland twice with Annie to meet her family near Cork, on the west coast. A rare friendship because Annie was not educated, quite ornery at times, a character in her own right, with not the slightest feeling of inferiority. But, quite simply, she loved Sarah and Sarah loved her. All the planning for meals was done by those two together, and Sarah never forgot to include Annie in a sail now and then, took time to sit down and talk with her, and every Sunday took her over to the mainland to Mass early in the morning.

So whatever "class" might mean on the mainland, it did not exist on the island, and that was one of the small miracles every guest witnessed and all children learned by osmosis.

By the time the Speedwells were expected, Annie and Sarah were settled in, and when their call came from Southwest Harbor, Captain Fuller set out at once in *West Wind*, and Lucy, Jane, and Sarah got ready to go down to the dock to meet them.

"I forgot all about flowers," Jane said as they ran down. "I meant to pick some. The trouble is there isn't very much yet."

"It will be chaos while they settle in," Lucy said. "I doubt if they'll miss flowers."

And in a little while, standing on the dock, they could see

West Wind turning into the channel and already hands were waving.

"What a thrill to see them!" Jane said, thinking that the last minutes of waiting were almost intolerably long. But at last they were within hailing distance and Jane could lift her long arms in a wide arc, up and down.

"Hi, Aunt Jane, hi!" Bobbie called out from the prow, where he was sitting.

"Where's Nancy?" she called back, for only six people were visible.

"Inside," John, who was holding little Amy in his arms, called back. "She's got a lame back."

Captain Fuller made a smooth landing right against the dock and threw the rope to Jane, who tied *West Wind* up. And by then everyone was tumbling out, laden with rucksacks. Little Amy, holding a huge teddy bear in her arms so she could not make the jump, had to be lifted off by Captain Fuller while John helped Nancy.

"Welcome, welcome, my dears," Jane said, an arm around Bobbie's shoulders. She and Bobbie had always been an alliance. Tom, the eldest, who was now sixteen, was the shy one and was busying himself with endless sleeping bags, baskets, bundles of every shape and kind, and handing them to Wylie on the dock.

"Nancy, dear," Jane said, going to meet her and looking into her face with concern. "How did this happen?"

"I don't know. Isn't it stupid?"

"She's just tuckered out, I guess," John said. "Nothing the island won't cure."

"It's going to be a tight fit in the little house," Jane said, exchanging a glance with Lucy, who, reading her mind, gave a firm nod. "I think we'll just kidnap Nancy for a day or so," Jane said. "What would you think about taking over, John? Think you can manage down there with only five to help you?" she teased.

And before Nancy knew what was happening it was all settled. The children were loading bundles into the wheelbarrow and Lucy had volunteered to go to the little house and help settle them in while Jane and Sarah carried Nancy's bag up.

"It's quite incredible," Nancy said, an hour later, lying in the big bed in the guest room between Jane's room and what would be Frances Thompson's in a day or so. "I feel like a child who has been carried off on a broom by a beneficent witch. How did it all happen so fast?"

"This is your chance to rest," Jane said, standing by the bed and giving Nancy's foot under the covers a pat. "I think sleep is going to help that back more than anything."

"I don't know what's the matter with me."

"Well, I can guess," and Jane smiled. "Packing for seven people might explain quite a lot."

"And then it's always hard at the end of the school year"— for Nancy taught in a kindergarden, as well as all the rest she managed to do. It was clearly comforting to imagine for the moment that her back was only fatigued. Smiling, she closed her eyes, and after gently touching her forehead Jane slipped away.

At nearly forty, Jane was thinking, Nancy looked amazingly young. She was very small-boned, with curly black hair cut short, and a narrow, intense face that lit up when she smiled and her very dark eyes twinkled. But there was strain. Nancy had always carried the world on her shoulders and Jane suspected that the war in Vietnam and all the protest meetings and marches had taken a toll. It had been a hard year all round, and the demands on good Quakers like John and Nancy were heavy.

She considered all this on her way downstairs to see about a

309

tray for Nancy's lunch, with suddenly a warmth of thanksgiving about her heart, because, after all, this was what the island was for, to give a hard-pressed friend a respite, to shelter and make well. As she set up a tray, choosing a lovely cloth with flowers embroidered on it, she was singing "Over the sea to Skye. . . ."

It was after one when Sarah, Lucy, and Jane sat down to their lunch out on the big porch, the first meal out there since Sarah had arrived.

Lucy had been amused by the chaos at the little house and decided finally that she was not being a great deal of help, as the children fought over who would sleep where and John struggled to get the kerosene stove working.

"John seemed quite relieved when I reminded him that they would all be expected up here for supper at half-past six."

"I bet he was," Jane laughed. John, a teacher of math in a high school, was not the most practical of men.

"And is Nancy all settled?" Lucy asked then. "She did look pretty wan, didn't she?"

"The best thing is that I remembered the board for the bed. We had it years ago when I had trouble with my back—and Sarah remembered it had been stowed upstairs. What luck!"

Sarah suggested it might be a good idea to make some plans for the next day. "Maybe Sylvie, Tom, and Wylie could help me with the boat—it's going to be about three days' work, I'm afraid, before we can put her in the water and have a sail."

"Well," Jane mused, "I'll take Bobbie and Amy on a walk through the woods."

"Last year," Lucy reminded her, "Bobbie was crazy about making a Japanese garden, do you remember?"

Sarah smiled and Jane caught her smile and asked her what that was all about. "Don't you remember how you really hated his pulling up a tiny spruce tree?"

310

"Oh dear," Jane laughed. "It's quite true. There are literally thousands of tiny spruces, but I did mind. How foolish can I be?"

"Quite chauvinistic when it comes to the island," Lucy said.

"Am I?" Jane looked dismayed. "Do you think so?"

"Reedy, I'm only teasing! You treasure every blade of grass, and why shouldn't you?"

"I suppose it has become a sort of country in itself, this island," she mused, then she laughed with Lucy. "I pledged allegiance to this country, Wilder, a long time ago."

But over brownies and tiny cups of coffee she was still thinking about what Lucy had said. And it turned into quite a discussion about chauvinism before they separated, Sarah to go down to the boathouse, and Lucy and Jane to have a nap, stopping on the way to tell Nancy the news and to take her tray out.

"Now rest, dearie, and no one will whisper a word to you until suppertime, when your brood will all be coming over, you know."

"It's an awful lot for you to do," Nancy murmured.

"Nonsense, that's what a holiday is all about."

It was after three when Jane got down to the little house and rescued John, who had stayed with the little ones while Tom, Wylie, and Sylvie went down to the boathouse to help Sarah get *Siren* ready.

"Where have you been?" Bobbie said quite crossly, "we've been waiting and waiting. . . ."

"We thought you were dead." Amy said, giggling uncontrollably and rushing to hug Jane.

"I have to pick you up for a proper hug, don't I?" Jane lifted her up and swung her around in her arms.

"Let's go," Bobbie said.

"Bobbie, thee had really better learn patience," John admonished. And then to Jane with a shake of his head, "I've been trying to read."

311

"Well, I see you have two tyrants to contend with. We'll be off to the moss drawing room and see what we can find. What do you suppose I was doing that took so long?" she asked Bobbie as they set off, Amy holding Jane's hand and dragging her big bear along on the other side.

"It's not good for that bear to be dragged like that," Bobbie said. "You had better leave him at home."

"I don't want to," said Amy firmly. "He needs exercise."

"He does seem to rather drag his feet," Jane said. "Maybe he needs a long snooze on your bed."

Amy considered this, wrinkling her nose. "I think I'll let him lie here on this big rock. Then he can rest his back. It hurts, you know."

"What were you doing so long?" Bobbie came back to the subject with determination as they made their way along the lumber road.

"Want to guess?"

"Talking with Mummy?"

"No, she's fast asleep, I hope."

"Writing a letter?"

"That's what I should have been doing," Jane said. "Oh dear. Well, I have to confess that I went fast asleep after lunch."

"Do you sleep a lot?" Amy asked.

"She's old, Amy, of course she does," Bobbie said with conviction.

"Aunt Jane is not old," Amy said with sudden passion. "She's not. She's not."

Bobbie frowned and Jane laughed. "The truth is, kids, I usually take a nap after lunch, don't you?"

"Not on the island," Bobbie said at once. "There's too much to do."

"I can't walk so fast," Amy said. "Please wait for me."

"You can run ahead if you want to," Jane said to Bobbie. "See if you can find the moss drawing room and give a shout when you do."

But Bobbie stopped to kick a stone, catching up with it and kicking it again. "I think I'll stay with you," he decided, and Jane realized that the deep woods, quite dark even on a sunny afternoon like this one, might be rather scary.

So they came upon it together, the secret, enclosed place carpeted in many kinds of mosses.

"Let's take off our shoes," Jane suggested, "so we can feel how soft it is."

When Amy had finally managed to untie her sneakers and slip them off, she lay on her back while Bobbie walked very softly off to try out the mosses. It was such a silent place; the silence enveloped them and no one said a word for a few moments. Jane was lying down beside Amy, looking up into the trees and through them to the blue sky. "Smell the smells," she murmured. "Isn't it delicious?"

But as she turned her head to see where Bobbie had gone, she saw that he was uprooting one of the pale green rounded cushions. "Oh Bobbie," she said sharply. "Must you do that?"

"I want to see what it is like," he answered.

"But it will just die without its bed of pine needles and loam. If I were you I would try to put it back exactly where it was. Do you think you can?"

"I'm *not* you," Bobbie said crossly, "and besides I've lost the place where it was."

"Bobbie, thee is being very bad," Amy said with some satisfaction, sitting up to survey the scene. "Thee kills moss."

"Good-bye, then. I'm going home." Bobbie was red in the face with rage. Jane swallowed a smile. It would never do to laugh.

"Come on, little brother," she said, "let's go to the house and find a cookie, and maybe your mother would like a cup of tea, who knows?"

"It's very hard to have Amy for a sister," he announced to the world at large, as he ran down the path and away from the other two. So much anger to run out of his system, Jane thought, as she watched him.

They found Lucy sitting out on the porch mending a pillow-slip, but when Jane went out to the kitchen with Bobbie to make their tea, she found the tray all laid and the kettle boiling . . . and that was Lucy's doing, of course. Bobbie helped by eating two cookies in about thirty seconds. "It might be a good idea to leave a few for your mother," Jane observed with a twinkle in her eye. "Besides, at that rate you might burst like the frog in the fable! Lucy, you wizard, I'm going to take a cup to Nancy before I have mine. I'll be right back," she said, laying the tray down.

"Take your time," Lucy said, smiling. "We'll try to do without you."

Nancy was sitting up and looked quite pink, Jane was glad to note. "That's just what I needed."

"Shall I bring mine up and have it with you?"

"That would be lovely."

So Jane sat in the flowery armchair for a half-hour and they talked about Bobbie and Amy. "It's been hard on Bobbie because Amy came as such a surprise and I'm afraid she is rather spoiled. He was the baby and now has to be a good brother to what he must feel sometimes is an impossible little person whom everyone loves for reasons he cannot imagine." Nancy smiled her charming smile thinking about this.

"You are feeling a little better?"

"That wonderful sleep . . ." Nancy sighed. "Sheer heaven. It's so silent."

"Yes, I always feel enveloped by the silence when I first

arrive. It might be a good idea if you didn't try to come down for supper, speaking of silence; there won't be much!"

"Do you think I could? It's an awful nuisance bringing up a tray, I'm afraid."

"Dearie, it's no trouble at all. John can bring it up and you'll have a chance to talk about the day."

"Good," Nancy sighed and slipped down into the the bed to lie flat. "He wants so much to do some work while we are here, so I am letting him down, I'm afraid."

"But Sarah and I can keep the children from bothering him most of the day and the three older ones are working away on the boat. My idea is that you must have at least three days without moving around. Isn't that a good idea?"

"It is the most extraordinary place . . . imagine taking seven people in and putting one of them to bed. You are so marvelous, Jane." Nancy had tears in her eyes.

"Not quite as marvelous as you are, dearie," Jane said.

"Half the time I fail," Nancy said. "I'm always being taken by surprise by things I should have foreseen." Again she was close to tears. "This back . . . I know I did too much last week. The Vietnam War. It seems as though the country were being torn to pieces. I felt I must take part in the vigil the Quakers organized, but we had to stand for four hours."

"And that was a bit much," Jane said. "How hard these decisions are, when to push beyond the limit and when to be careful. I know a little about backs, you know. A couple of years ago mine just gave way and I had to waste a month of that summer in bed here. It taught me a lot, as I think back on it now. My body has not let me down before; how lucky I have been! And I had to learn what it feels like to be dependent, and, gosh, I felt such new understanding of what people bear!" And she smiled. "How hard it is to be cheerful through pain and frustration."

"We so rarely have time for a talk," Nancy said, "so my poor old back has provided one real pleasure already."

"Blessings on thee," Jane said as she got up, then stood for a moment looking out at the sound. "One thing that sometimes is hard here, because there is just so much going on, is to find time for real talks. I long for that."

"But somehow you manage to make each person, young and old, feel cherished. That's the miracle."

"Do I?" And Jane laughed. "I guess I am always hungry for more."

They were interrupted then by a loud knock on the door. "And who can that be?" Jane asked with a twinkle in her eye as she opened to Bobbie, who charged in with a small sailboat in his hands.

"I just wanted to know if I can take this down to the pool and sail it!"

"And maybe you just wanted to know how your mother is," Jane said, smiling at him.

"Maybe," Bobbie admitted, giving Nancy an anxious look.

"I'm being terribly spoiled," Nancy reached out an arm to give him a hug, "and I'm feeling a lot better already."

"Has it ever occurred to you, little brother, that sometimes mothers need mothering?" Jane said, "and what your mother needs is to be allowed to rest?" But this was too much for Bobbie to answer. "You may take the boat down and sail it, of course, as long as you bring it back before you leave. Come along, it's time to get ready for supper. Want to help me set the table?"

"Outdoors?"

"I think it's warm enough if everyone brings a sweater." And off they went, Bobbie dispatched to the little house to get the others, carrying the boat in his arms. "Tell them to make it snappy," Jane called after him. "It's nearly time now."

But when she went into the kitchen Annie teased her. "It'll

be a piece of luck if they get here in an hour. I know Sarah when she's working on that boat!"

Nancy was amused to discover, as she lay in perfect peace and listened to the laughter and thumpings around downstairs, that it might be one definition of heaven to be as she was, high up, happily aware of what was going on somewhere below, but not to be for once a participant, a responder to half a dozen human personalities and needs for her attention. She was wide awake, and as long as she lay still, not in pain, so she lay there quite blissfully until her own supper appeared on a tray and John sat down for a moment to tell her what was happening.

"Jane is going to read some of *Charlotte's Web* after supper. We decided that was a book we could all enjoy, after some rather hot discussion," he chuckled.

"Can you manage for another day or so?" Nancy asked. "It still bothers me rather a lot to move around."

"Jane and Sarah are wonderful about keeping the kids busy, so I even got some reading done this afternoon. Not to worry, dear."

Nancy reached out to take his hand and squeeze it. "Good," she sighed.

"I guess I'd better go down."

"Maybe Sylvie could bring my dessert."

"I'll send her up. Sleep well, won't thee?" and he bent down to kiss her mouth. "We can manage, but thee knows how much thee is missed."

Another thing Nancy was discovering was that when one is awfully tired, any emotion is a strain. She was relieved when John had closed the door. She was suddenly hungry. Roast lamb, mashed potatoes, and peas tasted very good indeed. As well as a large glass of milk.

"Oh Mummy," Sylvie said when she brought apple pie a little later, "are you getting a real rest?"

317

"Wonderful . . . are you having fun?"

"Well, we're working hard on Sarah's boat so we can have a sail. She is such a fine workman herself, she holds us to a high standard and sometimes Tom rebels. This afternoon he just went off and had a swim!"

"How did Sarah take that?"

"Oh, she just laughed a little and said maybe he heard a different drummer. You know, Mummy, there is something about this island . . . people are allowed to do what they feel like without feeling guilty. I love that."

"Jane has that gift—Jane and Sarah together. How lucky we are to be here!"

"Mummy, please get well soon."

Nancy caught the anxious look. And minded. "Mothers are not supposed to be ill," she said with a rather wan smile.

"Because they hold everything together. When you're not there, the center seems to go, you see."

"I expect to be down at the little house after tomorrow. So hang in there, darling."

"I'm not good at being the mother. I get awfully irritated with Amy and Bobbie saying, 'What do we do now?' "

"Family life is overrated, isn't it?" Nancy teased.

"Maybe, by people who don't know what it's really like. Jane seems to take it all as a lark. But she doesn't really know."

"Or she has a talent for making things into a lark even when they are not."

"She loves little children. I don't."

"I think you'd better go down, Sylvie."

"It's nice to be with you alone, Mummy. That's one good thing about your being ill. But I guess I had better go down before the dishes are all washed."

*   *   *

When there are nine people at work things get done very fast. By the time Sylvie joined them the dishes were dried and put away, and Sarah had lit the fire and was busy getting the Aladdin lamp lit.

"Are we going to be too hot with the fire?" Jane asked as she came in.

"I couldn't resist it," Sarah said. "Firelight just seems part of reading aloud after supper."

"And it was quite chilly on the porch," Sylvie said as she joined them and slipped in to sit on the sofa between Tom and Wylie.

Jane sat down under the Aladdin lamp, Lucy on the corner bench with a basket of Jane's stockings to mend in her lap.

It was a grand end to the day, this gathering-together to read something aloud. For a moment Jane's eyes rested on the group and the firelight on their faces, on Amy, who had fallen asleep on the bear rug, as she herself so often had done when she was five or six. Then she took out the worn copy of *Charlotte's Web* and began to read, savoring each word, a smile coming and going as some familiar sentence delighted her again. It was now really dark outside and the night had become a presence, as people sitting in firelight must have felt it since time immemorial. After a few chapters, a yawn took her by surprise, and she laughed at herself and closed the book. "If you are as sleepy as I am, it's time I stopped."

"Just one more chapter," Bobbie begged.

"But we have to leave some for tomorrow," Lucy said, rolling up a stocking she had finished mending.

Sarah, who had been having a talk with Annie in the kitchen, appeared then with an armful of flashlights and offered to go down to the little house with them.

"Is it dangerous?" Bobbie asked, his eyes very bright.

"No bears have been seen," Sarah assured him.

"Sleep well, all of you," Jane said at the door.

"Frances and Erika tomorrow," she said to Lucy as they lay in the dark talking a little. "Oh dear, and in a few more days you'll be gone. Can't you manage a week?"

But that, it seemed, would not be possible. Lucy always helped launch the summer and came back at the end to help close everything down, but she could rarely stay. Her own nieces and their children came to be with her in her little house in the country near Philadelphia.

"It will seem like an awfully empty space over there," Jane murmured.

Next morning, while Lucy was still dressing, Jane sat in the kitchen with Sarah and Annie making plans for the new arrivals.

"My idea, Jane said, is to take all the Speedwells for a picnic on Baker's Island tomorrow—that will give Frances and Erika time to settle in in peace."

"What about swordfish for dinner?" Sarah asked.

"Too early for swordfish," Annie, busy at the stove poaching eggs for Jane and Lucy, reminded them. "How about stuffed baked haddock with a tomato sauce?"

And by the time Lucy came down a lot of planning had been achieved, so she and Jane decided to have their breakfast in the dining room.

It was quite a surprise when Nancy appeared in her wrapper to join them. "It's time I began to cease being a pampered invalid." She slipped into a chair and sat stiffly, leaning against the straight back.

"Oh dearie, I bet you're starving! Have your breakfast with us. But do, if you can, go back to bed for one more morning, will you? This is your chance, after all."

"But there are only five more days!"

"You must do what you feel you want to do," Jane said firmly.

"I want to get going," Nancy said, "but my ornery back is still rather reluctant."

"Scrambled eggs and bacon for the invalid." Annie set a plate before her. "And more toast for all of you."

Lucy suggested then that Nancy have a try at getting up for midday dinner and maybe go down to the little house in the afternoon, "but tomorrow there's a picnic on Baker's Island . . . and maybe you could sleep here tonight and take that day in perfect peace with Frances and Erika."

"The children will mind," Nancy murmured.

"But getting in and out of that rowboat is not the best thing for a lame back," Lucy insisted.

"I'll just have to see," Nancy said. Jane felt she was depressed, near to tears perhaps. She got up and put an arm round her shoulders and kissed the top of her head.

"This is the place where you can let down, dearie, so don't let the gremlins plague you. What the children need more than anything is a rested mother."

She looked at her watch. "Good heavens, it's after nine. We'd better go and find some flowers for Frances. Where does time go on this island? It just vanishes!"

Luckily, perhaps, the search for flowers—there were none yet in the formal garden—led Jane and Lucy down to the pool, and on the way they noticed that a rowboat was out near the dock with Bobbie and Wylie in it alone.

"Come on, Lucy, we can't have that!" At seventy-five Jane could not run as fast as she used to do, but she outdistanced Lucy and was on the dock waving and calling, "Come right back, boys!" by the time Lucy caught up with her.

The currents were quite strong, especially when the tide was going out, and it was clear that Wylie, who had the oars, was not finding it easy to bring the boat around.

"That's it," Jane called, "pull on the right oar. There you go . . . now pull hard on both oars!"

"It's all right, Jane," Lucy said as she caught up. "They'll make it." But she saw that Jane was flushed, and her unusually sharp commands showed that she was angry and upset.

"It's not all right," Jane answered. "They know perfectly well what the rules are."

"What's the matter?" Wylie said when the boat was firmly tied up and he and Bobbie were safely on the dock again.

"Wylie, you know very well that no child is to take a boat out without a grown-up. You found out that the current is strong, and if I hadn't happened along you might be drifting away now and not able to get back!"

Wylie put his hands in his pockets and stood his ground. "I'm twelve," he said, "after all. It's a foolish rule."

"Last summer a boy drowned right out there. You were risking Bobbie's life."

"I have my Junior Lifesaver's badge. I could save him."

"Wylie," Jane said quietly, "I think you have to accept that there are rules on this island, and whether you like them or not, they have to be obeyed."

"I'm too hot," Bobbie announced, ripping off his tee shirt. "Let's have a swim."

"Not without a grown-up, I'm afraid," Jane said. "We'll all be down around noon and then you can have a swim."

But this edict was apparently the last straw, and Wylie glared at Jane with something like hatred in his face. "It's stupid," he said. "We can't have any fun."

"There are only five more days. You'll just have to stick it out," Jane said, smiling now.

"What *can* we do?" Bobbie asked.

"In about half an hour you can come down to the main dock with me and welcome Miss Thompson and Erika. Right now we must pick some daisies and buttercups for Miss Thompson's room."

"Come on, Bobbie, let's go to the boathouse," Wylie said, and off they went without looking back.

"Well," Jane laughed, "that was quite a row!"

While they picked the flowers, Jane stopped for a moment and stood looking out to the bay. "It's awfully hard to be stopped short in the middle of an adventure."

"Children have to rebel, you know. It's part of growing up . . . but you were very effective, Jane, I must say."

"I'm remembering one bitter moment in my life, the summer before Vassar. I wanted desperately to see an old school friend to say good-bye, over at Northeast Harbor. Pappa absolutely refused to let me row over! I *still* mind," Jane said ruefully. "I was outraged. And, you know, I could have done it perfectly well."

"That, I expect, is what Wylie is telling Sarah now."

"Yes, but I was grown-up, Lucy, after all!"

"Some people might say you're not quite grown-up even now," Lucy was laughing. "Oh Jane!"

"At seventy-five? I'm afraid I'm a hopeless case." But then Jane looked at the straggly bunch of flowers in her hands. "What can we do to make this look a little less forlorn?"

"A little laurel might help,"

Jane looked at her watch. "Mercy, we'd better hurry!"

It was always like this, a slow start to the morning and then at some point a wild rush. But by half past eleven they were all waiting at the dock, Lucy and Jane sitting and talking on the benches at the top before the steep descent to the float itself, for the tide was low. Even John had come with Amy on his shoulders. Bobbie and Wylie were down on the rocks examining the mussels that clustered on the pier supports.

"Hey," John called, when he saw them, "maybe we could find a pail and have mussels for lunch."

"I bet it's not allowed," Wylie said, looking up at Jane.

"Oh yes, it's allowed," Jane answered, "if you like mussels, go to it, kids."

But just then *West Wind* was sighted in the distance and everyone ran down onto the float and started waving.

"It's a perfect day," Lucy said. "What luck!"

Every arrival was momentous on the island, as though they had been marooned and were now about to be rescued. Such shouts of joy and hugs and lifting-out of luggage and large containers of the food Captain Fuller had fetched and, of course, the leather mail pouch.

Frances was helped out by Jane, who treated her like Venetian glass, for Frances did look awfully tall and frail these days, laughing as she nearly stumbled when she stepped down off *West Wind.*

"I'm here!" she said, holding fast to Jane's supporting hand. "How wonderful!"

Erika was already carrying her bag up, waving off help with a characteristic nonchalance. "I can carry it perfectly well. It's the briefcase that is heavy."

"It will all fit in the wheelbarrow, won't it, Captain Fuller?" And once on land, it did, so they all walked up slowly, without impediments, while Captain Fuller followed, taking his time. Frances was a little out of breath after climbing the porch stairs.

"Come and sit on the porch for a minute," Jane suggested. "It will take a minute for Captain Fuller to get your things stowed away."

"Erika is going to do nothing but work," Frances said, "and I am going to do nothing but sleep and read."

"I do have a horrible load of papers," Erika said, "but I intend to have some swims, willy-nilly."

"Splendid! I told the Speedwell boys we'd be down at noon. The water will still be rather cold, I'm afraid. But do let's go!"

"I think I'll just settle in," Frances decided. "It's so lovely to be here. . . ."

"Maybe a glass of sherry and a biscuit before you go up?"

"That would be welcome."

Was Jane herself aware of some almost imperceptable changes in the customs of the island? No liquor had been served in her parents' day. Now there was always a bottle of sherry to be produced on special occasions, and most of the older guests, like Frances Thompson, brought bottles of Scotch or Bourbon in their luggage.

But for the moment the four sipped infinitesimal glasses of sherry, while Erika and Frances heard the island news, and promised to look in on Nancy, who had before her marriage taught at Warren, so she and Frances were old friends.

As always when Frances came, there was a complete change in atmosphere. She was a highly charged presence, quite unconsciously a star who brought out Jane's homage and chivalry as perhaps no one else did. Lucy sometimes resented this. She didn't like to watch Jane being as deferential as she became when Frances was present. And something in Lucy obviously felt prickly when the conversation became intense. Yet she had to admit that Frances in her eighties was remarkable, still so involved in world affairs, still so caring, still on innumerable committees having to do with education all over the world.

It made Lucy feel in an odd way diminished, and silent. She had sensed the same atmosphere in Germany, as though Jane were not quite in the same league as Erika and Frances. She had certainly been invaluable through the years of negotiating to get the *Nachbarhaus* going, but she had not, Lucy had to admit, been at the center of power.

Here on the island, a tiny microcosm of a world, she was at the center of power, and Lucy sometimes wondered whether anyone really saw with what skill and tact that power was used, by means of how many small decisions and inummerable acts the atmosphere was created in which so many and such various people found rest and nourishment.

She was thinking these thoughts as she followed Erika and Jane back from the pool, where they had all had a glorious swim and were now hurrying back, late as usual for dinner, as it was after one. Then, as their animated voices preceded her, Erika saying how amazing Frances was, Lucy admonished herself not to be as defensive as she felt about Jane. For Jane was clearly both happy and at ease, and that, after all, was what mattered. On the island Jane flourished because here all her gifts could be used. Here she was *empowered*.

Nancy was striking the three-tiered Japanese gong on a long rope that announced every meal as they walked into the house.

"Ah," Jane called out. "She's up and downstairs!"

"And high time," Nancy laughed.

"We'll start without Sarah," Jane told Annie, "she'll be along soon."

Sarah slipped into her chair just as Jane was saying grace. *"Benedictus bendicant,"* she said with a smile. "Short because we are all starving."

And for a moment all eyes were fixed on the haddock as Jane very carefully sliced and passed along one portion after another and Lucy passed the vegetables, summer squash, and mashed potatoes.

"John is having trouble with the stove," Sarah explained. "I wanted to help him get it started. They've got a big pail of mussels to cook."

Nancy looked around the table and said, "It has been a

blessed time, a respite, but I'll go down right after lunch and hear all the news, especially what mussels taste like!"

"They've been doing very well," Sarah said reassuringly. "Amy had a swim in the shallow end of the pool this morning."

"I can't believe that baby is old enough to swim!" Frances said.

"She paddles like a little dog." Nancy smiled across at Frances, who was eager to hear about all the children, and also about Nancy's job at the kindergarden.

"Even those little kids are aware of the war," she was saying, "and it's hard to explain what is happening."

"Awfully hard," Frances said earnestly, "especially since we ourselves don't know what is happening, do we?"

"It's a horrible war," Erika said, "horrible."

"I feel sometimes it will never end . . . that we are being sucked into quicksand," Nancy said.

"As indeed we are," Frances was quick to agree. "We are busy destroying a civilization, for what? The chimera of communism!"

"Has a war ever been stopped by people rising up against it?" Nancy asked. "I mean after Kent State surely people must see that it's not possible, that something is cracking inside the country."

"But how to end it? No government can afford to admit defeat, and we have five hundred thousand men now engaged," Lucy said. "I really feel for Johnson these days."

"He won't be re-elected, that's for sure," Erika said.

"I wonder." Frances was leaning forward in her chair, intensely absorbed by the conversation. "It is rare to change administrations in the middle of a war—some would think not possible—even after Kent State and all the violence of feeling in the colleges and universities."

And so the discussion went on through dessert and coffee,

327

until they parted to go and have naps and Sarah and Nancy to go down to the little house.

It was hard to keep quiet after the disturbing talk. Lucy and Jane, lying on their beds, did not feel able to relax for a while.

"What am I going to do without you?" Jane said, looking across at Lucy. "You always manage to pour oil on troubled waters."

"Do I? I hardly said a word."

"I know, but somehow when you are there it creates an island of peace even when the discussion gets hot. Isn't Frances amazing? She is just as intense and involved as she ever was."

"Yes." Lucy thought this over. "But so are you. And you never make one feel guilty and upset."

Jane sat up. "That's it," she said. "I never have admitted it, but you're right. It's that intensity. I always feel attacked by it. But," she added, "it's wrong, for that is not what Frances intends, Lucy. That is not in her mind at all."

"But that is sometimes her effect. Nancy looked so relaxed when we got back from the pool, but I saw how tense and upset she was at the end."

"I'm not a very good lion tamer, am I?" Jane chuckled. "I wanted to change the subject, but I didn't know how." She lay back then and crossed her arms under her head, looking up at the ceiling. "We can't shut out the world, Lucy. The island just has to be able to contain everything, I feel, and still give all these warriors a chance to rest."

"You do manage that, you know."

"The island does it."

"Yes, but you hold so many threads in your hands, Jane. You hold it all together and make it work."

Jane sighed. "Tomorrow's going to be a big day. We'd better have a rest if we can. I'm still all stirred up, I must confess."

*　　*　　*

After tea Jane for once went off alone to the formal garden to do a little weeding and thinking. She was so rarely alone that it seemed a peculiar pleasure to get out tools and a basket and set to, thinking of Muff, for this garden had been her particular pride and pleasure. When a thrush began to sing, high up in a tall copper beech, and Jane answered him with as thrushlike a sound as she could muster, it seemed a perfect moment. She was so absorbed, her back bent over the flower bed, extricating the frail salpiglossis from an invasion of spreading weeds, that she did not hear footsteps on the grass.

"Hi!" It was Tom, she saw, as she straightened up. "Want a job?" she asked. "It's always a mystery to me why weeds are so much stronger than flowers!"

"I don't want a job," he said, smiling at her, and Jane was amazed, as she looked up, at how tall he had grown in a year. "We've worked pretty hard on that boat of Sarah's, you know."

He sat down on the bench and looked around, not at all self-conscious at watching Jane work; but having started, she was determined to finish at least the front so the border would look less ragged. "I'll just keep at it," she murmured.

Then there was a silence and Jane sensed that maybe what Tom wanted was to talk about something. She really didn't want to stop, but after flinging a last bunch of weeds into the basket, she straightened up. "I guess I'll give my ancient back a rest and sit down a minute myself." And so she did. "You'll be off to college before we know it, Tom. Do you remember when you were a kid how fiercely we played parcheesi one rainy day?"

"I hate losing," he said, giving her a sidelong glance, but not amused. "I still do."

"Well, I hear you're doing awfully well in school. You're not a loser now."

"Oh school . . . that's nothing," he said, rubbing his knee as though to rub out something there.

"What's on your mind, Tom?"

"I don't really know. That's the trouble. I can't seem to connect."

"It must seem sometimes like a rather long journey ahead," Jane ventured.

"It's not that. It's that I don't have the foggiest idea what I want to be or to do with my life. I don't have a destination if it's a journey, a life, I mean. You have to have some idea where you are going, don't you?"

Jane considered this for a moment. "I didn't have the foggiest idea either when I was your age. I found out only in college, I guess, that I wanted to be a teacher more than anything."

"My parents are just too damned *good!*" he exploded then. "I'm tired of all the good deeds and everything. I would like to make a lot of money and not give it to the poor Africans! I'm sick and tired of worrying about conscientious objectors. We never have a meal in peace these days." Then he added bitterly, "Everyone expects so much of me because I'm the oldest. Those brats are never off my neck!"

Jane couldn't help smiling at this outburst, it was so natural. Amy and Bobbie, the late arrivals, must have been hard to take. "It's no joke being the oldest," she said. Then she was thoughtful, looking out through the trees at the field and the brilliant sunlight there. "Would you like to go away to school, I mean for these last two years? Would that help?" Then she laughed.

"What's funny?"

"Not you, my dear. I was just remembering that Yeats poem about the cat and tame hare who he says 'eat at my hearth and sleep there,' and he prays to God 'to ease his great responsibilities.' It's amusing because cat and tame hare are hardly great responsibilities. . . . I am not making sense," she said. But she was still amused by what had flown into her head, a poem

330

Marian had often quoted with a twinkle in her eye whenever things got to be overwhelming at school. "What about a last two years away from home?"

"My parents would say we can't afford it," he said shortly.

"I have an idea you might get a scholarship."

"Much too late for that. School starts in six weeks!" Tom was sitting with his head bent, closed in, Jane felt.

"So you've got to find some way to come to terms with family life, I guess . . . and that cat, Bobbie, and that tame hare, Amy."

"Animals would be a lot easier," he said. "Oh well . . . I'm a hopeless person. "But I just don't see that we are responsible for the whole world."

"I sometimes get overwhelmed, too," Jane confessed. "When the talk gets so intense about the war, I just want to run away and be left alone."

"You do?" Tom looked up, relief on his face. "I didn't think anyone but me felt like that."

"Is it cowardice, do you suppose? Or is it just that a human being can contain only so much pain?" She asked herself as much as him.

"I don't know. You're supposed to be able to handle it if you are a Quaker. But that's where I don't connect."

"Well, we're not alone, Tom, that's for sure. Your parents are such extraordinary human beings, they always make me feel ashamed. Most people can't take a great deal of reality, as someone said the other day. But there's your mother with a large family and a job and she still seems able to open the door to every need."

"She does try," Tom granted, "but I almost never see her to talk to the way we are talking . . . and my dad . . . well, he needs a lot of time to think, you know."

"We just have to accept—accept each person as he or she is,"

Jane said, looking out to the bay, "and that, I guess, is the hardest thing of all." Then she turned to Tom. "I have to swallow quite a lot of things I don't like about my own family, even here on the island. Most people have no idea how much patience and tolerance is needed in a large family on a day to day basis. You know, Tom, Alix and I were the youngest of five girls, and I expect our sisters sometimes got pretty irritated with us!"

"But you had Snooker," Tom said, "I mean you were not on their necks all the time, were you?"

"Yes, we had Snooker and she was the one who really brought us up—you are quite right. It's much harder for you."

"I was not cut out to be a governess," Tom said, smiling now. Somehow he was feeling a lot better. He got up and stretched. "Want to see if I can beat you at croquet?"

Jane looked at her watch. "If we play hard and fast," she said, "I can just make it. It's really time to go down to the pool and see what's going on there."

"Even you are caught, aren't you?"

"I don't feel caught," Jane answered, "because I suppose everything I have to do I want to do."

"And nothing I have to do I want to do," Tom said wryly, daring her now.

"Except maybe to beat me at croquet?" Jane teased. "Let's give it a try!"

It was one of those difficult choices she had talked about with Lucy, but Jane was not sorry that she decided to give Tom what he wanted even though they would be late for lunch. They played a mean game, with only an occasional shout of victory or a groan and the sharp click of mallet on wood. Tom had met his match, and much to his astonishment, Jane won.

"You're a wizard, Aunt Reedy," he said, throwing down his mallet.

332

"I've been practicing for about seventy years," she said, laughing at him. "Anyway, win or lose, it's a fine way to let off steam, isn't it?"

"Yes, but an even better way was to talk. Thanks, Aunt Reedy," he said, as they walked down the field to the bath-houses in a congenial silence.

We did have an extraordinarily carefree childhood, Jane was thinking, and that was—Tom had hit the nail on the head—in part because of the always available Snooker. Not until World War One did the world break in on the perfect heaven, and by then they were grown-up, she and Alix. Tom was far more grown-up now than perhaps she had ever been. Out of these thoughts she said, "You're such a great person already, Tom. It took me years to grow to where you are now."

"Why? I don't believe it."

"Because we were so safe, you know, so shielded from everything you already have to cope with and face."

"I don't get it," said Tom. "All I've done is complain."

Jane felt she had said enough, and anyway it would have taken some thinking to come out with what she was feeling about this boy, who was having to grow up very fast into a heartbreaking world, and was not afraid to be honest.

"Look at that schooner," she said. "Isn't that a glorious sight!" Under full sail the craft was outward bound, and watching it, tears came to Jane's eyes.

Early the next morning, while Frances and Erika were still asleep, Lucy, Sarah, and Jane were already busy organizing the expedition to Baker's Island, surrounded by the large baskets they would fill with cans of corned beef hash, Thermoses of milk and coffee, enameled blue mugs, cookies, plums, peaches, bottles of ketchup, loaves of brown bread, forks, spoons.

333

"What else?" Jane asked.

"Plates," Annie, who had been observing the goings-on closely, said firmly.

"Of course. Where are the paper plates and napkins, Sarah?"

"In the pantry, underneath."

"You'll need a can opener," Lucy said.

"Mercy, what if we forgot *that?*" Jane laughed.

"*And* the skillet," Sarah said. She had a list in her hands and crossed items off as they were stowed away.

"Now you'd better get out of the kitchen," Annie said, "or you'll get no breakfast. I can't make pancakes in total disorder and chaos."

"It looks like splendid weather," Sarah said when at last they sat down on the porch. "The fog is already melting away."

They would be ten, Jane figured, if Nancy decided to go, and it might be a good idea to phone down to the farm and see whether Bruce could come along in the work boat and take the boys and Sylvie with him.

Baker's Island faced open sea. Wilder and several other islands were sheltered by Baker's and did not get big surf. So the bay itself was ideal for sailing, but there was excitement in going out to rough water, to the edge of the continent with no land until Spain somewhere thousands of miles away. Mr. Reid had bought a piece of Baker's for this very purpose. One came out of thick firs and underbrush along a rough trail to soft brown rocks flattened by the winter storms, so this open place had been named "the dance floor," so smooth and open it was, smooth enough to dance on.

But it was a real expedition to get there, not the least hazardous part of it gathering the clan together at the dock near the pool.

"Let's go, kids!" Jane called. "We've got to catch high tide at Baker's."

The boys piled into the work boat with alacrity. John lifted Amy down into *West Wind* and joined them, and they chugged off, towing a dinghy.

"You're brave to come with us," Lucy said to Nancy. "I hope it's wise."

"I just couldn't not go. Imagine being here and not going to Baker's!" She was pink with excitement and looked, Lucy thought, a lot younger than when they had arrived.

Jane, standing beside Captain Fuller, was exuberant and soon they were all singing "Men of Harlech" at the top of their voices. Then for a while there was silence. Amy fell asleep half lying on her mother's lap and Jane and Lucy sat down on either side to talk.

"I was thinking," Nancy said, "how many wars your island has survived. I mean, so much has happened in the world, but the island is just the same. That is rather wonderful."

"Yes," Jane said, her eyes very bright. "Children have come who are grandparents now—and of course Mamma and Pappa are always somewhere in the background. When I come back in June I find them again. And Edith, Alix, and Muff."

"I guess that continuity is rather rare," Nancy went on. "So many people move right away from their parents, I mean in spirit as well as physically."

Jane smiled. "I guess it does seem a little strange that the furniture has not been replaced, that the same old photographs and paintings hang on the walls . . . and the bear rugs. We did have to replace one, you know, because it was too moth-eaten. I couldn't believe how expensive it was!"

Lucy was more aware than most of Jane's friends how much the cost of living had affected things. "A lot has changed," she said. "There used to be more help. What Jane is doing— and it takes some doing—is to manage to keep the essential machine, if one can call it that, in order and working without a lot of people who were taken for granted fifty years ago."

"But some things are easier—a gas-run refrigerator, for instance; there used to be an ice house in Pappa's day. I can still smell that smell of sawdust and the freezing cold there when you opened the door!" Jane said.

"What I sense," Nancy said, "is that it used to be a family island for your family and now it has become an island for a lot of other families—how lucky we are!"

"Yes, there are fewer elegant young men playing tennis and golf than when we were five young women, that's for sure!" And she laughed. "How I resented them when I was a child! They seemed a threat then."

"Why?" Lucy asked.

"I wanted our family to stay exactly as it was. I didn't want my sisters to marry. I wanted to stay a child forever."

"And maybe that's why you invite so many children now? Just imagine being able to take in seven people on a holiday!" Nancy said vehemently.

"That's my idea of luxury," Jane said, "and it's all thanks to Pappa."

Amy was awake now and got up to stand at Jane's knees and look up at her, filled with curiosity. "Are you very rich?" she asked.

Jane exchanged an amused look with Lucy. "Not very," she said, "but rich enough to invite my friends to the island."

"Oh," Amy said. It was not the exciting answer she had hoped for. But then she was distracted, as they all were, by a schooner under full sail coming into the bay.

And within a half-hour they were approaching Baker's and could see that the work boat had anchored and the boys and John were clambering into the dinghy. But instead of rowing toward the shore they turned about and came alongside

West Wind, just as Captain Fuller was throwing out the anchor.

"I thought we could help Nancy," John called out. "Bruce thinks we can lift her."

But Nancy felt sure she would be better off doing it with just a hand from John, and indeed she managed very well, and everyone was relieved.

"Hurrah!" Jane said. "Well done, my girl."

After that John lifted Amy off into the dinghy and Jane and Lucy passed the baskets to Captain Fuller, who had clambered down to *West Wind*'s dinghy, and all made a safe landing. With Bruce and Captain Fuller carrying the heaviest baskets and bringing up the rear they made a single file along the rather rough trail. John took charge of Amy, and when Jane saw that Nancy was moving rather cautiously over rocks and fallen branches, she asked Sarah for her knife and made a staff out of a fallen branch.

"Take this, dearie, it may help over the rough places. I had meant to remember to take one of Pappa's canes for you."

The boys had already disappeared far ahead.

Jane adjusted her pace to Nancy's. "Are you all right?" she asked as they came out into the cleared space around the old lighthouse and stood for a moment looking up at it.

"I'm doing very well," Nancy said.

The little house beside it was all boarded up, with some wild vine creeping up along one wall and along a windowsill in a rather ominous way. And for a moment they stood and listened to the silence.

"There's something lonely about an abandoned lighthouse, isn't there?"

"A little spooky," Jane said, taking a deep breath. "We used to bring doughnuts over for the lighthouse keeper and his wife —think what it must have been like in winter!"

The trail now entered deep woods, a suddenly dark, wild

337

world. "Right about now Alix and I used to pretend we were witches and made sounds as horrible as possible!"

"Make one now," Amy said. She and John were waiting for them at a turn in the trail and she had caught Jane's last words.

"Shall I?" Jane asked, and gave Lucy a conspiratorial glance. Then she took a deep breath and an extraordinarily loud, strange howl was heard ricocheting through the woods.

"What was that?" Sylvie and Bobbie ran back to find out. "We heard an awful scream, didn't we, Bobbie?"

"It was Jane being a witch," Lucy explained.

And everyone laughed, as people do when they have been frightened a little.

"Come on," Jane said, "we'd better get going. Anyone who sees a dry branch for the fire had better start collecting."

"I'll tell the boys," and Sylvie ran off with Bobbie close behind her saying, "Wait for me!"

Soon after they had traversed a marshy place at the edge of the woods and stopped once more to listen to a thrush, they found themselves spread out on "the dance floor," great golden, flat rocks with open sea before them.

"Isn't it great?" Jane said, standing very tall and taking deep breaths of the salty air. "Listen to that surf!"

Sarah was already busy laying a small pile of brush and some dry branches over the black spot which marked the site of many fires over the years, a declivity between the rocks somewhat sheltered from the wind. Bobbie and Tom had found a quite large log which they were dragging along, and very soon Bruce and Captain Fuller made their appearance with the baskets.

"Good work," Jane said. "Now you two can relax while we get things going."

John helped unpack the baskets and was given the can opener to start opening cans of corned beef hash. Jane got hold of the box of matches and knelt down beside Sarah—it was she,

THE HOUSE OF GATHERING

of course, who must light the fire. That was one of the traditions.

Nancy was lying flat on her back on the warm stone, where Amy joined her, amused by this rock bed.

No one noticed that Bobbie had climbed down, fascinated by the waves, and was dangerously near the water until Captain Fuller, sitting smoking a cigar with Bruce beside him, called out, "Hey, Bobbie, you'd better watch out, boy!" Just then a big wave broke and covered Bobbie with spray. Sylvie ran down to pull him back.

"I'm all wet," he laughed. "Mummy, I'm as wet as a fish!"

"Come and lie in the sun and dry off," Nancy said, sitting up with some difficulty.

"Thanks," Jane said to Captain Fuller. "We do need someone to keep a watch!"

Bruce said, "Kids never know how dangerous the ocean can be, do they, Captain?"

"I'm not scared," Bobbie boasted.

"Well, maybe you should be," Captain Fuller admonished him. "A boy drowned out here last summer." He said it quite severely and Bobbie flushed. A severe word from the always kindly Captain Fuller could not be taken lightly.

And Jane whispered to Lucy, "Good for him. I'm so glad I was not the one, for once, to scold."

Lucy had the mugs all out and ready for coffee or milk, with the paper plates and napkins held down by a big rock.

"Let's light it, shall we?" Jane said, bending to the rite, sheltering one match after another with one hand; but they all blew out in the stiff breeze. Finally a satisfactory blaze ran along through the brush. "Now if you'll give me the skillet, I'll start the hash."

By this time everyone was hungry and the whole clan had gathered to watch the proceedings, which were inevitably rather slow. Luckily the big log did catch and at last Sarah could pass a plate to Nancy and Amy, and one by one, with long intervals between, all the others were served while Lucy filled mugs and then passed bread and butter and knives and forks.

"It's quite an operation, isn't it?" Sylvie said, sitting down by her mother. She was one of the last to be served, as after rescuing Bobbie she had gone off by herself to read a book of Robert Frost's poems she had tucked into her windbreaker.

"A lot of planning and organizing, but Jane loves it. She is in her element," Nancy said, watching Jane put another branch on the fire, her face flushed from the heat, so intent on the job she was doing that she looked a little like a priestess.

"Fire does seem to have something sacred about it," Sylvie said following her mother's eyes. "Jane might be a Druid."

"A hungry Druid," Jane laughed, as she caught the words. "Come along, Lucy, Sarah, this is our batch."

Captain Fuller and Bruce were allowed by special dispensation to cook their own, and so they did.

"Earth, air, water, fire," Jane murmured as she sat down with her plate and looked across to the horizon for a moment. "We seem to have all the essentials."

"Rocks, birds, trees," Sarah murmured.

"I do hope Frances and Erika are enjoying perfect peace with loved ones far away," Jane said, smiling.

"It was good planning to give them this day," Sarah said.

"I hope so—the only hard thing is that it meant Annie had to stay home."

"I'm going to take her for a sail," Sarah said, "as soon as *Siren* is in the water."

"John looks very comfortable over there smoking his pipe," Jane said, her eye roving around the group. Then the silence fell, everyone full of hash and contentment by now. Jane sighed, a long happy sigh.

It was Sarah's idea then, the observant Sarah, to ask Sylvie to read a Frost poem before they gathered things together for the trek back. Sylvie looked quite startled, then pleased as she leafed through the book. "I don't know how to choose," she said looking across at her mother.

"How about 'The Gift Outright'?" Nancy suggested.

"By all means," Jane said. "I think about that poem a lot."

"Maybe if you stood up," Lucy said, "we could all hear it."

"I feel awfully shy," Sylvie confessed, but she did stand and read the familiar words very well, and they all listened with the long roar of surf in their ears as well as Mr. Frost.

" 'Such as we were we gave ourselves outright,' " Jane repeated when Sylvie had closed the book.

"What are you thinking?" Sylvie asked.

"Oh, I don't know," Jane said, suddenly embarrassed. "I guess that's what we want to do . . . and often can't or don't." Then she added, " 'Something we were withholding made us weak.' "

"That's not a way of describing you," Nancy said, smiling across at Jane.

Lucy wondered what had been in Jane's mind; she so rarely talked about herself. Perhaps she would ask her later on. Now Jane was mustering the clan to collect the rubbish and the utensils for the trek back.

"I suppose," John said as he collected empty hash cans, "giving does make one strong, but I can't say I always feel that on school days!"

"Oh, I know. I remember well that drained feeling one gets when there is no let-up because there are papers to correct and next day's classes to plan." Jane paused for a moment and placed a hand on John's shoulder, fraternally.

"Sometimes, as Nancy well knows, it's a matter of knowing when too much giving throws a monkey wrench into the works," he said.

Nancy was struggling to her feet. "Balance," she said, laughing because she had just nearly lost hers. "It's learning how to balance it all, isn't it? That's what is so hard at times, when to say 'no.' I can't."

"And when can a mother say that?" Lucy asked.

Captain Fuller was stamping on the remains of the fire and Jane put her whole attention on that crucial matter for a moment. "Do you think it's really safe? Maybe we should fetch some good salt water and pour it on?"

"No need," said Captain Fuller. "See, there's no spark."

"Well then, *en avant, mes enfants!*" Of course, after Jane had spoken French words, singing the "Marseillaise" became irresistible and they filed off singing, her alto soaring out until she was out of breath.

They all agreed when they were back at the farm dock that it had been a perfect day, and what luck that the weather had held!

"Only one more day. I'll never finish my raft," Wylie mourned.

"But can we get *Siren* into the water tomorrow? You promised," Tom reminded Sarah.

"I'm hoping," Sarah said cautiously. "It all depends on the weather, you know."

"I can't believe a whole week has gone," Sylvie said.

And Amy wailed suddenly. "What's the matter, Amy?" John asked, lifting her up and kissing the top of her head.

"I don't want to go," she said. "Why do we have to go? Can't we stay a little longer?"

"Oh, I wish you could," Jane said, taking a small hand in hers and holding it tight, "but you see the Stevenses are moving in day after tomorrow."

"Into *our* house?" Amy said incredulously.

"Come on, children, we'd better get going," Nancy said quite firmly, for everyone was tired, and it was really time they separated.

"It's been a glorious day," Tom said. "Thanks, Aunt Reedy."

"I just can't believe those children are growing up so fast. Tom is suddenly such a grown-up person," Jane said as Lucy and she carried the baskets up to the big house.

They stopped in the field to take a last look at the mountains across the bay, dark-blue and purple, making an outline as of huge sleeping animals, Jane thought, such ancient and comforting mountains they always seemed. And she and Lucy didn't need to talk. It was good to walk on in silent intimacy as they did.

Sarah had gone on ahead to speak to Annie and they walked into an amazingly silent house and went upstairs.

While Lucy went into their room to change for supper Jane slipped along the hall and tapped on Frances' door. Erika opened it. "Come in, come in. We're having a drink on the balcony," she said.

"Has it been a good day?" Jane asked. On the balcony Frances was stretched out on the chaise longue with a blanket over her knees, a glass of Scotch and water beside her on the railing.

"So peaceful," Frances sighed. "I slept all afternoon."

"And I have nearly finished correcting papers." Erika came back unfolding another light chair for Jane.

"Oh dearie, thanks, but I must really wash up before supper." But she stayed a moment sitting on the rail, just the same, feeling an immense joy in seeing that already Frances looked less drawn. Frances caught her look and smiled back.

"And how was the expedition?" she asked warmly. "All those Speedwells must have had a great time!"

"Oh, we had a roaring good day of it," Jane answered. "It's

awful that they have to go day after tomorrow, but Nancy does seem to be fit again, I'm glad to say." Jane yawned then and laughed. "I'm awfully sleepy," she said. "I don't know why."

This amused Erika. "No, you have no reason at all to be sleepy after organizing that trek and getting everyone fed and safely home, no reason at all to be sleepy, none at all."

Jane laughed then too. "It's great sport, you know."

"But perhaps a little arduous." Frances smiled at her.

"Nothing on the island feels arduous," Jane said quickly. "It's all fun, a perpetual holiday these days."

"Some people might call it rather hard work," Erika said.

"I may get sleepy, but it's not like getting tired," Jane responded.

And after she had left them to change her dress, Frances and Erika sat silent for a moment, drinking their drinks and watching a sailboat glide past.

"She is in her element," Frances said then. "It's wonderful to see her here, isn't it? So free and so much herself."

"I have never known a rich person like her," Erika said. "She is such an aristocrat in an American way . . . in Europe it would not be like this."

"I suppose not," Frances said thoughtfully, "but that's not quite it either. Very few rich women in the United States are anything like Jane. Many do feel a responsibility about using wealth with wisdom, many give to the arts and all sorts of social organizations, as they did to Warren when they were parents in the school, but the difference is partly that Jane was always one of us, she chose to be a teacher. And that made all the difference."

"It would," Erika understood. "Not a Maecenas but a fellow worker." But then she looked across at Frances. "Yet you said in the last years she had lost her skill with the children."

"Oh, so painful," Frances sighed. "The children in some way had outgrown her. . . ."

"She is so childlike still in some ways. That is part of her genius, isn't it? That is also what makes me wonder . . . how she has kept this child so alive into old age." She smiled. "Let's face it, Frances, neither you nor I have done that. We are awfully grown-up, I'm afraid."

"Jane will never be entirely grown-up," Frances said, after thinking this over, "and I think it's because for her childhood was so intensely happy and fulfilled, and when she is with children she draws on that treasure inside her, and finds it again."

"Yet she is very understanding of the burdens people carry, isn't she? I could feel how she cared about Nancy."

"Oh yes, I can't tell you how many women she has managed to give respite to for a day or a week or a whole summer. But why do we say 'not grown-up'? I wonder whether that is it."

"What is it, then? She is not an intellectual, of course. I am always surprised at how little she manages to read," Erika said.

"She is too busy living," Frances said at once.

And just then they heard the gong being struck, three notes, and knew it was time to go down.

"A great woman" was Erika's last word. "And I myself can't put my finger on all the reasons why!"

Without Nancy they seemed a very small family gathered in the dining room for supper before the fire. Sarah lit the tall candles while Jane and Erika brought in plates of chicken soup and hot biscuits.

"Ah." said Jane. Then she looked around at the four faces on either side of her and added, "But first we must have a grace. Let's have a silent one this evening. Silence gathers it all together," she said when they had bowed their heads for a minute, "doesn't it?"

Then she said, looking across at Lucy, "Alas, tomorrow will be a hard day because Lucy leaves the island, having accomplished the usual miracles in a few days."

"Lucy sees everything," Sarah was quick to agree. "It's just amazing what gets done when she is here."

"I can give you a list of what I have not accomplished," Lucy teased. "It would be quite long."

"We had better not know," Sarah said.

"The fact is that without Sarah and Lucy it could not be managed," Jane said. "Oh how lucky I am!"

"I'd be awfully happy if the subject were changed," Lucy said. She was clearly the least self-assuming at the table.

"But I must just tell them about the lights!" Jane pleaded. It seemed that Lucy had arrived bearing lights, battery-run, that could be attached to any wall in a dark closet. "No more fumbling for newspapers in the hall cupboard!"

"No more carrying of a candle to the downstairs toilet," Sarah added.

"Where do you ever find out that such things exist?" Jane asked. "It's a mystery to me, but you do." Then she smiled. "I can just hear Pappa saying 'great minds invent small improvements.' That was when someone told him about a gas-run refrigerator and stove. He was quite astonished." Instinctively Jane glanced up at the photographs on the mantel, Pappa in his Palm Beach suit sitting on a rock looking amused. "There have not been many changes," Jane said as though to reassure him.

"So many changes in the world since your father bought the island," Frances said thoughtfully, "and still you keep that safe, secure past alive here so the past flows into the present, and that is very restful . . . and rather rare in these United States, where we so often feel we have outgrown our parents' taste and sometimes even their values."

"But the present," Lucy said, for Frances put her on the

346

defensive as far as Jane was concerned, "flows into the future all the time and that is what keeps it so alive, isn't it? Think of all the children who came here years ago and now bring their children. . . ."

"And grandchildren."

Jane turned to Sarah then, her eyes shining, and said, "You know, I think this is the year to unbury the treasure we hid on the mountain one fine day at least twenty years ago. I am waiting for the right child to go with us. That day it was Cam and her dear mother and Matthew, Viola's youngest. He found it rather a hard climb, but he was the one to find the little niche in the rocks where we hid it."

"What was the treasure?" Frances asked.

"Ah, that is a secret," Jane said. "Of course we imagined someone finding it a hundred years from now, but I'm afraid I can't wait that long! What do you think, Sarah?"

"Maybe when Angela comes her little boy might be the right child."

"I don't know why I talk about the right child. Any child will do."

After supper there was talk of reading something, but Lucy felt she must pack and Jane admitted that she felt rather sleepy, so after doing the dishes they took their candles and climbed the stairs to bed, only Sarah staying in the warm kitchen to have a little time with Annie.

Of course the next morning was one of those wrenching ones when beloved people had to leave, and rather a hustling and bustling one at that. Sarah was off just after dawn to meet Bruce at the boathouse and get *Siren* launched and the sails up.

Jane would drive Lucy to the airport, so at least they did not have to say good-bye at the dock, where she pinned the traditional sprig of spruce in Lucy's lapel and Frances and Erika were the only ones to stand and wave till they were out of sight.

"I wish I were going to be here to help you get the little house ready for the English invasion," Lucy said.

"Dearie, Sarah will help and it will be done in no time."

They stood on *West Wind* and enjoyed seeing the sights of the harbor, full of boats of all sizes and shapes and Old Glory flapping in the breeze as they passed the Coast Guard station.

"Any day now the Wellens should be turning up in their lobster boat to spend a night at the dock. I do hope the weather will hold and their little boy is well again. He had a long siege of pneumonia last spring and I know Esther worries about him."

"It's good to see Erika and Frances letting down. Erika was pretty tense when they arrived, didn't you think?"

"Everyone works so hard," Jane said, "and I feel I do nothing at all these days."

Lucy chuckled at this and slipped an arm through Jane's. "Your nothing at all would exhaust some people I know."

Captain Fuller was easing *West Wind* in through two or three boats tied up at the dock by then, and the first lap of Lucy's journey back to Philadelphia was over. "I'm so glad we don't have to say good-bye yet," Jane said as they followed Captain Fuller with the luggage up to Jane's car.

After several weeks of walking around the island, where the only vehicle was an ancient jeep, it was rather fun to be driving, Jane felt. And to see all the people on the streets as they flashed by. "We're continentals now," she announced. "We have left the timeless world and I had better look at my watch."

They knew each other so well, these two, that it was taken for granted that Jane would not wait at the airport. A long farewell would be too painful, after all. So a quick hug and "Write soon" and she was on the road home again, singing the whole way to keep up her spirits.

* * *

For once there was no one at the dock when Jane and Captain Fuller got back. She decided to go over to the pool and see if the Speedwell kids maybe wanted a swim, and on the way stop in and say a greeting to her niece Daisy and her husband. They lived in Alix's house all summer but there had been no time so far to see how things were with them and their large, happy Newfoundland dog. The house, gray-shingled, with blue-green trim at the windows, was visible from the dock but there was no one in sight.

"Halloo, halloo," Jane called as she climbed the porch steps. "Anyone home?"

Perfect silence. No bark even. So they must be on the mainland. John and Daisy were curators of a small marine museum, and maybe this was one of their days over there, she surmised. Had Captain Fuller made a special trip for them? Otherwise how did they get over? Jane didn't like things to happen on the island without her knowledge. Orders to Captain Fuller should go through her, so others who might want to do shopping or take a walk in town could go along. "Maybe I shouldn't be so proprietary," she admonished herself. "I guess I can be pretty stiff-necked myself when you come right down to it." So nothing would be said this time, she decided.

In a way it was lovely to be walking the familiar path through the blueberry bushes and up into the field alone. "Rarely, rarely comest thou, spirit of delight," she murmured. Marian had always said that you knew who you were only when you were alone. Jane looked about her, noting once more how amazing it was that one heather plant smuggled in from Scotland by a cousin years ago had flourished and spread, so now a large area would soon be purpled over among the wild cranberries along the edge of the woods . . . and wondered if that statement of Marian's were true. She herself never felt as lit up alone as with a beloved friend, did she? Yet this morning, with the strong feeling aroused by Lucy's departure still alive in her, she saw that it was true. The rush of the last days, the battle with Wylie over the boat, the expedition to Baker's, the hot discussion about Vietnam, Nancy's valiant determination to get well—all this that had been stirred up on the surface now began to sink deep down, to coalesce into some large, vague question as to what life was all about. In the large arena it did often seem a very small achievement to do what she tried to do here on the island, to maintain something created long ago for the pleasure of friends . . . and to pass along the values it represented.

Here Jane stopped in her thoughts, for she had always found such generalities bothersome. And her instinct was to probe the words . . . values, for instance, a rather glib word, she felt. What did it really *mean?* It was more to the point to consider that without Sarah none of it would be possible any longer. Lucy did a wonderful job, of course, but Sarah was the pin that held it all together through the whole summer. I have always wanted to be independent, to be my own man (why do I say man, not woman, Jane asked herself?), but these last years I have had to accept how dependent I have become, and sometimes I react badly, I know. Jane had been quite sharp with Sarah about some decision she felt she ought to have been asked about only the other day. I am dependent on Lucy too, but that is different, goes back fifty years or more, is the entirely voluntary dependence of true friendship and love. Whereas Sarah and I sort of inherited each other—and there are bound to be prickly times.

So then what is life all about? Some weaving together of all this, and the values, she supposed, as she received a wave of scent from the rugosa roses by the boathouse, have to do with holding it all together, living it from moment to moment . . . but just then Amy ran out and hugged her round the knees. "Can we swim now?"

"Let's!"

"The others are all sailing with Sarah . . . Mummy's packing. I did hope you would come!"

Next morning, the day of leaving for the Speedwells, Jane woke late because it was raining and even at eight it felt very dark, and a little lonely without Lucy. But this is the morning to pay bills, she told herself, and I had better get going. Sarah had lit a blazing fire in the dining room so breakfast with Frances and Erika turned into a cozy time. When the weather was not at its best the house itself was, and became a comforting ark. Frances and Erika decided to stay downstairs and write at the big table and enjoy the warmth. Sarah put on a slicker and went off with her rucksack on her shoulder to help the Speedwells burn rubbish and get themselves together.

And Jane settled in at her father's huge roll-top desk in the office just off the big living room, picking a bunch of bills from one of the pigeonholes where everything got stuffed. She never ceased to be astonished by the grocer's bill. Pappa would not believe what food costs these days, she thought, as she made out a check. And the big cylinders of gas for the refrigerator and small auxiliary stove had gone up astronomically since Jane had taken over on the island.

The trust fund her father had left for the general maintenance took care to some extent of the three year-round men who worked there, and of the boats. The trust was run by a board composed of members of the family who made all major decisions together. Jane swallowed a smile as she considered how much heat had been generated over the golf greens. Some members felt that it was an unnecessary expense to keep the grass cut, but John and Daisy, who liked to play golf, were upset and it was finally decided to do a rough job, just enough so a real aficionado could still play, although Pappa would have snorted at how inadequate it was. "Only a lunatic would play there now," he might have said. Sarah, on the other hand, felt it was worth all the work because a few exquisite harebells grew along the edges and would be swallowed by long grass if the greens were not kept cut.

Jane was interrupted by the sound of feet on the back porch. Bobbie, with Amy in tow, thundered in. "It's awfully wet out," he announced. "Here's the boat I borrowed."

"Well, thanks to that plastic bag, it's dry as a bone. Thanks, Bobbie."

Amy had gone over to Alix's bear, which sat in a small rocker dressed in a middy blouse, and held it in her arms. "My bear wanted to come so badly," she said, "to say good-bye, but I was afraid he would catch a cold."

"You look like an owl," Bobbie said to Jane.

"I do?" Jane wondered why, then realized it was her horn-rimmed glasses and couldn't resist giving several owl-like hoots before she took them off. This reduced Amy to helpless laughter. "We might send your bear a message," Jane suggested. "I'll see if I can find a postcard." And she turned back to the desk to rummage around in a pigeonhole where there should be a card.

"Mummy said to tell you that if convenient we would be ready to leave at eleven," Bobbie interrupted.

"Good, I'll tell Captain Fuller right away. He held off going for the mail and he'll be anxious to know." When the call was made, and Jane had looked at her watch and realized they had better hurry, she asked Amy what they might tell her bear. They decided after several tries on "See you next summer, dear Bear," and this was written in Jane's beautiful round hand. "How shall I sign it?"

"Yourself."

"Well, maybe Aunt Reedy for Alix's bear." When that had

been accomplished and the postcard had been carefully stowed in Amy's pocket, Jane said, "Now kids, you'd better go back. Tell your mother I'll meet you at the dock in about twenty minutes."

Jane took a slicker from the hall closet and put a pair of scissors in her pocket with which to cut seven sprigs of spruce for the seven buttonholes on her way down, and went in to see how Erika and Frances were getting on and to warm her hands at the fire, for they were quite stiff from the cold in the office.

"I hate to see them go," she said. "It doesn't seem possible that a whole week has flown . . . nor for that matter that the English family will be here tomorrow."

"How do you ever keep it all sorted out?" Erika asked.

"Oh, I don't even try. I seem to get along very well by not looking ahead more than a day at a time!" Her eyes twinkled. "Then it's all a surprise," she added. "Next week is the distant future. The present is what matters . . . and I had better run or I'll lose it."

It was a wet search for perfect little tips of spruce, for as Jane reached up to cut, water poured down from the branch and trickled down her nose and felt very cold.

Captain Fuller had the curtains up on *West Wind,* she noted, as she came out on the pier. No sails out today, only a few motor launches and fishing boats.

Sarah was the first to emerge from the path, laden like a camel with boxes and bags of this and that. Then John, with a pipe in his mouth and an enormous rucksack on his back with Amy's bear sitting on top of it, covered by someone's jacket. Then Nancy, not carrying anything, Amy's hand in hers, and finally Bobbie, Wylie, Sylvie, and Tom, each with a canvas tote bag swinging along.

"There you all are," Jane said, "a sight for sore eyes. You

look like pilgrims, a medieval band on their way—where, I wonder?"

"It's awfully wet," Tom said rather crossly. "Why did it have to rain?"

"Much better to leave on a rainy day," Sylvie answered, smiling at Jane. "It would be too hard on a beautiful day."

"I do hate to say good-bye," Jane said as they reached the float down the long gangway, and she slipped a sprig of spruce into each buttonhole or pocket, and, when she came to Nancy, gave her a warm hug. "It's only till next summer," she said then.

"I'll be thirteen," Bobbie said. "It's a whole year away."

"And I'll be six," Amy lamented, close to tears, Jane saw. So she lifted her up and swung her around and set her down again, laughing.

"All aboard," Captain Fuller called.

And then it was all much too quick as they passed him all the bundles and boxes and finally scrambled in themselves.

Sarah untied the rope and threw it to John, and very slowly *West Wind* turned out into the bay, with everyone standing and waving, until they were out of sight and Jane and Sarah stood on the float alone, stood for a moment in the sudden immense silence.

"Well done," Jane said then. "They really did have a good week, didn't they?"

"A splendid week," Sarah said, "though I worked them pretty hard to get *Siren* in the water." She chuckled. "Sylvie and Tom learned quite a lot about caulking and painting, maybe more than they wanted to learn."

"Well, dearie, what next? I guess we'd better go down to the little house this afternoon, check the stores down there, take fresh linen down."

"It's a perfect day for a snooze, so don't think of going till after tea. I'll meet you down there."

It was not possible, Jane realized, to say in words to Sarah what a comfort she had become. But it was much in her mind as they walked up to the house together in companionable silence. Whatever tensions there sometimes were in the apartment in Cambridge, here on the island she and Sarah were in perfect accord. Little by little, Sarah was taking on more of the work to be done, and especially where the English families were concerned, for after Muff died she had become an intimate part of their lives in winter as well as in summer, something between a beloved governess and a mother, Jane thought, glancing over at Sarah as they walked. She had not changed in the ten years or more since they moved into the barn, looked amazingly young and boyish still, a timeless person. But such a reserved one, so deep inside herself, that even now Jane found it difficult to show the real affection she felt. Perhaps it was also, she considered, as Sarah went off by herself, no doubt to see that *Siren* was all right, that gratitude is the hardest emotion to express—and why was that? Marian would have known the answer. "I guess it is," Jane told herself, "that I am a rather prickly character when it comes to independence. I don't really like being dependent . . . so it is hard for me to admit it."

It flashed through her consciousness then, one of those moments when something in the past is suddenly illuminated by something in the present, that maybe just that reluctance had been at the root of Marian's withdrawal in London so long ago . . . perhaps she, too, found it next to impossible to admit the financial help Jane was providing to make that summer possible. Acknowledging that possibility brought Marian very close again, and Jane, on a wave of happiness, burst into an old French song she had sung with the children in Normandy.

The rain had almost stopped, she noted. But she must resist the temptation to walk down to the vegetable garden and must finally get the desk in order and those bills paid. There was a whole blessed hour before lunchtime and this time she would not be interrupted. "Perfect peace," she said aloud to Alix's bear as she swiveled her chair around and began to sort papers out, and to jot down things "not to forget" on a little pad as they rose into her consciousness. "I must remember to write a birth-day word to Laurel Whitman," and that was noted down and underlined. In fact, it might be best to do it right away and get it done.

The problem on the rare days when Jane could work in the office was the number of things that should be cleared away, and this morning she finally bogged down as she went through a pile of requests for money, from Appalachia, from Africa, where there was starvation, and twenty or more others to be considered. She wondered sometimes if, in her father's day, he too had had to cope with quite so many needs?

The whole room had filled in the last half-hour with desperate human voices . . . and the hardest thing was to make choices. This was almost the only thing now that made Jane feel ex-hausted, and when she had done all she could, she got up and stretched her long arms and then took refuge in the warm kitchen to have a little talk with Annie, since Erika and Frances had gone upstairs, and the fire was almost out.

"What is that heavenly smell?" she asked. "Chocolate some-thing?"

"Brownies," Annie said, smiling. "I sometimes think you have a chocolate nose, Miss Jane."

"Ah," Jane said, inhaling the chocolate-scented air, "smelling them is almost as good as eating one."

They had a long talk after supper about Vietnam, and read aloud an editorial from the *Times*. It was after ten when Jane got to bed. For a moment before she fell asleep it occurred to her that one of these days Esther, the daughter of one of her

Vassar classmates, and her family would arrive in their boat and tie up overnight at the main dock. Esther and Dick were very independent, almost never came up to the house for a meal. Jane well understood their love of a gypsy holiday, and she herself rather enjoyed an arrival for which she had no responsibility for a change. Her last thought was about Tony, the little boy, who had had pneumonia in the spring, and whether they would be able to make the trip this year.

She was fast asleep, and had been for hours when she thought she heard a hesitant tap on her door, waited a second, and was sure she heard it again.

"What's that? Who's there?" When she opened the door a flashlight in her eyes blinded her. Who in heaven's name could it be at one in the morning?

"Aunt Reedy, thank goodness I got the right door."

"Esther! Good heavens, child, what's up?" Jane whispered.

"It's Tony. He has a temperature of a hundred and five. I'm terrified that he has pneumonia again."

Half asleep still, Jane acted from some subconscious level. "You're tied up at the dock?"

"Yes."

"Let me think." Then after a moment, "Come downstairs. I think I can reach a doctor in Northeast Harbor." So they tiptoed down to the office.

"You'll freeze without a wrapper," Esther said, for Jane was in pajamas.

"Never mind. I'll dress if we can find him and if he can meet the boat at Northeast . . . it would take about a half-hour. Is it still raining?" she asked as she found the phone, Esther holding the flashlight so she could see to dial.

"No. It's foggy, though."

"Not good."

The doctor did answer, bless his heart, and after talking with Esther agreed to meet them at the dock in Northeast in three-quarters of an hour.

"Oh, what a relief!" Esther said, tears in her eyes now.

"I'll take a candle up and be down in five minutes," Jane said. "It's going to be all right, dearie."

It was strange how shock can slow one down, Jane thought, as it seemed to take an eternity to dress, and in spite of her comforting tone with Esther, she could not help wondering how they would make it through the fog. Did they have a powerful light on the lobster boat? She tried to remember what buoys to look for once they were in the sound. Dick would have a map, she supposed. What felt like hours later they were setting out, Jane with a powerful flashlight because they had, as she had feared, no floodlight on the boat.

Luckily Dick had got the *Tiny Tot* stove going in the cabin and it was very warm, lit by an oil lamp. Jane had to laugh when she saw that not only little Tony was in there, all wrapped up and very pink in the face, but also a basket of kittens. "We couldn't leave them," Sonny said.

"It is rather a gypsy caravan, I'm afraid," Dick said. "We'd better get going." He decided that Jane could stand on the ten-inch wash deck beside the cabin and light the way with her flashlight while he was at the wheel on top of the cabin, "my flying bridge," he called it. Sonny and Esther sat down on the deck, leaning against the cabin door.

"Bear left a little," Jane called up as Dick righted the boat after the turnabout from the dock and crept into the fog.

It was pretty scary, she had to admit, with visibility very poor indeed. But there was nothing to do now but do the best they could and just hope. . . . And farther out across the sound the fog lifted, what a miracle! So they made it to the town dock guided in at the end by the lights of a car, which must be the doctor's, Jane thought.

And indeed it was. Dr. Sherman turned out to be very young, and not at all dismayed by having been routed out in the middle of the night. "Let me see that boy," he said at once. And congratulated Dick on the warmth in the cabin when he went down. "It's pretty chilly outdoors."

Tony looked at him with drowsy eyes, as he sat down on the bunk, "Who are you?" he asked in a sleepy voice. "Please go away and let me sleep. I am awfully sleepy."

"It's the doctor, Tony."

"My legs hurt," Tony said. "I think I'm sick."

The cabin was awfully hot, and Jane took Sonny out on deck with her while the examination proceeded. When it was over the doctor suggested they go outside. He laid a cool hand on Tony's forehead and said, "You're going to be all right, son. Now you go back to sleep."

"Well?" Esther asked, when they were all outside in the cool darkness.

"My guess is that it's a virus, not pneumonia. The temperature is high—you were quite right to call me—but I expect it to go down within twenty-four hours. But he can't stay on this boat."

"Where can we go?" Esther asked. "We were on our way north—it's a holiday."

Jane had been listening intently and wondering where she could bed them down, all four. Why not Edith's house? Angela would not be coming for a week or so.... "I think I can put you up, dearies," she said.

"Oh Aunt Reedy, that would be wonderful!" Esther breathed.

"It seems like an awful imposition," Dick said.

"It's a bit of luck that the nieces and family won't be coming till a week or so. Of course we can manage. She turned to the doctor. "Do you think Tony would be warm enough in the boat till tomorrow? It will take a bit of organizing, you know, to open a cold house and get fires going."

"Oh, he'll be better off tonight right where he is," the doctor said reassuringly. "I wouldn't think of moving him in this night air."

"Good," Jane said, "so all we have to do now is get back to Wilder."

"Wilder, is it? I've always wanted to land on your island. Maybe I could pop over tomorrow and see how Tony is getting on."

"Could you?" Esther said. "Oh, how kind that is of you!"

"Glad to do it. Now you keep the boy warm. Keep him on liquids and I'll be over in the afternoon after my office hours."

"Good night, then, or rather good morning," Dick said, "and so many thanks."

They watched the doctor's flashlight cast a beam on the car, then the car lights go on, and he was off and away. They were alone in the dark while Dick fiddled with the motor, but finally it did start. Jane took up her position; Sonny went to the bow and Esther down to the cabin, where Tony fortunately had fallen asleep.

"We are homing pigeons," Jane said as they rounded the dangerous turn and just missed a buoy. "It does seem a lot easier now."

It was three o'clock when Jane got to bed again in the silent house. She did not feel tired, only elated that the whole expedition had been brought off. Wonderful what the adrenal gland will do! But the problem now was to get it to quiet down. It was dawn before she had got all the logistics together in her mind about the morning. She must call Bruce before seven and tell him to bring the jeep down to the dock so Tony could be driven to Edith's house. And also carry up their provisions, sleeping bags and such. But finally, as the first birds were cheeping, she fell asleep, with the alarm set for half-past six.

"What an adventure!" was her last conscious thought.

It was a great comfort next morning to find Sarah and Annie having their breakfast when she went down in her wrapper to call Bruce. She had quite a tale to tell as she drank down a cup of coffee at the kitchen table. On occasions like this, Sarah's quiet efficiency and imagination were simply invaluable and Jane gladly let her take the reins in her hands. The English family were expected at noon, but Sarah would take charge there. "And we'll have the Wellens settled in long before that," she said. "What time did you say we'd go down and move them?"

"I think I said nine. It all seems like a dream now, so I'm not sure. But I know I told Bruce nine, so that's it."

"My guess is they'll sleep late, so if we go down at nine, all will be well."

"Miss Jane," Annie intervened, "you just go up and have an hour's sleep . . . that's what you need."

"Oh," Jane laughed, "I'll never wake up if I do. I'll have a good breakfast and a hot bath and that will do the trick."

By next day, a brilliant morning, everything was smooth sailing: the Wellens settled in and Tony feeling a lot better; the English family happily ensconced in the little house and Christopher, their eldest, delighted to find a playmate his age in Sonny Wellen. Dick planned to take them fishing in the lobster boat, and Jane came down to breakfast after eight singing "Oh What a Beautiful Morning" and quite herself again.

"Sarah, we've got the right boys to go treasure-hunting . . . what do you think? Tomorrow maybe. I'm just dying to see if we can find it!"

"It's a piece of luck that Sonny and Christopher get on so well," Sarah agreed. "And why not? Shall I suggest the plan when I go down after breakfast?" Then she added, "What is your thought, Jane? A massive expedition or a secret treasure hunt with only the boys?"

"I hadn't thought," Jane said, eating a second piece of toast.

"If we all go it will be a great public scramble," Sarah said. "Why not just you and me and the boys, after all?"

"Then we shall have great tales to tell when we get home, and I think we had better invite the English over for supper, and Dick and Esther if they feel they can leave Tony. But," she stopped, remembering Frances, "it might be a little much for Frances, all the brouhaha . . . maybe we'd better wait for a big gathering until after she leaves; what do you think?"

Annie chose to answer this by saying rather gloomily, "Miss Jane, you expect too much of yourself. Bad enough to climb that mountain at your age, and you had better do it this year, by the way. And what about my sail, Sarah?"

"Annie, we'll go today while they are out fishing. I know I promised, but things have been rather thick and fast lately," Sarah said.

"They always are," said Annie. She had occasional black moods and today apparently was brewing one of them. "One of these days you'll kill yourself if you don't take care. You are not immortal, Miss Jane."

"I know," Jane said, laughing happily, "that's why every day seems such a gift. But I don't feel old, Annie. Do I really seem on the brink of collapse?"

"No, you don't. And that's the worst of it; the way you behave you might be fifty! And all these people come and expect the impossible! Half the time I go to the cookie jar and it's empty. They eat you out of house and home."

"The island does seem to create huge appetites," Jane said. But she was aware that Annie would be quite disappointed if no one sneaked in and stole a cookie. "After all, it's you, not I, who is the great provider, Annie. And what about roast chicken for supper?"

"I'll need celery for the stuffing," Annie said morosely.

"And here's Captain Fuller to take the order," for Captain Fuller was pushing open the screen door just then. She sat down with a cup of coffee to go over the list with Sarah. Already the new day was gathering momentum. Frances and Erika would be down at any moment for their breakfast. "I'll just run over to Edith's and see how Esther and Tony are getting on. Do you suppose I could steal four blueberry muffins for them?" Jane asked.

"You could but I'll have to make another batch for Miss Frances and Miss Erika."

"I think maybe not," Sarah murmured. "If we're going sailing Annie will be pretty busy, you know, this morning."

"Never mind," Jane said, "they'll never know what they missed!" And off she went. Then she came back a moment later to ask Annie to tell Frances and Erika it looked like a fine day for a swim or just to sit in the sun by the pool and she would hope to see them there at twelve.

She didn't walk quite as fast as she used to, but that meant she noticed a lot of things she used to miss, Jane thought. The pyrola was in flower near a fallen log, such a magic sight, as it flowered after all the spring things like checkerberry were over, and she stopped to examine its tiny white spires, a little like lily of the valley, but not obscured by large leaves, each delicate frond standing upright. It had been a favorite of her mother's, she remembered. Maybe on the way back she could pick one or two to place on the mantel.

Edith's house, a large one built to contain her large family, stood a little back from the steep ledges on that side of the island, with a roughly cut lawn in front of it. And there Jane found Esther lying in a deck chair reading.

"Oh Aunt Reedy, you blessed person!" she cried out when she saw Jane approaching, and ran to meet her and be enfolded in a warm hug.

"How is the patient?"

"Ever so much better. Dick thinks we could take off maybe day after tomorrow. The doctor was very pleased. He said, 'That son of yours is a resilient fellow.'"

"Well, that's great news."

"It's been simply wonderful to be here," Esther said. "Yesterday Tony lay out here in the sun and watched for the ospreys. He was so excited when they flew over I think it made him well, not an invalid any longer, but a bird watcher." She looked at Jane shyly and then asked, "Could you sit down for a moment? Do you have time?"

"All the time in the world, dearie," Jane said, sitting down on a folding chair and stretching out her long legs. "Let's seize the chance for a real talk. It seems ages since we've had one."

The tide was rising and they could hear the murmur of waves breaking on the rocks below.

"Such a restful sound," Esther said. "You never get the big surf, do you? That's what I love about the island, the gentleness. Time seems to stand still." Then she smiled, "Are you still sometimes a witch in your red cloak? When we were children we used to beg you to be a witch for us!"

"I'll try to remember to wear it before you go. Once I have it on becoming a witch appears to be irresistible."

"Mother still has hers. I guess all Vassar girls hang onto them, don't they?"

"How is your mother these days?" Jane asked. "I feel badly

that I didn't manage to drop in to see her more often last winter." They were exact contemporaries, had been in the same class at Vassar and had made several trips to Europe together, but Snooks, as everyone called her, was gliding into senility. The idea of possibly losing one's mind in old age was not something Jane could contemplate, and she dreaded a visit.

"Oh Jane, she just isn't there anymore."

"I wish I could understand what happens . . . what goes on in the mind. Snooks had such a brilliant, original mind. She was so vital."

Suddenly the tears Esther held back most of the time just could not be stopped. "Pay no attention," she said, blowing her nose. "I don't know what's the matter with me."

"It's awfully hard, dearie. . . . I know."

"Hard on all of us, but much worse for Daddy. I don't know how long he can go on being a full-time nurse. That is what it amounts to, after all. Sometimes she is quite affectionate and grateful, you know. Then it's bearable. But sometimes she gets cross and pretends she doesn't know who he is."

"Maybe she doesn't," Jane ventured.

"Daddy says the only time he has any peace is at night, when she's asleep and he lies down beside her and holds her hand."

Jane was weeping herself. But she was not ashamed of tears; perhaps weeping with Esther was the best she could do. And for a second she reached over and held Esther's hand in hers. When she let it go, she said, "Sometimes tears are the only answer one can make to tragedy like this. There's no shaking it off, is there? There's no easy, pious response."

"Dear, dear Aunt Reedy, what would we all do without you?"

"You would do very well," Jane smiled. "I'm not essential, you know."

"Maybe not, but you sure are a comfort. Just to know you are here and the island is here—how few people care the way you do, how few are quite simply always there." Esther was all right now and happy that she could say something she had always felt but never quite dared put into words. "I'll never forget that summer when I broke my leg, your reading *The Wind in the Willows* aloud and making paper dolls."

"Did I do that? I've forgotten that completely. But I do remember your laughing when I made noises like Toad's car."

"Poop! Poop!—which reminds me that I had better go and see whether Tony feels like getting dressed this morning."

But before she got up to go, Jane talked over the treasure hunt plan and whether she could kidnap Sonny for the day. Esther was delighted, and so clearly longed to go along that Jane quickly agreed that it would give Dick a chance to do something for Tony, for Sonny, out fishing with his father, had been getting all the fun.

Jane walked back slowly with a full heart. One of the moving things about a long life, she was thinking, was the chance to grow into real friendship with an adult whom one had known as a small child. She had known Esther, after all, since she was a red-faced infant in her cradle. She had been one of the first tiny babies Jane had ever held in her arms. And here she was, such a mature, devoted person, so aware, so quick to respond to other people's needs—much of what she had become was surely due to her mother's influence—and now living close to her father's devotion. "Devotion," Jane was thinking, is surely one of the most beautiful words in the language. And she wondered if it existed in just the same way in any other language. *Dévouement* had, she felt, a slightly pious note in it.

When she got back Frances and Erika were still at breakfast and Jane sat down with them for a moment and talked about Snooks a little, for Frances had known her at Vassar, of course.

"I wonder whether Harry could consider a nursing home. How long can he go on?" Frances asked.

"I suppose it's one of the hardest decisions anyone ever has to make," Jane answered, leaning her cheek in her hand.

"But at a certain point," Erika said, "it just has to be faced. I see this all the time in my work. It sounds like Alzheimer's disease, and if so, there is no hope."

"It's downhill all the way, then," Jane said.

"The time comes when the person afflicted really does not know where they are, you see," Erika said. "When the cost to the family or those nearest is simply too great."

"Devotion," Jane murmured. "That's what is so moving about Harry. Could they have someone live in and help, for instance?"

"But Jane, it might go on for years and mean a night nurse eventually," Frances said. "Can they afford that?"

"I could help," Jane said at once. For some reason she felt rather stubborn in the face of Erika's experience and logic. Something in her rebelled against what she saw as depriving Harry of his determination to stick it out to the end. And suddenly she remembered something the philosopher who had founded the Warren School had told her when his Irish wife was, like Snooks, simply not there. "Ernest Hocking told me that he spent a half-hour every evening with Agnes when she was unable even to recognize him. He sat with her and held her hand and said a poem or a prayer . . . and he felt sure that we do not know, we simply can't, whether or not something may penetrate the shield of senility. He felt he had to take the chance, that his voice alone might be a comfort. That, I think, is what Harry feels. He can't bear to let Snooks be among strangers, you see." She had flushed as she recounted this, and it was clear that she had not been persuaded.

"*Ach,*" Erika said, "it's hard." Then she turned to Frances. "Jane is so generous, but I think too of all the deprived children we see, of the immense need for help with preschool and Headstart programs . . . has one the right, weighing it all, to give to someone who is not there at all, when there are so many needs?"

"No one can do everything," Frances said quietly, sensing that Jane was upset. "We all have to make choices."

Jane felt all churned up by the discussion, close to tears and close to anger at the same time. She could not rid herself of the image of Harry holding his wife's hand through the night. Deprive him of that? But with her instinct to keep her balance she pulled herself together and smiled. "Sometimes the right thing just seems the impossible thing, you know. So I dangle on the horns of a dilemma—though it's not up to me to make the decision, so . . ."

"I've been too sharp, haven't I?" Erika said. "I am sorry."

"Don't be sorry," Jane said, "for heaven's sake, Erika! I asked for advice. I needed to know, and if I can't agree with the advice I expect it's just the old mule in me. Mamma used to say, 'Jane is stubborn as a mule'—but, oh dear me," she added, "old age is no joke, is it?"

"We are just not prepared," Frances mused.

"So I guess the real problem is that I don't want to face it," Jane admitted. "Snooks is my age."

"But, dear Jane," Frances said gently, "you do not have Alzheimer's! And really," she went on half to herself, "one trouble with all the statistics and all the generalities is that old age is as singular an experience for each person as childhood is. I used to be amazed at Warren to see over and over again that in a class of twelve there was such a wide gap in learning ability, for instance." Then she smiled at Jane. "You simply are not old at all, although, at over seventy, you really should be, you know!"

"Incredible, what you manage to accomplish here all summer," Erika said warmly. "Frances and I talk about it all the time."

"Well," said Jane, getting up, "that reminds me that it's

nearly eleven and we had better get down to the little house and see how they are getting on down there."

Frances decided to stay, as she felt that the walk down to the pool and back would be enough exercise for her. It was hard for Jane to remember that this very thin, very tall person risked breaking an arm or leg if she should fall. Frances never complained about osteoporosis and refused to behave like an invalid, lifted up on her insatiable curiosity about and love of people of all ages, throwing herself wholeheartedly into any and all discussions, still inside herself, a flame of psychic energy encased in those fragile bones.

On the walk down to the little house, Jane had a chance to talk a little with Erika about Frances. In fact, Erika was anxious to talk, and as soon as they were out of earshot she confided that she felt some plan should be made about how Frances could be helped to stay in her apartment in Cambridge.

"She's so alert and so on fire. I find it hard to keep in mind that she is over eighty, you know," Jane answered. "Do you really believe she needs help?"

"Nothing like a nurse yet," Erika answered, "but perhaps someone to come in every day, do the food shopping, cook her dinner, and tidy up."

"Yes," Jane said thoughtfully, "that could be managed without her feeling she was being taken over. I guess that's what we all fear, to lose control of our own lives, isn't it? Going to a nursing home is going to prison."

"I gather Frances is all right financially . . . she never talks about it."

"She was instrumental in setting up a foundation for one of the old supporters of her father's settlement house in Chicago, is still a member of the board, and manages to get to the meetings. That foundation is at her back, and I and a half-dozen other people could be relied on, so money is not a problem."

Jane stopped as they came out of the rather dark tunnel on the path to where the bay opened out before them and the old elephant hills, in sharp outline against the blue sky.

"Well, that is a relief," Erika said. "I have been anxious about that. After all, the head of a private school does not retire on much to live on!"

They shared an ironic laugh about that fact. And then Erika gave Jane a probing look. "I have an idea this is the last time she will be able to come here . . . hazard a fall."

"Oh." Jane felt the shock and showed it. She had tears in her eyes.

"It's been such a good time, Jane. I hope you know that."

"Yes, but . . ." The sentence was never finished, but the reality was folded away in the back of her mind, like a letter she would have to reread and ponder. Frances never to come back to the island! That hurt.

The next day was a gift from the gods, Jane felt, a perfectly calm blue sky, with just a little stir in the air, which might turn into a cool offshore breeze later on. Sonny and Christopher had arrived a half-hour early and were now playing parcheesi (all the games available were pretty old-fashioned, Jane realized, and Christopher had grumbled about this, but they were now thoroughly absorbed nevertheless). Esther and Sarah were busy making peanut butter and jelly sandwiches and filling Thermoses with milk and coffee, and Jane went to pull a thin jacket from the hall closet. It was hard to define to herself why this expedition had taken on a powerful magic in her mind. Would they have even a chance of finding the secret place? She supposed that it was partly the knotting-together once more of the past and the present, the recapturing intact, if they succeeded, of a moment in past time. She invoked Eleanor as she thought about it, so full of humor and life that day, and now dead. And

Cam, who had been at a loose end then. And Matthew, an awkward and unhappy little boy, married, a father, and working away in a bank!

It was unbelievable how life had gone on for more than twenty years, how wars had been fought, children had grown up, but the three little gold pieces in a crack in the granite cliff had—it was possible that they had—remained intact, unchanged, as in a fairy tale, a treasure waiting to be found, a secret waiting to be told. And the secret was more than three gold pieces—but what was it? Jane asked herself.

They were all four aware of Jane's excitement, her eyes shining, her long stride so young still, as they finally made their way down to embark on *West Wind*, Sarah and Esther each with a knapsack, carrying their lunch, Sonny and Christopher running ahead in a race to the dock.

"What a day!" Jane said. "The gods are kind."

"We are the luckiest people in the world," Esther said. It seemed like some apotheosis of the island life, given them like a present after the awful anxiety about Tony, a special reward.

On the way over the boys sat on the stern with their legs dangling down into the cabin. "Tell us what the treasure is, Aunt Reedy," Christopher said. "Is it a real treasure or a joke, for instance?"

"It's a real treasure, I can promise you that. But I can't promise that we'll find it," Jane said, and she looked at the two boys, Christopher so English with his pink cheeks and blue eyes, so sure of himself, and Sonny, a plump child with wide-apart brown eyes that always seemed to hold a shade of anxiety in them, and younger by a year, following Christopher's lead. As Jane sat with an arm around Esther's shoulders, contemplating them, she felt immensely happy. They were the right boys, she felt sure, for this adventure.

"Can we have it if we find it?" Sonny asked then, "and can it be divided in two?"

"Oh dear," Jane smiled, "I haven't thought about that. We had better make up our minds, hadn't we? I can tell you one thing, though: it can't be divided in two, only into three."

Christopher and Sonny exchanged a look, pondering this. "I thought it might be a ring," Christopher said.

"But a ring couldn't be divided in three, you dummy," Sonny said.

"Well then, what can it be, you dummy yourself!" Chris gave Sonny a light punch on the arm.

"I'd rather not guess," said Sonny, frowning. "I'd rather have it a secret until we find it."

"But who'll get it if we find it?" Christopher pressed. "What if I find it first; will it be mine?"

"Well," Jane said, refusing to be pushed, "I guess I haven't made up my mind about that. Maybe," she smiled across at Sarah, "we could share it and each have a piece, we three."

"We might decide to put it back for someone else to find, some boy not even born yet," Sarah ventured. This was so like the wise Sarah that Jane laughed her pleasure in it.

"There speaks wisdom," she said.

"What's the use of finding it if we can't have it?" Christopher asked.

But Jane was enchanted by Sarah's idea, the thought that the treasure might go on being discovered and then hidden again, every twenty years forever.

"And how would anyone know there was a treasure?" Sonny said, anxiously. "I mean, if you died, who would know?"

Strange what a shadow that thought cast, but Jane pushed the shadow off. "You and Christopher know," she said. "Imagine what fun if you came back some day with your children!"

"It's no fun at all to think about our children," Christopher said, suddenly cross.

"No fun at all," Sonny echoed.

"What if we can't find it?" Christopher asked then.

"Ah, that's the adventure," Jane said, "we don't know if we can." She had turned to look out ahead and for a second wondered if she was imagining things, but, sure enough, the small brown head with enormous eyes appeared again, "Look, boys! A seal!"

"Where?" They got up and bounded to the side, leaning over Jane as she pointed. "There! There!"

"Those human eyes," Esther whispered; "no wonder sailors thought they were glimpsing a mermaid."

The seal was curious, disappeared underwater and reappeared in the boat's wake, and for the rest of the short ride across to the dock at Northeast Harbor they were entirely absorbed in seal watching.

"I guess we'll have to divide the treasure after all," Jane murmured to Esther. "The boys will feel cheated otherwise."

"I wonder." Sarah, who had caught this, ventured, "I would wait and see . . . it has to be a legend, doesn't it? If they get inside the legend they might change their minds."

"And the whole point of a legend is that it goes on from generation to generation, like the island," Esther said.

"Well," Jane said, thinking about this, "it can be told, after all. Roland blew his horn only once, but it has gone on and on for centuries in people's minds because it became a legend and was told."

But now it was time to stop wondering what was going to happen or not happen and to begin making something happen, right away. Captain Fuller tossed the rope to a helpful young man and *West Wind* glided in to the dock.

"When shall I come back, Miss Jane?" Captain Fuller asked.

"I should think three o'clock would be safe."

"I'll be here. Good luck, Miss Jane!"

"Thanks. We may be on a wild goose chase, after all." And she gave a wave which Captain Fuller did not see because he was lighting a cigar. "Now kids, let's go. And my advice is," she said as they ran down the dock, "take it easy. We have a steep climb ahead."

It was a half-hour walk to the beginning of the trail, and there Jane, Esther, and Sarah caught up with the boys.

"You'll be way ahead of us," Jane announced, "so I had better tell you now what we are looking for." And she explained that the treasure was hidden in a small cliff about six feet high, where they would be looking for a round stone with a white line across it. It was not a smooth cliff or ledge, but one with irregularities in it where there were patches of moss and tiny firs found places to root.

The boys took their sweaters off at Esther's suggestion and tied them around their waists. The sea breeze had not materialized and it had suddenly become a hot July day.

"You take it slowly, Jane, won't you?" Sarah exhorted. Jane did not like to be reminded of her age.

"I've climbed this trail a thousand times," she answered. "Don't teach your grandmother to suck eggs!"

"Annie charged me to keep a firm hand." Sarah smiled. "I'm only following her orders." She strode on ahead then, and Jane and Esther followed at a slower pace.

"You're in a lot better shape than I am," Esther said, stopping to catch her breath after the first steep ascent.

"I have longer legs," Jane said. "Look back . . . we begin to see the island."

Esther stopped to look out across the bay. "Yes, there it is, like a long dark furry animal asleep. How many people have stood here and wondered who lived there; the big house is hardly visible at all behind the firs!"

"Muff used to fight against any tree being cut, so it has become less and less visible. And without the hurricane in thirty-eight it might have disappeared altogether!" And she turned to Esther. "You are too young to remember that."

"I was four, and I remember it very well . . . the way the trees in Cambridge fell without a sound, like feathers."

"The island was decimated. We came up a week later to see what was what and we wept." Jane quickly recovered from remembering that agonizing scene. "The men set to work and in a year or two wildflowers we had never seen before began to show in the cleared-out places among the ragged stumps."

They walked on. The silence took over. Below them the shining blue, and ahead the path rising into a section of small trees and bushes.

"We must be close to the place now," Jane said quietly, aware suddenly of why they were here on this day. "Where are the boys?" She stopped to cup her hands and give a long "Halloooo!"

"We're up here!" Sarah called back.

Could it be that she had found the place? Jane and Esther hurried to join her, wherever she was. Jane stumbled on a root but luckily did not fall. And there they were, the boys sitting on a jutting rock, swinging their legs, and Sarah, her knapsack flung down beside her, standing beside the cliff.

"You've found it! Great stuff!"

Instantly the boys were at her side. "Is this it?" Christopher cried out. "Really?"

"But we can't find the stone," Sonny said, "so we thought this couldn't be it."

"Maybe we're not tall enough," Sonny said, looking up at Jane.

"Matthew could just reach it," Jane said, "and he was about your size."

"I thought you should be here for the final search," Sarah said, "so I suggested that we all wait."

This was it all right, the crucial moment, and Jane wondered if there was the slightest chance that she could lay her hands on that small stone. But then it was the boys' adventure, she realized, and they must have a try first.

"I tell you what," she said, laying a hand on each of their shoulders. "Let's go at this with the utmost care. Each of you start at one end of the cliff and very slowly feel your way across till you meet in the middle. One of you has a chance to find it and it should be at about your height, Sonny, so Christopher had better look about a foot lower."

"Remember," Esther said, surveying the scene, "it's not a race, boys," for Christopher had lunged at the wall as though he would pull it to pieces. Sonny, always cautious, was feeling his way slowly. Pebbles trickled down. When a jay screamed he jumped.

"How could it be here?" Christopher said. "Someone else must have found it by now."

Sonny had reached a small fir pushing up through a crevice and was feeling around it when he noticed just above it, almost hidden by a tree—could it be?—a small aperture with a round stone pressed into it, a stone with a white line through it.

"Eureka!" he shouted. "It's here . . . the round stone! What shall I do now?"

"Let Jane be the one to unearth it," Esther suggested. "Don't you all think she should be the one?" And Sarah agreed.

"Shucks," said Sonny, turning around to face them. "I thought it was finders keepers. Didn't you, Christopher?"

"Yes," said Christopher.

"Go ahead, Sonny, you pull it out." Jane conceded. She was

not about to take over the crucial moment. But before he could, she had to say, "But remember, it's magic, and none of us can possess magic or keep it forever."

Sonny had to pull quite hard to dislodge the stone, but at last it came and he could slide his fingers into the hole and feel a small leather pouch there. "I've got it! Here it is!" he said, dancing up and down and waving the pouch.

"What's inside it?" Christopher, consumed by curiosity, asked. "Open it, you dummy!"

Sonny shot a glance at Jane, holding the pouch in the palm of his hand. "One, two, three, magic, it's me!" And out tumbled the three gold pieces, shining so brightly in the sunlight they might have been minted that morning.

"It's gold!" Christopher said. "Pure gold!"

"One twenty-dollar piece and two ten-dollar ones," Jane said, a twinkle in her eyes. "So you see, although in one way it can't be divided to two, in another way it can. Sonny, because he found it, can choose whether he wants the twenty-dollar piece or the two tens."

"So I haven't lost after all," Christopher breathed.

"I want the twenty-dollar one," Sonny said. "I'll keep it for a million years," he added solemnly.

"I want the two tens," Christopher said, "so I can jingle them in my pocket."

Jane beamed. It did seem like a wonderful bit of luck that the treasure had been there for twenty years, and could be found after all those winters and snows and high winds. "Shall we make an oblation to the gods of this place, who maybe helped us find it?"

"But what can we make an oblation with?" Sarah asked.

"Milk," Jane said at once. "I have an idea the gods are fond of milk, milk and honey, but today they will have to accept just milk." Sarah handed her the big Thermos and she let fall a few drops of milk on a round of moss at their feet. "There," she said.

What with the climb, the excitement, the marvelous climax, everyone was ravenous and they decided to sit down right where they were and lean their backs against the cliff. After they had devoured two peanut butter-and-jelly sandwiches and were eating grapes and drinking milk while Sarah poured out coffee for herself, Jane, and Esther, Sonny asked, rather warily, "Aunt Reedy, what did you mean about magic . . . you said to remember that no one can possess it? Can't we keep the gold pieces?"

Jane laughed. "I don't know exactly what I meant. I guess I was thinking about this day in all its glory, and that we can have it now, but we can't keep it forever." She looked out to the bay below and a white sail floating past. "Anymore than Eleanor, Cam, and Matthew could keep that day when we hid the treasure . . . we had to let it go, you see."

"But we can keep it, can't we? The gold pieces, I mean," Christopher said.

"Can we?" Esther broke in. "The gold pieces will last forever, maybe, but we won't. Is that what you meant, Jane?"

It was impossible, Jane felt, to articulate what exactly she did mean. But what came to her mind was a de la Mare poem Marian had often said, and she recited it now:

> "Look thy last on all things lovely
> Every hour. Let no light
> Seal thy sense in deathly slumber
>   Till to delight
> Thou have paid thy utmost blessing;
> Since that all things thou wouldst praise
> Beauty took from those who loved them
>   In other days."

Esther had tears in her eyes as she whispered, "Thanks, Jane."

"I don't understand it," said Christopher, "but I like the way it sounds."

Sonny pushed away the sadness he sensed in the air, the aftermath of so much excitement and triumph, and asked if he and Christopher could go on ahead to the top. And off they went.

"What a triumph!" Esther said then.

And Jane laughed. "I was so afraid it wouldn't work!" And she added, "It might be the last chance, you know. I'm not the mountain climber my father was at my age. And then," she reached out to touch Esther's shoulder, "Sonny and Christopher are the right age for magic. It just seemed a chance I had to take!"

"I wish they had wanted to put the treasure back," Sarah said.

"I know," Esther assented at once.

"Yes," Jane said thoughtfully, "but I think that was too much to ask, don't you? Children live in the present . . . we were asking them to imagine something very far away that they could not really imagine." Then she smiled. "And since I too am one who lives in the present, I understand that very well. It is so hard for me, for instance, to imagine the island forty years from now. Will it still be in the family? Will it be possible, financially speaking, to keep it all going? All I know is that we have it now, the secret treasure."

"And all the memories of it," Esther murmured.

Epilogue

I find that I have come to the end of what I had to say about Jane Reid. She lived another six years. During that time she fell and broke her arm, and she was so sure-footed even in old age that I have come to believe it happened because of a small stroke. After that, she found it hard sometimes to find a word, although she never lost an instant response to any friend and especially any child who came to call at the barn in Cambridge, and, with Sarah's help, she spent every summer on the island. Sarah, with infinite tact and discretion, was then always at her side, helping her to dress when that became necessary, setting the scene at teatime so that many friends were hardly aware of any change, as they stopped by, as they always had done, to be cherished and to bask in the atmosphere of pure love.

During those years Lucy died, and I myself retired from college teaching and came back to Cambridge to live in an apartment not far away.

The time came when Jane was in bed most of the day and Sarah told intimate friends that she would die probably very soon, as her heart was failing. We came one by one to find her, her hair in a long pigtail, lying in her great bed under the eaves, her eyes still very blue, her hand reaching out to clasp the hand of a beloved friend. How warm a clasp it was! I have held the hand of people Jane's age whose hands felt like ice, but Jane's was vitally warm and alive as one held it for a moment, like a blessing.

Those last years had been a long, radiant sunset.

And then she was gone.

LaVergne, TN USA
08 September 2009
157223LV00006B/50/A